CHILD OF ASH AND FLAME

───❀───

MAUREEN FLYNN

Copyright © 2021 Maureen Flynn
Text © Maureen Flynn.
Cover art © Holly Fung & Tim Dunnett.
No part of this book may be reproduced or transmitted in any form or with any means, electronic or mechanical, including photocopying, recording or by any information storage and retrieval system without prior permission in writing from the author.
All events and characters portrayed are purely fictional and any likeness to any persons living or dead is purely coincidental.
Visit my website at https://maureenflynnauthor.com
First print edition 2021.
ISBN (Paperback): 978-0-6453518-0-4[1]
Written and edited in UK English.

For my family

Prologue – Ten Years Ago

"TELL ME THE STORY, Daddy," Claire insisted. "It's not my bedtime yet." She pointed at the clock on her bedside table.

"Hmm? Didn't your mother say tonight's an early night, Claire-bear? Something about punishment for racing the horses without parental supervision?"

Snuggled under her quilt, Claire suppressed a grin. She and her brother had been so *bored*. They'd taken Peony and Walter and ridden from one end of the dusty paddock to the other. The timber post-and-rail fence around their white-washed farm with its rickety verandah, crooked chimney and corrugated iron sheds had drawn nearer and nearer, until they'd veered away at the last second.

"I only fell off twice. I didn't cry and they're small bruises, promise." She pushed her quilt back and sat up. "The story! The story!"

"You'll wake your brother," her father teased.

Claire glanced to the opposite side of the room, where Marcus hid with his dark blue covers pulled over his head. "Don't be silly. We were talking right before you came in. Check if you like."

Marcus threw his quilt back, black headphones over his ears and an iPad balanced on his stomach. "Why'd you have to give me away, Sis? I'd just started watching the latest Marvel." He reluctantly pulled his headphones off and placed them and his iPad onto his bedside table. Claire and Marcus weren't meant to watch anything after lights out.

"Come on. It was obvious you weren't asleep because you weren't lying down properly." Claire stuck out her tongue as one of the cows sounded a sleepy moo from the paddock like it agreed with her. She turned back to her father. "Are you going to tell us the story or not?"

"What story?" her father teased, but he sat on the edge of her bed like he did every evening.

"You know the one," she said, just like *she* did every evening. She waited for him to get comfortable, a hand resting on each leg and a smile on his lips.

"You're in trouble, remember? You're meant to go to bed early. Still, I suppose I can give you the brief version. Happy with that?"

"I suppose," Claire grumbled.

He laughed. "Once upon a time, there was a princess with red hair exactly like yours, Claire."

"Yeah," Claire said, touching a strand of her own wavy locks and forgetting about her disappointment as she began to pre-empt her father's tale.

Marcus groaned. "This is such a lame story."

Before Claire could reply, her father smiled. "You don't have to listen, mate." He cleared his throat. "Now, where was I? Ah, yes, the princess ... She lived in a land far, far away, not at all like ours, in a world called Kelnarium. She had everything she needed; riches and beauty, fun and friends and family, but she lacked one thing."

"Love!" Claire said.

Her father hesitated. "Yes. So, she looked for a face in the flame, for she could make visions that way, with a little help, and at last she saw the handsome man she would wed. One day, she and her friends wove their magic together and summoned her prince from our world."

"And they lived happily ever after?"

"And they lived happily ever after," her father echoed.

"I don't buy it," Marcus said crossly. "They didn't know each other!"

Marcus was forever picking holes in her father's stories. Claire found it best to ignore him. "What did the prince look like?" she asked. "I bet he was handsome. What about where the prince and princess lived? Was it an enormous palace?" Claire knew the answers, but she liked the way her dad told the story, almost like he'd been to Kelnarium himself.

Her father glanced sideways at the bedside clock and then at Claire. "Distracting me with questions won't work. I promised your mother you'd be in bed early." He shot Claire and Marcus stern glances. "Next time *ask* before you race the horses."

Claire sighed, but let herself slide further under the warm covers, lids heavy. "Do you think I can be a magical princess when I grow up?" She pictured herself in Kelnarium, an idyllic land of verdant green, dressed in rich robes and a gold crown perched atop her head, and smiled sleepily.

Her father kissed her forehead. "Definitely."

Chapter One

CLAIRE KNEW MAGIC WASN'T real. It was a shame. If it were, she'd blast everyone out of existence and there'd be no one in Shale but her parents and her and Marcus. Her knuckles whitened as they clutched the handles of her family's shopping trolley. If only her mother would hurry up with choosing a peanut butter brand. Another minute or so and *someone* from Shale High was bound to run into them.

"Come *on*," she muttered.

"What have I said about taking more care with your manners?" Suranne asked, placing a hand to her messy bun to touch it back into place. She needn't have bothered. Strands of auburn were already falling out of her hair tie. She turned with a half-dazed expression, like she was seeing the aisle for the first time, her baggy green cardigan sliding off one shoulder to show the butter-yellow t-shirt beneath.

Claire had expected her mum's vague look. When she was a kid, she hadn't minded her mother's almost mystical air, thinking it exciting rather than embarrassing, but these days it was yet another thing that marked Claire and her family out as different.

"Your mum's such a hippie," the kids had said to Claire on her first day of high school. "Will she sell us some of her stash?"

Her dad had been furious when Claire had come home repeating that question, eager for a quick buck and pleased by the sudden attention of her fellow classmates.

Claire and Marcus had learnt not to ask about Suranne's half-there looks or to repeat what the kids at school said, but the truth was, Suranne was a little weird with her odd way of speaking and her permanent aura of having her head in the clouds. She looked at Claire now with a faint smile and a tinge of sadness in her eyes.

Oh, no, Claire thought. *Here we go.*

"I began to tell you a tale earlier. When we were foraging for cereal?"

"Nope." *Honestly, Mum. Who uses the word, "foraging" anyway?*

"Don't mark me for a liar, child, I was telling you a story. Your father stole my heart and me both, though I thought at first that I was stealing him. I still miss them sometimes—"

Claire sighed. "Who's 'them?'" Suranne was no born storyteller the way James, Claire's dad, was. Her stories came out garbled, like she thought other people knew what she was talking about. They didn't.

Suranne didn't answer. She blinked, inspecting her shopping list. "I forgot about the milk when we were in the diary aisle," she said. "We'll have to venture back."

Claire rolled her eyes. It had been like this for most of Claire's sixteen years; her mother would start a story but never finish it. "Stuff the milk. What's next on the list?"

Suranne checked. "Bread." She smiled as Claire steered the trolley towards the bakery section. "James finishes work in an hour. I fancied we could make something hot for the homeless shelter. James and Marcus can see the dish safe to them later."

Claire's mother didn't join craft groups or gossip at the shops, she didn't do the tuckshop roster, but she did insist on making food donations to the local not-for-profits. Claire liked helping, as long as Marcus and James took the stuff where it needed to go.

Where *was* Marcus? He'd spotted Laura with her older sister and headed off in the direction of aisle seven *ages* ago. Marcus had always said he liked hanging out with Claire after school, that he didn't need anyone but her, but ever since he'd started training for the big regional footie match – well, he had mates now, and Laura, the prospective girlfriend.

Adults moved out of her and Suranne's way, glances skidding past them and noses slightly upturned. If her dad were here, things would have been easier. James had grown up in Shale and he knew how to be polite, how to deflect the questions and the nasty comments in a way that made people laugh and forget their animosity. And if Marcus were here, he'd shoot them a roguish grin they couldn't resist ...

As things were, Claire passed two school mums she recognised, her gaze unable to meet theirs.

"The O'Connors are an *artistic* family. Temperamental, you know," one of them said in a stage whisper to the other.

"They can't help it, I suppose," her companion agreed.

Suranne didn't say a word, her hand against Claire's elbow, guiding her forward. Claire felt her cheeks burn, wishing she could pull away and disassociate herself from her mother, not that it would work, since Claire looked so much like her. But then they were past the gossips, moving silently towards the bakery shelves.

Claire went to grab some rye bread, skirting around the fruit and vegetable section. Right in front of the bread were kids from her year. She stopped and turned to face a pile of apples, hoping they hadn't noticed her.

School was never fun for Claire or her older brother Marcus – although people stopped picking on him when they discovered he could kick a ball. Though Marcus had been a gifted painter, he'd soon given it up when he'd realised how much attention football got him. It made up for a lot of sins in Australia, being good at sport. Other kids had tried to bully Claire but once Marcus found out – well, no one tried it again. She didn't have any friends, not really, but at least she wasn't actively targeted.

No, she and Marcus weren't the other kids' problem. It was the stigma of having Suranne for a mum that stuck; endless looks and whispers, and only the four of them to deal with it. Claire had never known Suranne's parents to ask them if they knew where things had gone wrong. They'd died in an accident before Claire was born and the rest of that side of the family – all city slickers – didn't talk to her family either. James's parents, Maggie and Dermot O'Connor, had been nice and kind and a bit vague, the way old people got, but they were both dead now too.

Instead, Claire had gathered rumours, eavesdropped in the library and the local shop, anywhere she could really, trying to understand. The gossips said that James and Suranne had met in some big town like Sydney or Melbourne, then eloped to the sleepy town of Shale where James had grown up. There was a scandal, they reckoned, but they couldn't say exactly what – only there *had* to be a scandal because who'd come to Shale willingly? Apparently, Claire's grandparents were tight-lipped about their daughter-in-law as well and none of the rumourmongers got any joy out of them while they were alive. Anyway, the point was, Claire didn't want to face kids from school with her mum.

"Whatever is wrong, dearest?" Suranne asked. "Why don't you try and converse with some of those nice kids?"

"Nothing," Claire muttered. Her mum was the worst. It was bad enough Claire looked so much like her, but did she also have to sound so stiff and formal on top of being off with the fairies? Not to mention, she literally had no idea of what kids Claire's age were really like.

Before Claire could change the subject, Marcus reappeared. "Sorry, Sis," he said. "I wanted to catch up with Laura."

She shrugged, not wanting to show him she was bothered. He saw Laura every day in class but that wasn't enough these days. "Want to go for a walk later?" she asked him.

"I wouldn't miss it for the world," he said unenthusiastically, but his acceptance was an apology.

Suranne smiled at Claire and Marcus, unaware of the tension between them. "As long as you return home with enough time to help with the cooking."

"Sure," Marcus said. "Right, Sis?"

"Yeah." Claire was distracted. Ella, a girl from her year, hurried towards them, messy brown hair pulled back in a ponytail and tanned face shining. She was a quiet sort, but that didn't mean Claire wanted to stop and chat. It was the shy types like Ella who gossiped in their little cliques at recess and made Claire feel like she stuck out like a sore thumb. Claire was shy herself, and when she tried to talk to the other kids, her conversation was always clumsy. She was constantly missing social cues.

"What else did you say we needed, Mum?" Claire asked. "For tonight's recipe?"

"I was contemplating baking a shepherd's pie. You could acquire some mince if you like?"

Claire sped off. She didn't need other people. She did get lonely, but at least her family had each other. All of Claire's life they'd been a unit, links in a chain. She could rely on them no matter how different they were.

Marcus opened the gate that connected the dry National Park land to the family farm. The electric fences marked the end of their property. He glanced up at the cloudless sky, scowled at the absence of any sign of rain, then jogged onto the track, turning back and waiting impatiently for Claire. "You and Mum are too alike," he said, his joggers kicking up orange-brown dust as he scuffed his shoe into the dirt like he couldn't wait to get going.

"What do you mean? We're both mad gingers?" Claire asked as she carefully latched the gate before the more inquisitive cattle could escape, then walked to join him up ahead. She glared at her brother, gum trees surrounding them either side. She was *nothing* like Suranne.

"Well ... I don't know ... but *I'm* not like you and Mum. Dad and I are just so *ordinary*," Marcus said, but he didn't meet her eyes as they set off together along the trail.

"As far as I can tell you're a big weirdo like the rest of us," Claire snapped, scaring a blue tongue lizard sunbaking on the side of the track into the undergrowth.

"Ha, ha. Thanks, Sis. But seriously, you don't have to avoid everyone like Mum does. Maybe it's that?"

"I can't help it," Claire said, kicking at a rock. "I don't like anyone but you guys."

"You had friends in primary," he said quietly. "What happened to them?"

"Turned out they weren't my friends." She could never admit it to Marcus, but those girls had only been nice to Claire because they'd wanted to get close to him. They'd giggled about his muscles and his height and when Claire had said she wouldn't introduce them, they'd dropped her.

"What about Liz? There was that week you guys hung out."

"I don't want to talk about it," Claire said.

Unwilling to push things, Marcus smiled and started to run instead. "Race you!"

They were going to "The Big Dam," twenty minutes into the National Park. It had been their special spot since they had been little kids. No one got lost on the track; the path was well marked out thanks to generations of hikers lured onwards by the historic mushroom tunnels an hour on. Plus, people were forever going exploring in search of the ghosts that had been there since the 1840s; apparently, a coal miner had gone mad and killed his wife. "If you're quiet, she'll come out, all clad in white," Claire's dad always said.

Whenever Claire and Marcus wanted a bit of peace, they'd sit side by side on a bush gum stump, right beside the brown waters. One time, in a drought, Marcus rode his bicycle right through the mud to the other side. Suranne had been furious. She'd had to stop working on a painting to hose Marcus all over, and even then she couldn't wash all the black muck away. It was a place of special memories.

"Come on," Marcus shouted from a long way ahead. "Last one there has to wash up tonight."

Claire laughed and started after him. A few minutes later, she stopped running, clutching at her side and trying to catch her breath as she watched him vanish around a bend. There was no way she could catch him, not with all his football training. The sunlight caressed the treetops, trying to find a way to reach tendrils to the ground. A bird called as the sound of her brother's footsteps came to her from further along the path.

She began to jog again. "Slow down, Marcus. It's not a sprint," she called.

There was no response. "Damn!" She tripped on the steep, rocky scree. When the area wasn't in drought, this part was difficult to navigate, with a tiny stream running between rocks. At the moment, it was a tiny trickle, moisture seeping through her joggers as she rushed on.

She heard his footsteps slow in the distance. "Marcus! Wait up!" But then: nothing. That was odd.

She sped up, scratching past bushes and trying to keep her balance as she leapt from uneven rock to uneven rock. She couldn't hear Marcus at all now.

Rounding a bend in the trail, she saw a clearing ahead. Marcus was grinning as he waited for her beside a big gum on the far side of the clearing. As she paused to catch her breath again, ready to tell her brother what a pain he was, the sun concentrated like a spotlight directly on Marcus, on his gleaming white joggers and brilliant red t-shirt.

His mouth was a wide-open slash, his screams cutting through the air. Claire cried out, but he didn't respond. She ran blindly, closing the gap between them and stretching out one arm to touch him.

Before she could reach Marcus, a loud *crack* rattled through her, knocking her off her feet. She hit the ground with a thud, surrounded by bright light. She would have screamed but nothing came out. In desperation, she crawled forward, temporarily blinded, scraping her palms against stone, her jeans ripping at the knee.

The sizzling sound and the smell of smoke brought panic to her throat in a low growl. She looked up as a scrap of red cotton floated down, almost caressing her face.

She reached out again but there was nothing there. Marcus was gone. The gum he'd been standing next to had cracked in half, a neat split ripped right through its thick middle.

Chapter Two

"SHOULDN'T WE CALL THE police? Why aren't we calling the police?" Claire couldn't understand her parents' lack of action.

She'd raced the whole way home, slamming the gate shut without stopping to latch it properly, and dodging grazing horses, cows and sheep in the paddocks. Her father had listened grave-faced as she'd rattled off her tale at one hundred miles an hour. Now, to Claire's surprise, his hands didn't shake, and his face didn't twitch like it normally did when he was angry or frightened.

She felt thrown off balance. "Don't just stand there, Dad. We've got to do something."

He shot her a measured glance, then pulled on his big, bushman's boots. "I'll be back soon." The screen door slammed shut behind him.

"Shouldn't we call the police?" she repeated, turning to her mother, who'd sat on the sagging, dusty old couch like a pre-Raphaelite figure from a painting and said nothing since Claire had come racing in the door shouting.

Suranne's face was bloodless. "Something terrible is unfolding. That's why they have taken him."

"What's happening? Wait? Are you saying someone *took* Marcus?"

"Sit with me, Claire," Suranne said, and her voice shook so much that Claire obeyed, even though she wanted to demand answers. She wrapped her arms around her mother's shoulders as Suranne stared into the distance.

Time stretched onwards and still James hadn't come back.

"Mum? Should we call the police now?" Claire touched the back of her mother's hand. 'Mum?'

In response, Suranne gripped Claire's wrist hard. At Claire's cry of pain, she let go, drooping back into the cushions.

Claire stared at her arm, shocked. Her mother, who had never hurt anyone or anything, had left red marks.

"There is no point, Claire," Suranne said.

"No point? But he's your son!"

"You think I am not aware of that?"

Claire began to cry. "What's going on? Where's Marcus? Why don't you *care*?"

Her mum's green eyes were flinty. "Of course I care! But ... we promised my family, your father and me, when we were young. We started to believe that this day would never occur, that everything had worked out. Well, time has finally caught up with us."

Claire sensed she was at the edge of the mystery that had shaped her family's life in Shale. "Tell me, Mum," she asked in a softer voice, "how did you and Dad really meet?"

Her mother paused for a moment, and Claire thought that the words were about to tumble out in a rush. But then Suranne pursed her lips. "You are too young, Claire. Given your age, this is beyond your comprehension."

Too young? That was like a physical slap. In frustration, Claire felt her temper rise, but before she could reply, the door opened, and her father clattered into the lounge. He didn't remember to wipe his boots and left dirt tracks on the worn carpet.

Claire's mother stood expectantly, and then wilted as her husband slowly shook his head. "There's nothing but burn marks against the tree and the ground." He rubbed his hands over his face. "Claire, go to your room. Your mother and I need to talk."

"But, Dad—"

"Just go, Claire! For once do as you're told!"

Claire reluctantly climbed the stairs. She slammed her bedroom door but stayed in the corridor outside. When she heard the murmur of her parents' voices, she crept back to the top of the stairs to watch them and to listen. Her mother paced back and forth, her red hair tumbled over one shoulder, strands sticking to her face; her father stayed rooted to the same spot.

"We cannot ring your police," her mum said. "What would we tell them?"

Claire's dad scratched at his black beard. "I don't know, Suranne, but we can't act like nothing has happened. People will start asking questions."

"Tell them he went away to study," her mum said, stopping abruptly. "He just applied for the exchange program. We will say he went early."

"It'll never work."

"School holidays commence next week. That gifts us two weeks before anyone asks any questions," Suranne snapped. "What else would you suggest we do?"

"Tell the truth. Someone will notice he's not here eventually. Admit he went missing. Say we don't know what happened."

"Do not be a fool, James. We *do* know what happened. There will be an investigation. People already talk about us. Can you imagine the rumours that will manifest if this gets out?"

James clenched his hands into fists. "What else can we do?"

"Say nothing for the moment. Until the end of the holidays. Maybe … maybe he will be returned by then." Her voice broke a little at that. "We should have stayed."

Claire's father flinched like he'd been hit. "Don't say that. Don't ever say that. We had eighteen happy years, didn't we?"

"But to lose our son?"

"We knew this might happen. *You* promised."

Suranne twisted her hands together. "You know I had no choice!"

"We raised him to be strong like you." He gripped her shoulders. "He'll make it home."

"I don't know if I can live with this; the waiting, the not knowing …"

"We'll pull through this together," James said.

"What if we never see him again?" Suranne sobbed openly. "Are you sure you are not mistaken about where he's gone?"

James sighed. "No chance. I could still sense the crackle of magic in the air. It was your family's work. I'd recognise the signs anywhere."

Claire rubbed her ears, certain she'd misheard. Magic only existed in people's imaginations, didn't it? Her dad must have meant something else. That was the sensible explanation.

Her mother sucked in a rattled breath. "What do we tell Claire? We have to tell her something – she saw Marcus taken."

Claire's father sighed. "I'll tell her tonight. Leave it to me, Suranne." He quickly wrapped his arms around her, then broke away.

Claire shrank back against the banister. When the town of Shale had spoken of scandal surrounding her parents, she'd never imagined it would lead to her losing her brother. And just what had her father meant by magic? She couldn't get the word out of her head, the possibilities equally exciting and frightening.

Claire hid under the covers, shaking. Outside, an owl hooted, cows mooed and the crickets made a cacophony, but even those familiar sounds didn't comfort her. Fear gripped at her throat: what had her parents done?

There was a quiet knock, but she didn't answer. She heard the bedroom door open and the sound of her father's footsteps. She started as he pulled the quilt back from her face. "Claire-bear, I need to talk to you."

He reached out to stroke her hair, but Claire knocked his hand away before she could stop herself. "I'm not ten. You can speak to me like I'm an adult."

"I guess I can. Sorry."

"What happened out there? One second, Marcus was in front of me, the next, he vanished." She couldn't keep the fury out of her voice. Somehow, this was her parents' fault. All of it.

"He was magicked away," James replied.

"Dad! *Magicked?* Really? You know magic doesn't exist!" But even as she said it, she knew there was no other explanation. Marcus had literally disappeared in a flash of lightning and a puff of smoke.

"Remember the bedtime story I always told you? About the princess of Kelnarium and how she summoned her prince?" He chewed his bottom lip. "Well, that's all true. Obviously, I'm not a prince, I exaggerated that bit."

"You're not making any sense," Claire said, but the rage ebbed. "What does that old story have to with Marcus?"

"Everything," he said.

Claire shifted upright, hugging her knees, unable to hide the fact that she was a little bit intrigued.

"When I was much younger, I was summoned into another world. Your mother and her friends wove a spell and there I was. Just like that." He clicked his fingers for effect.

The dramatic gesture made Claire smile despite everything. She loved tales of people finding themselves elsewhere, especially when James read them aloud, his little quirks making each telling unique. Not only that, it would be so cool to find yourself in a completely new place, no expectations or people who knew you.

"It happened when I was at the back of the farm checking a horse's shoe," James went on. "I smelt smoke. When I looked up, the sky was greasy with the stuff. It'd been a dry year and the paddock was parched and brown. I expected a bushfire. And then the lightning hit, and my stomach went cold, like something gripped me from the inside. I tried to scream, but I was already flying into the air, up, up, up into a colourful void." He paused, wonder lacing his voice. "Reds and blues and greens and yellows, all brighter than the colour of your mother's paints in the shed, and then it was over." He smiled. "I was face to face with Suranne in a land of mountains and lush green, nothing like the dusty, dry landscape here."

Claire's skin tingled. This tale was real to James. She could tell from the way he sounded, because his voice always shook a bit when he recalled a precious memory. Was it possible Suranne was from another world after all? It would explain *a lot*.

"I was taken before her people," James said. "They needed me, you see. A prophecy claimed that it was important for someone of Dorran blood – that's your mother's family name – to have a child by someone from another world to protect Kelnarium's future."

"Wait. Mum wanted you just so she could have your kid?" This was *not* how Claire had imagined her parents falling in love.

"Yeah, I wasn't too happy either, but you've got to understand how seriously they took prophecies."

Prophecies? This story was getting more and more like a fantasy novel by the second. She grasped for something to say. "Why was Mum important?"

"She's the daughter of a powerful magical family." He shrugged. "Anyway, despite everything, your mother and I fell in love and were married. But I grew unhappy. I missed my parents. I missed my job at the *Shale Herald* and telling tall tales at the pub on Fridays. Suranne understood. She'd given me no choice when she'd stolen me away. Living here was something she could do for me."

"Give up everything she knew?" That seemed pretty unfair on Suranne, and Claire didn't really get her dad. It would be cool to go to another world, especially if it had magic. Why would anyone want to come home to boring old Shale? Adults. They were so weird.

"Yes. We spoke to her parents. They were hurt at first, and sad, but in the end, they let us go."

"I thought my grandparents died in a car crash before we were born," Claire said, eyes narrowing. The more her father went on with his story, the more he revealed how much he'd withheld from his kids. "Did you lie to us?"

"It was easier that way," James said. "Less painful than you thinking they were in the city but didn't want anything to do with you."

"You could have told us about Kelnarium."

"We had our reasons not to. Will you let me finish this story?"

Claire nodded, though she smarted inside. Her family didn't keep secrets from each other. They just *didn't*.

"Your mother had to promise that our firstborn would return if Kelnarium was in danger. It was the only way they would help us leave through the Rift."

"The Rift?"

"It's a scar, but it's also like a ... a highway between there and here. Those colours I saw when I travelled to Suranne and again when we returned home to Shale together were part of it."

Claire thought for a bit. "But didn't people in Shale notice you'd been gone for ages? Weren't your parents frantic?"

"Yes, but it wasn't as bad as you're thinking. Time passes differently there, kind of like, well, Narnia," he said, looking a little embarrassed. "I was in Kelnarium for two years, but in our world just over two weeks had passed. I told Mum and Dad the truth, of course. I had to with Suranne in tow, but we put it about town that I'd run away to the city for a bit and had come home with a bride after a shotgun wedding."

As interesting as all this was, it was getting away from the point of their discussion. "So, Mum's people want Marcus to ... to help Kelnarium? How?

With magic?" Claire could barely contain her enthusiasm. What if she had magic in her veins? Could she use it in Shale? She couldn't wait to ask Suranne about it.

"I don't know, but I imagine yes, it'll have something to do with Dorran fire magic," Claire's father said.

"Fire magic?"

"That's your mother's family's speciality. Suranne lost the ability when she came to live in Shale."

"Cool," Claire said breathlessly, her eyes going wide. She couldn't help imagining shooting flames from her fingers at the older kids who sometimes laughed at her in the playground. She was definitely asking Suranne about spells later.

Her face fell. Her brother had been summoned to a whole other universe and all she could think about was herself. He would be so frightened and alone. If only they'd gone to Kelnarium together. "When will Marcus come back?"

"Who knows, though if he succeeds in doing whatever has to be done, he'll be sent home one way or another."

Claire's heart pounded. "And if he fails?"

James closed his eyes. "It'll be just us, Claire-bear ..." He couldn't go on, his voice rough with unshed tears.

Claire gave his hand a gentle squeeze. "We can't let that happen. We could find a way through and help Marcus. We never do anything alone in this family and—"

"It's impossible. You can only get there if you're summoned."

"I'll find another way. I'll try. I'll do it."

He put a firm hand on her shoulder. "Don't! I couldn't bear to lose both of you. Nor could your mother. Promise me you won't ever try. Promise."

"But—"

"Promise me, Claire!"

"But ... Oh, Dad." She crossed her fingers behind her back and did something she detested: lied to her father, telling herself that it was payback for him keeping such a big secret from her for so long. "I promise."

Chapter Three

CLAIRE COULDN'T STOP seeing her brother's face as she inspected the spot where he'd vanished. She let her fingers trace the split in the tree and the fading scorch marks on the ground, but they revealed nothing new. She'd trekked here every day for the last four since Marcus had gone. It was the same each time; a burst of hope followed by crippling defeat.

It was a hot day, the sun making her squint, rays reaching out for her bare arms. She suppressed a yawn. For most of the last few days, no one had slept, her family enveloped in a bleak silence. In the daylight, her parents threw themselves into work while Claire stayed home from school and after dinner, they'd hold tight to Claire's hands as they watched TV together on the lounge. At night, they let her go to her bedroom reluctantly. Claire would pause outside Marcus's room before she went to her own, staring at the vibrant green bedroom wall she and Marcus had painted together when they'd shared a bedroom as kids. She would watch the way muted starlight fell on her window, the way the moon peeked between ghostly boughs, until she drifted into fitful sleep.

This afternoon had been the first time anyone had woken from their stupor. Suranne had returned to the old sheep shed to paint. She'd asked Claire to join her. Normally, Claire would have jumped at the chance – painting together was one of the few activities that made Claire feel close to her mother. But instead, like an itch she couldn't help but scratch, she'd come here.

Besides, there was a growing distance between her and her parents that she couldn't shake. It had taken Marcus disappearing for them to finally tell her the truth. If that hadn't happened, would they have ever told her? And she couldn't stop thinking about Marcus – he hadn't known about magic running through his veins. What emotions was he experiencing in Kelnarium, finding out it was a real place instead of a story and discovering a whole past he hadn't known about? At least Marcus would be good at magic. He was good at everything. But that didn't make what her parents had done – or not done – right.

"We didn't want you feeling different to the other kids," Suranne had said. "Or having the burden of such a big secret at a young age." She'd shaken her head. "Knowing you could be snatched away at any minute ... we couldn't have left that hanging over your heads."

Claire begged to differ. Even thinking about it now made her chest tighten. She could have handled it. She and Marcus both could have. Her heart rate increasing, she tried to think of something else. It was no good getting worked up again and again.

"I wish Mum could still use magic and she'd taught me," she said to the air. "Then I could get to Kelnarium and help Marcus with this stupid task." Suranne had said she'd lost the knack of using magic when she'd travelled with James through the Rift. She'd explained wistfully that no matter how hard she tried, nothing happened here. She'd also said that if Marcus or Claire had magical abilities, they hadn't demonstrated them in Shale either.

Claire kicked a pebble through the crack in the tree. It was no use. No one was going to summon her and until someone did, she'd have to wait like her parents, hoping Marcus would be sent home soon. She tried to remember the last time they'd been separated for more than two days. Probably on school camp last year, and she hadn't enjoyed it then either. If he wasn't sent home, life would get a whole lot lonelier, and she couldn't even access the magic in her blood to make it more bearable. Her throat ached, but she was too old to keep crying. She had to be brave, like adults were when things went wrong. She wanted her parents to know that she was mature and courageous. She wasn't a little girl clinging to her soft toys anymore.

She sat beside the damaged tree, arms wrapped around her knees. She felt cooler. The sun had gone behind a cloud. She thought about magic, imagining being able to light a fire to keep herself warm and putting bushfires out with a single thought. If only she could try it ... Claire shook her head. It was no use going over the same thing. She'd have to get home, or her parents would get worried.

As she got to her feet, she tasted it in the air; the tang of meat when it's been overcooked on the barbecue. Her breath caught. When she glanced up, the sky was white.

Suddenly, lightning flashed, striking next to the tree. Claire took an involuntarily step backwards. It had been like this when Marcus was taken.

There was another flash of white light. And another.

Her vision funnelled in on bright, primary colours, pinning her to the spot, just as James had described.

Was she really being summoned? Was she to find Marcus so easily? How proud her parents would be and how relieved when she walked home with Marcus in tow! They wouldn't call her a child or keep secrets from her again. She didn't have time to feel scared as her feet slowly rose off the ground.

She put her arms out to steady herself, somehow staying upright even with the wind tearing at her hair. Her skin smarted as dust whipped into her face. *Breathe, Claire, breathe*, she told herself, skin goose-pimpling as she picked up acceleration. *Dad managed this. You can too.*

Taking a deep breath, she made herself stare at her surroundings, the speeding whirl of kindergarten-crayon colours making her stomach churn. She wondered how much time had passed. She hadn't thought to ask her father how long the journey had taken.

Thinking about time and how it flowed in this place, it took Claire a moment to notice something yellow-brown flickering beside her. At first, she thought she was imagining things, but the harder she looked, the more she could have sworn it was some kind of living thing. Its form flickered as though it wasn't quite corporeal, making it hard to see, but she could just make out the thin line of a mouth.

Before she could scream, its mouth opened, stretching wider and wider until it took up the space beside Claire. The creature laughed shrilly, thin tendrils of mud-coloured *something* reaching out from the edges of its ill-defined form to meet her.

"Betrayer."

The word echoed in the colourful space of the Rift as she tried to lean away from its billowing body.

"Wha—?"

Chapter Four

CLAIRE RUBBED AT HER hairline, swearing as she pressed into a growing lump. She'd woken up in a crumpled heap, a hard surface poking into her back, and blackness slowly receding. At first, she'd thought she'd imagined the journey and the creature, that she'd been struck by lightning in the National Park and sailed into unconsciousness, but now she sat up she saw that wasn't so. For one thing, the land around her was flat and devoid of even small shrubs, nothing like the uneven terrain and trees crowding out the park's skyline. She waved a hand in front of her eyes, but the scenery didn't change. No greenery or hills as far as her vision extended. No insect or bird noises. She shivered at the emptiness.

James had woken up face to face with Suranne somewhere lush. Where was Claire's welcoming party and why was the land nothing like what he'd described? She shifted her legs to one side, wincing at the pins and needles as squashed muscles came to life. Her hands pressed into something cold and hard. Perhaps the land she sat on would give her some clues as to her whereabouts? Claire looked down, blinking past the swimming headache forming.

She gasped, involuntarily pulling her hands away. The ground was black and glassy, like Shale after a bad bushfire had passed around the town, only there wasn't the burnt-out vegetation for people to crush underfoot. Instead of charred foliage or even dirt, the ground felt hard like ice too, though it wasn't slippery. She wouldn't want to fall off her horse here. She'd get some sweet bruises. This place gave Claire the creeps, everything tinged with a sinister Alice in Wonderland unreality that could snap at any moment.

She took in a deep breath of air to steady herself, relieved to find it was clean and crisp. Looking up nervously, she hoped the sky would be normal too.

"You have got to be kidding me," she said, her eyes widening.

Instead of shades of blue, Claire stared straight up at a sky filled with colours of the rainbow, but turning her head, she saw that this brilliantly coloured patch didn't extend all the way to the horizon. At its rippling edges, what presumably was the ordinary, moody grey sky was visible. The colour burst had blocked out the sun and clouds.

If the sky wasn't usually a kaleidoscope of whirling colours, then maybe not all of the ground was hard and black. Maybe the land her father had described was just out of view.

Claire's teeth chattered and she wondered how long she'd been unconscious. Hugging herself, she realised how damp her navy cotton t-shirt was, and her jeans for that matter. Her journey to this place must have been the source of the moisture. She tried to think of a plan. She couldn't stay in this wilderness, that was certain. Without shelter and dry, warm clothing, she'd freeze to death. Not to mention that she'd need food and drink eventually.

She looked around. Had Marcus come this way? She hadn't seen any sign of him, but then, she couldn't see signs of any living thing. Running her tongue along the back of her teeth, the way she did in school when she was nervous, she struggled to her feet. To her far right, she saw what looked like dark shadows, possibly mountains. They were the only feature in this vast flat plain, and her father had mentioned seeing mountains when he'd first arrived in Kelnarium, so that way would do. She smoothed wrinkles out of her jeans and shirt, then set off.

She'd been trudging for what felt an age, the mountains in the distance getting closer, when the crashing of hooves caught her attention. She squinted – she could see silhouettes to her left out of the corner of her eye. She counted eight, no, nine figures on horseback, heading straight for her. Soon, they'd be parallel, but they weren't looking her way at all. Her ears rang as hooves kicked against hard ground. Were these people friend or foe? Dad hadn't mentioned any baddies in Kelnarium, but she hadn't exactly asked either. But she was hopelessly lost so she didn't really have another option except to try and get their attention and hope for the best. She counted to ten, trying to slow her speeding heart, then jumped up and down, waving her hands over her head and yelling, "I'm over here."

There was an answering chorus of shouts as the riders drew nearer. The galloping slowed to a trot. Tears of relief sprang into her eyes. She'd been more scared than she'd admitted to herself about being stuck in a strange world all alone. She hastily wiped her tears away. "Please, I'm lost."

They were only a few feet away now. A man who looked a few years younger than her dad led the group, his hair hidden under a scuffed metal helmet. As he leapt from his horse, flinging the reins to the boy behind him, Claire looked enviously at the man's thick crimson cloak. He glanced at her bare arms, then turned back to the boy, pointing at a leather saddlebag attached to his saddle. The boy twisted around to pull a bundle out of the bag, then clicked his tongue, prompting his horse to move closer to Claire. With a shy smile, he put the cloak into Claire's outstretched hands with a murmured, "My Lady," and a small bow.

Before Claire could express surprise at the strange way he addressed her, the leader of the group stepped closer and the boy fell back. "I apologise profusely for our delay, Lady Claire. It was unintentional, I assure you," the man said. "We tried to summon you closer to the Manor, but ..." He shrugged apologetically. "Magic is an imprecise art these days. At least we had our salamanders to guide us."

"*You* summoned me?" Claire couldn't help the note of incredulity creeping into her voice. She was too surprised to even question the man's use of "Lady Claire" or his casual mention of lizard-like creatures (which she couldn't see) leading them to her. For some reason, she'd been imagining a magic user as someone with white hair, covered in weird signs and symbols, and with an intense energy that crackled. This guy was obviously a leader, but he seemed like any other authority figure from Claire's own world. In spite of his clothing and the odd things he said, he seemed kind of boring and, well, *ordinary*.

He laughed nervously, fingering his leather belt, and stroking the edge of the knife tied to it. "Not I, no. Best let your grandfather explain. He's expecting you." He took her limp hand in his own and bowed his head. "My name's Rael. I am the captain of the Dorran Guards and we'll make sure you get home safe." Behind him, men and women half-bowed in their saddles towards her. "It's good to meet you at long last, Lady Claire," he said as he released her hand.

"Thanks," she muttered, questions clamouring, but only one mattering. "Is Marcus with ... with my grandparents?"

"It's just Lord Dorran now. Your grandmother, Lady Dorran, died six years ago." Rael glanced around warily. "Come. No one wants to spend more time in the Riftlands than they have to." He turned from her, and before she could protest at his evasion of her question, he remounted his steed. When he waved his hand impatiently, a woman with green eyes like Claire's kneed her own horse forward. She was leading a spare mount, saddled but riderless.

"Can you ride like your brother?" the woman asked brusquely.

"Yes. I'm a better rider than he is, but—"

"Perfect," Rael said. "We'd best be off." With a soft command, he turned his mare as Claire grasped her own horse's leather stirrups. The men and women formed their horses into a semi-circle around him and Claire as she mounted.

"Her name's Shera," Rael explained. Before Claire could say anything, he sat up straight and dug his heels gently into his horse's flank so that the mare began to trot. Her own horse, Shera, fell into line right behind Rael's as two other riders hemmed her in from either side. She patted Shera's neck affectionately. If she gave Shera free reign and closed her eyes, she could imagine she was riding with Marcus on the farm.

Claire didn't know how much time had passed. An hour or two? The landscape they rode through was still bare, though the air felt less icy and her lungs had lost their dull ache. At least they were on a proper trail now, dry dirt underfoot instead of that odd black glass stuff, and there were spindly shrubs either side, albeit grey and brown. Mountains tinged with cloud and mist rose in the distance and ahead, the land dipped into a valley.

"Is it much farther?" she called ahead to Rael. There was still no sign of the verdant richness her dad had described.

"We'll be home by dinner," he yelled back.

"And?" Claire couldn't help but feel that getting information out of Rael was like expecting her horse, Shera, to answer her back. He'd barely spoken to her this whole trip.

He swivelled around in his saddle to face her, rubbing at the red-brown stubble on his chin. "Things will be clearer soon enough." Glancing away from her, back to the path ahead, he muttered, "Best keep an eye on the road. We're about to pass through one of the camps."

Something in the tight control in his voice made her shiver, like he was a wire pulled too taut. She rose in her stirrups to crane over Rael's shoulder. In the distance, she made out dull, weather-stained fabric flapping in the wind. She wanted to ask what Rael meant by camps but something in his voice warned her not to; it was the same kind of strained tone James used when people in Shale prodded about Suranne's past.

Soon, the party rode beside ramshackle lean-tos and dirty animal skin tents; about twenty in total, creating a rectangular scar on the landscape. Claire steered Shera around a pile of refuse and three children playing as Rael pinched the bridge of his nose with two slender fingers. The other riders muttered to themselves.

"Animals," Rael said in a low voice.

Claire glanced at him in surprise as Shera drew level with his mare. She wanted to ask what these people had done to piss him off, but she didn't know the guy and was new to this world. Besides, she was too busy trying to avoid cooking pits, makeshift washing lines and children to say something.

As the horses carefully picked their way around obstacles, people came out of stained tents. Dressed in undyed sheep wool tunics over threadbare pants and covered in sores, they stared at the party. Claire reckoned there were about sixty people in total.

One woman ran forward, flinging herself in front of Rael's horse. Her hands touched the tips of his boots. "Just a little money, kind sir, good man. Just a little to use at Pleath Village." Her lips were cracked and dry, her words slurred from a swollen tongue.

"Even if I give you coin, you are no more welcome to buy there than you are at Dorran Village and Manor," he said coldly as he pulled his horse away to brush past her.

He undid the top tie on his cloak, revealing a thick scarf beneath. He unwound it from his neck and tied it over his mouth and nose. "I have a spare for you," he said to Claire, his voice muffled.

Claire shook her head, hearing rustling behind her as the rest of their party followed suit. She was shocked at Rael's callousness. Why were these poor people living in such squalor? "Why don't you help them?" she asked.

Rael looked at her blandly. "This is their punishment, Lady Claire. It is justice."

"I don't know what they've done but isn't this a little extreme?"

"With all due respect," Rael said. "You were not born here. You don't know anything about us."

"But surely my grandfather doesn't support this." She thought of Suranne making soups and fresh bread and hotpots for the homeless shelter. "If he's anything like my mother I know he'd want to help."

"You don't understand," Rael snapped. He took a deep breath. "Apologies. I shouldn't have barked at you, Lady Claire. It's not your fault. Your grandfather is good at explaining things. After you speak to him, everything will be clearer."

Claire didn't bother arguing. She'd made the mistake of thinking about her parents and now a terrible lead weight sat in her stomach. She hoped she'd find her brother soon and get home, so they could all be reunited. They'd be going spare with worry. Still, this was a world of magic, she reminded herself. She couldn't help a small grin. Surely no one would blame her if she went back to Shale *after* she'd had a chance to experiment with it a bit.

Chapter Five

THE RIDING PARTY HAD left the camps and the hills beyond them far behind, passing through countryside marked by low green bushes and softening earth, dotted with farms and fields of crops as the sky turned a more natural blue. As they'd ridden by, farmers had looked up and smiled or called out in greeting.

Now, they crested a small mound behind a village. Red poppies bloomed on either side of the road. Claire gazed at them swaying gently in the breeze and smiled as a warmth spread through her.

Glancing at her, Rael smiled too. "I see you enjoy these vibrant flowers," he said, all the hostility gone from his voice. "The gardeners planted them to represent the fire of our House, the fire that is your birthright."

Remembering what her father said about her mother's family specialising in fire magic, Claire wondered again what kinds of spells these people could use. Suranne hadn't said much, saying the memories were painful now she couldn't touch her magic and James had told Claire not to pry. A shiver ran through her as she looked to the top of the hill where the flowers came to an end at a wooden palisade. She couldn't wait to find out.

They were soon outside the gates. Rael smiled as men dressed in bright red tunics, a flame symbol painted on the chest, stepped back into the shadows to let them pass.

Claire's eyes widened as they passed through. This place was huge. She couldn't see where the estate ended, with the outbuildings sprawled every which way, reminding her of the haphazard demountable classrooms at her school. Some buildings had purposes she recognised: a stable, a barracks for the soldiers who'd escorted her, a blacksmith's with smoke puffing from the chimney, a laundry where men and women laboured over tubs of steaming water. Others she guessed were storehouses.

And there were people everywhere, all of them hurrying from one task to another. At least half of them were redheads. Claire had never seen so many gingers in her life. Any last shred of doubt vanished – now she knew she was in a different universe. In Shale, she and Suranne were the only gingers and she was forever made fun of at school with nicknames like "carrottop" and "freckleface".

A group peeled away from the others, making straight for Claire and the rest of the riding party.

"We leave the horses here," Rael said. He watched with approval as Claire dismounted Shera and handed the reins to one of the men who'd approached from the outbuildings.

"Who are all these people?" Claire asked.

"Dorran House servitors," Rael said.

"Slaves?" She was thinking of the people in the camp.

He gave Claire such a look of contempt that she felt red rise in her cheeks. "We have no slaves. Some are retainers whose families have lived here for generations. Some have come from the nearby villages for apprenticeships and the like. Some have married into the clan and some of us are cousins from outer branches. Dorran isn't just a House, it's a *family*."

He turned back to his party. "Dismissed. Clean up in the barracks and then the evening is yours. Come, Lady Claire, we are expected at the manor house." Without checking if she was following, he strode ahead.

Claire trailed after the leader of the guards, determined to tread more carefully from now on. There was so much that she didn't understand about her mother's world, and she didn't want to cause offence.

As the last of the outer buildings fell away, she goggled. The structure in front of her was nothing like the sagging, ramshackle farm she'd lived in her whole life, or like any other building in Shale. Not even when Claire had gone to Sydney for an overnight excursion to Hyde Park Barracks had she seen a house the size of this one. It was bigger than a two-storey house, bigger even than a mansion. This was like something out of a book she'd read on English royal homes, like the really old ones.

As they drew closer, she saw the building was made of red stone and there were windows made of dark glass set in black wooden frames on the lower levels; she couldn't imagine that much light would get inside. Her grandfather could be looking out on her now and she wouldn't know. What would he make of her?

She followed Rael. With every step she felt more and more nervous. The roots of her hair tingled and itched as they headed for a set of carved ebony wooden doors decorated with bas-relief flames; a long time ago they must have been painted brightly, but now the colour was faded. A man and a woman stood guard outside, each wearing light leather armour, a sword at their waist and a staff in their hands. At a nod from Rael, the guards pushed open the doors, and she followed him inside.

She was immediately grateful for the cloak she was wearing. The entry hall, deep and long, was bare and ridiculously cold for a place owned by a family possessed of fire magic. She pulled the woollen fabric tight around her, eyes adjusting to the gloom within. Torches flared in brackets, but gave no heat. There were no floor coverings, only the rosy flagstones, and there were no paintings or tapestries on the stone walls.

"Welcome to Dorran Manor," Rael said with a grin as he half turned towards her. He continued into the hall.

Sticking close behind him, Claire passed the entrances to multiple corridors that ran left and right, with more doorways visible along them lit up by lamps in brackets along the walls. It was a rabbit warren; she just knew she'd get lost. Rael, though, seemed to have no trouble – why would he, it was his home – as he picked the third corridor from the left. Claire counted doorways, trying to remember directions while she also tried not to lag too far behind, but it was no use. She could never remember the route they'd taken.

At last, Rael paused before a plain wooden door. "How are you feeling?"

It took Claire a moment to answer. Where should she start? "I ... it's chilly. Why doesn't someone warm this place up?"

"You'll get used to it. Your blood will remember soon enough, and then you'll mind it as little as I do."

"Is Grandfather inside?"

"What?" He blinked. "Oh, no. This is your room. It's next to ours. It used to be your mother's. She and Kiera would talk all night."

"Kiera?"

"My wife," he said. "Anyway, there's a hearth inside and you can wash before you meet with Lord Dorran." He stepped forward and pushed the door open.

Claire squinted at the sudden burst of light. Flames from a blaze set in a hearth made of pink stone illuminated a middle-aged woman with brilliant red hair that tumbled down her back in soft curls, bound up from her face in a black kerchief. She stooped over a fire-blackened cauldron. As Claire and Rael entered the room, the woman straightened, smoothing her thick woollen dress and stepping over a pile of rags towards them.

Her gaze slid past Claire. "You took your time, Husband."

Rael stooped to kiss her on the cheek. "It was worse than when Marcus was summoned. The Rift spat her out closer to its centre. Thank the Saura we found her."

Kiera grimaced. "This water's almost done. I'll draw the bath." She turned to Claire. "Stand closer to the warmth, child." She jerked her head to her right.

Claire moved towards the hearth. To her left, near a small window, was a bed surrounded by thick red curtains with a woven carpet beside it and a wooden chest at one end. Between the hearth and the bed was what Claire took to be a washing tub. It could have been any luxury bedroom. Though this had once been Suranne's room, nothing of her remained.

She started as Kiera coughed. "I was friends with your mother, you know," she said.

"The best of friends," Rael interjected.

"Yes."

Claire didn't know if she should react to the strange bitterness in Kiera's face. Before she could find something suitable to say, Kiera began to size Claire up, the way the older kids sometimes did in the playground. Claire stiffened, her first instinct to get someplace quiet that was her own – like the school library – but that place didn't exist here. She felt powerless. If only Marcus were with her. He'd know the perfect thing to do and say. She dug her nails into her palms and counted silently to ten. The sooner she had a wash and met her grandfather, the sooner she'd be reunited with Marcus.

"If you don't mind, I'd like to clean up now," she said as steadily as she could.

Kiera smiled. Was it Claire's imagination or was there a nasty edge to it? "Of course. As for you, Rael," she said with a quick glance over one shoulder, "I've already drawn your bath, so you can bathe, then get changed to take Lady Claire to Lord Dorran." Her expression softened at the mention of Claire's grandfather.

Claire wasn't too keen on Kiera staying in the room with her. She wished she'd go away with her husband. She didn't think she imagined the animosity she sensed from Kiera and she hated conflict. At school, she kind of withered up and didn't look at people and hoped they'd leave her alone. She didn't think that would work with an adult.

Rael didn't seem to notice the tension between them. "Come out into the corridor and knock on our door when you're ready," he said, then departed.

Kiera returned to the hearth. Wrapping a rag around her hand, she bent over the cauldron, grasping the handle.

"Let me help you," Claire said. She picked up a rag from the heap beside the cauldron and grasped the other side of the handle. She struggled to keep time with Kiera, but soon they'd hauled the cauldron to the bath. It already contained some cold water. Using a pitcher, they filled the rest of the bath with hot water.

Kiera straightened, rubbing at her back. "You look more like your mother than Marcus." She said it like it wasn't a good thing.

"Where is Marcus?" Claire asked, grasping her courage. "Is he OK?"

Kiera blinked. "You'll have to repeat that," she said. "I could barely hear you. I thought you said is he 'oakey' ..."

Confused for a moment, Claire suddenly realised that Kiera didn't know what "OK" meant, just like she didn't understand some of the things Kiera and the others said. What, for instance, was Saura?

Before Claire could reframe her question about Marcus, Kiera had turned her attention back to the tub. "Is that warm enough?" she asked. "I can heat it up with a bit more magic if you like your baths piping hot."

"What? No, thanks." Part of Claire wanted to lie about the temperature to see a spell in action, but she felt pretty gross so didn't want to have to force herself into scalding water. "But do you know if my bro—"

"There's clothing here," Kiera said, cutting her off and pointing at folded red garments on a chair. Before Claire could speak again, Kiera pulled a screen made of folded wooden frames strung with painted sheep skins away from the wall and arranged it around the tub, saying as she did so, "When you're dressed, I'll do your hair."

"Do my hair?" stammered Claire. She patted at it awkwardly.

"You can't see your grandfather like that," Kiera replied coldly. "We don't always expect ceremony, but this is a special occasion; the return of another of Suranne's children." She emphasised "Suranne's children" in a way that let Claire know she didn't think much of them.

Claire swallowed. She hoped she wouldn't be paraded in front of all of Dorran House. She knew she'd turn bright red and chew her nails trying to think of something to say. She waited as Kiera reached inside a small bag tied to her belt and sprinkled some kind of sweet-smelling herb into the water. Just as Claire recognised the lavender scent, so similar to the kind her mother put into her own baths, Kiera moved outside the screen, rearranging it back in place so Claire had some privacy. She stripped off her clothing as fast as possible and stepped into the tub, thinking of Suranne. Had her mother picked up her love of lavender from Kelnarium? Claire sank into the lovely and warm water, wondering.

She waited for the tingles all over her body to subside as her skin adjusted to the warmer temperature and lathered herself in soap. She couldn't stop thinking about Suranne and how she must have had to adapt to Claire's world, just like Claire would have to adapt to Kelnarium. Grime scudded the water as she sponged herself with a cloth Kiera had left her for that purpose, then she jumped out. If her mother had survived in a new world, then Claire could too.

She wrapped herself in the plain brown towel beside the pile of clothing Kiera had left her, then sorted through her new attire. Beside the chair were some leather shoes that came to a point at the toes, and resting on top of the chair was a crimson shapeless tunic that went to her ankles when she held it up, a pair of dark woollen stockings and a bright poncho thing with ties and ribbons and gold embroidery that Claire couldn't make head or tail of. There wasn't a bra or underwear in sight. With a sigh, she placed her old ones back on and resolved to hand wash them later, then put on everything else except the weird poncho. She folded the screen back, the confusing garment under her arm.

Kiera waited on a wooden stool beside the hearth, a small pile of what looked like jewellery – it glittered – in a small open chest at her feet. She nodded briefly at the poncho in Claire's hands. "I can help you with that," she said dispassionately, like she hoped Claire would go away.

Claire suppressed resentment. What was this woman's problem? She and Marcus hadn't *asked* to be summoned here.

As Kiera rose, Claire passed her the poncho. Without speaking, Kiera shook it out, then placed the linen-like fabric over Claire's head. Poking and pushing, she smoothed the edges on Claire's arms, tied the golden ribbons together, then rethreaded the gold ties at the bodice and laced it up tight. Finally, she reached for a belt of metal links, tying it around Claire's waist and letting it sit like a girdle. She stepped back. "There. You look better."

Claire bit back a frustrated retort. Kiera was clearly one of those people who delivered a compliment like a knife to the back. Besides, her new clothes were rough and made the back of her neck itch. She felt ridiculous, like a character in a Shakespearean play.

Kiera pulled up another stool. When Claire sat, she passed her a hunk of bread and some hot soup that she took from beside the fire. "You must be hungry and it's still a while before dinner."

James had taught Claire to be painfully polite in the face of rudeness, so she shot Kiera her widest smile and tucked in, the delicious warmth from the food spreading through her as she ate.

Kiera waited until Claire was finished, her hands folded neatly in her lap. "Did your mother ever talk about me?" she asked.

"She never spoke of Kelnarium." Claire knew so little of her mother's life before she'd arrived in Shale. Maybe this was a chance to find out more. "How did you know Suranne?"

"I *thought* I knew her. She was my cousin. Lord Dorran's brother, Kelt, was my father."

"What do you mean you 'thought' you knew her?" Claire asked.

Kiera's voice was hard. "She was my best friend and she left me for another world. You wouldn't understand."

Claire said nothing, turning her face away in embarrassment. She'd never had a real best friend. There'd been Liz but she'd turned on her and—

"Let me do your hair," Kiera said, as though nothing had happened. She moved her stool behind Claire. "I cut and arrange everyone's in the manor. I used to be a Lady-in-Waiting to Lady Dorran. I can make elaborate peaks and curls and even swans and crowns from a person's hair." Her pride was obvious. "Tonight, I think I'll pin yours back. It's a perfect fire-red, just like Suranne's was." She held up a hair clip with a salamander carved on top in gold.

Claire thought about how different things were in Shale. No one ever complimented her hair at home except for her family and they didn't count. Kiera used a delicate comb to brush out the tangles, then pulled Claire's hair into place and it got too hard to think about anything but the short, sharp stabs of pain at her scalp. Claire could have sworn Kiera was rougher than she needed to be and when she got to the salamander hair clips, she let them dig into Claire's skin. When Claire protested, Kiera told her not to be a baby. "They need to hold your hair properly."

When Claire tried to touch one of the clips, Kiera batted her hand away. "You'll ruin it. I've arranged them just so. There. Done."

Claire's roots tingled worse than when she'd first approached the Manor, her forehead feeling stretched from the tight bun.

"Now for the headpiece." Kiera carefully drew the chest close and selected a small gold tiara from inside, a rearing salamander stuck to a flame as its centrepiece.

This was too much. She'd look like an idiot wearing that. "I don't need it," Claire said firmly.

"It's tradition. You must show respect for your people and for the Saura." Kiera's tone brooked no argument, even if Claire had no idea who or what the Saura might be.

Two guards waved Claire and Rael past wooden doors covered in the same carvings she'd seen on the front door of the Manor. As soon as Claire entered the throne room, her slippered feet sank into a plush crimson rug which led all the way across the stone floor to an old man seated on a cedar wood, leather upholstered throne on a dais. Eight other men and women, all dressed in stiff embroidered tunics and dresses with gold salamanders stitched over their chests, stared at her from their vantage point behind the throne. Claire had once auditioned for a regional dance performance. The way these people looked at her now reminded her of the way the judges had looked at her then. None of them were Marcus.

Reaching the throne, Rael quickly bowed to the seated man then moved ahead to join the standing group. Claire had to stop herself from putting out a hand to keep him by her side. She could have done with the moral support.

The seated man – her grandfather she presumed – smiled, his eyes warmer than those of his impassive courtiers. "Come closer," he beckoned, and Claire couldn't help but notice a gold ring with a red opal centrepiece on his left thumb.

Claire did as she was told. She didn't know if she should bow or curtsey, so she met him stare for stare instead.

"At last, Granddaughter," he said. "It's good to finally meet you."

Claire pressed her hands into the folds of her dress. "Um, you too." She hesitated then added a tentative, "Your Lordship." She didn't know how to address a grandfather who was a lord. She studied her grandfather's face. He didn't look like Suranne, but then, he was very old; his skin wrinkled and parchment-like and his hair grey.

"Your blood hasn't adjusted yet," he observed, frowning. He pointed a finger at an enormous grate to his left. With a sudden whoosh, flames burst to life.

"Cool!" Claire said, the word echoing in the enormous space. She flushed as some of the courtiers behind the throne shot her stern looks.

Her grandfather laughed. "Give yourself a few days and you'll be able to do the same." He waved at the people ranged behind his throne. "These are my advisors. On my right-hand is Maen; remember him for he'll teach you magic. He's taught everyone with talent, large or small, for the last twenty years. On my left is my younger brother, Aed. The rest you'll meet properly at dinner; all of them are related to you."

Claire tried not to stare at Aed, a man who looked almost identical to Lord Dorran, except that he seemed younger, standing straighter, his hair thicker and with strips of brown alongside the grey. He even wore a matching ring. It was kind of nice to know she had relatives after all, even if she'd had to travel to a whole new universe to find them. This whole thing felt weird, like a dream. "Why did you summon me?" she blurted out before she could stop and think, desperate to know why she was in Kelnarium.

"We must have given you a nasty shock," Lord Dorran said. "I apologise. We thought Suranne's first-born would have strong abilities, but Marcus was a disappointment." He smiled. "Don't worry. I'm sure you're who we need."

"What do you mean, Grandfather?" She wished her voice was steadier.

"Marcus had the smallest of talent for magic. What do you know about us?"

"Not a lot," Claire admitted. "Dad said you'd only have taken Marcus if Kelnarium was in danger."

"Kelnarium *is* in danger," Lord Dorran explained. "That's why we need *you*."

She shifted from one foot to the other, uncomfortable at her grandfather's conviction that she could save anyone from danger, let alone a whole world. "You must have made a mistake about Marcus. He's good at everything."

"There's been no mistake. He is one of the weakest *learth* users Maen has ever tested."

"Where is Marcus?" she asked. She'd burst if someone didn't tell her soon.

"In the capital," Lord Dorran said. "I was sick of his endless moaning about being good at things in Shale. Councilman Eidan gladly took him off our hands, thanks to his talent for painting. Marcus is teaching the next generation of artists, or so I'm told."

Claire couldn't help smiling, even though the situation was clearly serious. That sounded about right. If there was one talent her family had in spades, it was art.

"Maen tried teaching him for a fortnight. That was enough to make it obvious he was never going to get anywhere. He's been in Kelnariat for just over a week, thank goodness."

Claire hoped her bewilderment didn't show. Marcus had been gone in the real world for four days and yet he'd been in Kelnarium for nearly a month already? Then she remembered that her father had said time ran differently here. Still, she was puzzled. Marcus made friends with everyone. If he hadn't, there must have been a reason. "Take me to him and we'll do whatever's needed to get out of here," she said. As soon as the words left her lips, she realised how blunt she'd sounded. "That is, I don't mean to be rude, but I don't belong in your world. Take me to Marcus and we'll both help you but then we need to go home."

"He's in Kelnariat and that's too far a journey." Lord Dorran grinned. "Besides, haven't you been listening? We don't need him."

Claire's stomach sank. He seemed convinced that she could somehow fix this strange world. "How exactly is Kelnarium in danger?" she hedged.

"There was a war forty years ago between the magical Houses and the Council. Your mother was still a young girl." He flung up a hand before Claire could interrupt. "Yes, I realise this means nothing to you. I'll explain the history properly later, but for now, you need only know that the Houses went to battle with the Council and united to use their magic in dangerous ways. As an unintended result, they created the Rift. Now, nothing lives in the Riftlands. The sickness spreads more and more each year. One day all of Kelnarium will be uninhabitable. But that's not all. It's been foretold that the Rift will explode this year, taking all Kelnarium with it. You must stop that happening."

"How?" Claire's head swam.

"Promise you'll learn the magic of this House and help us close the Rift. Then we'll reunite you with Marcus and send you back to your parents."

"Do you really think I'm capable of doing that?" she asked. "I'm ... I'm nothing special in Shale."

A slow smile stretched across her grandfather's ancient face. "You're Suranne's daughter, aren't you? She was one of our best, and Maen and I will help you."

Claire wasn't so sure, but the thought of her mother and father, burning up inside with fright and worry because they had no way of knowing what was happening to both their children in Kelnarium, raised a lump in her throat. She bowed her head, staring at the carpet to hide her face as she thought about never seeing them again. Life in Shale might not be great, but she loved her parents. She'd die here, and Marcus too, unless she found a way to stop this Rift thing from exploding. What choice did Claire have but to help?

"All right. I'll try," she conceded. No, she could do better than that. She made herself meet his gaze, shoulders back and spine straight. "I'll do it."

Chapter Six

CLAIRE SAT ON A WOODEN bench in the huge Manor kitchen beside a woman she'd met last night: Kiera's mother, Meghan. Her long silver hair laced with threads of auburn hung over one shoulder bound in a leather thong. Claire thought she was about sixty-five or so. Meghan smiled, her eyes the same shape as Kiera's, only they crinkled with an instant friendliness her daughter had never shown Claire. One of the best Dorran cooks, she was constantly in and out of the kitchens.

Overhead, bunches of herbs and cured meats hung by strings. The air smelt of fresh cream, oats and bread baking and the big open space was loud with the sound of chairs scraping, chatter and pots clanging.

Claire wondered if she should tell Meghan about her nightmare from the night before. In it, the same thing she'd seen in the Rift had floated before her; it had laughed as Claire had tumbled impossibly forward into the deep caverns of its wide, open mouth ...

Next, she'd stood in a small, dark cell with the sounds of cockroaches and spiders scuttling in the shadows. A boy sat on the floor, legs drawn up under his chin, dirty and thin.

The boy's pain-dulled eyes searched her green ones. She called out, but he shrank back. Then, she'd gotten a clear view of his face.

It was Marcus.

The creature had laughed again, shriller than before, as one thin tendril wafted towards her. Its mouth stretched upwards, fixed into an unnatural grimace. "Betrayer."

The word seemed to echo, even as shock had catapulted her awake. She'd clutched her covers in fright as the thing's voice had followed her out of the nightmare. "Do not try to take his place."

Was it just her suspicion that her grandfather had gotten things wrong with Marcus that had led to the dream or did it mean something more? Meghan seemed kind in a way her daughter wasn't, but still Claire wasn't sure she wanted to be distracted by talking about the dream right before her first magic lesson.

Meghan's gentle voice cut through Claire's indecision. "You haven't touched your third slice of bread."

Claire groaned. "I never have more than two pieces of toast back home."

"But did you perform magic then?"

"No." She sighed, shredding the bread between thumb and forefinger.

"You must eat," Meghan explained for the umpteenth time. "Working magic takes a toll on one's body." She tapped her fingers against the table. "One more bite and we'd best be off." She rose an arm and one of the cooks swung past with a bowl of hard-boiled eggs. He placed one on Claire's plate as Meghan smiled her thanks.

"Really?" Claire protested. Her stomach felt so stretched she was sure she could pass for Father Christmas.

"Yes, really."

Obediently, Claire shovelled egg into her mouth.

Meghan nodded approvingly as she pulled a stray silver hair out of her hazel eyes. "So, you slept in your mother's old bed last night. Does she still paint? There are three of hers hanging in that room of yours, all ringed with tiny salamander borders. She had a fine eye for detail."

What? Claire, her mouth still full of egg, shook her head. The room she'd slept in was bare of any personal trace of her mother. She'd lain awake last night wondering how different her mother might have been if she hadn't left Kelnarium, but it had been hard to imagine without a hint of her old personality available. No objects, clothes, photographs (though maybe they didn't exist here) or other memorabilia. It was as though Grandfather and Dorran House had erased her existence from the place.

Meghan frowned. "She doesn't? Suranne loved painting more than anything. Many was the time I scolded her for dripping paint onto the floor."

Claire swallowed hastily. "No, she paints in Shale. I meant there aren't any paintings in my room."

"Hmm." Meghan pursed her lips. "No matter. Are you done? Let's get you to Maen."

Claire brushed crumbs off her knee-length tunic, then swung her legs over the bench. She'd woken to find her own clothes removed. Kiera hadn't said where they'd been sent, but Claire felt funny about it, like she'd lost her last link to the real world. She was glad she'd held onto her underwear, even if she was wearing them inside out.

Before following Meghan out of the kitchen, she loosened the decorative brown leather belt around her waist. There. That felt better. She'd never been so full in her life.

"Come along, child," Meghan encouraged, as Claire lagged.

They walked through corridor after corridor lined with lit candles in sconces. It didn't seem as cold as last night, which was a small mercy.

At last, light streamed in through the windows. Yesterday she'd seen that the ones on the upper level were made of clear glass, so Claire knew they were rising higher and higher in the Manor. The passageway widened as Meghan led Claire through an arched doorway into a wide cloistered deck, open to the air and jutting out from the side of the building. The space was edged with carved timber that rose so high Claire couldn't see over them to the outside world. Shrubs and poppies grew in narrow raised garden beds along the edge of the deck.

Maen stood by a small wooden bench holding some old pots and a small pile of kindling that Claire assumed he'd gathered from the nearby shrubs, his hands clasped over a tunic that matched Claire's.

Meghan patted the small of Claire's back, nudging her forward. "There's no need to be shy. I'll see you at the feast tonight." She waved at Claire's new teacher, before turning and hurrying back the way they'd come.

Swallowing nervously, Claire stepped forward to join Maen. He said nothing. Instead, he put out a hand, his outstretched fingertips almost touching her cheeks. His eyes closed and sweat beaded his forehead as he concentrated on feeling the air in front of her face. She flinched and had to stop herself from stepping backwards.

Maen dropped his hands, clasping them in front of his stomach as he opened his eyes. He looked pleased. "The *learth* is very strong in you."

"*Learth?*"

"There are four Houses, all of which use elemental magic. We call this unique power *learth*."

"Can anyone have *learth* in their blood?"

"No. It's a mixture of inherited ability and individual mindset. The Houses test the populace regularly and those with the talent and desire to learn come to their respective manor."

"And you say I'm strong in it?"

"Yes."

He'd given her the perfect opening. "But you tested Marcus too and I think you've made a mistake about him."

Before she could tell Maen about her dream, he gave a short, scornful laugh. "Young lady, I know a good deal more about magic than you do," he said dismissively.

His words stung. He reminded her of her sarcastic maths teacher, Mr Hart, who made her shrivel up with a look. She definitely wouldn't tell Maen about her nightmare. He'd think she was being silly. "Will you teach me how to light fires with my fingers like Grandfather did yesterday?" she asked instead.

That would be an awesome tale to tell back home. Her face fell. Except she couldn't tell anyone but her family. What would it have been like for her if Suranne and James had stayed at the Manor? She would have had relatives at birthdays and Christmas for one thing - if they celebrated Christmas here, that is. She would have also been respected as a relation of Lord and Lady Dorran. She'd have had friends. Life would have been proscribed but simpler.

"Certainly," Maen said. "I'm a good teacher. By the time your grandfather starts working with you, you will have mastered the basics. We will begin with attempts to call fire in these pots. Do not think it simple. Magic has its cost."

"It causes exhaustion, right? Meghan stuffed me with food earlier because of that."

"Yes, there's that," he said, yet somehow Claire knew he wasn't telling her everything. For one thing, he looked at her with a strange recognition she couldn't understand.

"What kind of magic stuff can Dorran House do?" she asked.

"All sorts, young lady. We can conjure fireballs and shoot them at enemies. We can make a wall of flame. We can heat metal in soldiers' hands. We can turn mud molten."

Claire's mouth hung open. *Wow!*

"But we rarely need to do such things," Maen went on. "Not since Councilman Eidan took over Kelnarium's government and brought peace. Rael and his guards can manage the odd religious spy on the rare occasion they do manage to infiltrate our compound. They think magic is sedition against the gods but everyone else tolerates us and stays away."

"Those things all seem ... well ... super violent," Claire ventured, "and more useful against people. How will this stuff help with my task?"

"I don't know," Maen admitted. "No one does, but we'll teach you as much as we can, and something will come to you."

Great. No pressure, Claire thought.

"Now, there are two types of fire: hot and cold. Obviously when we want to melt, we'd choose hot, but cold is useful for generating a lot of steam quickly. One can also create an illusion to scare people off and—"

Urgh, he's exactly like a teacher at school, Claire thought as her brain checked out. *Never any fun and spouting boring theory.* She wanted to get to some actual spells.

Maen droned on and on. It was harder and harder to concentrate when the sun was hot on her face and the air warm.

A sudden tap stung her wrist. "Pay attention, girl. Mistakes happen when you don't concentrate. What did I just say?"

"I ... I don't ..."

"As I thought," he said. "Perhaps something more practical will wake you up." Raising his arm, red sleeve hanging down, he pointed towards a large wide-mouthed clay pot. "Gather kindling and place it inside."

She hastily gathered a handful of sticks from the pile near Maen and threw them into the pot.

Maen clicked his tongue behind her. "Not so fast. Neaten them up, like this." He bent and rearranged the sticks like he was a Boy Scout. "Now, watch me."

He closed his eyes and breathed in and out, slow and steady, both hands lightly touching the pot. He was graceful as he swayed, and a low hum reverberated in the air. Within seconds the kindling was alight. Maen opened his eyes.

"How did you do that?" Claire asked. "How do *I* do that?" It would be so cool if she turned out to be good at magic after all. It might explain why she'd always been so different in Shale.

"Close your eyes and breathe deeply, slowly, and with purpose. Think only of the flames. Shape them in your imagination. Let them flow through you as though you are a conduit. Try."

Claire placed her hands on the side of the pot as Maen had done, and did as she was told. She didn't want to let him down, but for every moment of stillness and inner quiet, a thousand thoughts drowned out her purpose. The images she tried to hold were replaced by her mother and father but most of all her brother, like the flickering pictures cast by an old projector.

She heard Maen sigh and opened her eyes. To her surprise, he merely said, "It takes time. Go again."

The breathing exercises seemed to go on forever. No matter how hard Claire tried she couldn't seem to conjure anything. She was about to tell Maen that the whole thing was a waste of time when she thought again of Marcus. Thought of their parents. Thought of them waiting for their children to come home. *I have to do this.*

Claire closed her eyes once more. She sucked in deep breaths and tasted the fresh air on her tongue. She remembered a camping trip with Marcus and the roaring campfire they'd made; she held the glittering yellow-orange in her mind, the memory vivid.

Whooosh. Her skin tingled as scalding heat rushed through her hands where they rested against the pot. A burnt meat scent curled up her nostrils. She leapt backwards, trying not to cry out in terror, gasping for breath as her eyes sprang open.

A fire leapt merrily in the pot.

"That smell," she said. "Was I on fire?"

"No," Maen assured her. "That is the smell of fire *learth* when it has manifested. I knew you would succeed when the salamanders first gathered to watch."

Claire stared around her teacher, perplexed. She couldn't see any amphibians on the ground or in the air, but everyone kept bringing them up.

Rael had mentioned salamanders helping his party find her when she'd first reached Kelnarium, some of the clothes and jewellery worn in the Manor featured them and just this morning Meghan had mentioned Suranne painting some.

"Salamanders? Where?" she asked. "And why are they significant?"

"Each magical House has its own elemental creatures to assist them in all things. Ours are the salamanders that live deep in the rock beneath the Manor, inside a cavern full of red opals and smoke." He pulled the neck of his tunic aside to reveal a gold chain with a tiny egg-shaped stone pendant, its clear centre shot through with crimson veins. "This stone is from their home. Each true Dorran is gifted one to connect us to our brethren and ensure we do not sicken and die away from our natural place in Kelnarium. You will be given one by your grandfather when he deems you ready."

Claire blinked, trying to process so much new information. "But you said there are salamanders watching us now. I can't see them."

Maen laughed. "Because you haven't learnt enough to be a true Dorran. Not yet. In time, you will see them as I do, and they will guide and protect you." He shot her a wide grin. "Trust me, you won't have to wait long. You did well with that spell. You were quick to make fire."

"Quick?" Claire protested. "We must have been at it for hours!" Her stomach rumbled.

"Trust me; that was quick. I—" He broke off, looking behind Claire to the doorway that led back inside the Manor.

Claire spun around. Her grandfather strode towards them, his ring winking in the noon sun. Behind him was a small woman with blonde hair and icy blue eyes. She held a plain wooden bowl in her hands and wore a white cotton dress which billowed at her feet like frothy milk. Claire couldn't remember seeing her at last night's dinner, though she was sure she would have noticed her.

"How goes training, Granddaughter?" Lord Dorran asked.

"Good, I think," she said.

"More than good. Lady Claire is a natural," Maen added.

Claire couldn't help a grin. She didn't feel talented, but she'd take Maen's praise. He was a tough task master, but maybe not a second Mr Hart after all.

The pair drew level with Maen and Claire. "This is Gwenivere," Dorran explained. "She and some of her fellow Dream Mages came from Kelnariat to help summon you."

"I-I'm sorry," Claire stammered, worried she was going to cause offence. "I met so many people at dinner you've slipped my memory, Gwenivere."

"Oh, I wasn't at dinner," Gwenivere explained. "My people and I had our food in private. All six of us were exhausted after the summons."

"Pardon my ignorance, but what are Dream Mages? What do you do?"

Gwenivere looked from Lord Dorran to Claire, her expression critical.

"There hasn't been time to explain much," Dorran said hastily, "and her mother told her nothing."

Claire hoped the flicker of hurt that rippled through her didn't show. Her parents should have told her more. They should have trusted her, the way they'd done with everything else.

Gwenivere nodded, turning back to Claire. "We're one of the three human magical brethren of Kelnarium left. We have visions of past, present and future across time and space. We knew of other worlds long before anyone else in Kelnarium did."

"Did you help my mother summon my father? He said she had friends with her."

"Yes," Lord Dorran answered for Gwenivere. "We need the Dream Mages to focus our working, so we can see the location of the other person being summoned and guide them safely through the Rift." He looked like he wanted to say more but Gwenivere got in first.

"But that's not the only reason *I* came to visit."

Claire stifled a laugh as Lord Dorran's bushy brows beetled upwards.

"Eidan wanted me to make sure things ran smoothly." She glanced at Lord Dorran. "He'll be along in a week or so, but I wanted to see our saviour with my own eyes." She fixed Lord Dorran with a hard stare. "She looks as much like your brother as she does Suranne. Are you sure of her?"

Claire smarted silently. Wonderful; first Kiera and now this Gwenivere clearly distrusted her. Also, Claire looked nothing like Great-uncle Aed.

"Yes," her grandfather said. "Besides, she's just a child."

"That's what I'm afraid of," Gwenivere said. "She isn't really one of us."

"I *am* still here you know," Claire broke in. If Suranne had told her more maybe she'd have felt less like a fish out of water and Gwenivere would be nicer now. Honestly, she was going to have hard words with her parents when she got back to Shale.

"Indeed. Then tell me, can you know how it feels to watch the land die, ghost towns dotting all of northwestern Kelnarium? Can you know how it felt for those in the Riftlands to watch people they loved snatched away into the Rift's growing centre; babies out of mother's arms, lovers from each other's embrace, family members pulled away? All spat out in another time and place, stranded." She looked sadly into her wooden bowl. "No, how can you possibly understand?"

Claire thought of Marcus vanishing in front of her near the dam. "Maybe I can."

"The Riftlands' spread is accelerating as the Rift itself widens," Gwenivere went on, as if Claire hadn't spoken, her voice trembling. "More and more people must flee. And to make matters worse, magic has become unstable. It was hard enough summoning you here in one piece. That's why I've stayed after the summons, leaving fifty of my people in Kelnariat without their leader, and why I'll be supervising your training from now on. I can watch for any signs of danger." She took a deep breath, her trembles slowly subsiding.

Claire glanced at Lord Dorran and Maen. Both kept their expressions blank. The silence grew until Dorran clapped his hands together. "Well, I'd best be off. I'll leave my granddaughter in both of your capable hands."

Maen looked at Gwenivere. "Lady Claire had just managed to light some kindling when you arrived. I had intended to go on with that this afternoon, but are there things you wish to show her?"

"No. I'll keep watch for you-know-what." Gwenivere's icy eyes caught Maen's before Claire could ask what she meant. She reminded Claire of her English teacher, expecting a lot and disappointed by the slightest failure. She couldn't help but feel nervous.

Maen cleared his throat. "Let's continue. Claire, see if you can light more than one pot in a row. This time, imagine lighting them using thought alone. Forget about touching them." He stooped to line three up in front of her. "Now, listen closely. To do this, you need to hold the correct breathing technique the whole time."

Gwenivere's mouth was a thin line. "Isn't that a little advanced for her first day?"

"She's powerful, but her stamina's good too. That's a rare combination." He stared at her significantly and Claire felt a surge of solidarity with her teacher. He wasn't going to let Gwenivere walk all over her.

Gwenivere held his gaze for a moment, then nodded.

Claire closed her eyes and commenced the breathing exercises Maen had taught her. It was the work of moments to remember the time she and Marcus had built a bonfire at the back end of the farm. The tell-tale tingle spread from fingertips to upper arm and the air tasted of meat and smoke. *Whoosh*. One fire lit. She heard a murmur of approval from Gwenivere. She ignored the rush of heat and the fast beat of her heart and pictured the bonfire again. This time, she had to hold the image for longer as the sticks in the pot stubbornly refused to catch alight. Finally, a snap and crackle sounded to her left, her arm feeling like it was waking up with pins and needles. She heard Maen stumble out of the way.

"Ignore us," he called. "Concentrate on the last one."

This time it took a full ten minutes for anything to happen. Claire's stomach felt hollow and her muscles loose, but at last, the tell-tale sound of twigs crackling let her know she'd succeeded. She opened her eyes to see Maen smiling with the exuberance of a young child.

Then, exhaustion hit. The last thing she saw was Maen and a pale Gwenivere peering anxiously at her as she blacked out.

Claire woke up in bed, warm and tucked in up to the chin. She rolled to her side, coming face to face with Kiera, who was sitting on a stool, concern in her eyes.

"You're awake at last," Kiera said. The unkindness in her voice from yesterday had vanished. "Maen said he pushed you a bit hard, but you'll be fine by the feast. I have watered down mead and bread and meat. Let me help you up."

Claire managed to push the thick covers back, though her muscles felt heavy, and let Kiera support her as she sat up. The room spun as Kiera held a goblet to Claire's lips. She took three sips of the sweet honey-like mead, then turned to the plate of fresh bread and strips of venison and gravy, cramming a third of the stuff into her mouth before she realised what she was doing and started chewing properly. Claire's vision steadied as she focused on the back wall.

"It's all right. You used a lot of energy," Kiera said. After a pause, she went on. "Maen says he's never seen anything like it." Her voice dropped as her mouth worked in odd directions. "Not even Suranne ..."

Claire leant back against the pillows, unable to hide her curiosity. "I know you miss Mum, but why are you so angry with her?"

At first, Kiera merely wiped a tear from her cheek and tried to smile, but then she found her voice. "I did everything with her. I lost part of myself when she went away."

Claire pictured Marcus and thought she understood.

"And then I told myself it wouldn't matter. *I* didn't need her. Dorran House didn't even need her. Rael and I have talent. Maybe our children would be strong enough to close the Rift and the prophecy could go rot. Of course, that was before I discovered I couldn't have children."

Claire tried to think of something to say as the painful silence grew. She wanted to rub a hand against Kiera's back but wasn't sure if it was the right thing to do. "I'm sorry."

"Don't be." Kiera tilted her chin. "Rael and I are happy enough and I have found other ways to build a family."

"I noticed you and my grandfather weren't apart for long at last night's dinner," Claire observed softly.

"Yes. Suranne was his only child and my own father, his older brother, is dead too. When Lady Dorran passed it felt almost like a curse. He's experienced too much loss. His younger brother, my mother, Meghan, and my brother and his wife, they are his family now. But he and I always had an understanding that went deeper."

"Then I showed up."

Kiera laughed, but not unkindly. "Yes. I thought because you look like Suranne you'd be the same as her. Everyone loved her. She was beautiful, funny, kind and the life of the party. And the mischief we made together ..." She flicked her loose long hair over one shoulder. "We were the most popular girls in the Manor."

Beautiful. Funny. Kind. Popular. Claire might have been her mother's daughter if she'd been born here, but she couldn't be sure. Besides, Claire couldn't tally the woman Kiera painted with her scatter-brained and awkward mother. "She isn't that person anymore," she said. "Everyone thinks she's weird in my hometown." A lump rose in her throat. "She doesn't have friends or go to parties. She even lost her magic."

Kiera didn't say anything for a long time. "I was upset that she hadn't taught Marcus about his heritage. I thought he was lying when he said she hadn't taught him a single spell."

"No, he wasn't lying." Claire picked at the bed cover, willing away tears. "But I wish she'd told us more." It might have helped Claire feel less like a pariah in Shale. But it was no good going over the same thing again and again.

She thought about her conversation with Meghan instead and looked about the room. She hadn't noticed them yesterday, but now she knew to look she saw small holes in the stone, with areas around them that were lighter than the rest of the wall, like paintings had once hung there. "My mother lived here, but there's nothing of her left. Why?"

"Lord Dorran put some of her things in a chest and kept it in his bedchambers, though he hasn't looked at any of them since your grandmother died. The rest of her possessions were left to me. I stashed them in a wooden cupboard and locked the door."

"Is that where the paintings ended up?"

Kiera jerked away from Claire, like her words had physically hurt. "I tried turning them around, but it wasn't enough," she whispered. "There was a painting of me, you see, and paintings of our special places. I didn't want you to see them ... to have even more of her ..."

A lump formed in Claire's throat. She didn't know what to say.

"I wanted to hate you, but I don't, and especially not now, after you've shown so much affinity for *learth*." Kiera smiled, taking the empty plate out of Claire's hands and standing up to place it on the fireplace mantel. Once the plate was disposed of, she turned back to Claire. "Now, we must get ready for tonight's feast."

"I won't have to do anything, will I? Back home, I ... I didn't like talking to people much."

"You'll be fine," Kiera said firmly. "Your things are on that wooden stool and I can do your hair again."

"Can I do yours?" Claire had always been jealous of the girls in primary school giggling and braiding each other's hair on lunch break.

Kiera stiffened, then grinned. "You can, but it'd better be perfect. I have a reputation to maintain."

Chapter Seven

CLAIRE SAT AT THE MAIN table in the dining hall, between her great-aunt Meghan and Lord Dorran. She and thirteen others sat on the raised dais, served first, and seen by all. Spread across the dining hall were a good hundred or so people sitting at tables. Some of them were related to her. She felt as if she'd never get to know all their names if she lived here a million years, but many of them smiled at her now. No doubt they'd heard how well class had gone with Maen. A couple had already hurried up to her on the way to dinner offering her thanks. She'd almost started believing she was the saviour they needed. She waved at some of them now – there was little Sasha, Blaise and Clothilde's daughter, and over there, grabbing a hunk of bread and stowing it in his pocket, was her roguish cousin Maet, and three seats past him were Liesel and Toam – she couldn't keep track of everyone if she tried.

She took a sip of apple juice from the goblet in front of her and tried to be more alert. Her grandfather was telling her about Dorran House's place in Kelnarium as servitors holding tureens took turns heaping roasted turnip, carrot and potato onto her plate.

"We weren't always so isolated," he explained. "We used to send envoys throughout the land, helping anyone who needed us. But for the priests, most had no issue with us."

"It's because we don't worship Brighid and Lugh," Aed interjected. Claire liked him best of her relations other than warm-hearted Meghan; he was shy and unassuming and had made time to listen to Claire's questions when they'd walked through the gardens earlier. He winked at her conspiratorially. "We magical users know our powers are natural, not gifted at the whim of the gods."

"Indeed," Lord Dorran said. "The common folk make wooden carvings of the god and goddess and we leave them to it. We are left alone, except for the odd mad priest who tries to score points with his makers by attempting an assassination." He smiled at Aed. "Luckily, I have my brother to act as my faithful double. We look so similar that they attack him instead of me and pay the price for their mistake. Aed is a mean warrior for all his mild manners. But before the Rift, there was a lot more suspicion. It was fuelled by priests who had Selk's ear in Kelnariat."

"Selk?" Claire asked.

"He was elected Council Leader of Kelnarium forty years ago and didn't like the fact that more and more folk were apprenticing to learn magic or work with us in some way. He feared the growing towns around us would threaten his power. He demanded the four *learth* Houses—"

"Wait, who are they? There's the Dorrans and the Dream Mages—"

"No," Gwenivere interrupted from the other end of the table. "We don't use *learth* magic like you Dorrans do." She smiled thinly. "Our magic, *anam*, is sourced from within rather than from the external elements. It is something deeper than blood, it is in our very souls. Anyone in Kelnarium might have the skill, regardless of their bloodline."

"As Gwenivere alluded," Lord Dorran added, "the four *learth* Houses represent the elements. Dorran House represents fire, Maellwyn House represents water, House Domain represented earth and House Ushanan represented air. The last two were destroyed in the war." Lord Dorran turned to his brother, who placed a hand on his shoulder.

"You mentioned a war when I first met you," Claire said. She twisted around in her chair to point at one of the five paintings on the rose-coloured wall behind them. "I noticed that painting last night. Is it a scene from the war?" The scene depicted a battle, the artist capturing the expressions of agony on people and horse's faces alike.

"Yes," Lord Dorran answered. "Your grandmother painted it."

Claire stared at the painting. The style was so different to her own or Suranne's. If she looked hard enough, perhaps she'd be able to perceive the personality behind it.

"Now this is important, so listen carefully," Lord Dorran said. As Claire swivelled back around, he continued, "Selk demanded that the four Houses sign the Corpus Treaty—"

"It was meant to be for all magical brethren in Kelnarium," Gwenivere said, pushing meat fretfully to one side of her plate. "Not just the Houses."

"Yes, it all stemmed from a bid to regulate the size of magical communities by restricting how many people we could take in, whom we could marry and when we could use our magic without penalty. Maellwyn House, the Dream Mages, the Enchantment Weavers and our people signed the pestilential thing. We thought we'd be able to renegotiate once a new Council Leader was elected." He sighed. "House Ushanan and House Domain refused to sign. Selk rode to their territory in northwestern Kelnarium with an army loaned to him by the priests to force them to sign the treaty. For better or worse, we made the decision to sit tight, hoping good sense would win the day."

"Wait," Claire realised. "This is the war that led to the creation of the Rift, right? I swear you said that, too."

Her grandfather couldn't meet her eyes and his cheeks grew pale. "Yes, and Dorran House was responsible."

Claire let her fork loaded with potato and gravy hang in the air. "What?"

"I'd only been lord for a few years when the split between the Houses over Selk's treaty happened. Not all Dorrans agreed with my decision to sign it."

Aed frowned into his steaming vegetable pile. "Kelt was too hot-blooded and hasty. And he was spoilt to boot."

"Hush," Lord Dorran said gently. He glanced at Meghan and with a start, Claire remembered Kelt had been Meghan's husband, Kiera's father. Was he the man who Gwenivere had compared her to earlier?

Meghan's eyes bored into the glossy wood of the table like it would rescue her from the bad memories she was reliving.

Lord Dorran looked at her pityingly. "He was the eldest but didn't have the magical or leadership skills required to lead Dorran House. I was appointed leader, and he resented it sometimes." He shook his head. "When my brother disagreed with me over Selk, I thought if I left him alone, he'd calm down. I figured he'd talk to Meghan and they'd ride away for a few days, as he'd done over other arguments."

"Only I was away visiting my sister," Meghan said, so softly Claire had to lean in to hear. "She lives in Dashun Village, on the coast to the south, two-day's ride from here. She'd just had her second child."

"Kelt never told me. I was a fool." Dorran's voice broke. "I left him alone with his rage."

Aed took over. "He rode away. Most of our best soldiers vanished with him. By the time we realised how many had gone, we were too far behind to catch up and talk sense into them. We rode out anyway and picked up Lord and Lady Maellwyn on the way. Turned out some of their people had thirsted for battle too. When we got to Ushanan Manor, the fighting was well underway. Selk and his men, the priests and their assassins on one side, Kelt and his rag-tag gang on the other."

"More than underway," Dorran said in a tone that made Claire certain he and his brother had engaged in this call and response before. "Kelt had combined magic with the other two Houses, creating firestorms and earthquakes, rockfalls and windstorms all at once. Selk and his men were killed but there was too much magical energy and it had to go somewhere. Kelt lost control."

"He was responsible for the Rift?" Claire couldn't believe someone she was related to could be to blame for such a terrible thing. Now she understood why, if she did indeed look like Kelt, Gwenivere mistrusted her.

"It's my greatest shame," her grandfather replied, fiddling with his goblet. "I tried to untangle him and the others he'd dragged into his working, but even with the Saura and her salamanders helping me, I couldn't save him. The manors of House Ushanan and House Domain were destroyed, their lands now the Riftlands in the northwest."

"You are not the only person who shares blame for what happened," Gwenivere broke in.

"Not this again," he laughed, but there was a hint of exasperation beneath it, as if they'd had this conversation a thousand times before. "Isn't living in Kelnariat penance enough for you?"

Claire looked between the two of them. What were they on about? How could *Gwenivere* be responsible for anything? Before she could ask, the conversation flowed on, Aed taking one glance at the tearful Meghan and skilfully praising her baking prowess as dessert was brought out.

Claire ate almond tart, some kind of cheese pie and a pudding studded with raisins and let the conversation wash over her. Around the hall, alcoves flickered with candlelight, casting shadow pictures and, if Claire tilted her head, she could observe the cut of the dark wooden beams criss-crossed over the diners, making high elegant archways. She finally came to admire the enormous painting of a glowing white-hot salamander against a backdrop of crimson flame and let her mind wander. How warm and full and content she felt right now. She thought of her mother back home making dishes to feed the hungry and wondered how much waste there would be from this meal. She hoped Dorran sent it to those who needed it. Thinking of hunger and poverty made Claire remember the camp she had ridden through on her arrival. Those people had looked so pinched and starved.

She waited for a break in the conversation, then cleared her throat. "Who were those people in the camp I saw with Rael? Between the Riftlands and your farmland and villages? I felt sorry for them."

Meghan's breath came out in a hot rush at Claire's ear. Aed shifted uncomfortably in his seat. It took Claire a moment to notice the whole table had gone silent, all eyes on Lord Dorran.

"Are they survivors of those who rode off with Kelt?" She looked at the others eagerly, then paused, noticing the sudden tension around the table. What would her father or Marcus say in such circumstances? "I can tell this is a sensitive subject. It makes sense why you're angry with them if they were part of Kelt's army."

Her grandfather frowned. "Everyone who rode with my brother from our House was killed. There were no survivors."

"Then who are they?" Claire insisted. She didn't want to upset her newly found relatives and friends, but she had to know.

"In the immediate weeks after the Rift's creation, people thought the priests and Selk were justified," Lord Dorran explained. "It was magic that had made it, after all. Things were volatile, but luckily people were afraid of more violence. They elected a moderate to lead the council. Praine told us to lie low and we've done what she asked ever since."

Claire bit back frustration. Why was her grandfather hedging? He hadn't answered her question at all. "I'm afraid I don't quite follow. What does the past have to do with the people in the camps?"

Gwenivere sent a look to Lord Dorran, as if seeking permission to reveal the truth. He shrugged, so she elaborated. "Years before Selk, the priests paid commoners a lot of money to form a team of hired assassins to do their dirty work for them, often against magical Houses and those who supported us. When the priests gained influence in Selk's Council, we were afraid things would get bad, but we never realised how bad until it was too late. Selk wouldn't have had a big enough army to attack House Ushanan and Domain without the priests' assassins, simply because the people of Kelnarium had a lot of respect for us, despite the angry diatribes of the few. Praine rounded up the priests in Kelnariat who'd pushed Selk into war and their entire network of paid assassins. They were just as responsible as any of the Houses were. Praine banished them to permanent exile in the Riftlands." She picked at the edge of a tart. "It's why the priests have far less power these days compared to back then."

"And it's why those exiles eke out the existence they deserve. No one sells to them or gives them shelter. No one speaks to them," Lord Dorran said with a bitter vehemence that made Claire sad.

Meghan clasped Claire's hand. "I know it's hard to understand, but we lost so many in that terrible battle. My husband and my daughter, Sheree." She nodded to Kiera and Rael who sat further down the table. "Rael lost both his brothers. Those people in the camps are responsible. They started it all."

Claire knew that some of the people she'd seen at the camps were too young to have been involved in the war. She had to say something. "But to punish even their descendants?"

"We lost two magical Houses that day and ever since magic has been unstable," Lord Dorran said. "Any kind of major working is a hazard. Not to mention that we users of magic have been splintered ever since. Lady Maellwyn died in the Rift's creation, caught up in Kelt's madness before she could pull back. It took all my energy to prevent a second war."

"Meanwhile," explained Gwenivere, "we Dream Mages were invited to join Praine's councillors, a tradition that has continued on with Eidan. As far as Praine was concerned, we'd had nothing to do with the war and she wanted to show she stood with us, so to Kelnariat we went. As to the Enchantment Weavers—"

"The Enchantment Weavers? They've been mentioned before. Who are they?"

Dorran answered before the Dream Mage could. "They live in the far east of Kelnarium. While the four Houses used the magic of the elements, and Gwenivere," he nodded her direction, "has visions, they weave birth, life and death according to patterns only they can interpret. For as long as anyone can remember, they've lived in the remote Arras Ranges and after the Rift they withdrew from everyone altogether. I doubt anyone has seen them for years."

Claire tried to keep hold of the thread that mattered, the camp. "OK, I get that things were tense, and emotions ran high -" she paused at the table's closed expressions. "Are still running high - but making children pay for the mistakes of their parents is wrong. How many years have they lived this way?"

"Thirty," Aed said sternly. "And they'll stay living as they are until doomsday."

Claire was startled. She hadn't expected such forcefulness from her kind great-uncle.

She jutted her chin. "Mum wouldn't like it."

"Really? Suranne knew about it and accepted the situation," Lord Dorran said.

Claire thought of her mother donating to charity every week, making food, the sponsor child they'd supported through Oxfam. "She's had time to regret that," she said. Tears caught in her throat as she rose from her bench. "I'm going to bed."

Chapter Eight

"WAKE UP," CAME KIERA'S voice, cutting through the image of a snarling face that filled Claire's mind. She sat up in a hurry, knocking Kiera's hands from her shoulders, heart racing.

Kiera perched on the edge of the bed, furrow lines of concern across her forehead. "You were shouting in your sleep. Something about Marcus."

Claire shuddered. The demon thing had haunted her dreams yet again, this time taunting her with the prospect of Dorran House finding out she was a fraud. She'd screamed at her grandfather in front of hundreds of Dorrans, reminding him that she'd warned them it was Marcus who they'd needed all along. He and the others had watched her, stony-faced, as she'd waited for her punishment.

"It was nothing," she lied as Kiera peered at her.

"Should I have a word with Maen?" Kiera asked, patting Claire's hands gently. "Perhaps he's working you too hard?"

Claire had been to lessons with Maen for five days now and every day he kept her practising for hours on end. A servitor would stand by her, holding a tray of bread and cheese and she'd scoff mouthfuls between trying to put out multiple fires at once or create cold flame. And it didn't end there. She'd finish practice with just enough time to wash and change into the more formal dress her grandfather insisted on for dinner. Then her meal came with a side of complicated politics, courtesy of Lord Dorran. She had to concentrate on what was being said to avoid his disapproval if even days later she hadn't remembered the name of a battle, a priest, a noble or any other small detail. And it wasn't over then. Kiera would review the day's discussion one more time before Claire went to bed. It would be believable to claim her rigorous timetable was to blame for her fitful sleep, but Maen would see through the lie. He and Gwenivere were always going on about her magical stamina.

"It's my brother," she said instead. "I miss him."

Kiera looked away. "What was he like? In your world, I mean?"

"We're super close," Claire said. "We loved mucking about on our farm and with the horses and in the bush." She paused at the confusion in Kiera's face. "Erm, sorry. The bush is another term for like, a forest. Anyway, Marcus was always there for me." She couldn't wait to see him again. She'd throw her arms around him and he'd be so proud she'd come to Kelnarium to help.

Kiera's voice shook. "He didn't like us very much. Me and Rael especially."

Claire was baffled. "I don't understand. You remember the time you told me Suranne was the life of the party? That's Marcus back home. He's the charmer."

"He was a sulky thing when he arrived at the Manor, nattering on about something called football and his girlfriend and how we were barbarians. I suppose Rael could have been more circumspect in how he explained Kelnarium to Marcus, but how was he meant to know that ... Anyway, once Maen tested him and told Marcus he was a weak magical user, he wouldn't give us the time of day," Kiera said sadly. "I don't think he liked being bad at something."

"There has to have been a misunderstanding," Claire said firmly. "Like I said, Marcus gets along with everyone."

Kiera looked doubtful. "He wouldn't talk to Rael and me and the screaming matches he had with Lord Dorran had to be heard to be believed. He didn't care about our heritage or history. He didn't want anything more to do with us." She put a hand to her heart. "We are his relations. We felt it keenly."

Claire plumped up her pillow to occupy her hands. The picture Kiera painted didn't tally with what she knew of her brother. If Marcus and Dorran House had started off on a bad footing, had Maen and the others tested him properly for magic or merely seen what they'd wanted to see – a failure? Was that what the strange beast was trying to tell her? And what kind of thing was it? She wished Gwenivere was easier to approach. After all, strange visions were her forte, but the Dream Mage spoke to Claire with an acerbity that led Claire to make mistakes. Still, perhaps Kiera would have some ideas.

She picked at the embroidery on the bed covers. "Mum had visions of Dad in the flame. Maen hasn't mentioned visions being a Dorran power though."

Kiera blinked at the sudden change in subject. "We can, with help from the Dream Mages," she said. "It was Gwenivere and her bond mate, Rinn, who helped Suranne find James."

"They can't send you visions without your consent, can they?"

"Don't be ridiculous!" Kiera drew back, her mouth a thin line. "What's this all about?"

"Nothing," Claire said quickly, getting out of bed. "I'd better get ready for training."

This time Claire's training took place in a plain hall on the lowest floor of the Manor, just above the basement. As she entered the room, she could see that candles lit every corner. Maen had explained during one of her lessons that the reason for the dark windows and poor lighting on the lower levels was because the salamanders liked such conditions. They were less likely to come out and interact with their human friends if the sun shone brightly. On the back wall hung a painting. Claire had to squint but even in the poor light she recognised the style as her mother's. She didn't recognise the woman in the painting, who had heavy lidded eyes, red lips in a perfect bow and chestnut hair pulled back in a bun.

Maen stood with two other people under the picture. One was Gwenivere, the other, whose back was turned towards the door, was a tall woman with black hair and a green dress in the same style as Gwenivere's. Wicker baskets and wooden bowls peeped out from behind the stranger's flowing dress. Before Claire could say something, the stranger turned and smiled.

Maen broke off mid-sentence and strolled over, the woman trailing behind him as Gwenivere looked on. "This is Rinn Taccala, Gwenivere's second in command."

"Pleased to meet you," Claire managed, even as Gwenivere's shrewd look threw her off.

Once the niceties were over, Maen commenced the lesson. "Today, we're going to focus on cold fire again. Once you get the hang of that, Gwenivere will take over." He nodded the Dream Mage's, untroubled by her aloofness when it came to Claire.

At least she's not openly hostile like the first time I met her, Claire thought. The veiled dislike was easier to ignore.

"Pay attention!" Maen clapped his hands close to Claire, making her flinch. "So, Lady Claire, what are the principles behind cold flame?"

This had been drilled into Claire the way maths equations were at school. "Correct breathing technique, hold the image of a fire the way one does for hot, but overlay it with ice or some other cold thing." Cold fire was kind of like merging two images together.

"Good," Maen said. "Begin."

Out of the corner of her eye, Claire saw Gwenivere tilt her head, her eyes searching every inch of Claire. It was like she was looking for Claire to mess up. Taking a deep breath, Claire tried to ignore her.

She began the breathing exercises, thankful her mother was obsessed with impromptu yoga sessions back in Shale. Rise. Fall. Rise. Fall.

She remembered sitting on the corner bench of the kitchen as a young girl. She'd watched James use the lighter on the stovetop. Next, she thought of ice cubes in the freezer. Now, for the hard part. She tried overlaying the image of the stove's flame with the ice, but the stupid demon from her dreams kept rising over the top of both. He grinned, dispersing both memories. Claire swore under her breath and opened her eyes.

"What happened?" Gwenivere interrogated Maen. "She's not trying."

Before Claire could react, Rinn put a hand on Gwenivere's shoulder and the angry Dream Mage went silent.

"Sorry," Claire muttered at the floor.

Maen passed her a glazed bowl full of candied nuts. "It's fine." After she'd crunched a few, he smiled encouragingly. "Let's go again."

Three more attempts went by before Claire managed to create a wall of cold flame from one end of the room to the next, separating her from the others.

Maen broke through the barrier she'd created with a brush of his hand. "You're distracted today," he said, but without judgement.

"I slept badly," Claire admitted, the smell of something charring curling around the room and her skin running hot.

"The world is about to end. Sleep may need to be sacrificed," Gwenivere retorted.

Rinn laughed, a sweet tinkling sound. "It sounds like you didn't get much either, Gwen. Why so grumpy?"

Claire was grateful. She didn't feel comfortable approaching Gwenivere about her dreams, but maybe she could find a spare moment with Rinn later.

"There's something ..." Gwenivere shook her head. "It doesn't matter." She smiled grudgingly at her bond mate.

"Let's have some lunch," Maen said, as if nothing had happened. He moved to the back of the room and sat cross-legged under the picture Claire was sure Suranne had painted. He pulled a wicker basket close, took out some bread and began to eat. When Claire sat beside him, he passed her another of the baskets. She peered inside at the pastes and dried meats and cheeses. *This magic business really takes it out of you*, she thought as she cut a large chunk of cheese from a round and crammed it into her mouth without thinking.

They ate in silence, Gwenivere looking across to Claire at odd moments, her brows raised like she was turning something over in her mind. Her stares made Claire feel like she'd been caught stealing loose change from her parent's wallet. Rinn shot the occasional warning glance Gwenivere's way.

At last, Claire felt full. She glanced at Maen, who scrubbed the remnants of his meal off his fingers with a napkin, seemingly untroubled by the tensions in the group. "Who's that?" she asked him, pointing at the painting above them.

"It's your grandmother," Maen replied. "Can't you see the likeness?"

Claire craned her neck. She guessed she could see the same lines of chin and cheek as her mother, and maybe herself. Her grandmother looked reserved, like one of those portraits of European royalty that she'd seen in one of her mum's art books, but that could be a style thing. "What was she like?"

"Gentle and kind, and very intelligent," Maen said. Claire heard the respect in his voice and felt a little proud. "She was the best healer we had. She tried teaching Suranne the skills, but your mother never had time for herbs and such." He sighed, placing his and Claire's baskets against the wall. "I'd love to sit and reminisce, but the day is getting on." He glanced at Gwenivere, who daintily wiped at her fingers with a white lace napkin. "Are you ready to take over?"

"Yes, I am," said Gwenivere. While Rinn placed their two baskets alongside the others, Gwenivere reached behind her for a plain wooden bowl, the same she'd been carrying the first time Claire had met her. Now that the bowl was on the ground, Claire could see it was full of liquid.

"We use this as a focus," Rinn explained, noticing Claire's questioning look. "We can use clouds and empty sky too, but inside, water is best."

"For now," Gwenivere said darkly.

"What do you mean?" Claire said, still confused.

"You've heard us say the Rift is unstable. None know it more than the Dream Mages. When we go into our trance state, we see the magical plane. Sometimes when we're seeking visions, a silent creature shatters our control—"

"You see it too!" Claire gasped. Even though the creature Gwenivere described was silent, she guessed it must be the same as the thing that appeared in her own nightmares. This couldn't be a coincidence.

"See what?" Gwenivere asked suspiciously.

"Nothing," Claire mumbled. She hadn't meant to say anything out loud in front of Gwenivere and Maen, who were intimidating enough individually let alone together. She'd corral Rinn in private later.

Gwenivere cleared her throat. "Right, let's get on if there is nothing more to be discussed," she said pointedly. "It is only when this creature appears that our people are injured or killed. Its appearances are unpredictable, but recently, we've seen it more and more often, regardless of what focus we use. Soon, we fear we'll be unable to have visions at all."

Claire looked from Gwenivere to Maen. "Does this thing attack Dorrans too?" she asked, daring another interruption. After all, she didn't want to die trying to work a basic spell. Why hadn't Maen said something earlier?

Maen gave her a look intended to soothe. "We didn't want to scare you when you first started training, but yes, it is possible. That's why Gwenivere's been attending sessions."

"We alone see the magical plane," Gwenivere stated. "I've been keeping an eye on things while Maen teaches you, but I have seen no sign of the creature I've described. It was unlikely with basic spells, however, from today, it's possible the creature will appear."

"Don't worry," Maen said.

"Don't worry? Are you crazy?" Claire's rising anger escaped like steam from a kettle. "I can't believe you kept this from me."

"There's no need to get upset," Maen said mildly.

She folded her arms. "What can I do to protect myself?"

"Not much for now. Be prepared to end the spell. Gwenivere and Rinn will watch for the creature and if it appears, we'll help bring you back immediately."

Claire looked wildly from one person to the next, but she knew she couldn't do anything but continue with the lesson. "Can we get this over with, please?"

Gwenivere nodded curtly, then rearranged her dress. For a moment Claire wondered if the Dream Mage was as nervous as she was. She pushed the idea away. It didn't seem possible for someone so regal and cold to be worried about what might happen.

"I'm going to teach you how to work with us, so that once you've closed the Rift, we can send you home." She paused. "Now Claire, listen carefully. When I first true-dreamt of the need for someone of Dorran blood to have a child by someone not of Kelnarium, I knew I had to break our long silence on the existence of other worlds."

Claire blinked. Just how old was Gwenivere? She looked younger than her mother and yet if she'd been the source of the original prophecy, she must be ... well ... old enough to be a grandparent.

"I rode to Lord Dorran and explained everything," Gwenivere continued. "Your mother was selected as the one most likely to fit the words of the prophecy, but how to find someone from another world? Suranne made a fire and we used it as a conduit for the vision. She saw your father." She drew in a quick breath. "That was the easy part. How to get him to Kelnarium was the problem. My people knew the Rift sucked people into the space between worlds and spat them into new ones. We saw it in our visions; their bewilderment and loneliness as they tried to make new lives." She swallowed and briefly shut her eyes, clearly remembering painful visions. Rinn, Claire noticed, looked on the verge of tears.

Maen took over. "We knew the Rift was forged by one of us and that another would close it, so it made sense for Dorrans to be involved in any working trying to transport someone from your world to ours. Your mother, Lord Dorran, Rinn, Gwenivere and I experimented for weeks to find a way to work together. Eventually, we figured it out: the flame was needed to break through the eye of the Rift, and Dream Mages had to show us the road to your world and hold it open long enough for someone to enter and make the journey in safety."

Claire mulled this over. "Does that mean you can bring people back from other worlds?"

Rinn shook her head. "At first, no one wanted us to. People were angry and afraid. They would have turned on us if we made even the smallest blunder, and what's to say we wouldn't have made one? It was a magical mistake that damaged Kelnarium. Then, with Eidan, Kelnarium's current leader, we might have tried, but travel has become too unstable. Each time we transport someone it gets riskier."

"You managed to bring me here safely."

"Wrong," Gwenivere said bitterly. "There's a man in Lord Dorran's infirmary, one of my Dream Mages, who was attacked by the creature in the Rift during our working to summon you. He's been unconscious since you arrived."

Claire didn't know what to say. She hadn't asked for Grandfather and his friends to summon her, but she didn't like the idea of people getting hurt on her behalf either. She wished someone had told her. She would have tried to sneak away to sit by the man and comfort him.

"But he knew the price," Gwenivere said. "So, let us begin, Lady Claire." She tapped the floor with her fingers. "Remain cross-legged. Close your eyes. Use the breathing techniques Maen has taught you. Picture the flames escaping from your body in a steady stream."

Claire did as she was told, excitement coursing through her. She felt different to when she used an ordinary spell; there was a rushing click click in her ears and a sudden mist enveloping her. She slowly opened her eyes and saw that the room had changed in a way that had never happened before with Maen. She saw different kinds of light flowing within the space obscuring the people around her. For a second, she even thought she could make out a small, pale salamander-like creature creeping across the floor towards her, but it vanished as soon as she tried to focus on its golden glow.

"That's it," Gwenivere whispered. "Reach for Rinn first."

"How?" Claire said, her voice shaking.

"Picture her."

As Claire obeyed, something painful twinged at her temples, like her mind hit against something firm. Rinn's essence? She saw her own magic, a dull red tinge, mingle with Rinn's gleaming gold. Before she could wonder what to do next, a knotted rope of silver wrapped around them both.

Good job, Gwenivere's voice sounded in her mind. *Get comfortable with this because you'll need to connect with one of us to travel home safely.*

Claire only half-listened. She felt refreshed, power singing through her veins. With Rinn's strength to draw upon, she sensed she could try the most difficult of spells and succeed. She imagined a wall of cold flame and was vindicated when a stream of silver fire ran horizontally across the room, separating Claire and the others from the exit. *This is awesome! If I could draw on lots of people, I'd be invincible!* She laughed. Maybe she *was* who Grandfather needed after all. She could take on anything. She could—

A sudden blow broke her concentration. Someone slapped her again across the face hard enough that Claire knew there'd be white marks. She opened her eyes. The strange light had vanished.

"How dare you," Gwenivere hissed.

"Wha-what did I do wrong?" she stammered, her hand touching her stinging cheek.

Rinn sat grave-faced. "You tried to take me over. We aren't teaching you these skills for you to make the same mistake Kelt did. I know you didn't mean to do it, but—"

"Use your own power, or work together with others of our House," Maen interrupted, "but never ever let me catch you trying to draw on any magic but your own again."

"She is her great-uncle's child," Gwenivere said sadly. "I warned you, Maen."

"It was an accident," Rinn said, rubbing Gwenivere's back.

"She has the hungry look he did. Didn't I say so after I first saw her?"

"I never even knew my great-uncle Kelt," Claire protested, stung at the injustice of being blamed for something she didn't understand. "You threw me in the deep end without an explanation. How was I to know what the purpose of your exercise was?"

"You should have waited for my next instruction," Gwenivere said through gritted teeth.

"OK, fine." It wasn't worth the argument. "What next then, boss?"

"We're finished," Gwenivere said coldly, rising and sweeping out of the room before a surprised Maen could protest.

Chapter Nine

"MAEN TELLS ME YOU IMPROVE more and more by the hour," Claire's grandfather said. They stood in the antechamber to his private rooms.

Four more days had passed since Gwenivere and Maen had first taught Claire how to become part of a magical chain for a summons. Each day began with an enormous breakfast to ensure she had energy to, quite literally, burn; then came training with Maen and Gwenivere. Then there was a big lunch; Claire never thought she'd eat so much, but she was always hungry and yet she'd put on no weight. In fact, after four days of training, her shift was getting loose. After lunch Kiera or Rael would walk her through the labyrinth of the Manor, introducing her to this distant cousin or that, trying to give her a sense of direction so she could navigate the corridors herself. Then they'd take her back to Maen and Gwenivere for round two.

Since that first day, they'd worked on Claire cautiously lighting fire and directing it where she wanted it to go without disconnecting from Gwenivere or Rinn. Though Gwenivere continued to co-teach lessons, she did so in stony silence, remembering civility only when Rinn prodded her. Even Maen had lost his temper with her yesterday, telling her to stop watching over his shoulder like he was a novice. As for Claire getting a chance to talk to Rinn alone about her weird dreams, it was impossible. She never left Gwenivere's side.

"You've well and truly earnt the right to learn with me," Lord Dorran said, bringing Claire back to the present, pride laced through his words.

Claire wished he'd share his easy confidence with Gwenivere. The half-lidded glances the Dream Mage kept shooting her made her feel guilty, though of what Claire couldn't have said. She clenched her fists by her side. She wasn't going to be a second Kelt.

Lord Dorran placed a hand on her arm. "Maen told me about Gwenivere. She takes her role as Dream Mage leader seriously. Some might say too seriously. Still," he sighed, "I understand her reasons. She blames herself for the Rift, just as I do, and doesn't want to be responsible twice in a row for magic going wrong."

"But you taught me the Dream Mages and Enchantment Weavers had nothing to do with it."

"Gwenivere had a kind of vision that warned of Selk, Kelt and the war to come. She decided to wait before telling the Houses, to see if events made things clearer. She's never forgiven herself for delaying." He stroked his chin. "I have often wondered if it is that which makes her uncomfortable around me. Do I blame her or hate her for failing to tell me about my brother's possible folly? No. But she never listens." He paused, then smiled. "But we have work to do. Come." He swept out of the antechamber into a private corridor.

As Claire followed in his wake, she admired the wooden panels on the corridor walls with their carvings of different faces, salamanders crawling through their hair and sitting on their shoulders. Perhaps they were her relatives. Before she could ask, her grandfather pushed open a cedar door and strode over to a wooden chair upholstered with dyed purple wool. He sank into the seat with a noise of contentment, indicating she should take the free chair opposite him.

Claire knew she was staring, but she couldn't help it. She hadn't ever seen a room so luxurious except in period piece dramas. The enormous four-poster bed featured purple velvet curtains at each corner tied back with golden tassels. A circular sheepskin rug covered the floor and wooden chests sat alongside one wall. The chest and the chairs, the small square table complete with ivory and ebony chess pieces, and the floorboards gleamed from constant polishing. Claire found the crisp scent of the polish comforting. At eye height, shelves of golden plates, goblets, bowls, necklaces, bracelets, and earrings glittering with jewels winked back at her. Between the shelves and the ceiling, paintings hung, three or four on every wall. A sword with an intricate scabbard hung on the back wall, in pride of place.

"I haven't had to use that other than at ceremonies for years," Lord Dorran said, nodding towards the sword.

"You mean you used to have to use your sword in battle? Were things really that bad?"

"We're powerful, Claire, and that makes people afraid. Religion stoked their fright. The towns where priests had a stranglehold would move against us from time to time and we Houses would band together to stop them." He glanced at a painting opposite them. Claire saw that it depicted four soldiers, two standing and laughing, one lying on the ground chewing a blade of grass and one sitting with chin in hand. One wore the red and black formal uniform of House Dorran, another wore silver and blue, yet another grey and purple and the final warrior woman wore garments of bronze and green. Claire guessed they were the official colours of each of the elemental Houses.

"We didn't just lose magical stability with the loss of House Domain and House Ushanan," he explained. "We lost real friends. We'd have mock tournaments, with prizes for those who showed the most skill in sword play, in the use of a staff, in riding, in arts and crafts. We'd switch location each year." He pointed at another painting: a riot of silken tents on an open field.

"And no one from either House survived? Not a single person? How's that possible?"

"They lived in Western Kelnarium and that's where the Rift began. Then of course, it was their war – they sent every woman and man they could spare to fight Selk."

"But surely some remained?"

"The children, the elderly and those others who couldn't fight stayed in their Manors and were killed when the Rift formed. Some of the servitors left earlier, coming to me and to Lord Maellwyn to adopt a new heritage. What else could they do?"

"But ... but," Claire began, thinking things through out aloud. "someone with magical blood could have survived. Must have done. Why didn't they rebuild the Houses?"

Lord Dorran's face darkened. "As with the exiles, you speak of that which you cannot understand."

His blistering tone made Claire look down at her lap. "I'm sorry, but—"

"But nothing. I have told you there is no more House Ushanan ... no more House Domain. There is nothing more to say." He fell into silence.

Claire pressed her tongue against her teeth to stop herself retorting. It hadn't been that strange a thing to ask and there was certainly no need for her grandfather to get so defensive. *Almost like he has something to hide*, she thought. His expression and the strange light in his eyes reminded her of Suranne the day Marcus had vanished.

"It bothers me that Mum didn't tell me about you and all my other relatives," she said casually. "It's like she didn't trust me enough." She waited for the penny to drop.

"Sorry for snapping at you," Dorran said, his voice gruff but kind. "It's a sore point. I've racked my brains for a way to restore the Houses, but the truth is, what's done is done." He tilted his head to catch her gaze. "Don't be too hard on Suranne. Any decision my girl would have made would have come from a place of love, even if it were misguided."

Claire couldn't deny her parents loved her. Not like Anthony Brown, who'd come to school with cigarette burns on his skin until the school counsellor had filed a report. Maybe she was being a bit harsh. She smiled. "Thanks. I guess that does help. A little. And sorry for pushing about the Houses."

"No. I'm too sensitive because I know it was my fault."

"A bit like Gwenivere," Claire said pointedly. "But Kelt was his own person and convinced he was in the right." She made herself smile. "It must be a family trait, that level of stubbornness."

"It certainly turned up in Marcus."

"What happened?" Claire asked cautiously. "Marcus wasn't the stubborn one back home. I was."

Dorran shot her a calculating look. "You look up to him. Everyone has told me that."

"With good reason," Claire said, defending herself. "No one likes me and Mum in Shale – that's the village we live in – but Marcus is popular. People are nice to me when he's nearby. Without him, I'm ... I'm ..." *Nothing*, she wanted to say, but she couldn't quite admit it out aloud.

"I wish we'd seen that side of him," Dorran said, "but he judged us before he even arrived. He wouldn't listen to me when I tried to explain our situation."

I bet you were rude and overbearing like you were with me when we first met, Claire thought.

"Hmph," Dorran snorted, like he'd read her thoughts. "Maybe I was a bit autocratic. When he carried on and on about wanting to be sent home even after I explained about the prophecy, well, I admit I lost my temper. It didn't help that Rael had been a bit too forthcoming about how we feel about the exiles on the journey here and Marcus saw us as the bad guys long before he met me."

Understanding dawned. That's why Rael had refused to tell Claire anything on the way to the Manor. He'd said too much to Marcus.

Lord Dorran turned away, moisture rising in his eyes. "Perhaps there was a bit of Leya in him. She was quick to make up her mind about things. She ruled Dorran House as much as I did."

"Was Leya my grandmother?"

"Yes. There was romance between the Houses, you know; all the way from the servitors up to yours truly." He turned back to face her. "Your grandmother wasn't a true Dorran. She was a House Ushanan servitor. She worked in their apothecary. My heart leapt whenever I saw House Ushanan's grey and purple garb at our gates, half-believing every time it was her. I couldn't believe it when she finally came to live here permanently so we got to know each other properly. We married a year later."

Claire thought of the painting she'd seen at training. "What was she like?" she asked. "Maen seems half in love with her memory."

"We all are. She was the best woman I've ever known." He paused, grinning. "With the exception of your mother of course."

"How did she die?" Claire asked cautiously.

A shadow crossed Dorran's face. "It was a winter chill six years ago. It hit the old and the infirm first. I was selfish. I told Leya I didn't want her tending to Dorran Village; that they could rely on their own herbalists and medicine men. She wouldn't listen. With a tilt of her chin and a wicker basket underarm, she was off all hours. I have often wondered ..." His eyes darkened and his lips twisted in pain.

"Wondered what?" Claire could tell from his faraway look that he'd forgotten where he was and who he was speaking to.

"Sometimes I think she risked herself because she'd already given up. She was heartbroken when Suranne went away and angry with me for countenancing it. She didn't see that—" He shook his head like he needed the movement to bring himself back to the present. His voice turned hearty with false cheer. "But, she had Kiera and Rael to fuss over and Meghan too. When Leya died, Meghan led the funeral procession beside me. The more vicious tongues thought we'd wait the appropriate mourning period and then marry, but we never have seen each other that way. If we had, maybe some things would have been easier."

Suddenly, Claire realised how alone her grandfather had been. Perhaps every bit as alone as she'd felt in Shale, only he hadn't had his family to comfort him as he aged. "Do you resent Dad for taking Mum away?" she asked.

"Resent? That's a strong word. No. He was in love. Perhaps it was a fair punishment, too. After all, James was an abstract in our plan, without emotion or life. When we brought him to Kelnarium, we ripped him from everything he knew without giving him a choice in the matter. I understood Suranne when she said she needed to return him home. It was a reminder. That kind of magic always has a price."

"You took Marcus and I away and we had no choice either," Claire pointed out, trying not to sound accusatory.

"And no doubt there will be a price for that as well." He lent forward with hands on knees. "Well, we've reminisced long enough. We should start practising. Maen tells me you catch on to concepts quickly but lack finesse."

Claire frowned. She couldn't help but feel a little bit hurt. Maen had never mentioned anything of the sort to her.

"You over or underestimate how much power you need and when you use it, it is uneven," he rushed on as Claire's frown grew into a scowl. "It's not an insult. He has taught many an apprentice in the same position you are now. The only reason I'm taking over is an old man's indulgence. You're my granddaughter, after all."

Her expression softened at Lord Dorran's obvious fondness for her. "Why does finesse matter?" she asked.

"The smoother your workings, the less exhausted you'll be, which matters in a sticky situation or a battle and we don't know—"

"What skills I'll need to beat the Rift," Claire said, finishing his words wearily.

"Indeed." He coughed delicately behind a thin hand. "So, how do you make your spells neater? The power in your blood makes it easier for you, but you still need to put in some effort."

"Tell me what to do," Claire asked eagerly, keen to prove herself.

"You must reach inside yourself and be comfortable sitting with your thoughts. Notice them but let them pass. Imagine you are watching pebbles passing beneath you in a stream. When you find the water rushing past too fast to notice the pebbles, pull back. I'll talk you through it."

Claire thought this didn't sound too bad. She'd done some meditation with Suranne when she'd started high school and what her grandfather described sounded like that. Mind you, she'd spent her time watching the clock when Suranne wasn't looking. This time, she'd make sure to keep her eyes closed so she couldn't get distracted by anything around her.

As Lord Dorran's gentle cadence washed over her, she tried to ignore niggling images and ideas; whether Rael would find the new recruit he sought on his trek to Newark Village today, whether Maen would enjoy teaching his other pupils as much as he did Claire, whether she'd have enough time after this session to join Meghan and Kiera in the kitchens and learn their spiced cake recipe ...

She blinked guiltily when Lord Dorran called her back to the present. "I couldn't do it."

He laughed. "Most people can't the first time."

It took her until lunchtime to get the knack and even then, her technique was shaky. Her breathing steadied and the tensions in her muscles eased. She heard the swish of his cloak as her grandfather shifted position, the soft footsteps of people in the hallway, the sound of her own heartbeat. She let her fists unfurl and fall softly to her sides. Instinctively, she held her palm flat and out from her body and went through the steps Maen had described. She knew it had worked when she felt her skin tingle and woodfire smoke tickle her nostrils.

"Nicely done," Lord Dorran said quietly. She opened her eyes to find him watching her in a way that unnerved her. "You don't feel the cold anymore, do you?"

Claire glanced at her bare arms. She hadn't bothered with the long-sleeved shirt underneath for a few days now. The flame continued to glow in her hand. "No." With a thought, she put it out.

"You've become one of us," Lord Dorran said. Claire could tell he was pleased because of the inflection of his voice, the same as Suranne's when Claire brought home a school award. "Your blood has heated as your magic has awoken." He reached into his cloak pocket to produce a glittering gold chain, an egg-shaped pendant hanging from it just like the one Maen had shown Claire. As she went to touch it, her grandfather smiled. "This was crafted from a reef of opal I selected from the salamanders' cavern last night and had shaped for you. I spoke to the Saura and she told me this stone is marked for you."

Claire gaped as she slipped the necklace over her head and the egg glimmered, streaks of red and orange seeming to flicker in the black of the stone, then it went hot against her skin. Suddenly, she could see five salamanders ranged around Lord Dorran, their tongues flickering in and out as their round eyes blinked her way. "I can finally see them," she whispered.

"You'll see more tomorrow when I take you to the caverns, our secret place where only true Dorrans may enter," he said solemnly. "The Saura wishes to meet you."

"The Saura?" Claire repeated slowly. Both Rael and Kiera had kind of sworn by the name, the same way some people in Shale swore by God, but she hadn't understood who or what it was, and now her grandfather kept referencing them.

"The Saura is the elemental leader of the salamanders, a spirit creature who lives in the deepest, darkest part of our caverns. I noticed you staring at the painting of her in the Dining Hall the other night. She's a powerful sight, with her huge legs and giant toes, her whip-like long white-hot tongue, her golden body that stings the eyes to stare at for too long and her eldritch red-hot flames that never go out and surround her beautiful head in a halo. It was she who gifted fire *learth* to the first Dorran. She only ever speaks to me, for I am leader of our House, but you are my heir. She wishes to see you."

He smiled at Claire's confusion. "Each House had their own elemental creatures and elemental leaders, though they never appear to anyone who isn't of their magic type unless in the direst of circumstances." He paused.

"And even then, they don't always aid us." He shook his head like he dispelled negative energy. "The Saura and her salamanders are ours and one day you will rule after me. It's natural they desire to meet you. As to your necklace," he pointed at it and his expression turned grave. "Never take it off or let it break. When you journey away from us, you won't survive long without it. You are a proper Dorran now, inheriting our weaknesses along with our strengths."

Chapter Ten

AS CLAIRE SLIPPED THROUGH corridors, she nodded at those she passed, though many ignored her in their rush. In the afternoon, a messenger had turned up to Claire's class on the balcony with Maen. Eidan had arrived early from Kelnariat and had called an immediate meeting with Lord Dorran and the Dream Mages over light refreshments in the dining hall. Maen had dismissed her and now the manor was in uproar. No one had invited her, but Claire had decided to find a way to listen in on the meeting anyway. Grandfather wanted her to learn about the history, politics and culture of this place, so she'd show him what she was made of. Besides, she'd been excited about him taking her to see the salamanders and the Saura. Now, their trip was delayed until tomorrow thanks to Kelnarium's political leader. Well, Claire wasn't going to let her evening stay ruined thanks to him.

As she tip-toed past the great doors that led into the dining hall she scarcely breathed. This was the trickiest part of her plan. Right outside the hall was a set of stairs that led to another landing. If Claire could creep up them unseen, there was a little door in the side wall that led to a cramped storage room where the candles for chandeliers were kept. Just off that was a narrow walkway which led out over the dining hall so the servitors could replace candles in the chandeliers. If Claire could get inside, she could eavesdrop on her grandfather and Eidan.

She glanced in every direction. She couldn't see anyone. She hurried to the top of the dark stairwell and tested the door. Sure enough, in their haste to light the hall in preparation for Eidan's sudden arrival, someone had left it unlocked. With one quick glance around to check no one was about to spot her, Claire slipped inside and hurried along the narrow thoroughfare, ducking to avoid hitting her head against the cartwheel-like chandeliers ranged above her.

She stopped in the middle of the walkway and peered out over the side, clutching at the wooden handrails as her head spun. It was a long drop if she lost her balance. She tightened her grip as a servitor carried a platter of cheeses, crisps and fruits into the room, glad she blended in with the shadows of the vaulted timber ceiling. He and the other servitors all left the room, closing the door behind them.

Looking down into the dining hall, Claire could see that her grandfather wasn't at the centre of the high table. Instead, he sat a place to the right. Gwenivere was to his left. Of the other six at the table, she recognised Rinn, Maen, Rael and her great-uncle, Aed. A third Dream Mage, a man, sat by Rinn's side. Another man Claire didn't know sat in Lord Dorran's usual place.

She squinted, trying to get a clearer view of him. She wasn't directly above him so she could just make out his dark brown hair and blue eyes, which reminded her of Marcus. His plain black shirt contrasted with the gold armband on his right arm and the brooch that glittered at his breast. His skin was tanned and weather-beaten, his beard was well-trimmed and there was a scar on his right cheek. The party around the table hung onto his every word.

"It's a shame I arrived so late," the man said, his voice smoothly confident. "I would have liked to meet your granddaughter. If she's half as delightful as Marcus, we'll get along."

Claire dug her nails into the wooden handrail. So, this was Eidan. She liked him already; his affection for Marcus was obvious.

"Indeed." Lord Dorran wouldn't meet Eidan's gaze and Claire wondered if he felt guilty about his lack of familial affection for his grandson. He cleared his throat and Claire knew that he was nervous. "What brings you in such haste, Councilman Eidan?"

"A week ago, on the outskirts of Kelnariat, raiders set fire to villages and farmland." He produced a piece of torn red and black fabric out of a fold in his clothing and slapped it on the tabletop.

Claire couldn't make it out from her distance, but Gwenivere pulled back, her chair scraping. Lord Dorran kept his gaze on Eidan's trophy, lost in thought.

"This was found in one village and I smelt the lingering crackle of magic at another." Eidan paused meaningfully but Dorran said nothing. "Come, my friend, what is this about? If some of your people have gone rogue, as this piece of a Dorran guard's tunic seems to indicate, I understand, but you must be honest with me." He sighed, placing his hands flat on the table. "I want to keep the peace. That's all."

Lord Dorran exchanged a glance with Maen, but Claire couldn't interpret it. She didn't like his furtiveness, like he was in the wrong, and she couldn't believe what she was hearing either. Dorrans harming innocent people? Why? Nothing made sense.

"I know nothing of this," her grandfather said at last. "But evidence can be planted and perhaps your mind played tricks on you."

Eidan's expression didn't change as he reached for his wine goblet. "There was no mistake. I have my sources." He turned the goblet by the stem. "Still, I want to trust you. Dismiss your men. The Dream Mages stay."

"What?" Lord Dorran was just as confused as Claire was.

"You heard me. I doubt you want anyone else hearing what I'm about to say."

"You can't order me about in my own home," Lord Dorran said with a hint of ice in his tone. "It's most irregular."

"I can and I have," Eidan replied quietly. "You elected me Councillor, so trust me. Besides, I did not tell you to bring along your retinue. That was your own doing."

Lord Dorran considered for a moment then nodded sharply at his men. Aed, Maen and Rael stood and filed out of the hall.

As soon as they'd gone, Dorran cleared his throat. "Well?"

Eidan laced his fingers into a steeple as he leant forward, addressing Gwenivere. "Can you look into the past, try to see what happened? Perhaps the priests ..."

"Yes," Dorran broke in eagerly. "Have you spoken to the temples in Kelnariat, Eidan?" Claire knew from one of her many history lessons that slowly but surely the priests were returning to Kelnariat, though they were meeker and less involved in public life than in the past, but Claire didn't care about that. She couldn't help but notice how Lord Dorran latched onto Eidan's words. Her unease grew. Was it possible her grandfather knew something about the destroyed villages after all?

Eidan stared into his wine. "Yes, but they swear they knew nothing about it." He frowned and looked straight at Lord Dorran. "This is a sensitive question, but I must ask it ... Where did Lady Claire arrive in Kelnarium? Is it possible she used magic before you got to her? People use the familiar to paper over what they don't understand, thus one confused girl using magic to wreak untold destruction easily becomes a horde of raiders."

Claire had to bite her tongue to stop herself from protesting out aloud. What a ridiculous idea! She wasn't capable of hurting anyone.

"She didn't know a thing about it until Maen showed her," her grandfather said, springing to her defence.

"Yes, but you would say that. According to Gwenivere's vision, she is Kelnarium's saviour after all, and how awkward it would be if our saviour caused such terrible injury. An honest mistake, but one hard to explain away to those who've lost their livelihoods."

Pandemonium ensued. Dorran and Gwenivere began to shout at once, as Rinn and the other Dream Mage whispered to each other, both twisting at their napkins.

"How dare you call me a liar?" Dorran cried, abandoning all attempts to keep his voice low. "I've stuck by you from the first, believed in you, and now you imply I'd mislead about a monstrous crime?"

"I accuse no one," Eidan said. He threw up a hand before Dorran could protest further. "This conjecture is pointless." He locked eyes with Dorran. "Let Gwenivere and her people determine the truth."

Lord Dorran broke the stare, looking away in defeat. "Fine."

Eidan turned to the Dream Mages, motioning for them to stand. They did so gracefully and descended from the dais to begin pulling some tables and chairs to the side of the dining hall. Claire winced as they scraped furniture against the floor. Suranne was always telling her off for doing that back home.

"We must be careful, Tarn," Gwenivere said to the man Claire hadn't recognised. "The Rift is unstable and ..." She glanced over her shoulder at Eidan, who looked on from the high table with arms crossed. Claire wondered what he was thinking. The Dream Mage named Tarn muttered something to Gwenivere that Claire couldn't hear, and Gwenivere shook her head in response. "I don't need to lecture you," she said. "You've as much experience in these matters as Rinn and I." Returning to the high table, she bent forward and reached beneath it, surfacing with her wooden bowl, then descended once more to seat herself on the floor cross-legged. The other two followed suit, creating a circle.

They placed their bowls at their feet and Gwenivere and Rinn arranged their dresses so that the fabric billowed out on the floor. Tarn tied each of his loose silk shirt sleeves in a knot at the elbow.

They closed their eyes in concentration, as Claire gazed down, fascinated. Training with Rinn and Gwenivere was one thing, watching them bring forth a vision was another.

Gwenivere started to sway gently, and soon the others moved in tandem. Gwenivere's head jerked, and she opened her eyes wide, staring intently into her bowl of water.

In the same moment, Rinn let out an agonised cry. She began to writhe where she sat, bending forward and now back, her arms flailing as if at some unseen creature. Her arm struck at the bowl with such force that Claire's heart leapt with fright. With a crack, the wood split.

In a confused babble, Rinn described images of Pennarth Village, men, women and children screaming, brandishing pitchforks at their magical attackers who wielded fire. "And they lift the helmet ... they lift ..." She gasped for air. "It's watching me. It's laughing at us."

Eidan lent forward, his voice steady. "Who's laughing?"

"It's the silent creature, the unnatural product of the Rift," Rinn cried, her voice itself high and unnatural. "It warns me of Claire, of the betrayer! Beware the betrayer!"

Claire clutched the handrail so tightly that splinters were driven into her fingers. Could it be that the creature Gwenivere said disrupted spells and visions was also the creature Rinn described now and the creature of Claire's nightmares? She'd suspected it but hadn't wanted to think through the ramifications either. What was the significance of the creature, and how was *she* going to betray everyone? Perhaps, as she'd suspected, Grandfather *had* needed Marcus to close the Rift and Claire wasn't the important one.

Claire's stomach plummeted. Over the last week she'd stupidly convinced herself she was Kelnarium's hero after all. *No such luck*, she thought, *apparently I'm the "betrayer", just like in my nightmare, and now Grandfather knows it.*

Rinn was still talking. Claire took a few deep and steadying breaths to calm herself and better overhear what was going on.

Mid-sentence, Rinn froze, her body stiff. She choked on her own saliva, coughing, gasping for air.

Surely this isn't right, Claire thought. *Somebody help her!* But nobody did, as both Eidan and Dorran looked on with inscrutable expressions and Gwenivere and Tarn stared straight ahead, eyes vacant.

And then Rinn began to scream, high and sharp, and this time Gwenivere grimaced with pain. Claire bit her tongue to prevent a gasp as Rinn flung herself in odder and odder contortions. It was clear that something was wrong, because Lord Dorran had started forward and was being restrained by Eidan. "We can't interfere. No one of Rinn's power has ever been lost to this creature," he said, but as he released Dorran and resumed stroking his beard his gaze was one of alarm.

Claire squeezed her eyes shut, unable to bear the sight of Rinn's blotched face and jerking muscles. Rinn was nice and so few people were nice to Claire that … that … *Oh, this isn't one of Dad's fairy tales,* she told herself firmly. Bad things could happen to good people. She knew that. This was no time for cowardice. She made herself open her eyes.

Rinn's mouth was wide, contorted with pain, like some invisible hand pressed down on her. The sudden snap sounded like a gunshot from a war film. As Claire watched in horror, Rinn slid to the ground in a boneless heap.

Eidan leapt from the dais, falling to his knees beside Rinn. "Help the others," he yelled as he put two fingers against Rinn's neck.

Lord Dorran hesitated for a moment, face white, then got to his knees and clasped Gwenivere's hand, rubbing it with vigour. Gwenivere moaned, looking around her with confusion. Dorran helped her to take a sip of from his goblet. Beside them, Tarn stirred, then groaned, hands massaging his temples.

Eidan caught Dorran's questioning look and shook his head. "I'm sorry. She didn't make it." His voice turned hard. "Rinn Taccala is dead."

Claire felt sick. She'd seen magic as a game and closing the Rift as an irritation blocking her way back to her family. She hadn't seriously imagined people she cared about *dying*.

Gwenivere pushed Dorran away, flinging herself at Rinn. She cradled the dead woman, rocking backwards and forwards, face blanched.

"I'm so sorry," Eidan said, his voice breaking. "I'll arrange a state funeral and you'll be paid compensation."

Gwenivere looked up, somehow shrunken and pitiful. "Compensation ... Why?" Her voice was thin yet steady. "Rinn Taccala died performing her duty."

Dorran got up unsteadily. "I must ask you, Gwenivere, what was all that about my granddaughter?"

"This beast disrupted our vision and singled Rinn out," Tarn said, wincing with pain. "It told us that Lady Claire is Kelnarium's scourge, not our saviour."

Claire's cheeks were wet. This was so unfair. A moment later, she felt like someone had slammed the wind out of her as she realised something far, far worse. Lord Dorran, Gwenivere and Eidan would interrogate her. How could they not? She could claim that she intended to do her best for the people of Kelnarium all she liked, but it was her word against the Dream Mages. Not only that, she couldn't deny that she had dreamt of this Rift creature.

She had to get help – but from whom? Once this story got out, no one would protect her. She'd be an outcast, just like she was in Shale. She had to get out of the Manor right now.

She could manage it. Even if someone saw her, she could run. She had to if she wanted to see Marcus again. She'd run to a village and beg for help to get to Kelnariat and once she was with her brother, everything would go right, like it normally did back home. By the time Lord Dorran began searching for her, she'd be long gone.

It was now or never. Claire dashed back to the storage room, ignoring the sound her feet made as they pounded against the wood.

Chapter Eleven

CLAIRE SLAMMED THE storage door shut and kept running down the stairs, dashing into the atrium in front of the dining hall. Two men were deep in conversation on her left, while a woman carried a tureen of something on her right. The woman's eyes caught hers, brows furrowing. Claire didn't have much time. Already, confused shouts drifted out of the dining hall. Hair whipped in her face as Claire shoved past the Dorran servitor. The tureen she carried toppled and spilt across the floor. At the same time, the door to the dining hall flew open.

"Stop!" Gwenivere shouted as Claire raced for the stairs to the upper levels of the Manor on the other side of the atrium.

Claire picked up speed, risking a glance over her shoulder and seeing the long-limbed Dream Mage – apparently recovered from her ordeal – hot on her heels. At least Claire had one advantage over Gwenivere: she'd had time to get to know the maze that was the Dorran home.

She dashed up three flights of stairs to the royal rooms, then skirted sideways down a corridor, dodging past people as she skidded around corner after corner, left, right and left again. Her breath came out short and sharp and her sides ached, but she could no longer hear feet racing behind her. Gripping the edge of a wall for support, she took in her surroundings. Another few turns and she'd be at her room. She set off at a more sedate pace, wiping the sweat from her forehead.

Within ten minutes, she was outside her bedroom. At first, she moved cautiously, afraid Lord Dorran had sent someone to wait for her, but there was no one inside. She kicked her embroidered slippers off, sliding on the tougher outdoor boots she wore during training with Maen, and pulled a long-sleeved shirt over her head, lacing the ties at the front hastily. After a moment's thought, she wrapped a scarf around her neck and pulled a warm cloak from the cedar chest at the foot of her bed, flinging it over her shoulders to protect against the cold. *There. That will have to do.*

Pressing her advantage, Claire hurried to the closest Manor exit, going downstairs and out via the kitchens, stopping only to grab an apple for her horse, Shera. Luckily, supplies had been brought to the Manor that afternoon from a Dorran party who'd been sent to the village, so she was able to slip outside easily with all the people coming and going as they finished unloading the carts and preparing for a grand dinner in Eidan's honour. Still, her nerves shredded as her ears pricked for a familiar shout of recognition that never came.

Adopting a confident stride, she headed for the stables. When she arrived, Shera nuzzled her palm and then crunched on the apple as Claire saddled her up. When Claire was finished, she noticed a leather saddlebag stashed in a corner. She flicked back the flap and was relieved to find a flask of something sweet and alcoholic and some old bread, hard cheese, and nuts. No doubt it was a handler's supper. *Well, need's must*, she thought. Claire hitched the bag onto the saddle and walked Shera outside.

Mounting up, she smiled confidently at the people passing by. Marcus had told her once that if you did the wrong thing with confidence, no one would question you. At the thought of Marcus, she shivered with excitement. She couldn't wait to see him again.

As she approached the gate, one of the men on sentry duty turned and smiled, recognising her. "Lady Claire," he said, as friendly as usual. "Please make your ride a short one. The doors shut soon, and you'll be forced to sleep the night among the poppies." He laughed at his own joke but Claire said nothing, merely nudging Shera past him. As she passed through the gate, she heard him speak to the other guard, "She's turning as sulky as her brother. There's no need for her to be rude; I'm her cousin, you know? Only a distant one, but still."

Claire heard the other man mutter a reply but couldn't make out what he said. It was clear, though, that she'd offended them. But there was no time to turn back and try to justify her haste to them, as her grandfather or Rael and the guards could figure out what had happened at any moment and follow on horseback. She only hoped she hadn't made the men suspect she was up to something. Luckily, at that moment a farmer came in with a cart and she heard the guards greet him; at least now they wouldn't be likely to watch her ride off. She headed downhill, moving at a moderately brisk pace, not willing to make Shera gallop in case the guards were still watching. She followed the road she'd taken on her arrival with Rael, and once she reached Dorran Village, she began to gallop through the rolling farmland, the land greener than anything she saw back home in drought-ridden Shale, even as long afternoon shadows touched the landscape.

The road seemed to go on forever, and once she was out of sight of the Manor, she allowed Shera to slow first to a canter, then later to a brisk walk; the last thing she wanted to do was wind her mount in case she needed to speed up again to escape from pursuers.

An hour passed. She'd ridden far enough away from Dorran territory to risk approaching settled land to find shelter for the night. Sunset was casting muted oranges and pinks across the sky as the landscape was getting harsher, the grass sparse and dry, the trees thin-leaved, indicating she was close to the Riftlands. Stone and hard, dry dirt passed underfoot. She remembered from the journey with Rael that there should be another village just over the approaching hill. As she rode closer, the sky changed to a strange orange-red colour, a hint of ashy black to the cloud line.

Claire pulled Shera's reins in a bit. Best to take this slow. As the mare crested the hill, Claire's heart sank. Smoke billowed in columns from thatched cottages that had collapsed in on themselves, the grass around them black. Crops stank as they smouldered. Farmers lay face down in their own fields. Her eyes watered, but she made herself ride through the carnage as tiny salamanders winked into existence, sitting on her shoulders and looking solemn as they pointed their short, webbed toes at the horrendous scene, their eyes wide and sad.

Near the shell of a cottage, still radiating heat, a farmer clutched a pitchfork, his shirt torn and bloody from a knife wound. He was dead. So was his wife a few metres ahead. What had happened here? Tears pricked Claire's eyes. What was she going to do? If she went back the way she'd came she'd run into her grandfather and his guards, but this was the last village. Beyond it, there was nothing but the camp of exiles and the Riftlands. She had to get to Kelnariat and Marcus, but the only way she knew of to get to them was back the way she'd come. *My mind is going in circles*, she thought as she rode past the dead woman. There was nothing for it, she had to throw in her lot with the exiles. Sure, they had nothing, but they were unlikely to be friends with Dorran House either, which was the main thing, and they might be able to help her find her way to Kelnariat. As she urged Shera to ride on, she glanced at the salamanders. Surely they'd stop her if she was making the wrong decision, but they did nothing, She took that as permission to keep going.

The path went upwards, she remembered, and then descended into a dip. The valley where she had first seen the exiles when she'd arrived in Kelnarium sat at its foot. She rode on for another fifteen minutes as night fell properly, scanning the horizon for evidence of the people who had destroyed the farming settlement, but she was alone other than the elemental creatures.

As she rode, the air grew dirtier and dirtier. Ash fell on her arm, still alight. Shera's nostrils flared in fear and it took all of Claire's energy to direct her onward. The smoke grew thicker and greasier, and underneath it was the smell of flesh burning. Shera whinnied in terror. Claire leapt from her back and coaxed her forward by the bridle.

She crested the slope, crying out in despair as the gully came into view. The bustling camp she had seen with Rael was destroyed, its remnants scattering in ashes on the wind. The animal-hide tents that remained sat charred and blackened, the lean-tos collapsed in on themselves and still alight. Belongings lay in haphazard clusters. Flaming pits marked the perimeter of the camp, creating a kind of trench around it and allowing Claire to see the terrible destruction wrought, even in the dark.

Shera reared with a whinny as smoke flared. "Come on," Claire begged, trying to tug the frantic horse forward. With a great swing of her head, Shera wrenched her bridle out of Claire's grip, then galloped back the way they'd come, saddlebags and all. Holding back tears, Claire watched Shera vanish into the haze. *At least I still have the salamanders*, she thought, but even as she moved her fingers to stroke one, all of them vanished. She was alone. Desperately, she turned back to the sight of the camp. She needed help. Without supplies she'd starve. With no other option available, she walked down the hill towards the camp, stopping at its edge.

It's so quiet, she thought, shuddering. Her stomach churned at the smell and she clenched her fists against the urge to be sick. *Has anyone survived?*

As if on cue, the air filled with the sound of someone screaming. Maybe that's why the salamanders had left her. They'd known a non-Dorran was nearby.

Claire took a cautious step forward. "Where are you?" she called.

The person cried out and Claire ran to her left, following the voice. One of the flaming pits flared up as Claire tried to skirt its perimeter. As if by sinister magic, its fiery tip reached out across the blackened ground towards Claire's feet. Attempting to calm her terror, she took one step back and closed her eyes, then counted three even breaths as she tried to remember what Maen had taught her. *Grasp for the fire and take hold of it. Teach it to do your bidding.* She tried to relax, easier said than done in a real-life emergency, then did as Maen had instructed, feeling the flame's energy and directing it left instead of towards her. She knew she'd succeeded when the air in front of her cooled, leaving her fingers prickling.

The screams sounded again, closer now.

"I'm coming," Claire shouted, running forward and diverting or extinguishing flames as she went, trying to locate the source of the screams.

In front of her was a deep, long pit. Running to its edge, she nearly gagged when the stench coming from within it struck her. She covered her mouth and nose with her hand and strained to see through the haze but when she did, she turned and threw up. The pit contained piles of dead bodies with staring eyes and covered in blisters and sores. *How could anyone do this to somebody else?* She remembered Eidan talking about bandits with magic wreaking destruction near Kelnariat's capital and the furtive way her grandfather had looked, like he knew something about it. If Dorran House had done this, they were *monsters*.

From inside the pit came another cry, weaker this time. Claire made herself turn back to the pyre, knuckling sore lids. *There.* It wasn't a trick of the uncertain light or her eyes streaming and blinding her. She had seen the bodies shift.

The wind changed, carrying the smell of scorching skin away from Claire, allowing her to focus. Claire pulled her scarf over her face so that she could still breathe. *Pull yourself together. There's someone buried here that you alone can save.*

"Put your hand in the air," she managed to say. "I can't see you."

The only response was the sound of exhausted crying, which set Claire's teeth on edge. "I can't help you unless you show me where you are." She cringed at her own brutality, but her first aid course had taught her you had to sound confident and in control in an emergency.

She gagged as the entire pile of bodies closest to her twitched and fell back into place in a wave. "Oh, my God. You're not … you're all the way under …"

In horrified silence, Claire scanned the surrounding landscape for something that whoever was trapped could hold onto while Claire dragged them out. She scouted around and found the remains of a tree. With a great deal of exertion, she pulled a broken branch away from its trunk, which she dragged back to the pit.

"I'm so sorry," she shouted to the pile. "I'll have to jab until I find you." She lay on her stomach and edged forward on the dry and cracked earth, feeling like a scavenger as she poked at the pile of bodies, clumsily moving limbs aside to try and see what they might be concealing. At last, two soot-blackened hands reached out and held tight, eyes wide with desperation. Under the dirty face, Claire saw the girl was her own age.

"I'm going to get you out. What's your name?"

"Lotte," the girl croaked.

"Hold on tight, Lotte." Claire wrenched the branch backwards. Splinters lodged in both hands, but Lotte's head was free. Claire pulled back further, with Lotte gradually emerging, shoving and kicking at the corpses trapping her until she was free. Finally, Lotte had a foothold on the side of the pit.

Sudden heat seared Claire's back. *No!* While helping Lotte, Claire had let her magic subside and the fire had come up behind her. Flames rose hot as Lotte screamed, losing her handhold. With a curse, Claire closed her eyes, her mind slamming into a plume of fire too strong to divert. She'd have to use all her remaining energy to put it out. She imagined a waterfall near the dam in Shale after a lot of rainfall, the sound of splashing against rocks, the feel of cool spray on cheeks and smiled. Her mind connected with the blaze as she pinched it out, making her arm sting all the way past her elbow.

Opening her eyes, Claire reached for Lotte with the branch. With a wild cry, the girl extended blistered fingers and caught at its end. Coughing, lungs longing for clean air, Claire helped Lotte crawl to safety beyond the perimeter of the camp, away from the fires.

Lotte retched and choked, gasping and struggling to breathe, before falling to her knees, then onto her side with her eyes closed, her chest barely rising and falling.

Claire tried to ask if she was OK, but her own voice was a mere croak. Her body ached as a terrible lethargy stole over her and she too collapsed, entirely spent.

Chapter Twelve

RAYS OF LIGHT PRICKED at Claire's eyelids. She batted a hand across her face, groaning. "It's too early, Kiera. Close the curtains." But whatever was shining on her felt too bright to be coming in through the window. She opened her eyes, puzzled by the greyish light of dawn staring down on her. Then it came back in a rush; Rinn dying during a Dream Mage working, Claire escaping Dorran Manor and then ... then ... it was too much. Claire's stomach heaved at the memory of the burnt husk of the valley, the pits, the dead exiles and the girl ...

Lotte! Had she survived the night?

Claire turned her head, ignoring the muscle cramps and the hole in her stomach telling her she needed food after all the magic she'd expended and losing what little food she had eaten. Lotte was awake, shifting this way and that in a bid to get comfortable on the hard ground. She was crying. Claire wished her parents were here. They'd know what to do, but since they weren't, she'd have to do her best.

"It's OK. I'm not going to leave you," she managed, though her throat was dry and sore and her tongue too thick.

Through choked sobs, Lotte gave a short laugh. Claire didn't need to see beneath the soot on her face to sense her derision.

"Hey," Claire said. "I'm serious." She made herself sit up, knees tucked to her chin, hands massaging her legs. "I'll take care of you."

"Dunno what 'OK' is, but yer kind don't care for mine."

Claire froze. No matter how hard she tried to suppress her suspicions about her grandfather, they hadn't been far from the surface since she'd first overhead Eidan's tale. "Who did this to you?" she made herself ask, dreading the answer she knew was coming.

"Who'd ya think?" Lotte replied bitterly. "I see what yer wearing. I know ya for what y'are. And then there's yer hair – red like a Dorran fire."

Claire's gut twisted. There had to be a misunderstanding. She could imagine her grandfather, Rael and the others attacking these exiles, but conducting mass murderer and throwing children into a pit? That was evil. Besides, what reason did Lord Dorran have to destroy ordinary villages, and all the way to Kelnariat too.

"It wasn't my grandfather's men. It can't have been."

Lotte snorted, making Claire start. She hadn't realised she'd revealed her thoughts aloud.

"I saw 'em!"

"But how do you know?" Her voice wobbled. "I mean, are you sure?"

Lotte turned to her properly, blue eyes the colour of a tropical ocean wave and dirty blonde hair framing a small pixie face. "O' course," she replied as she sat up. "They was wearing red and black Dorran colours."

"It can't have been Grandfather's men," Claire said, but her voice had lost any conviction. Lotte didn't look like she was lying.

"Who're you?" The girl asked, suspicious now.

"I'm Claire." She paused for a moment, weighing up what else to say.

"I'm no idiot. Ya said, 'Grandfather's men.' Who exactly is yer grandfather?" Lotte's eyes turned hard. "Tell the truth."

"It doesn't matter. I ran away." Claire hated that her words caught. "They didn't want me."

"It does so matter." Lotte gripped Claire's arm, pinching so tight Claire held back a yelp. "We begged 'em to spare us, but they didn't listen, and yer one of 'em." She pulled her hand away suddenly, like Claire's skin had branded her.

"Only half, my father isn't from here," Claire protested, "and I didn't know about this. I swear!"

"Who's yer grandfather then?" Lotte asked, turning her hand palm upwards and blowing on it where the skin was raw and blistered.

"Lord Dorran," Claire admitted wearily.

"I s'pose I should thank ya for saving me, but yer'll have to forgive me for not declaring undying gratitude to the enemy."

Lotte's bitterness felt like a knife blade to Claire's chest. "I'm not the enemy," she said, trying not to feel hurt. "Seriously."

"But yer a Dorran and Mam said I should never trust one."

"Who else can you trust, Lotte? Besides, I pulled you out of the fire!" Claire looked towards the camp. "You must have family and friends? We should check if anyone else survived and then let's get out of here." Lord Dorran would know she'd run away by now. They'd have to head east towards the capital. Maybe Lotte knew the way. If she didn't, Claire had to hope they'd come upon a farmer journeying the same way who would give them a ride. Claire knew it was a weak plan, but she couldn't think of anything better.

"We? I ain't going anywhere with ya."

"Come on, Lotte." Claire pressed a hand to her aching forehead. "We're in this together. You're the closest thing I've got to a friend now – and frankly I'm the closest thing you've got to one too. So, we stick together, and maybe we get out of this alive. After all this, you never have to see me again."

Lotte's mouth pursed sulkily, but she didn't reply.

"Suit yourself then." With a shrug, Claire got to her feet. She trudged towards the perimeter of the camp, even as she knew it was hopeless. Smoke inhalation would have killed any survivors by now if the fires and the blades of the unknown soldiers hadn't gotten them first. Still, she had to check for survivors just in case, and then she'd get away. She shuddered. If even one person was alive ... "Hello?" she called. "Is anyone there?"

Lotte dragged herself to her feet. She wouldn't meet Claire's eyes, pacing to the other end of the camp. "Jan? Mam? Da?" she cried.

The pair spent agonizing minutes on their search, but it was no use. The exiles were dead. Claire picked her way back to Lotte, who stared at nothing, collapsed onto her knees. She had to try one last time to convince Lotte to leave with her. Anything less was a death sentence.

"Lotte, I'm sorry you've lost your family but—"

"Don't," Lotte said.

"But—"

"Just ... don't."

With a sigh, Claire sank onto her heels, throat rasping from thirst. They couldn't stay here, but how to persuade Lotte to trust her? She puzzled for what felt like ages, cold stealing over her despite the sun shining. She glanced at the sky. It was darkening like it was about to storm. Beside her, Lotte muttered something under her breath as wet fog descended. The back of Claire's neck prickled. "What's happen—"

Before Claire could scrabble on hands and knees towards Lotte, something formed in the growing mist.

Not something. Someone. No. A lot of someones.

They were almost transparent, long and thin, both male and female, hair tangling in soft silvery skeins. Some knelt by Claire's head, putting careful spectral fingertips to her lips. Some of them grinned as they touched her cold cheek. They reminded Claire of her dad's story of wraiths.

Claire tried to bat them away, but the more she struggled, the more they crowded around her. Every time she allowed her gaze to glance upwards, wraiths filled her vision. She felt them like an icy stab to the heart. Her breath cut sharp and shallow. She would die here, and her family would never know.

As her heart constricted, Claire noticed her fingers had turned blue-purple, and her muscles began to ache from the struggle and the cold. The mist was all pervasive. She couldn't see more than a few centimetres to either side of her.

Then, just like that, the wraiths vanished. Fear slammed through her like a metal fist. Towering over her was something else.

She looked like a queen; tall and slender, deathly pale as the fog. Her silver-frost hair cascaded down her back like liquid, her lips were an impossible cherry-red against her blue-white face and her eyes, all pupil and black, were the strangest eyes Claire had ever seen. Her slender hands reached out for Claire's own. Claire flinched, shrinking back.

The woman's mouth curved into an amused smile. Claire gasped. Pointed teeth peaked out as she tilted her head, considering Claire like a cat did a mouse. She made an impatient gesture and hissed, "Get up."

Claire contemplated refusing, but she didn't like her chances of survival if she disobeyed. She tried to stand up but her legs wouldn't obey her. The lady smiled and held out a hand to help. Claire grasped it, finding it surprisingly solid. Once on her feet, she noticed that the lady was gazing beyond Claire.

Lotte! Claire had forgotten all about her. She swung around. The exile stood behind her with arms folded. She didn't look afraid. "What's this about?" Claire demanded.

"Ya wanted me to trust ya." She nodded at the wraith. "Claire says she's a Dorran, but she wants to help."

The lady cocked her head to one side. "And do you?"

"Yes, but who are you?" Lord Dorran had never mentioned such a creature in any of his many lectures at dinner.

"She's the Crian, ruler of the Melinor, and my friend," Lotte said.

The Crian gripped Claire's chin with icy hands and pushed it up so Claire looked into her strange eyes. She said nothing, studying Claire's face. Claire rubbed her cloak over her arms and tried not to flinch at the scrutiny. At last, the Crian nodded. "So, you are Lord Dorran's granddaughter, and yet you rescued Lotte. Why?"

Something about her seriousness compelled the truth. "I haven't lived in Kelnarium long and my mother taught me punishing people for what their parents had done was wrong. I argued with Lord Dorran about it. When I ran away and found Lotte's camp and heard her begging for help, well, I couldn't leave her."

"No. You are the child born of two worlds, the one who was to come in our greatest hour of need."

Claire felt sudden hope warm her veins. She'd run away in despair, certain Dorran House had made a terrible mistake about her importance to Kelnarium, but this spirit was claiming otherwise. She breathed easier. Maybe there was a simple explanation for the Beast's words and she could go back to her grandfather and everything would come right.

The Crian sighed, looking over Claire's shoulder to Lotte. "There is no evil in this girl's heart."

"Thanks," Claire whispered, relieved someone believed her. Still, her heart sank. Even if she was able to fulfil the prophecy, her grandfather and Dorran House were murderers. "I don't know what to do next," she admitted. "I have to close the Rift before it explodes and takes all of Kelnarium with it but—"

"The Rift is going to explode?" The Crian's brows shot upwards. "Who told you this, child?"

"Gwenivere and my grandfather," Claire said. "I thought everyone knew about the latest prophecy. That's why Marcus and I were summoned."

"Ha!" Lotte laughed from behind her. "What clap-trap are ya talking now?"

"It's the truth," Claire said, staring the Crian down.

The spirit gazed deep into Claire's eyes. Claire didn't dare look away.

At last, the Crian broke the stare. "Lotte, there are no lies in this girl's face or heart. If she says she is to close the Rift and save us, I believe her."

"Hey, I didn't call on ya to fawn all over her," Lotte protested.

"You don't understand, child. I—" The Crian looked to the sky as though hearing someone speak. Her form shuddered and flickered, and her eyes turned blank. "You must return! Danger! Death!"

Before Claire could say a word, the Crian wrapped the girls in her icy essence and the exiles camp fell away as they rose into the sky.

Chapter Thirteen

CLAIRE DIDN'T REMEMBER much of the journey except whiteness, fog and an icy clutch in her lungs. She found herself, seemingly seconds later, lying on rough ground. Lotte sat beside her with the Crian nowhere in sight. She looked up, amazed to find they were on the path that led to Dorran Manor. She saw the outer palisades, the gates ... and smoke rising from inside the compound.

She twisted to face Lotte. "Something's wrong." Claire blinked. Lotte's skin had healed on the journey; it was now clean and white instead of scarred and covered in burns, though her clothes were still filthy and ragged.

"Where're we?" Lotte touched Claire's arm, which was also clean and unblemished.

"The Crian spirited me home," Claire said, shocked. "She must have sent you too, because she thought you'd be safe with me." She heard clashes and strained to listen. It sounded like metal striking metal, like people training on a battlefield in a movie or ... Screams punctuated the air. Claire sat up straight. "My family needs help. Can't you hear it? I'm going in."

"Wha— but I can't follow ya there. They'll finish me off." Lotte sounded on the verge of tears. "Them's the one's that *murdered* my family."

Claire stood up as a new theory formed. "I don't think it was Dorran House that attacked you," she said. "It's easy to dress up as someone else, and when I think about it, I didn't smell Dorran magic at the village or the camp. Whoever got you is after my people now. That must be what the Crian meant by danger and death. I have to help them!"

She turned and ran up the hill, all her aches and pains gone, all her energy miraculously returned. The gates were open with no one standing guard. The sound of fighting was louder; from this proximity, the screams and the wailing became more urgent. Claire pressed herself against the wall inside the gateway, peering in. Tears prickled as she thought of her grandfather, Aed, Meghan, Rael and Kiera.

From behind her came the sound of footsteps, and she turned as a hand slipped into hers. "If I help ya, will yer people reward me? A handful of coins would gimme a chance to start again," Lotte whispered with a sniff, her face scared and pinched, but also determined.

"Yes, whatever you want. I have to get closer. People I care about are in there."

"Careful," Lotte said, but she edged alongside Claire through the gateway, past the smouldering buildings, the horses bolting this way and that, past the granary, past the dye vats, past the storage sheds, past the dead servitors, past the stamped earth and flattened grass.

The sound of battle grew louder the closer they got to the entrance of the Manor itself. Claire's mind filled with images of metal piercing and tearing flesh, the sound of fists striking skin, of the sickening crunch and snap as someone was thrust against stone or fell on the rosy flagstones. *Maen can blast any intruder, and Rael trains his soldiers every day for something like this,* she told herself. *So why,* a doubting voice insisted, *are people dead in the outer compound and Dorran buildings in ruins?*

Panic gripped as she ran for the great doors, but Lotte pulled her wrist out of Claire's grasp, forcing Claire to slow. Lotte pointed at a bush to their left, pressed against the Manor wall, then hurried over to it.

She waited for Claire to join her. "This gives us a bit of cover while we talk. We can't just barge through those doors. We ain't got no weapons and no idea of what's really goin' on." She wiped her nose. "Do ya wanna end up like Jan, my mam and da?"

"My grandfather," Claire began through clenched teeth, "I can't leave him. Not when I know he's in trouble." She paused, in her mind adding, *and his people are my best chance of finding Marcus.*

Lotte blocked Claire's way. "Calm yerself, stop and think. Let's move up the side of the building an' find a place to scale a wall or a quieter entrance. We need to know what's goin' on. If we walk in the front door whoever's attacking will catch us right away." She gripped Claire's wrist. "I've survived when the rest of my family hasn't. I gotta make that count for something, an' walking into a death trap ain't my idea of it."

"I don't have time to chat. My family are getting killed in there," Claire hissed, then immediately wished she could take it back. At least Mum and Dad were safe in Shale. Lotte had lost everyone.

The exile looked like she'd been slapped. "Claire, listen. We gotta be sensible. I can't lose ya now." She flushed and looked away. "Yer right; yer all I've got."

A fireball the size of a soccer ball illuminated the sky, coming from one of the outhouse buildings. New cries punctuated the sound of weapons clashing.

What the heck is going on? Claire closed her eyes, trying to formulate a plan. "We should head to our right. There's a walled garden the kitchens use. We can scale the wall and get inside the Manor that way."

Lotte tugged at Claire's scarf. "Lemme tie this about your hair; bright as a flame, it is. That way if people are killing Dorrans they won't recognise ya," she said as she tied the silken fabric around Claire's head. "The granddaughter of Lord Dorran would be a grand prize." Then Lotte picked at her own undyed woollen tunic. "Gimme your cloak so yer people won't know I'm an exile." She waited as Claire did as she asked, then bent down and rubbed her palms in the dirt, drawing upright to rub it into Claire's cheeks and forehead. She bent a second time and did the same for herself.

"Right. This way," Claire said. She took an uncertain step forward as a second smaller fireball missed her by inches.

She threw herself to the ground, mouth half full of dirt, as a third landed right in front of her. Her heart pounded as she extinguished another with magic before it could land on her head. Someone must have spotted them. They had to move. Fast.

Lotte flung herself beside Claire as new bursts of light flickered above them.

"Hurry," Claire whispered, scrambling back to her feet, her hand outstretched as she shifted fire magic away from them both. Lotte let herself be hauled upright and dragged along the side of the Manor. At last, they reached the right-hand side of the building, where creepers draped against a stone balustrade concealed the kitchen garden from view. "You go first. I'll cover for you," Claire said.

Lotte climbed up the vines in a flash, her feet and hands rustling against the leaves. Soon, Claire could barely see her. The exile summoned Claire with a soft hoot, like an owl. It must be safe wherever Lotte was inside, or at least it was for the time being. Muscles straining, Claire gripped the vines with her hands and crept up slowly using her feet and knees to climb as well. With agonizing care, she clambered from the vines onto the edge of the walled garden and swung both legs over, jumping onto the soft grass below.

Lotte waved from where she waited a few feet away. "I think most of the noise is comin' from the entrance. Mebbe yer people are tryin' to get out? If we can get to their attackers from behind, we might be able to stop them with yer magic." She paused. "What will ya do if the people attacking are farmers upset about what we saw yesterday, if Dorran House *were* responsible and this is the result?"

Claire hadn't thought of that. "I have to help them anyway. They're my relations, but then when it's all over, I'll demand the truth and decide what to do next." She gripped Lotte's hand. "Either way, I'll make sure you get your money. It's the least I can do. Let's go. We should hurry. Try to stay in the shadows."

They tiptoed through the Manor, diving behind alcoves whenever they saw a man or woman with a sword scurrying past wearing browns and greys and blues. Claire remembered the colour scheme from lessons with her grandfather and Eidan's visit; they were Eidan's people from Kelnariat. Claire didn't know what to think. They were allies of Dorran House, so maybe they were trying to help her grandfather and Lotte was correct about angry villagers. She didn't want to believe it.

Raised voices echoed down the passageway. They were almost at the Throne Room. Claire pushed herself into a dark corner, dragging Lotte beside her.

"Don't kill him!" a voice, Gwenivere's, called out, firm and commanding.

"Be silent," a man answered. Claire recognised his voice immediately. It was Eidan.

"The Council does not harm a man who has surrendered," Gwenivere insisted. "Think, Councillor."

"Dorran has betrayed us," Eidan replied. "He helped his granddaughter escape, knowing that it was her who would betray us all. It was a Dorran who began the Rift and a Dorran who is continuing to let it destroy my world and yours."

Claire put a shaking hand to her chest, breath catching. *What a mess. Eidan's misunderstanding could destroy Dorran House and it will be my fault for running away.* She sidled closer to the door, a single salamander suddenly appearing overhead to point frantically towards the Throne Room. *I know, little fellow,* she thought. *I'll do my best to help everyone inside.*

"Take him back to Kelnariat, Councillor," Gwenivere was reasoning. "Let the Council hear his case in a fair trial. Fairness is what your government is about. That's what makes you different from the corrupt days of Selk." Her voice softened. "I know you are upset, but don't let emotion cloud your judgement. Give him a chance to explain."

Claire was filled with a sudden warmth for the usually distant Dream Mage. She prayed Eidan would listen. She edged closer to the doorway, holding up a hand to signal that Lotte should remain in hiding, hoping at the same time that no one would turn the corner and find her eavesdropping.

Eidan's tone brooked no argument. "Don't question me, Gwenivere."

Someone, probably Eidan, made a kind of clicking sound, like fingers snapping. Something else banged against the flagstones. *Boots,* Claire realised.

"Seize her," Eidan commanded, "while I kill him."

The blood rushed to Claire's head. She couldn't just stand by as Eidan murdered a member of her family.

"No," she shrieked, running towards the Throne Room doors before Lotte could reach out and stop her. "You can't."

She stumbled into the Throne Room to see two guards restraining Gwenivere while Eidan perched on her grandfather's throne, a sword sitting lazily across his lap. Lord Dorran slumped before him, face to the ground. Blood trickled out of one ear. Another salamander, unseen by everyone in the room but Claire, patted at the sticky substance in confusion, then dug webbed toes into her grandfather's arms. There was no response. Claire wanted to run and fling her arms around her grandfather, but something stopped her. His hair wasn't quite dark enough and his ears were too wide and long. It wasn't Lord Dorran before her, but her great-uncle, Aed.

Hope surged. Had Lord Dorran escaped after all? But new grief washed over her. Aed had been kind to her. His life was just as important. She flung herself at his side, careful to avoid squashing the salamander now curled against his neck.

Eidan looked at Claire lazily. "And which scullery lass are you?"

Claire's hair was still covered beneath the tightly wound scarf Lotte had arranged before they'd mounted their rescue effort. Her face was covered in the dirt and soot of her recent adventures. Her own mother would be hard put to recognise her without a second glance. No wonder Eidan thought her a servant.

She opened her mouth to introduce herself and start explaining, but something in his too-hungry expression stopped her. In spite of his lazy voice, he had a madness to his eyes that reminded her of a wild dog. Maybe he didn't need to know who she was just yet. "I beg you, Lord Eidan, let Lord Dorran go free. He's not guilty of whatever crime you think. Someone's been telling lies."

He sneered. "How can you be sure?"

"I saw Lady Claire run away," she half lied. "She had no help."

He considered her for a moment. "A convenient tale," he said, getting to his feet with sword in hand. "How much money did Lord Dorran pay you to spread it?"

"None," she said, tears threatening to overwhelm her. "Please believe me, Sir."

Eidan grinned as he neared Aed. She froze as he roughly flipped her great-uncle onto his back, the salamander scuttling along the floor as Eidan bent, sword pointing over his stomach. Behind him, Gwenivere screamed. Claire had to do something and fast. She reached within for fire, aiming for Eidan's cloak. As smoke unfurled from its end, she heard his sword plunge, Aed grunt and then a wet squelching sound as the metal blade came back into view dripping red, breaking Claire's concentration.

"Kill Gwenivere and the girl," Eidan said, turning away from Aed's body and striding towards the door.

There was no time to lose – Claire estimated the distance between herself and the two men holding Gwenivere. "Dodge!" she screamed at the dazed Dream Mage, as she hurled flames a metre in front of their feet.

One of the guards shoved Gwenivere to her knees as he ran through the door after Eidan. The other dropped to the ground, rolling sparks out of his shirt sleeve, then he too was up and out through the doorway. Gwenivere crawled along the ground, coughing, to escape from the flames. Claire raced forward, gripping Gwenivere under the arms and hauling her to her feet. "Let's go!" she screamed.

She raced out of the Throne Room to the corner where she'd left Lotte. The exile had slid to the flagstones, tears staining her cheeks.

"It's OK. They didn't get me," Claire said, "but we have to move. Eidan's mad! There's no way he'll listen to reason."

"Hurry!" came an urgent voice came from around the corner. "There are at least five of his men to every one of ours." Then the owner of the voice appeared: Rael.

Claire simply stared as a small group in Dorran colours followed him. Her breath came out in a rush of recognition. Kiera, Maen and Meghan were among them; at least they had survived the initial attack. Seven salamanders swam through the air in their wake, sparking orange-red and gold.

Rael gestured to one of his guards and the pair peeled away to peer through the door of the Throne Room.

"Eidan's already gone," Claire called out. "The body on the floor is Aed. I don't know where Lord Dorran is."

Rael spun around, then acknowledged her with a brief nod. "Follow us! Move!" he said, as he led the way down a hall, a sword in one hand and a dagger in the other.

Claire tried to ignore the dead bodies littering the corridor, bewildered salamanders crawling everywhere. Rael led them through an arched doorway that led outside. They picked their way through overturned carts, discarded baskets and yet more bodies, stopping when they reached the fortification wall.

"Blast on my count," Maen shouted, taking Rael's place at the head of the group.

Heavy boots clattered behind them. There was no time to ask questions.

Claire stepped forward with Rael, Kiera and Meghan. Maen held up fingers as he counted, "One, two, three."

She closed her eyes and called up the biggest fireball she could manage in unison with the others. *Boom.* The impact pushed her backward as sudden heat flushed her face, arms, legs.

"Help move the wreckage," Maen called. He stood to one side, working a new spell.

Claire guessed he was cooling the fire-blasted bricks. She rushed forward with everyone else, eagerly throwing debris out of their way alongside Lotte. Within seconds, they'd made a hole big enough for people to clamber through.

"Go," Maen said, waving Gwenivere forward.

Claire helped Gwenivere and then Kiera through the gap in the wall. She choked on smoke as she dived through herself, eyes smarting from fumes, but she made it to the other side with little more than a graze.

They were at the back of the Manor enclosure. Many of the escapees were already descending the hill through a field of flame-red poppies that only ended at the edge of the thick forest. Embers from the blast flickered around them, but she and Maen quickly had them out.

So much fire in two days, she thought. *If I ever get home, I'll get an instant job as a firefighter.* Giggles escaped before she could stop them.

Maen glanced at her as he directed the last of the party down the slope. "Head for the forest," he instructed.

Claire swallowed, anxious to know about her grandfather. "Is Lord Dorran—"

But Maen shook his head, taking her arm and guiding her hurriedly after the rest of the group. "He's no longer with us."

Chapter Fourteen

THE ROCK AND CREAK of the horse-drawn canvas-covered cart made Claire sleepy, as did the chorus of shod-feet clip-copping on the dirt road. She couldn't believe it when Maen had led the survivors to a small ramshackle barn in the woods well away from the estate walls – it was so perfectly hidden that you could only find it if you knew where you were going. Two carts had been waiting, attended by a pair of startled retainers and the Dream Mage, Tarn. Maen had sent the servitors to a second section of woods, an evacuation point for those who lived in the Manor in case of attack, to regroup anyone else who might have escaped. "They can explain all is not lost, that you and I live, and that our party will continue to the Riftlands."

Now she chewed on the dry bread Maen had handed out once they'd gotten underway. He sat beside her, staring into space. Tarn was up front, driving their cart. Lotte, looking shellshocked, huddled beside Claire on the floor that had been padded with blankets and old quilts. Just outside the Manor, Claire had introduced the exile as a visitor to a farm whom Claire had rescued from some of Eidan's men. She'd stood her ground with Maen and insisted that not only was she refusing to go anywhere without Lotte, they'd travel in the same cart too. After Maen's initial feeble protests about not taking innocents on such a dangerous journey, no one had questioned the arrangement again.

Kiera, Meghan and Gwenivere were in the other cart behind them, which was driven by Rael. Her own cart was approximately five metres long and two across – not a lot of space for three people, but enough. There were packs up the far end, filled with food and coin for a longish journey. The Dorrans had been prepared.

Claire fixed Maen with a sharp gaze, her bread forgotten. "So, when were you planning to tell me we were going somewhere?"

Maen smiled. "We intended to travel to Kelnariat via the Maellwyns in a week's time when you were better trained. Lord Dorran never told Eidan of his plan, hence the hidden carts in the forest."

"We're going to Maellwyn Manor? I thought there was no love lost between our Houses." Her voice trembled. "That's what Grandfather said." Maen had told her not too long ago that Lord Dorran hadn't made it out of the Manor. He'd seen him collapse with a knife to the gut; his last words had been to find Claire and run.

"Ah, he exaggerated because he didn't want to tell you all of our secrets at once. It's been to the advantage of both Houses to pretend we fight. In truth, your grandfather and Lord Maellwyn exchanged regular letters and met in secret in Autun every year or so." He frowned at Claire's untouched bread. "Eat up! You used a lot of energy back there!"

She did as she was told, despite the crumbs catching in her throat.

He waited until she'd swallowed the last morsel. "Now, I have a question for you. Where have you been the last two days? It was like you vanished. Don't tell me there's a hidey hole on Dorran grounds I don't know about."

Claire stiffened. She'd assumed Gwenivere had told Maen and the others what had happened with Rinn and the Beast, but apparently not. She decided to keep quiet until she could speak to Gwenivere, who must have reasons of her own for withholding information.

Still, someone had set fire to villages and Lotte's camp. She had to make sure it wasn't the Dorrans. She searched quickly for a way to frame her reply, looking at Lotte, who pressed against a bulge under her borrowed cloak. Claire knew she fingered her sheepskin pouch, the only thing of value she had left.

"I made Great-Uncle Aed tell me what your meeting was about. I felt left out." She silently apologised for the lie, but Aed was beyond caring. "He told me about the places burnt near Kelnariat, the scrap of Dorran uniform. I ran away to ... to the outhouses to think. I slept overnight in a stable. Horses comfort me." She caught Maen's gaze defiantly. That last part of her tale wasn't even a lie really. In Shale, she felt like she did understand animals better than people. "I wasn't ever comfortable with the way you talked about the exiles and I thought if Dorran House spoke like that about them, maybe you didn't care about farmers and poor tradesmen either and so you might have been responsible."

Maen's eyes were baggy and shadowed from lack of sleep and Claire could have sworn there was grey in his hair she'd never noticed before. "You did us a great disservice," he said. "Dorran House does not murder. Someone has set us up to take the blame."

Claire narrowed her eyes. "Swear it."

Maen sighed. "I swear."

She sank back against a folded blanket. Maen didn't look like he was lying. "I wonder who set you up?"

"I don't know."

They fell into silence. "Grandfather said Eidan was a good leader as well as a friend," Claire ventured finally. "Yet he was wild back there. I saw him murder Great-Uncle Aed."

"And his men were camped a mere half day away ready to storm the estate," Maen said grimly. "He'd decided we were guilty before he arrived. Praise the Saura one of the guards had the presence of mind to shut up the secret passageway to the caverns before Eidan's men could find it. Our elementals, at least, will be safe until we can return to rebuild the Manor." His voice rose. "But we shouldn't have to skulk about Kelnarium. We should be united in dealing with the Rift, not turning on each other. Someone in Kelnariat is behind this – probably whoever is paying those bandits to masquerade as us – but why?"

Before Claire could reply, the cart ground to a sudden halt, jerking her forward. Tarn poked his head through the yellow, red and green patched fabric separating the wooden seat where the driver sat from the interior. "There's a clearing ahead where we can make camp. The river crossing near Autun isn't far now, I'd say half a day's ride at most."

Maen glanced at Claire. "I suggest we get changed into less conspicuous attire, so we're not recognised. If people think we're responsible for razing settlements, who knows what they'll do to us on the road, where we can be attacked easily and without consequence." He paused significantly.

"Don't we want to be recognised? I know people are upset about the so-called Dorran raiders," Claire said, "but why can't we tell them who I am?

Surely once they know we're saving Kelnarium, they'll look on us more kindly."

"That part of the prophecy has never been publicised."

Claire remembered the Crian's surprise at the mention of the Rift exploding. "But why not?"

"Only the Dream Mages, key people from Dorran and Maellwyn House and Eidan know the extent of the destruction heading our way unless we can stop it fast. We all agreed we didn't want to spread mass panic and cause issues for Eidan's Council." He ran a hand over his face. "Maybe that was a mistake, but it's too late now. People know someone part Dorran and part from another world will arrive in our time of need. People know the Riftlands spread wider and wider every year, but they do not know the rest. So," he sighed, "what would you have us do? Change into something less obvious or publicise that we are Dorrans?"

As Claire pressed her lips together realisation struck. Maen wanted her to make the decision. With Grandfather dead she was the new head of Dorran House. Yet, she was a teenager. What did she know about leading people, especially in a world she'd never known existed until a week or so ago? Best to do what the guy who understood Kelnarium suggested.

She cleared her throat. "We get changed and we rest," she agreed, "though let's keep it a brief stop. I can see why we don't want anyone to stumble onto us."

In no time at all, the two carts were stationed on either side of the small clearing; Kiera had a fire lit and meat turning on a spit, Claire helped with the horses and then she and Lotte lay out some of the older woollen blankets on the damp grass. Leather bags with clothing half-hanging out of the loosely closed flaps sat in a heap beside them thanks to Maen and Rael's forethought.

Claire drew nearer to the fire and sat on a blanket, the birch and spruce trees towering over them and blocking out the stars. Munching on bread and hard cheese, Claire took a plate of meat from Kiera.

There was little conversation as the party ate – without the distraction of the mundane tasks of setting up camp, it was obvious everyone was exhausted and ravaged by grief. Tarn and Gwenivere were the only Dream Mages who'd made it out of the Manor, and who knew how many Dorrans had escaped? Though Rael had sent some of his guards to take children and the vulnerable away from the estate when the attack had commenced, no one knew if they were safe. Meghan and Kiera sat with knees touching, heads bowed. Rael's face kept screwing up like he was about to cry and Maen's had gained new grooves. Claire's own heart felt heavy as she thought of Aed and the way he'd sounded when the sword had slid from his chest. Lotte sat so close to Claire that their shoulders touched, and Claire could feel Lotte's occasional sobs.

Maen put aside his dish and rose to his feet. He indicated Claire should join him at the centre of the circle beside the fire. Wiping tears away, she put her own finished meal aside and did as requested.

He put a hand on her shoulder when she reached his side. "When Eidan turned on us, Lord Dorran gave me his ring for safe keeping, as he normally did when Aed was called upon to act as his double. As you all know, both brothers are dead. I saw one of Eidan's captain's strike Lord Dorran down and he screamed at me to fight my way out of the room. I wanted to stay with him, I would have died with him, but he knew Dorran House is more than its leader alone." His grip on Claire's shoulder tightened. "Lady Claire is head of the Dorrans now. Her grandfather knew that men and women like me would help her. I know we will all serve her well." He put his free hand out, revealing the gold and opal-veined sparkle of her grandfather's ring, a thick cord looped through its band.

She was meant to take it, Claire knew, but she felt so inadequate. It was hard enough being responsible for her own actions, let alone a party of people. Once, she'd gone to Girl Guides and they'd been made to do a stupid exercise where everyone took turns to lead a survival scenario. Claire had been terrible; no one had listened to her and she'd gotten so anxious she kept changing her mind about what to direct people to do. If Maen and the others had longer to get to know her, they'd probably choose someone else.

But Maen was nodding encouragingly. "We know this is overwhelming, but you aren't alone. We'll guide you when you need it. Take the ring. It's rightfully yours."

Claire looked around the solemn circle, struck by the trust and encouragement in most of their expressions. Maybe it wouldn't be so scary, after all. At least she wasn't dealing with high school kids. She plucked the ring from Maen's palm and put the cord over her head, tucking it and the ring under her shirt alongside the pendant necklace Lord Dorran had gifted her. As she did so, something flickered in the corner of her vision, something that looked suspiciously like a giant white-gold salamander encased in flame, but then she blinked and the image was gone. She turned her attention back to her fellow survivors, remembering where she was.

No one moved, like they expected something more from her.

"I'll do my best for this House," she said. "No one else should have to die. We continue to Maellwyn Manor. Finish eating and get changed." She pointed at the bags of clothing.

Rael cleared his throat.

"Yes?" She inclined her head to the captain – her captain now.

"We can't continue on without changing the patchwork canvas we have over the carts. People will recognise us. There are plainer animal skin covers in that bag." He pointed to one that bulged at every seam.

Claire nodded. "Switch the coverings. The rest of you get changed, pack up and get ready to leave." She was pleased her voice didn't tremble too much. *Fake it until you make it*, Marcus always said.

As they chose clothes to get changed into and got ready for the next part of the journey, she had a few words with each of them, trying to keep their spirits up. Meghan especially seemed grateful. She and Kiera couldn't stop thinking about their young relatives. Not knowing if they lived or died had taken its toll on the pair. Meghan's wrinkles looked deeper and she stood almost doubled over, while Kiera's cheeks were pinched.

There was one person left Claire hadn't spoken to in the clearing. She went in search of Gwenivere. The Dream Mage stood in the darkness apart from the others, leaning into a tree bough, some of its branches brushing against her arm. Even in the bad light, Claire could see her cheeks were too pale. "Do you have a minute?" Claire whispered.

Gwenivere froze, but she didn't move away.

"You know I spied on your meeting with Grandfather and Eidan. You know what Rinn saw," Claire said. She took Gwenivere's silence as consent to go on. "Why haven't you denounced me to Maen and the others? You could have just now when he gave me the ring. You would have been well within your rights."

Gwenivere's gaze remained fixed on Rael and the carts.

"Talk to me," Claire hissed. "Are you going to tell him that the Beast said I'd destroy instead of save?"

Gwenivere's eyes crinkled at the edges. "The man I believed to be good and righteous above all others turned on us. Four out of the six I brought with me to Dorran Manor are dead. The rest are trapped in Kelnariat, and yet you question me? How dare you."

"All right, all right," Claire said hastily. "I didn't mean to be insensitive, but I don't know what to do. I've been having weird dreams with the Beast in them. That's one of the reasons I ran away from the Manor. I was scared it was right and you'd all punish me. I know you have no real reason to believe me, but I don't want to betray anyone. I want to save this world, get Marcus and go home. That's all."

Gwenivere took a step towards the carts, brown and grey horsehair skins finally over both, then turned to look straight at Claire. "The creature you describe is no friend of ours given how it injures and kills magic users across Kelnarium. I trust it even less than I trust you. That's why I've said nothing to Maen. I suggest you don't either for the moment. We can't afford to have dissent amongst our party."

Claire nodded her agreement. She didn't like keeping the truth from people, but Gwenivere's reasoning was sound. She headed back into the clearing, skirting a large log, when a hand reached out and grabbed her ankle. It was icy cold – Claire felt it even through her tights – and made her stumble.

"Get down for a sec." It was Lotte. Claire repressed a twinge of guilt. The exile had been the furthest thing from her mind with everything else going on.

"It'll have to be quick," Claire said, but she dropped to sit on the log, with Lotte still in the shadows behind her. "Well?" she said, not looking at the exile girl.

"Ya said yer'd keep me safe, that yer'd give me coin so I can start again."

"Lotte," Claire whispered. "We're safe for now."

"*Ya* are," she said. "Yer important. At the first sign of danger yer'll be protected, but me? I'm nuthin' and no one." She paused. "I can't stop thinkin' about how they died—all of 'em. It's different for ya. Ya didn't know yer grandfather all your life like I did my parents, my brother and everyone else in that camp."

"I'm so sorry," Claire said miserably. "Tell me about them." She got up quietly and climbed over the log to sit beside Lotte.

Lotte had pushed her cloak back to dip long fingers into her sheepskin pouch. "My mam were an orphan. She stumbled into the camp and my da took her in. He never asked any questions about why she didn't have somewhere else to go. He said she bewitched him with her lovely voice. She'd sing to Jan and I and sometimes we'd have dancing and she'd tap out the beat with Da and some of the others." Lotte opened her clenched fist. In it sat a string of carved wooden beads, grimy pink quartz and feathers, bits of rusting silver twisted around the rope cord. Claire recognised the style. No Dorran would ever mistake it for anything but an exile's work. "This was hers. She told me to keep it on me always. It's important, she said, though I dunno why. Da said she were sentimental that way."

Claire closed Lotte's fingers over the necklace. "Keep it to yourself. I don't know if I can protect you if someone finds it."

"I know."

As Lotte reverently placed the necklace back in her pouch, Claire thought back on how they'd met. So much else had happened, they'd had no opportunity to discuss why the Crian had sent Lotte to the Manor with Claire. For that matter, Claire hadn't had a chance to ask about who the strange spirit was.

"Oh, her?" Lotte said in answer to the question. "She's always been around. Said she were friends with my mam, but she helped me more than her."

"Helped how?"

"She and her Melinor would leave gifts of berries and dead animals for us and she'd warn me if I were in danger from farmers and the like when I went a-stealin'."

"Why'd she send you off with me then? None of this is particularly safe."

"I dunno," Lotte admitted. "I think it were my fault. I got startled when she said 'danger' and I grabbed at yer elbow. I guess I got transported with ya 'coz I was touching ya."

Claire shrugged. "It makes sense."

But Lotte's eyes widened with fright. "Ya can't tell the others about her, though. Promise."

"Sure," Claire said, "but why?"

"I've heard Dorran guards mention her before and they hated her. Dunno why." She poked at the dirt with a stick. "Probly 'coz they know she's friends with exiles. If you tell 'em, they'll know who I really am. Promise ya won't."

"As far as Maen and the others know, I was never anywhere near your camp. I can't tell them about the Crian or about exiles without revealing I lied to them. So don't worry, I won't tell them a thing. Now, get changed here. Then leave your sheepskin behind."

"I'd already thought of that. I pilfered an outfit when everyone were distracted." She tapped her fingers at her side and Claire noticed the dirty skin was underneath her.

"What about the pouch? It'll make you stand out."

Lotte snatched her hand away from Claire's. "It's mine! Ya ain't taking it from me."

"I wasn't about to suggest it," Claire said wearily. She thought for a moment. "I told the others you were only visiting this area. Let's tell them you come from one of the villages clustered around Kelnariat and are used to their warmer climate. That way, when we get to Autun it won't be weird for you to break away from the rest of us because you're simply going home. I saw a woollen cap in one of the bags. Put your pouch on top of your head and the cap over it."

"What about my money?" Lotte asked. "Ya people don't have much left. Do you think they'll give me coin?"

Lotte had a point. Maen wouldn't give them money without a good reason. They needed it too much themselves. Claire ran a shaking hand through her fringe. "I'll have to steal some from the back of the cart when we get to the city." She didn't know how she'd manage it or what she'd say if she got caught, but she'd made a promise and her family didn't break their promises.

Chapter Fifteen

CLAIRE SAT AT A CROWDED trestle table at an inn as evening fell in Autun, along from Lotte and a young cattle breeder. He'd bought her and Lotte two brimming tankards already, and they were onto their third, uncaring that the beer was watered down. It warmed Claire's insides and left her with a buzz that numbed the hardships of the last two days. Candles fixed into an iron ring and held to the roof by chains cast shadows onto the dice they rolled. Behind them hung a shield with the symbol of Autun City; blue river, brown mountain and the yellow of wheat.

The party from Dorran Manor had left the dense forest and crossed the narrow stone bridge that spanned the Teranth River, and had intended to take the road around Autun, but the weather had turned foul and the horses had started slipping, the carts bogging in ruts. Though she knew it was risky heading into a big city, Claire had no choice in the end but to direct the party into Autun for shelter.

They'd arrived early afternoon. Maen had paid precious coin to enter at the quiet Southern gate and had led the party through cobbled streets, past a pungent fish market and the livestock pens into a bustling alleyway. "Innkeeper Giers knows us well," he'd explained, before vanishing to settle lodgings for the night.

Claire and Lotte had gripped each other tight, mouths hanging open. Claire had only seen old inns like this on the TV and Lotte had never travelled far from her camp. The inn was made of brick that had been whitewashed, a lantern hanging over the door, plants on either side with purple flowers adding colour. Raucous laughter drifted through the glass windows.

While the others took care of the horses and Maen and Rael went in search of news, heavy rain allowing them to cover their head and faces without comment, Claire and Lotte went in search of a good time, eager to drown out bad memories. Claire had wrapped a scarf around her bright hair, but as the room grew warmer and warmer and no one said a word about her presence, she'd let it unravel without much care. She'd told everyone her name was Clera and no one had batted an eyelid. She hadn't felt so safe in days.

"Ha!" Lotte said, throwing another two sets of six. "Looks like it's yer unlucky night." She pulled the small pile of bronze towards her as Claire and the cattle breeder groaned. Before he could demand yet another rematch, a man with long blonde hair and a dark green cloak shoved his way towards them, easing onto the bench. His hand gripped Claire's as she tried to slide out of his way.

"Hey!" She elbowed him in the ribs, but his grip merely tightened. "Let go!"

The table went silent as Claire's pot of beer went flying, splashing up the man's cloak. He pulled the dripping plaid back to place a dagger onto the table, its blade jagged and sharp. People's eyes slid away, and the bench quickly thinned out.

"Do what Clera asked. She's a friend," the cattle breeder said. The stranger aimed his dagger the breeder's way, poised in his hand for a close-range throw. Claire's so-called 'friend' was on his feet in a flash. "See you later," he flushed, tipping his hat at Lotte and avoiding Claire's disgusted glare as he headed for the lodgings upstairs.

The man sank onto the bench, brows quirked at Claire, his left hand still gripping the leather binding on the dagger.

"What do you want?" Claire asked cautiously. She didn't think Maen would be happy about all the unwanted attention she was attracting, and she wished she'd adjusted her scarf when she'd had the chance.

The man's hand pinched her arm. "Where've you come from, Clera? You're not from round here." Claire felt his suppressed rage like an electric wire touching skin.

A tall woman opposite, with sleeves rolled up to her elbows and a stained apron over her plain grey dress, leaned over. "It's a big city, mate. Let her be."

"What would you know, Hillarth? You don't hear much baking bread all day." The man spat on the table in front of Claire. "And when's the last time we've seen red hair in these parts? Don't tell me you don't recognise this Clera's look?" The man's lips pulled over his teeth into a snarled grin.

Claire's palms felt sweaty. "I don't know what you mean. My cousin and I are from ... from ..." She couldn't remember where she'd decided Lotte came from near Kelnariat. She twisted to Lotte, begging her to understand what she needed.

"Yes?" The man prompted, acerbic and mocking.

"Corinth Village," Lotte said quickly as sweat trickled down Claire's back.

"Corinth Village is it?" He turned his grin on her. "Sure you didn't mean Dorran Manor?"

The inn was emptying. Those who stayed to watch the show gasped.

Claire shook her head, hoping she looked convincing. "No. We're ... we're from Corinth, as my cousin says."

"With that pale skin?"

Damn! She should have remembered her grandfather's lessons when she'd concocted Lotte's cover story. The climate in Northern Kelnarium *was* warmer and the people's skin darker. Claire willed her legs to stop shaking under the table. If he noticed ... She had to cover her slip-up and fast. "I ... I ... my mother married a southerner."

"The thing is, Clera," the man insisted, pushing his tanned face closer to hers, "I don't believe you." He pinned those around them with a cold stare. "Haven't you heard the news? Dorrans have destroyed good crops and farmland from one end of Kelnarium to the other. How can you stand for this?"

"She's no Dorran," Lotte said, voice shaking, but the man ignored her.

He shoved his free hand into Claire's hair, tugging her head back violently. "Go check the posters in Temple Lane. Rewards offered for Dorrans captured and sent to the militia."

"He's telling the truth," an old man with a long-white beard said, rubbing his hands together. "Are there others in your party, lass?"

As if she was going to tell him. "For the last time, I'm not a Dorran!"

"And I haven't run the merchant guild for six years," the man gripping her hair said. "I've dealt with enough of you scum to recognise you on sight." He let her go with such roughness she reeled.

"Shut it, Val," the innkeeper, Giers, said from someplace behind Claire. "Not all of us have the stomach for a religious rant before noon. Have a free drink on the house and we'll say no more."

The man, Val, stabbed his knife into the table, so that it quivered point down near her thumb, making Claire flinch. "You'll regret helping people like her. Eidan's men rode through the city a few days ago and I learnt many an interesting thing."

"Like what?" Claire asked. She couldn't show she was afraid, and this might prove to be important information she could share with Maen and the others.

"Your people are finished, Clera. Eidan's finally seen sense. Dorran House is no longer welcome in Kelnarium. You show up in any major city or town, you'll be hanged and if you dare enter Kelnariat ... well, I've been told Eidan is concocting a special punishment for your kind in the capital." Val laughed. "And as to the other magical brethren ... it's only a matter of time until the priests convince Eidan to target them too. Good riddance to bad rubbish."

Claire couldn't breathe. She'd known Eidan had lost it, but this was something else. To put the safety of this world second to his rage at a crime Dorran House hadn't even committed was madness. Her palms sweated and her heart pressed too hard against her rib cage as she realised something worse. She'd witnessed how her grandfather's imagined betrayal had affected Eidan. He'd show no mercy to any Dorran who crossed his path and Marcus *was* a Dorran *and* stuck in Kelnariat. He could be imprisoned or tortured or killed. She had to warn Maen.

In a flash, she tugged the dagger out of the wood and flicked it under Val's throat. "Let my friend and me leave."

Claire wrapped a green woollen blanket around her shoulders as she eased back against a goose feather pillow, shifting in an effort to avoid an uncomfortable dip. The mattress was threadbare and full of holes. Maen, Rael and Gwenivere steadied themselves as the whole rickety bed frame creaked. Lotte had backed up Claire's story of what had transpired downstairs, but now that they needed to discuss strategy, she'd been sent away. Claire hoped she'd understand, but it would look too weird if she insisted the "farm lass stray" she'd picked up sat in on private Dorran meetings.

"Is there anyone in Kelnariat you can think of who would have set Eidan on this path?" Maen was asking Gwenivere. "Did you see or hear anything unusual before you left the city and joined us?"

She grimaced. "Not that I can think of. Eidan was his usual self; good-natured and grateful that we Dream Mages took up Praine's offer of quarters in the Council Buildings and assisted him as we had her." Gwenivere considered, smoothing out creases in her dress. "He was excited, but so were we. We were about to meet the person who could save us, after all." Her eyes darkened. "Though I suppose there was ..."

"Yes?" Claire asked, sitting forward.

"Some of Eidan's councillors had started looking at me in a strange way. Wallis and Heath."

"How do you mean 'strange?'"

Gwenivere frowned. "I don't know, really. In hindsight, I'd say it was secretive ... like perhaps they knew something I didn't. I was going to mention it to Eidan when he joined us at Dorran Manor."

"Wallis and Heath have only ever tolerated Eidan's allegiance to magical brethren. They were of a hard-line cadre who tried to prevent Praine coming to power, but they supported Eidan grudgingly," Maen explained.

Claire knew it was for her benefit and shot him a grateful smile. "Then it sounds possible they put Eidan up to this. We won't know what they plan and how they got into Eidan's ear until we get to Kelnariat," Claire said quickly. "We can't spend long with the Maellwyns."

"What do you mean 'until we get to Kelnariat?' We should deal with the Rift first," Maen said.

Claire should have known this would happen. "No! We have to go to Kelnariat to rescue Marcus. I won't go home without him. Think of what Eidan will do to him." She couldn't tell her parents she'd abandoned her brother to the mercies of a madman and she'd never live with herself either if she did. She looked to Gwenivere. "And there are the remaining Dream Mages too. It doesn't sound like they're targeted for now, but perhaps it's only a matter of time ..."

"Much as I'd love to do as you ask, it's too dangerous," Gwenivere said firmly. "I don't know what game Eidan and his councillors are playing, but the world dies unless you do something about the Rift."

From the looks on Maen and Rael's faces, she could see that they agreed with Gwenivere and weren't about to change their minds. "We'll see," Claire said, dropping it for now. She'd have to come up with a clever reason for the detour to Kelnariat. Besides, she'd thought of something else in the hour or so she and Lotte had waited for the others to re-join them. "How exactly did Kelt make the Rift?" She held up a hand impatiently as Rael opened his mouth to speak. "Oh, I know he joined forces with other Houses, but I mean specifically how did he *do* it."

"Why do you need to know?" Gwenivere demanded.

"Because," Claire began, "surely I need to reverse whatever he did to get rid of it."

Rael and Maen exchanged glances, then nodded. Maen cleared his throat. "He used a spell we haven't taught you yet; hot and cold flame combined. He shot it straight into the sky and drew on everyone's power around him to sustain it." He rubbed at the rough bristles growing on his chin. "The Saura have mercy on us, we think he destroyed the barriers between worlds and made something new from the space between."

"It sounds like I need this spell to reverse what's happened. Will you teach it to me?"

"It's too risky to use on the Rift," Gwenivere said. "You could rip it wider or make a second one."

Claire curled her hand into a fist and plunged it into the mattress. "When are you going to trust me? You made me head of Dorran House."

"Be that as it may, Gwenivere's right," Maen insisted. "It's too risky."

Claire gave up. She'd push this again at the Maellwyns. She rearranged her expression to one of business. "I've sent Meghan to purchase ingredients for hair dye from the markets. Kiera will need to dye all us Dorrans and then we'd best be off at first light now the rain's easing. I will rest beforehand." She settled back against the bedhead, signalling the discussion was over. "You may go," she added as she closed her eyes.

As the others left, closing the door behind them, Claire wondered at herself. She'd never have spoken with such authority back in Shale, where no one had paid her any attention let alone done as she'd asked; she couldn't imagine her commands working at home when she didn't want to do the washing up. The thought made her smile.

A moment later, the door creaked open and her smile vanished as her eyes sprang open. "Yes?" she said loudly, as she scrambled to sit upright, the blanket around her shoulders half slipping off.

Then Lotte was there, holding a mishappen dagger to Claire's throat. The exile must have carried it in her pouch. The dagger Claire had taken from Val was all the way across the room on a desk. She had no hope of getting it before Lotte slit her throat.

"Ya gotta be careful," the exile said, eyes narrowing as she put the dagger against the blankets near Claire's thigh. "If I wanted to kill ya, yer'd be dead."

Claire's heart was hammering. She couldn't look away from the twisted metal dagger by her side, imagining how easy it would have been for Lotte to kill her if she'd wanted to.

"I was listenin' in on yer whole chat by the door," Lotte said settling herself on the end of the lumpy bed. "It's true about you and the Rift then? When the Crian said I weren't so sure 'coz she's a bit weird, ya know, but if yer own people think it ... an' I know they do 'coz I could hear it in their voices ..."

"Yep," Claire said with a grimace. "The person who is going to save your world is me."

"Ya don't sound thrilled."

Claire rearranged the blanket. "I was happy with my family in another world, but then my grandfather took my brother, Marcus. Turns out he didn't have the magical ability needed for the job so now I'm stuck doing it."

"Wait," Lotte considered. "Ya were born outta this *world*?" She whistled softly. "What's it like? How's it different? How – oh, blast. It ain't important right now." She pressed a hand to her forehead like it focussed her, then caught Claire with a grim stare. "I almost sold the secret of yer identity for the reward. Yer people meant nothin' to me. Yer'd have been hung and I'd have taken my coin and started again."

Claire couldn't look away from Lotte. She hadn't thought of that, but it made sense. "Why didn't you?" she managed, through a mouth that felt like sandpaper.

"Somefin' made me hesitate." Her gaze dropped to the mattress. "Mebbe it were that ya weren't like any other Dorran I'd met. Mebbe it were I kept seeing the Crian looking at me real reproachful. Mebbe it were deep down

I knew ya was telling the truth from the first. I told myself I'd eavesdrop on your council of war and then decide."

"And?"

"The seriousness of what ya discussed told me what I already knew. There's no point in me betrayin' yer. I'd have money, sure, but I'd die alongside everyone else. Besides, I don't think yer people did murder mine. Something strange is goin' on. Seems to me the best way of finding out who killed my family is sticking with ya."

"It'll be dangerous. You could die."

Lotte shrugged. "So could ya." She shuffled up the bed to sit next to Claire. "I'd rather face death together." She held out a hand to Claire. "I'll forgive ya for your people's hatred of mine if ya forgive me for almost betraying ya."

Claire thought of Liz and how it had felt to have someone to confide in, even if only for a brief while; she remembered laughter in the playground, choosing each other for reading group, making crowns out of grass and flowers, but most of all she remembered how it had felt to be less alone. In Kelnarium, without Marcus, the terrible emptiness inside was ever present.

She leant against her so their shoulders pressed together. "It's a deal."

Chapter Sixteen

CLAIRE WOKE UP WHEN Lotte shook her.

"We're here," the exile whispered.

Claire blearily rubbed sleep out of her eyes and brushed newly dyed brown strands out of her face. It had been a nerve-wracking few hours on the road; the path crowded with other wagons and carts all gossiping of Eidan's proclamation and what they'd do with the reward if they found a Dorran. It was lucky Claire had ordered everyone to dye their hair or they'd have been caught within ten minutes of riding out of Autun not long after dawn. They'd been questioned twice by over-eager men and women, but their party's superior number had prevented any serious conflicts.

She groaned as Lotte playfully punched her shoulder. "Come on, sleepy. I wanna see the Maellwyns. I wonder what they'll be like?" She lowered her voice. "Mebbe they're nicer than yer folk when it comes to exiles."

"I don't know," Claire said, then laughed, seeing her own half-awake expression reflected in Maen's as he stretched out stiff joints.

She fell into line behind him as he climbed out of the cart, admiring the pale red and white tessellated patterns on the road. Glancing behind her, Claire saw how steep the terrain had been as Tarn unhitched his tired horses from the cart. Talking softly to both mares, he led them behind the rest of the group.

"We'll take the horses but get the Maellwyns to hide the carts along the cliff later," Maen explained. "There isn't the storage space once we're through their gates."

Turning to look ahead, Claire shaded her hand in front of her eyes. For a second, she thought she saw a salamander sitting in the clouds, awe-inspiringly large. "Is that you, the Saura?" she muttered but there was no reply. Since that time in the forest outside Autun when Claire had first thought she'd seen the Dorran elemental leader, she could have sworn she'd seen her everywhere in the skyline, but the female salamander never spoke. *Grandfather told me elemental leaders spoke to their human counterparts. That's me now, so why won't she speak? Is it because I'm too new at the job?* Claire made herself look away with a shrug. She needed to be alert to her surroundings. The tang of salt hung in the air. To her left, the land stretched for miles, green and fertile, and it was squishy underfoot like the dirt was damp. To her right, the ocean crested the horizon. Ahead of her, a high wall of water extended from sky to road.

"How do we get through?" She gasped.

"The Maellwyns have no need of gates," Maen said. "If someone comes here with bad intent, they drown crossing through that. If Eidan came here with treachery in his heart, he won't have survived. If someone comes as a friend, it is as though the barrier doesn't exist."

Claire glanced at Maen. "Thank the salamanders we're on the same side then," she said as they approached. She watched as others in their party crossed the barrier unharmed, but still pressed close to Lotte. It seemed incredible that anyone could pass through without drowning.

She clutched onto Lotte's hand and held her breath as they passed through the water, but Maen had been correct. They didn't even get wet.

Ignoring her rapidly beating heart, Claire gaped at the vision before her. Maellwyn Manor didn't have outbuildings like those of Dorran Manor, and instead of being located on a hill it was built into the cliff, waves breaking far below. The building itself was much bigger than any castle or palace Claire knew of from textbooks in her world. The surfaces of Maellwyn Manor were so white and smooth that the sun reflected off them and hurt her eyes so that she had to shade them to take anything else in. She made out white colonnades and at the very top of the building, domed roofs of bright blue. Dark pots full of clambering plants and white and blue wildflowers were lined up at the base of the building, though she couldn't tell the type for the slowly descending mist coating everything. It lined her arms and she was sure her curly hair was frizzing something wild too.

She blinked the moisture away. Ahead of her was an enormous archway, dazzling in its pure whiteness. Palms clustered on either side of it. If she squinted, she saw a figure standing by the door. As their party drew nearer, he waved one arm in the air in greeting then strolled down stone steps to meet them. His long face was unshaven, and Claire noticed that he wore a silver and blue threaded tunic.

The man stopped at the sight of the rag-tag group, taking in their messy hair and plain, dusty attire. He stared openly at Claire's dark curls, then glanced over at Maen who gave a slight nod.

As though he remembered his manners, he jerked his head. "I welcome you to the House of Maellwyn. Do you come in the spirit of peace and harmony?"

He was looking at her, Claire realised, rather than Maen, because she was Head of Dorran House now. She'd better act like it.

She managed a clear, "We do," and the man extended his hand to her and then Maen.

Once the formalities were over, Maen grinned as he slapped the man on the back. "Good to see you, Jemroth. It's been too long since last I visited with Lord Dorran."

Jemroth laughed. "A good year or so I believe." He turned to Claire. "Forgive my rudeness. I'm Jemroth. Advisor to Lord Maellwyn. You must be Lady Claire." He paused while Claire nodded in a daze. "On Lord Maellwyn's behalf, I welcome you and your party." He paused and looked sideways at Maen before he went on. "I require some of your time right away, if it pleases you. Lord Maellwyn is eager to speak with the legendary Lady Claire." Jemroth shrugged at Maen's raised eyebrow and dropped his formal tone. "It's hardly that surprising."

Claire looked to Maen for direction but caught herself just as quickly. If she were going to be a leader, she'd better take a leaf out of Marcus's book and start acting like one. "We left our carts outside. Can you conceal them?" she requested.

Jemroth nodded. "Indeed, Lady. I'll send some lads to move them into our shed. As for your horses," he glanced over to Tarn and Rael who held onto reins tight, "some of our boys will stable them on our grounds. We have partly prepared the guest wing for you. You've arrived earlier than we expected." He clicked his fingers and men and women in light blue and silver cotton attire appeared from behind dark corners and tall palms. They silently reached for reins or headed down the path to the outside world. Still others waited for further orders, standing to attention with hands softly clasped in front of them.

"Take our guests to their quarters," Jemroth instructed these assistants.

Lotte scowled and kicked at a loose pebble as she was forced to separate from Claire and follow the others to the left where a smaller entryway opened. Claire mouthed "See you soon," and hoped she wouldn't be too long. Having Lotte nearby had lent her a kind of strength and without her she already felt a little lost.

Jemroth coughed politely and Claire blushed. He was waiting for her. Maen had already walked inside. Claire followed Jemroth dutifully.

Beyond the small stone steps, the atrium Claire found herself in was wide and bright, the ceiling so high Claire couldn't see what the roof was made of. Every few paces, huge windows went from ankle height to above her head, letting in natural sunlight. Brackets in the whitewashed walls held bronze lamps, but they were unlit. In the cool shadows, people moved silently, cleaning and polishing or gliding about with hands full. Their movements were smooth and graceful. As the group passed through an archway and headed down a corridor, a woman streamed water from her hand into a pot plant. Claire stared. The woman didn't hold a glass or a pitcher – she was using magic.

"We have arrived." Claire started at Jemroth's velvety voice. He took a few steps forward, pushing at two wooden doors painted periwinkle blue. They swung heavily inwards. Claire entered the room, the smell of brine and fish suddenly assaulting her, Maen close behind.

Jemroth bowed low. "Lady Claire and Maen to see you, my Lord."

A human shape shone in ethereal silver-blue light coming from an oval skylight overhead. She blinked, her eyes slowly adjusting to take in the man who was seated before her on a raised dais much like her grandfather's. The throne – made from timber bleached by the sea – had been carved to appear like a breaking wave. She kept her head held high as she stepped onto a dyed blue carpet which led to Lord Maellwyn. She was a Dorran. She must appear in control, no matter how out of her depth she felt.

Claire managed a sketchy curtsy as Lord Maellwyn stared at her with eyes that possessed disconcerting milky-white irises edged with dark blue. His hair and beard were white and his face aged, but even so, he seemed full of life and vitality, energy crackling out of him like dolphins leaping and performing for an audience. His smile was warm and disarming and though they looked nothing alike, she was reminded of her grandfather.

"Thank you, Jemroth. Please see to dinner," Lord Maellwyn said. As Jemroth left, he returned his gaze to Claire, and tapped a long finger against his throne. Claire saw immediately he wore a ring like the one her grandfather had gifted her, only this one was inset with a pearl instead of an opal. "What brings you to us, Lady Claire? It is evident that you are the bearer of bad news. Lord Dorran would tell me first if he were journeying our way. If he needed our help to close the Rift he would have asked, and you wouldn't be wasting your time stopping here when you could be in the Riftlands unless it was important."

Claire hesitated. She liked this strange man but how much should she tell him?

Lord Maellwyn studied her face. "Our two Houses have tried to put our magical differences behind us. I know that it is difficult for you to know what to do, but please, I beg you to trust me. It is natural for you to be reticent, but I need you to tell me everything ..." He took a deep breath. "... for only together can we discover what Eidan is up to."

"Oh yes," Maellwyn went on at Claire's obvious surprise. "Lord Dorran sent a messenger the day that the Councillor arrived to warn me of his early presence and of fears someone was setting up Dorran House for atrocities committed across Kelnarium. And now here you are. A coincidence? I don't think so. Now tell me, what happened?"

Claire gathered her thoughts. "Eidan razed the Manor, convinced I was responsible for the villages and farms burnt near Kelnariat. He killed my grandfather and Aed, thinking they'd helped me escape justice." She swallowed. "Dorran House is scattered, most of us murdered. Only eight of us have made it to you."

"So few?" Lord Maellwyn roared. "It must have been a massacre!"

Claire stared at the floor, trying to ignore the ache in her throat.

"I'm sorry, I forget myself. I did not mean to shout," Lord Maellwyn apologised, his voice softening. When Claire looked up, the gleam in his eyes had dulled, all his vitality fading. "This is terrible," he went on. "The worst news possible. I ... What can Eidan mean by it?" He fell silent. When at last he spoke again, he seemed old and tired. "I will consult with my advisors while you bathe. If there is anything else you desire ...?"

"I want to go home to my family, but you can't give me that, can you?" Claire said wistfully.

Lord Maellwyn frowned. "You are young to bear this burden, no easy task, even for an adult. Rest. Relax. Take comfort in the little peace your stay here can provide."

Claire was a little late to dinner. She'd sought out Lotte to make sure her friend was as well looked after as she was, then soaked longer in the bath than she'd intended. As she entered the huge dining hall, everyone turned to face her. She'd been left a floor length periwinkle-blue silk dress to wear, tied with a white sash and tan leather sandals with straps that wound up her bare ankles. Her dyed hair was loose, held back by silver circlets. Dressed like this, she felt like a lady, yet many of the people lying on cushions around the long rectangular table stared at her in open suspicion. She thought of Marcus as her cheeks warmed under her make-up. He'd have smiled and held up a hand and swept through the hall as though everything was normal. That was a mistake. The familiar pain in her chest thinking about him and what Eidan might be doing to him made it hard to concentrate.

Unlike the dining hall at Dorran Manor, where people sat on benches to eat, the Maellwyns had one big horseshoe lounge that ran right around the room. A diaphanous piece of linen draped over the polished wood and touched the tiles. Blue and silver cushions were plumped everywhere she looked, with people leaning on them with both elbows or placing them under a hip or their bottom.

There was an empty space between Lord Maellwyn and Maen. She headed in that direction, wearing a forced grin that fooled no one, wishing her sandals didn't slap so loud against the ochre and brown tiles. Whispers followed her as she slid past hard faces. She searched for Lotte and found her wedged between Kiera and Meghan a few places away from Maen and Lord Maellwyn. At her encouraging nod, Claire straightened her shoulders and swept the rest of the way to the vacant space.

Little insects had been tipped inside every lamp in the manor at nightfall. They glowed a pale blue and emitted a pleasant, low hum. Lord Maellwyn got to his feet, as did the young man beside him. Maen had mentioned a son. This must be him. His dark hair was as unkempt as her mother's kitchen mop and his wide eyes seemed to change from grey to blue to green and back again, constantly shifting like the colours of the sea. He looked as kind as his father. Both wore white linen shirts with a blue linen cloak flung over one shoulder and held in place with a silver brooch twisted to look like a wave. As they sketched a bow, she saw they wore a silver circlet like hers.

"Join us," Lord Maellwyn said.

She clambered awkwardly into place beside Maen, smoothing her dress. He held onto his silver goblet of wine as she nearly tipped it over.

"Sorry," she murmured. It took her a few seconds to get comfortable.

Lord Maellwyn reached gracefully for a clay pot that Claire knew from world history class was called an amphora and poured some wine into the goblet in front of her. Propped awkwardly on one elbow, she sipped delicately at her goblet as he glanced at his son.

The boy stretched his hand across the table to Claire. "My name's Gareth," he said. "Lord Gareth if you want to be formal, but most Maellwyns don't bother when it's just us."

"Good to meet you, Gareth," Claire said.

Maen nudged Claire gently and swept a hand around the top section of the table to take in Rael, Kiera, Meghan, Gwenivere, Tarn, Lord Maellwyn, Gareth, Jemroth and two other solemn looking men dressed in formal Maellwyn garb. "We were discussing Eidan with Lord Maellwyn when you arrived. Specifically, his new declaration against our House and who set him against us."

They noticed her stares and nodded, unsmiling. "We're advisors to Lord Maellwyn," one explained. "My name's Kress and this is Sleath."

She acknowledged them with a smile, then put down her goblet and reached for a purple plum from the large clay fruit bowl.

Lord Maellwyn cleared his throat. "Now, where were we?"

"You asked me if I knew anything about Eidan's past that isn't common knowledge," Gwenivere said, dark grief shadows under her eyes. She acknowledged Claire with a quick glance, "I'll start again for Lady Claire's sake."

Claire leaned forward, cupping her chin with her hands, both elbows on a cushion. This should be interesting. Her grandfather had explained to her how Eidan had risen to power, but he'd admitted he'd never known much about his beginnings for all they'd been friends.

"He was raised in Bambridge Village, near the mountains and a short day's ride from Kelnariat," Gwenivere said. "His father's grandparents were rich cloth dyers who fell on hard times and had to leave Kelnariat for a more modest existence, so he grew up with little. He always said that made him more compassionate." She sighed. "I can't understand what's changed."

Lord Maellwyn stroked his tangled beard. "Nor can any of us." He popped a grape into his mouth, chewing thoughtfully. "Are the rumours true that one of his ancestors was a Dream Mage?"

"Yes, he was their leader in fact, but that was long before my time," Gwenivere explained. "Eidan came to me for testing as a young man. He had a small amount of talent and a strong belief fostered by his misguided grandparents that he would one day take my place. I disabused him of that notion, and he left Kelnariat in a huff. Luckily, he never dwelt on it."

"No, he was apprenticed to a merchant, wasn't he?" Maen said.

"Yes, that man was his making. Cload taught him everything he knew and knocked his grandparent's arrogance out of him. Eidan ran his own successful business for years, which is how I found him again. I saw right away that he had a sense of morality and didn't support Selk. I introduced him to Praine, and the rest is history."

"We keep coming back to the same thing," Claire said, losing her shyness as she thought about everything that had happened. "Eidan is a man of fairness and justice. He *believes* in those principles. He's turned on us because he thinks we no longer uphold those values, a belief which serves someone else's purpose nicely." Her eyes narrowed as she turned to Lord Maellwyn. "What word is there from the towns and villages near you?"

He hastily swallowed a handful of honeyed nuts. "There's rumblings of discontent, but they cannot breach our defences. Most of their ire is directed at your House, truth be told. Eidan's quarrel is with the Dorrans, after all."

"And for how long do you think you'll be left alone?" Rael snapped.

"Peace, friend," Lord Maellwyn waved a hand, and servitors cleared the bowls of fruit and nuts. "Whatever happens, remember we have been allies for far longer than Eidan has known me."

Claire glanced around the hall. Though he sounded certain of his people's loyalty, she wasn't so sure. For one thing, there were the black looks shot her way. She frowned, puzzling over what they could be about, as servitors began placing bowls of steaming green vegetables and tender meat in front of the diners. For a few minutes, everyone's attention turned to the food.

Claire was starving. She took a bite, enjoying the unfamiliar spices. There was more flavour here than there'd been at Dorran Manor. She couldn't wait to tell her parents and Marcus about her adventures. Her mum loved to cook and – no, she couldn't keep thinking these things because the yearning distracted her. She made herself focus on the many hard stares still directed at her.

"Lord Maellwyn," she said, keeping her voice low, "why does everyone look at me like I'm a bad smell? If you're on our side, why aren't your people?"

Lord Maellwyn blinked, like he hadn't expected her question, then drained his cup to its dregs. "It's my wife, you see. She was as popular in her own way as Leya was with the Dorrans and it was Kelt who killed Nanami creating the Rift."

Ice slid down Claire's back. "If this is true, how can you be sure none of them will betray us to Eidan? There's a reward on our heads."

Lord Maellwyn glanced at his pearl ring like he took strength from it, then looked up again. "They don't hate you. They distrust you. There's a difference."

"I can't see it," Claire muttered.

"They're afraid," Gareth broke in softly, leaning past his father. "Afraid you look too much like Kelt, afraid you'll kill us all. They don't know you."

Claire couldn't meet his eyes. She thought of the Beast. Perhaps its repetition of "Betrayer" meant it knew there'd be a human cost to closing the Rift and that this cost would tear people apart. She pushed her bowl of meat and beans away. She was no longer hungry.

Chapter Seventeen

CLAIRE TRIED TO LIGHTEN the mood as she leant against Kiera's bedroom wall. She'd gone to Kiera's room after dinner, seeking her out to get her to talk to Maen and Rael about teaching Claire the magic Kelt had used to create the Rift. Yet Kiera had bustled about the room, saying little the whole time Claire attempted small talk.

"That's pretty awful, isn't it?" Claire said, indicating the plate of paste and bread on the dresser table that she'd tentatively tried a portion of in her own room. It was a custom of the Maellwyns to eat a light second supper in their private quarters.

Kiera pursed her lips and continued to fold the covers back on her bed.

"The lady that left it said it's made from *palila,* a fish with a strong flavour. I've never heard of it before, have you?" Claire went on desperately. Why was this so difficult?

Kiera continued to studiously ignore Claire.

"She showed me a picture. This *palila* fish—it looks like a rainbow fish from my world."

As minutes passed in strained silence, Claire felt her patience lessen and her face began to flush with annoyance. She'd noticed Kiera had been quiet on the journey to the Maellwyns, but she'd been civil, so Claire had assumed her behaviour could be explained by grief. Now, Kiera was acting like she was upset with her, which was plain weird; Claire hadn't done anything wrong.

Kiera sat on the plain wooden bed, a piece of bread in her hands. She cleared her throat. "There is something I don't understand," she said, looking directly up at Claire. "Maen said you were sulking in a stable at the Manor and that's why none of us could find you during the battle. Why did you hide instead of joining the fight?"

"I ... I ..." Claire fished for a good response as she shifted uneasily from foot to foot. She couldn't explain what had happened without having to answer some very awkward questions.

"I don't understand," Kiera repeated, sounding bewildered and a little angry. "Maybe if you'd helped, you'd have saved lives. I know you're young, but until now I'd have said you were brave, too."

"I was angry about what my great-uncle had told me, and I was confused about what was happening outside," Claire lied nervously. "I'm not proud of it, but it meant I survived."

"So many others didn't," Kiera whispered, letting the bread fall into her lap, "when with your magical ability to help them they might have lived."

"I couldn't have resisted that many men. Even Maen said it was impossible."

Kiera's head was in her hands and her shoulders shook with great sobs. "So many dead, just like that and the children ... that was the worst part ... their little bodies."

Claire sat on the bed and put an arm around the older woman's shoulders. She understood some of Kiera's horror. She'd seen the villages and Lotte's camp, after all, and the terrible wrongness of it sat on her like a heavy cloak. Claire would find out who was responsible, and they'd pay for this; for hers, for Kiera's, for Lotte's losses, and for everyone cut off before their time. But first she had to deal with the Rift.

"You're not angry with me," she said softly. "Not really."

Kiera straightened, her cheeks tear stained.

Claire gripped the older woman's hand where it rested in her lap. "You know I'm going to fulfil the prophecy. Deep down you believe in me." She hesitated, then decided to reveal the truth. "You believe in me more than I believe in myself. I'm afraid Kiera. I'm afraid I'll get the spell wrong, I'm afraid more people will die, I'm afraid Eidan will do something terrible to Marcus long before I can get to Kelnariat, but more than all of that, I'm afraid of what will happen if I don't try." She let out a long breath and released Kiera's hand. "That's why I came to speak with you. I need your help."

"My help?" Kiera's eyes widened, as she absentmindedly picked up the piece of bread again and started to tear it into tiny pieces.

"I've thought and thought about how to close the Rift." Claire paced between the wall and the window, suddenly restless. "The prophecy never explained how I need to do it, just that I will and, well, the only thing that makes any logical sense is for me to reverse whatever Kelt did."

"Rael said you spoke with Maen and Gwenivere in Autun about this," Kiera said, brushing breadcrumbs onto the floor.

"Yes, and they wouldn't listen. You're disappointed in me, but you still trust me to get the job done in a way they don't." Claire spoke faster. "Nothing else makes sense. I need to learn how to wield hot and cold flames at the same time, which means someone must teach me."

"I'm not the one to do it if that's what you're asking. I won't go behind Maen's back and I'm not as powerful as he is in any case."

"No, that's not it. I want you to persuade Maen that I need to learn."

"They know it already," Kiera admitted, "but they want Gwenivere to search for visions of the future in her bowl before they agree."

"What?" Claire exclaimed, her voice rising to a near shout. "It's too dangerous and we don't have time to waste. How many people have been lost already? Didn't Gwenivere say the Riftlands spread was speeding up? That by the end of the year half of Kelnarium will be desolate?"

"Hush," Kiera said. "Yes, but—"

"And didn't she also say that magic grows more and more volatile?" Claire continued, lowering her voice to a normal volume once more. "If we leave things too long, what if I'm unable to work any spell by the time we reach the Rift? Look, do you trust me or not?"

Kiera paused, considering. "I see the wisdom in what you say. I'll speak to Maen tonight."

Claire caught her up in a bear hug. "Oh, Kiera, you won't regret it."

Claire stood in a courtyard lined with trees and intricately carved archways, the sun beating down on them, ready for her lesson with Maen. Rael, Kiera and Meghan were off planning the next part of their journey and Lotte had decided to help them rather than watch Claire's training session, but she still had a large audience. Not only were Maen and Gwenivere in attendance, but also Lord Maellwyn and his son, and Jemroth and Lord Maellwyn's two other advisors, Kress and Sleath. At least she felt more comfortable with her newfound abilities given all the practice she'd had at Dorran Manor.

"Make sure you direct any spell to the centre of the tiles," said Maen as he stepped closer to Claire. "We don't want an accidental inferno," he added, waving a hand to indicate the plants around the perimeter. "Now, the spell Kelt used is complex. It doesn't matter if you don't get it right away, but the main thing you need to remember is to concentrate. If you feel like you're losing control, clap your hands or stamp your feet."

"Will ... will the Beast appear?" She'd managed to put the possibility to the back of mind on the journey to Maellwyn House but now she was training again, it could become a reality sooner rather than later. Part of her wanted to pull out, but then she thought of Marcus and her parents and her resolve hardened. She had to learn this. She was sure of it. Maybe the horrible thing would stay away.

"Perhaps," he said. "But that's why Gwenivere is overseeing things. She will protect you – and us. Now, what you must do is this: first, hold an image of your average hot flame in your mind and simultaneously overlay it with an image of something cold to produce ice. Once, you've done that—"

"That sounds hard."

"Yes," Maen replied steadily, "but anything worth the effort usually is. Where was I? Once you get the images in your mind, direct the spell where you want it to go and don't get distracted, lest it ends up elsewhere. Got it?"

It took Claire over an hour to figure out how to hold multiple images in her mind at once without getting side-tracked and lighting one type of flame before the other or getting frustrated and thinking of other things. The spell was different too; though the smell of charred meat was the same, her whole body felt like it fizzed and bubbled, and it took Claire a while to put the odd feeling aside.

The sun was high in the sky by the time she managed to create two small flames side by side in the courtyard's centre and she couldn't help a crow of delight. *What was Maen on about?* she thought. *This spell is a walk in the park*. She was going to rescue Marcus, close the Rift and go home. She found the magic within her, more focussed and refined than usual, less stubborn to shape too. It felt good, like she'd gone for a run and struggled through the muscle pain to push herself harder than ever before. She straightened her spine, set her shoulders back. She had this in the bag.

And then her spell shattered like hard candy dropped onto asphalt.

"Hey, I was doing great," she said, glaring at Maen. "I had everything under control, so why did you pull me back?"

He and Gwenivere were pale as they looked at each other. "It wasn't us," Gwenivere said. They glanced uncertainly towards Lord Maellwyn's party.

Lord Maellwyn shook his head. "We didn't do a thing," he said. He smiled at Claire reassuringly. "You must have let the spell gutter out without realising. It's natural when you're tired. Let's take a snack break."

Claire didn't feel the way she normally did when she was tired from working magic; her muscles weren't tender and her eyes weren't aching for one thing, but he was probably right. She couldn't think of another explanation.

Sleath hurried forward with a bowl of flat bread and honeycomb. Claire ate quickly, keen to get back into the lesson. If she'd achieved so much in a morning, what couldn't she achieve with more practice? She couldn't wait to share the story of how her magic journey had unfolded with her family when she got home. She'd be able to tell Suranne about magic and spells and her mum would understand. It sucked that she'd lose her powers in Shale, the same as Suranne, but at least she'd have the memories.

Buoyed up by thoughts of home, Claire closed her eyes, got the images she needed in place and tried to generate, then aim the flame. She couldn't do it. It was as though she'd hit a physical wall. She concentrated harder and tried pushing past it, but whatever was stopping her wouldn't budge. Then, before she could clap her hands, something crashed through her memory pictures. It was the Beast.

It snarled and jeered, green-tinged brown and disgusting. With each laugh it grew bigger, filling her vision.

Before she could stop herself, she fell forwards into its wide mouth; a city, spider webs, men and women spinning silk, Eidan standing at a podium, all whirling along beside her. When her world righted, she was in a poorly lit cell. She reached out and touched Marcus, but a different Marcus to the one she knew, a Marcus in rusty chains at the neck, with lips covered in sores, his clothing ragged. Her heart twisted.

"He'll die there," the Beast chortled. "What will you tell your parents? What will you tell yourself?"

"No!" Claire screamed, though if it were out loud or in her head she couldn't have said.

But the creature was gone.

She floated through emptiness, her body feeling weirdly separate to her mind, like she watched herself in a mirror. Had seconds or minutes passed? She couldn't be sure. She was lovely and warm, at least, though her stomach felt hollow. Maybe she could stay here for a bit, free of obligations and cares. It would be easy to close her eyes, let the fuzzy blackness claim her, and she was so sleepy.

Wham.

Her cheek smarted.

"Stop!" Maen's voice came from somewhere far away.

It all came back in a rush. People were depending on her. As nice as it might be to stay in this blank space forever, she had a task to complete. But how could she get back? She concentrated on the courtyard, on remembering the tiles, their blue and white sheen and the pattern of a dolphin they created, on how it felt to have a gentle breeze blowing in her face, the sun's rays on her lids ... She opened her eyes but everything was blurry.

"End the spell," Gwenivere screamed, waving both hands in Claire's face.

Claire blinked. What was going on? Slowly, painfully slowly, her vision cleared. Sleath rolled on the tiles in front of her, fire curling at his cloak. His screams broke through her sense of unreality. Hands at her mouth, her nostrils quivered at the smell of singed flesh, far more pungent than was usual for a Dorran spell. *Did I do this?* No, she couldn't have. In the past she'd stopped thinking about spells when she experienced visions. She shivered. It had to have been the Beast itself that had caused this disaster, but then, why had Gwenivere and Maen shouted at her?

"I ... I ..." She couldn't move and her lips felt heavy, like she'd been stung by a bee and had an allergic reaction. She staggered. Gwenivere's hand reached out to steady her.

The flames multiplied, surging after Sleath in a tall wall twice Claire's height. The fire moved fast, soon obscuring him from view. Claire heard the man's hair crackle. He was going to be cooked alive. He was going to—

Lord Maellwyn hurried forward, flinging his hand out, palm up like he was commanding Sleath to stop. Gareth ran behind the advisor and did the same. Two jets of glistening water exploded over the burning man. Within seconds, the unnatural flames went out.

Claire slumped to the hard tiles, heart and mind sluggish. Under the damp clothing, Sleath was red and wrinkled. Even as she watched, blisters bubbled up across his skin. One of Sleath's eyes was swollen shut, but with the one that remained open he saw her looking and tried to turn away.

Claire's skin crawled. She felt a thousand eyes upon her. She swivelled around to see the courtyard lined with Maellwyn spectators, all staring at her with open animosity. A terrible suspicion began to form as she turned back to Maen and the others. They too, looked at her with horror.

"What happened?" she whispered.

"You lost control," Maen said, "and wouldn't be called back for all Gwenivere tried. I couldn't touch your spell to end it either. It was as if something blocked me."

"Do you mean—" She couldn't stop thinking about Rinn contorting in unnatural directions as she spouted the Beast's words. *Betrayer.* If she'd done what she'd suspected, did that make its label right? She didn't dare look at Gwenivere.

Maen's words were a hammer blow to the chest. "You set Sleath on fire. If he dies ..."

Claire didn't need him to finish the sentence. Sleath's death would be her fault.

Chapter Eighteen

CLAIRE SAT ON THE EDGE of the courtyard huddled amongst plants, head in her hands as hot tears dripped down her nose. Everyone else had gone and she was alone. This was worse than the time she'd got caught cheating on a maths test, worse even than when she'd had to admit to her dad that she'd left their best horse bridle off track in the National Park. When Claire had first realised what she'd done, she'd wanted to tell the others about her dreams but Gwenivere had shaken her head, even as some of Lord Maellwyn's men muttered that Claire was as bad as Kelt. Instead, the Dream Mage leader had tried explaining to Maen that it was the Beast that had attacked Sleath, she'd seen it as she'd supervised Claire's spell in her trance state. The problem was no one had ever had it work through them before and that had caught Gwenivere off guard.

Maen had insisted it made no difference, that it was Claire's magic that had done the damage and now they'd have to find a way to prevent most of Maellwyn House turning against them. An ashen faced Lord Maellwyn had gone to call a meeting with Maen and Gwenivere to help explain things, including the full extent of Gwenivere's prophecies and the fate of Kelnarium, but Claire didn't hold out much hope that he'd turn things around. She didn't know if she wanted him to or not. What if she was the betrayer claimed? She was fairly sure saviours didn't set people on fire, but there was the fact she hadn't intended any wrongdoing either. The Beast had used her somehow. She wished Gwenivere hadn't hurried off with the others. As soon as Claire got the chance to speak to the Dream Mage in private, she would ask her to honestly tell her what had happened.

For now, with training ended, she didn't know what to do. She couldn't go inside to face the crushing disappointment of Kiera and the others. Besides, none of them could understand the guilt that burnt her throat and turned her stomach. She'd done the very thing she'd wanted to prevent; she'd harmed an innocent.

A gentle hand rested on her back. "I've brought you a handkerchief."

She looked up. Gareth crouched beside her, his outstretched hand proffering a silk square. She snatched it gratefully and blew her nose, even as questions loomed. Perhaps this was his final act of kindness before she was kicked out of his home? "You shouldn't help me," she said with a sniff. "Your people are right. I'm no better than Kelt."

"Father will curb their whispers. It was an accident."

His words warmed her like an elixir. Other than Gwenivere, no one had said a kind word after the incident. "I had no idea what was happening."

"I know. I believe you. We should have expected something like this after what happened to Rinn Taccala. It would seem that the more unstable magic becomes, the more that thing appears. Because you're powerful in *learth* and key to closing the Rift, perhaps we should have expected the results of its appearance would be more unexpected where you're concerned."

"We expected the Beast to attack me and my spell, not use me," she said miserably.

"Father will tell people that. Don't worry."

"But if magic is so unstable and this Beast can control me like that, how will I close the Rift? Maen said he couldn't stop the spell and I didn't know what I was doing to stop it myself. I can't use magic again. I'm a monster." Her mind filled with images of the mushroom clouds of Hiroshima and Nagasaki and her shoulders shook. She couldn't risk it.

"We'll find a way," Gareth insisted. "We don't have a choice." He jerked his head away so she couldn't read his expression. "Either road we take leads to death but only one destroys Kelnarium and that way is not yours."

"Is Sleath dead?" She had to know.

"No," Gareth said. "It will be a painful few months, but they think he'll live."

She couldn't speak for relief.

A servitor entered the courtyard with a bundle of rags to clean the charred tiles. Gareth frowned as the man stared openly at Claire rather than getting on with his task. "We should get out of here," he muttered. He chewed at his bottom lip and ran a hand through scruffy curls. "How would you like to see some of the lesser known parts of the Manor?"

Claire guessed he was offering in order to keep her out of sight until Lord Maellwyn could calm things a little, but she was grateful. Keeping her body and her mind busy would be a blessing. She took his proffered hand and got clumsily to her feet.

He led her through the courtyard and quiet corridors that inclined steeply downwards. Whenever a Maellwyn approached, Gareth would knit his brows together and shoot them his sternest expression and they'd soon scurry away. But they didn't run into many people. Most were still listening to Lord Maellwyn, Claire assumed, as she bumped into Gareth's back, not realising he'd come to a stop.

"Sorry!" she mumbled as she stepped back.

"That's fine," he said. With a turn to the left, he gestured towards an enormous tapestry that covered the whitewashed wall from floor to ceiling. "Take a look at this." The aged threads of the tapestry depicted a man with his feet in the sand, his hand outstretched to salute a pod of dolphins swimming in an impossibly blue ocean. The waves had been sewn with different blues, fading in and out of each other to make a strange pattern. The wave tips curled, with white foam stitched into the blue. The sand was a dirty and faded yellow. The man saluted the jumping dolphins and his expression reminded Claire of Lord Maellwyn. She wondered if each new Lord of the Maellwyns' took on the characteristics of the one before.

"It's beautiful, isn't it?" came Gareth's voice at her side. "It was done by one of our greatest artists. She alone of all four Houses chose to renounce the way of *learth*. Instead, she became an Enchantment Weaver. You can see, even in this earlier work when she could still feel the ocean, that her calling was for a different kind of magic."

"That must have been a great blow to your clan."

"No," he said softly. "We did not begrudge Marian her leave-taking nor the loss of her enormous talent. We felt for her deeply, for we knew the difficulty she would have juggling two identities. No matter how far we run from the sea, no matter how strong we think we are, its aching call finds us in the end."

"What happened to Marian? Her story sounds like a tragedy," Claire said, interested despite her own misery. The way Gareth told his story reminded her of her father. When he got caught up in the telling, his eyes shone just like Gareth's did now.

"It is," he said. "You see, my people cannot leave the sea for more than a few hours, so we take a part of it with us, just as you never go anywhere without a salamander opal egg around your neck." He tugged his tunic to one side to reveal a tiny glass vial, half the size of her pinkie and filled with clear liquid.

"Didn't Marian wear one?"

"Yes, she took hers to the mountains to learn the craft of the Enchantment Weavers. The Arras Ranges are so different to our home here and that took its toll on Marian. She was talented and learned fast, but she became restless. Despite many of her Maellwyn friends advising she return to her people, she would not do so. She felt that she had abandoned us, and in her pride, she would not come back, not for all the pleading or all the persuasion in the world. Besides, she was good at her work and she took pleasure in that. After a year, her links with the sea were broken, until she heard its song no more. Tired of living between two worlds, she smashed her vial, thinking she could fully commit to the Weaver way of life, but our blood doesn't work that way. She became ill, waning without the energy of the incoming tides that give my people strength. She died within two days of her vial breaking. Though she became skilled in the craft before her death, there is a naivety and simplicity in her earlier work, like this one, that is treasured far more than her later, more grandiose designs."

"You sound as though you knew her," Claire said.

Gareth laughed. "Oh no. She died long before my time. It is a story passed down from generation to generation, but though I did not know Marian personally, I have heard the sound of the waves, felt the soft sand under my feet and whispered to the creatures of the sea at twilight, and so I understand how deep her pain must have been without these things."

Claire wished that she could think of something intelligent to say, but her mind had gone blank. Time drew out, second by agonising second. Finally, she grasped at the one part of Gareth's story that was familiar to her. "Grandfather told me true Dorrans need to wear necklaces like you Maellwyns do." She fingered at her golden chain. "Did House Ushanan and House Domain do the same?"

"Yes. I've been told House Domain carried metal discs. The metal was dug at a mine near their estate. I don't know if they needed it the same way we need water. House Ushanan had some kind of quartz." He readjusted his tunic so his vial was covered once more. "But come. We have dwelt on the past long enough and I have more to show you." Without waiting for her assent, he turned and led her to the right of the main corridor and Marian's tapestry, and through a dark wooden door. The passageway beyond was softly lit by the strange blue insect-filled lamps and descended even more steeply than before. Claire touched a hand to the hard rock as her eyes adjusted.

"There's an extensive cave network under the building," Gareth explained. "Don't try coming here without me or you'll never find your way back."

After what felt like an age, the tunnel they travelled through opened out into sunshine and a small cove surrounded by steep rocks. The air turned cool and long afternoon shadows touched the beach and the seaweed scattered along the sand. Claire spun around. The Manor rose high above her, built partially into the cliff face, blocking out part of the sun. Claire turned back. Gareth had walked further onto the beach. Soft white sand crunched under Claire's sandals as she followed him.

Gareth sat on the grainy sand, the waves almost lapping at his feet, and looked up at Claire expectantly as he patted a spot next to him. "This is Merriam Beach."

Claire plopped down beside him, then followed his gaze out to the breakers, but she saw nothing along the horizon. Closer to shore, white spray crashed. It would be so easy to swim out as far as she could, until the water closed in and dragged her somewhere else. Then she pictured her head dashed against a rock and made a face.

"This is a nice spot," she said, wanting to be polite, "but are we waiting for something in particular?"

"Oh, you'll see!" he said with a mysterious grin.

Claire stared at the ocean waves as soft yellow light touched the water. There wasn't a cloud in the sky and the ocean sparkled, broken up occasionally by grey stone peeking above the surface.

And then she saw them—black dots, far out to sea.

"Dolphins!"

They leapt about, a whole pod of them, circling each other in a complicated dance. Claire watched them in silence as tints of rose and tangerine began to appear in the sky.

"They're lovely, aren't they?" said Gareth. "My mother used to love sitting like we are now. When I come here, it's like I'm closer to her."

Claire felt her mouth drop open. She'd thought Gareth her age, but that couldn't be right if his mother had been killed at the creation of the Rift. That was thirty years ago. Unless the Maellwyns aged differently to other people? She asked Gareth about it.

He smiled at her question. "Oh, no. Nanami wasn't my mother. My father remarried a woman named Gallia. She died giving birth to me." He turned his face away as his breath hitched. "By all accounts, they married more for companionship than for love, and she was too old for childbirth. I was a happy accident. Still, Father spoils me rotten." He dug his fingers into the sand. "Do you miss your mother?"

"Yes," Claire admitted, "even though I've only been gone for a fortnight or so." She saw how envious of their relationship Gareth was and felt bad for him. She tried not to think about all the times she'd complained about Suranne being too weird to Marcus and her father. If she got home, she'd never do it again.

"What's it like to have a mother?" he asked.

"Well, I don't know," she said thoughtfully. "She's ready with a delicious treat when I get home from school and we ride and go for walks as a family and we paint together and when she hugs me she smells like essential oils, especially if she's been doing a yoga session."

Gareth was facing her again, laughing. "I have no idea what half of you just said means. School? Essential oils? Yoga?"

Claire paused, trying to figure out how to explain such foreign concepts, but instead her breath caught.

With the sunset rich with colour, mermaids straddled the grey rocks and swam in the ocean, some floating right up to the sand close enough for Claire to almost touch. They weren't beautiful in the way they were in the storybooks of home. They were pale-skinned and naked. Their tails were rusty reds and dull greens, the scales blotchy and uneven colours with patches of sand sticking to them. In their long, dark hair, shells clung to the wet strands; some even sported a starfish or two strapped across one shoulder or on their slender necks.

Claire shivered as she looked into one mermaid's hard grey eyes, and then at her blue lips. She wouldn't want to cross these mythical creatures.

"Have you seen the Mer-people before?" Gareth asked quietly. "Do you have them in your world?"

Claire smiled as she stared at the strange, awe-inspiring creatures. "No. For me, they've only ever existed in fairy stories."

"They're a solitary race, but we are one with water, as they are, and so we respect each other. I think it was a kind of resignation on their part. Our people wandered all over this coast and discovered its creatures; it was easier for the Mer-people to come to a truce with the Maellwyn Clan rather than try to keep us away, just as it was easier for the salamanders to do the same with House Dorran."

Suddenly, Claire understood. "The Mer-people are your elemental creatures, aren't they?"

Gareth nodded, then pointed at a mermaid close to the shore. His white beard was long and flowing and blended in with the sea foam, his green eyes were wild, and his skin was nut-brown, tough and wrinkled with great age. On his nearly bald head perched a circlet of seashells. "The Nereus is their leader," Gareth said, as the great creature raised a bulky hand in silent greeting, sea snakes wrapped around his wrists and arms. "One day he'll speak to me as he speaks to my father."

Claire couldn't help but think of the Saura. She hadn't seen the powerful elemental since lodging inside Maellwyn Manor. She suspected it was because a being of fire didn't like the estate's closeness to water.

The sky continued to blaze with colour as sunset deepened. As Claire watched the mermaids, one ducked underwater and resurfaced with a crab in her hand. She put it in her mouth and crunched down with sharp teeth, swallowing the crab with a wild grin. Others stared and pointed at Claire.

"Can you hear them?" Gareth murmured.

"What do you mean?" If Claire concentrated, she heard a faint hum, like someone singing something tuneless far away, but that was all.

"They're speaking to you. Can't you tell?"

"No," Claire said. "What do they say?"

"They say that we must trust you."

"And do you believe them?"

"I believe every word." Gareth cocked his head to one side and put a hand behind his ear. "Listen. They tell me that you are from another place, aeons and aeons away."

"But you already know that," Claire insisted, laughing. "Everyone does. I think you're making it up so I'll feel better." Even if he was, she had to admit it was working. For this small while she'd been able to put the horrible events of earlier behind her.

Gareth went on as though she hadn't said a word. If he'd been offended by her accusation, he didn't show it. "They tell me that I must walk far with you."

His voice cracked and Claire saw with surprise that he was crying. She didn't know what to do or say. She felt small and silly as she put an arm around his broad shoulders.

"It'll be fine," she said, wishing she could believe it. "I'll beat Eidan in the end."

Gareth looked up with a sad smile. "It is not that which I fear." Before Claire could reply, he got to his feet and saluted first the Nereus, then the rest of the Mer-people, before turning back towards the tunnel.

Chapter Nineteen

CLAIRE SAT ON A STONE bench hidden by mulberry and cypress trees trying to stay out of sight. Gareth had gone to what he called 'the debating room' to see how his father's meeting to convince the rest of Maellwyn Manor that today wasn't a total calamity was getting on, but Claire hadn't been brave enough to follow. There'd been this time with Liz where they'd come up with mean nicknames for everyone in their class. Claire had laughed about it when she'd told her dad, but his look of disappointment had hurt worse than the anger of some of her classmates when Liz had told them about it later. She could just about handle the suspicion and rage of the Maellwyns, but the thought of facing Maen's and Kiera's disappointment was too much, and she was afraid Lotte would want nothing more to do with her. Besides, Merriam Beach had taken her mind off the Beast, but now she was sitting doing nothing, it occupied her thoughts with an irritating persistence. Her palms sweated and her gut twisted but she was pretty sure the right thing to do was to tell the others about her dreams and what Gwenivere had seen, and soon.

She put her chin in her hands and leant forward, admiring the plain white shells lining the garden bed. They almost glowed in the twilight. She wished she had her paints and her easel so she could capture the scene, but most of all she wished she were by Suranne's side in the shed, able to talk over her problems and get a hug. The real world felt further and further away, just like her old self, and she wasn't sure she liked Kelnarium much anymore. No wonder her father had wanted to go home to Shale.

Soft footfall distracted her. Claire looked up to see Meghan, a dark blue silken hood drawing back from her face, wisps of dark, silver-threaded hair escaping. She meandered through the extensive gardens towards Claire, moonlight outlining the parts of her figure the insect lantern she carried didn't.

For a second, Claire considered making a run for it in the opposite direction, but she was too tired. She waited expectantly, hoping her kinswoman would head elsewhere when she saw the Dorran pariah had taken up this space already.

Alas. No such luck. Meghan ducked through the foliage and waved at Claire. She knelt by a bunch of yellow flowers and sniffed their scent, before joining her. Claire shuffled to one side to make room.

"You don't have to be afraid of me," Meghan said, putting her lantern on the ground. "Of everyone, perhaps I can understand your situation best."

Claire didn't know what to say. Of course, Meghan had been married to the man who created the Rift. That must be a terrible burden to live with, and yet somehow, Meghan bore it.

Meghan folded her hands in her lap, staring determinedly ahead. "He was a good man. People don't like to remember that, and his family least of all. Aed and Dorran felt responsible so it was easier to remember Kelt as someone hot-blooded and dangerous." She sighed, adjusting the folds of her dress. "Yes, he was those things, but he was generous with his coin and a hard worker too. Most importantly, he was a loving husband."

"But he abandoned you and disobeyed his House for a battle that got him killed."

"It was one mistake. An enormous one, but it doesn't have to define my memories of him."

"Why are you telling me this? Why did you seek me out? You did, didn't you?"

"I saw you hurrying to the gardens and watched the direction you headed. As to why I'm telling you, perhaps because I can guess at some of what you're thinking. You think you are like Kelt. You fear you will make more trouble for us, rather than solve our problems. Perhaps you will, but it's better to try to do what you think is right than to do nothing at all."

"It feels so impossible," said Claire. "I'm just a kid and if the Beast can block everything I try and twist my powers against me—" *If it's foreseen I'm going to betray everyone ...*

"No one ever said this would be easy," Meghan said, "but Maen and everyone else seem to have been foolish enough to suppose it would be. I have told him so."

"He won't listen," Claire said, her shoulders drooping. "He was furious with me."

"You are too quick to fear the worst. Even as we speak, Maen is discussing with the others a way to try the same spell again."

"They can't make me," Claire gasped, fear threatening to choke her words. "I'll end up hurting someone else."

Meghan rose to her feet. "Come," she said as she picked up the lantern. Without looking back, she ducked through the trees and headed back towards the Manor. Claire followed dutifully. Meghan led the way through wide archways and past colonnades that gleamed softly in the moonlight, and into a passageway that led to the centre of the Manor. They brushed past servitors in increasing numbers and stepped through a huge archway.

Claire found herself in an enormous room full of benches arranged like the seats in the local theatre back home, curling right around the wall and stepping up with each new row. *Gareth's 'debating room,'* she thought. At the front of the room, Maen, Lord Maellwyn, Gareth and Gwenivere addressed the crowd.

Meghan pointed at the front row of empty seats, then gave an encouraging nod. As Claire followed Meghan to take their seats, she couldn't help but notice all eyes turn to her in the amphitheatre. It looked like everyone in the Manor had come to listen to Lord Maellwyn. As she glanced about the room, it seemed like every single spot was full. She noticed Kiera and Rael seated five rows behind her. Kiera shot her a pale smile and Claire felt a little less sick. At least Kiera looked like she'd forgiven her for the morning's disastrous mishap. She turned her attention back to the podium, where Gareth was addressing everyone.

"We should use our secret place," he was saying firmly. "It may be that the Beast cannot reach us there, and if nothing else, we Maellwyns will be stronger and able to put out any fires quickly." Dissent rippled behind Claire like a tidal wave, but he pushed on. "I know things went badly today, but as Father has said, we can't lay all the blame at Lady Claire's feet. She's still learning, and now that you know the full extent of the prophecies, you understand she has to learn to have any hope of saving us, but as to the rest, we were too complacent." He shot grim glances around the room. "All of us were. We should have expected that the Beast would adapt and attack in new ways, especially where Lady Claire is involved."

"But nothing went wrong at Dorran Manor," someone shouted.

Claire started guiltily. That wasn't true. Things had gone wrong. There were her dreams and Rinn's death, but somehow she thought blurting out everything in front of a hostile crowd mightn't be the best for Dorran and Maellwyn relations. She'd corner Gwenivere later and figure out a strategy to break it to key people, those who needed to know. She relaxed back in her chair a little. It felt good to make a decision.

"No, they did not," Maen agreed, stepping forward to stand beside Gareth, "but we were working simple spells for the most part and the one challenging spell we tested, Gwenivere watched over from beginning to end." He bowed at Gwenivere. "You were wiser than the rest of us, friend."

Gwenivere inclined her head. "In addition, we haven't considered the possibility that the Beast attacked in the way it did because Lady Claire was on the right track. It's possible that the spell she tried is the one needed to close the Rift."

"That's all well and good, but we've heard neither hide nor hair of Lady Claire since the accident," a voice came from somewhere towards the back of the crowd.

Meghan's elbow poked into Claire's stomach as silence fell. Though Claire was terrified, she knew what was expected of her. If Kelnarium was going to die anyway, she had no choice but to keep using magic, even if people got hurt, even if there was a chance the Beast hadn't been lying about her. She'd have to be extra thoughtful and extra careful. And then maybe, just maybe, she could rescue Marcus and get home.

Her throat clogged at the thought of her brother, but she got to her feet and made herself stride to stand beside Maen. "I'm sorry for what happened earlier today, but I agree with Gareth. I don't think I have a choice but to try again."

Chapter Twenty

CLAIRE STOOD BESIDE Gareth at Merriam Beach as the sun rose to its zenith, this time accompanied by Lord Maellwyn, Kress, Maen and Gwenivere. Claire had been surprised when Lord Maellwyn had led them down the same extensive cave network she'd traversed with Gareth yesterday. She looked around her. She'd sort of expected the Maellwyn secret place to be exceptional, not a boring, old beach, even if it did contain the Nereus and his Mer-people. Even as she thought of the Maellwyns elemental leader, she noticed the ancient king crest a wave.

Maen bowed low in Lord Maellwyn's direction. "My Lord?"

At least someone else was as confused as she was.

She glanced at Gwenivere. Though the Dream Mage kept her expression schooled to reveal little, Claire wouldn't have been surprised if she didn't know what to expect either right now. She'd managed to catch the woman last night, but Gwenivere asked Claire to hold off on saying anything about the Beast to Maen until after today's working.

Claire watched Lord Maellwyn walk to the shore, letting waves lap over his bare feet as he whispered something to the Nereus, who glowered at the strangers in Lord Maellwyn's party. At last, the Mer King seemed satisfied, and Lord Maellwyn turned back to face everyone. Claire's senses felt more alive than ever. She stepped forward, not wanting to miss a thing, not when something was finally going to happen.

"This is our greatest secret," Lord Maellwyn said gravely. "And no matter how far you journey and how hard you're pressed, this is one secret that you must never tell." Claire could barely make him out as mist seemed to billow inwards from the sea, moving quickly to tower high, high above their party, enclosing them in its damp embrace and shutting out the rest of the world. "The punishment for revealing Maellwyn secrets is death," he boomed. "No matter how far you run, my magic will find you and drown you." His orb-like eyes locked onto Claire's and he seemed to grow taller.

Claire shrieked as something icy pressed against her heart.

"Promise me you'll never reveal this place. Swear it on everything you hold dear!"

"We won't tell," Claire gasped. "None of us will ever tell."

His eyes bored into Claire's. After a few moments, he turned his attention to Gwenivere and the band squeezing Claire's heart eased.

"You too must promise."

Gwenivere managed to nod, even as she stepped back. He then asked the same of Maen.

As though satisfied, Lord Maellwyn seemed to shrink, and the air became less claustrophobic as the mist thinned. "Then we may begin."

Gareth and Kress stepped into the ocean beside Lord Maellwyn. The three linked hands and began to hum, making the same low and tuneless sound Claire had heard from the Mer-people. Soon, mermaids surfaced, only this time they were joyous, all waving at Lord Maellwyn and calling his name in their strange sing-song voices.

"These are my guests," he shouted to the Mer-people. "They have the Nereus's blessing and may cross."

As he spoke, a great wave flung itself at the shore, then curled backwards. The ocean parted as it retreated, as though Lord Maellwyn were Moses, leaving a pathway across the ocean floor, leading to ... Claire shaded her eyes with her hands but couldn't see where the path ended. There was no time to wonder. The others had begun walking, leaving her behind. She quickly stepped forward but as soon as her sandalled feet touched wet sand, the waves rose high above her head and hurtled down. *This is insane! We'll all die!*

Water closed over her head and she tumbled end to end. She'd gone surfing with Marcus at the local beach in the holidays, and the loss of control had been the same as sand had scoured her skin and she'd been sent rolling.

Claire flung her hands about her, certain she'd drown, but they struck only air and when she brought them back, they weren't even dripping. Her mouth was open but didn't fill with water. *I'm breathing*, she realised.

"Relax," Gareth called out from somewhere ahead. "The sea takes us where we need to go."

"But I'm not even wet," she called back.

"If you are invited, you will arrive safely."

Before she could reply, Claire shot above the waves, landing on all fours on something flat. Black rock. The strong smell of salt filled her nostrils and got down her throat. Sunbursts and rainbows swirled across her vision as water splashed onto a sparkling white structure rising from beneath the ocean just ahead. The building flowed and gleamed, like Lord Maellwyn's throne.

Claire got gingerly to her feet, tugging her shirt back in place before looking back to the beach. It was barely visible, the cliffs and Manor easier to make out. She'd never have been able to swim so far from shore without help back at home. She spun around to the strange building to see milky doors open. They gleamed like the inside of an oyster shell, pearly and reflective, creating bursts of purple colour against the white. As she stared in amazement, the others entered the building, led by Gareth and Kress. Lord Maellwyn waited on the threshold, beckoning to Claire, indicating she should follow him. The doors sealed them inside as they entered. Mist cooled her face as the ocean pounded against the walls. The Maellwyn secret place was like a hidden jewel. She wished she had her paints – she could have made a glorious picture.

As she caught up to Maen and Gwenivere who were whispering to each other, Lord Maellwyn, Kress and Gareth hummed in sync with each other. The sound was loud and came from deep within. The air grew cooler.

Claire's skin broke out in goosebumps as the air filled with condensation. Maellwyn, Gareth and Kress closed their eyes and threw their heads back at the domed roof. As she too stared at the ceiling and wondered what was going on, it took her a few seconds to realize that the sound she was hearing was not just waves around them, but also above them, pummelling the ceiling. She guessed the Maellwyns had returned this secret place into the sea. She clutched Maen's hand, fearful of being swallowed by the ocean, as the Maellwyns broke their concentration.

Maen's own cheeks were pale. He stared beyond her to the far ends of the structure. Claire followed his gaze. Seven Mer-people lounged in large clam shells; the biggest was salmon pink streaked with navy blue and contained the Nereus himself, his rusty red and seaweed green tail longer than those of his brethren, his muscles sheening from the sea. His green eyes pinned to Claire's, cold and empty and inhuman, and suddenly she was afraid.

"You are safe," Gareth said gently as he placed a hand on her shoulder. "Your own elemental leader would be just as frosty towards us. It's natural. I could count on my fingers the number of non-Maellwyns who've entered this secret place. The Nereus honours you by allowing you inside at all."

Claire remembered the caverns beneath Dorran Manor with a pang of regret. "I never had the chance to see our own secret place." She choked a little. "Grandfather was going to show me."

"I'm sorry," he said, looking sad. "But here, at least, in a place of great *learth* power, I do not think the Beast will follow you. We can practise with more confidence. Our Mer-people have agreed to watch over us all."

Gwenivere's lips were parted with wonder. "I'd still like to observe the proceedings. Is that possible in this place?"

"Yes," Lord Maellwyn broke in. "This building won't make it difficult to work magic." He smiled at Maen. "Kress, Gareth and I will stand at the ready should something go wrong, but I don't think it will. We'll test what happens when you use magic first, then run through the whole spell."

"Well," Claire said awkwardly. "I guess we begin?" This was like entering Peony into a dressage competition all over again. Having loads of people watching her had been nerve-wracking, but once she'd started, she'd been too engrossed to notice anyone.

She closed her eyes and breathed in and out, images of toasting marshmallows at the back of the farm colliding with the burn of dry ice, her hand pulsing as the air moved around her fingertips, and she heard Gwenivere gasp.

Gareth, Lord Maellwyn and Kress doused her flame with their own spells, the scent of brine counteracting the burnt meat air.

Maen asked her to try again and this time it was easier. As was the next and the next and the next until she could direct the flame wherever she wanted with little effort.

"Let's try once more," Maen said, obviously relieved. "Then we'd best get back for a big lunch." Now Maen mentioned it, Claire's stomach did feel hollow.

He signalled to Gwenivere, who sat cross legged by a Mer-person. She unwound herself from the ground and headed over, smiling. "I've seen nothing."

"Thank goodness," Claire said. She didn't know if she could handle another accident. "Where should I aim the flame for the grand finale?"

"Directly overhead," Maen said. "You'll need to stand right under the Rift and target the spell directly above you, as Kelt did, so that's what we might as well practice."

Claire took a deep breath, and did as she was asked, confident nothing would go wrong. Yet as she held the images of flame in her mind and aimed upwards, something strange happened. There was a loud click, like the noise of a stapler, and then, though her eyes were closed, she saw the white domed roof above her. Before she could snatch herself back to reality, grey clouds whirled overhead, then parted to reveal a deep rent marked by greens and reds and slashes of indigo. It was the Rift.

Like an old cinema reel, an image sketched within the crack overhead faster than Claire could keep up. Four men and women stood in a human chain. At an unspoken word, they flung hands out in unison, sparking a wildfire in the sky, then waterfalls cascaded over land, rocks fell, and wind swirled around it all. The Rift dissolved, sunshine and normal sky restored, leaving Claire with a warm feeling inside.

Before she could bring herself back to the others, a brown shadow suddenly blocked out the sky and the rest of the vision unfolding. Darkness blanketed the blue as it reached down to touch her. The shadow rearranged itself, dirty, thick and choking, with an open mouth gaping at its centre directly above Claire.

The Beast had found her, even here.

Every part of her froze. Maybe she'd destroy the Maellwyns secret place. Maybe she'd kill everyone inside and die alone. Her chest ached and there was a ringing in her ears. Things couldn't end here. There was something she was on the edge of knowing. The vision she'd just experienced had shown four people with four different kinds of magic. She suspected they each represented the four magical Houses of Kelnarium destroying the Rift, but if that was the case, she knew it was impossible. Two of the Houses no longer existed, so Kelnarium would die and she'd never see her family again. She needed time to think, but how could she with the Beast about to strike? She was doomed.

Yet even as despair choked her, nothing happened. Instead, the hideous creature glowered at her. "Why would you murder me?"

"I ... I don't want to murder anyone," she gasped.

"You will," it said, in a voice so mournful she almost felt sorry for it.

"How do you know?"

"Aren't you going to close the Rift?"

"Yes."

"Then you condemn me, for I am its very soul."

That wasn't possible, was it? No one had mentioned such a thing to Claire before. Her mind raced. "If what you say is true, I'm sorry, but this world will die unless ... unless ..." She couldn't go on for guilt, but she knew she had no choice. Too many people's lives depended on her doing what must be done.

"Unless you destroy me," it said.

The Beast rifled through her brain with a sensation like nails dragging against chalkboard. She wanted to cry out, but her tongue glued to the ridge of her mouth.

"You are determined," it spat as the sudden probe withdrew.

It watched her as she shrank backwards, something calculated in its countenance. Then it rushed upwards. She felt its fear like a physical thing as it stretched. She could have sworn she saw pictures moving between the wisps of the Beast and from the way it stretched as wide as it could, Claire suspected it didn't want her to see what was happening in the ongoing vision ... which meant ... which meant somehow, she was seeing how to close the Rift.

Claire strained to see past the Beast's undulating mass, certain that whatever pictures scudded by were important.

Though her line of sight was unclear, she could just make out the four people once more. This time she recognised one of them. It was Marcus, wearing the grey and purple tunic of House Ushanan, standing in a wide field. He pointed his finger and air billowed in a mini cyclone. He joined hands with three others; two in blue and silver Maellwyn House attire, though one cracked the earth beneath his feet, and the third person, why, it was herself, flames crawling across her open palm. Water, flame, air and earth converged then shot into the sky.

The Beast roared, diving onto her fast. She couldn't dodge as it lifted a long finger and touched her forehead. Knife blades drove through her skull and she was pulled sideways, spinning out of control.

Chapter Twenty-One

CLAIRE DRIFTED UP AND down ocean waves, Marcus beside her, the gentle rolling motion soothing. In the distance, Mum and Dad called out from the shore, their laughter turning to alarm. They pointed behind the pair. A huge wave built, about to crash over her and Marcus. "Dive under," she screamed, as the wave broke, and her world tilted …

The sudden drop jolted through her stomach. Marcus grabbed her in a tight grip, his fingers slipping.

"Careful," a male voice sounded somewhere above her.

She blinked as the sun beat against her skin instead of waves and a hand pressed against her forehead. "Where am I?"

"Merriam Beach," Maen said. "Your spell shattered when the Beast appeared, but don't worry. No one was hurt, though you won't feel well for a little bit. Can you walk? Lord Maellwyn has sent for servitors to assist."

She nodded, fighting back exhaustion as she sat up. Maen crouched beside her while Gwenivere, Gareth and Kress waited in a huddle. They broke apart at Claire's sudden attention. Kress and Maen helped her to her feet, then over to a rock to sit and wait. Memories came flooding back as her strength returned.

She gripped Maen's sleeve. "I know how to close the Rift. I'll convene a meeting with Lord Maellwyn when we get back to the Manor."

"How is that possible," Maen began, but Gwenivere cut across him. "Do as she says." The Dream Mage looked at Claire differently, something almost like trust in her eyes.

Before Maen could protest, Lord Maellwyn appeared through the cave opening with two servitors. Claire let them walk on either side of her as they commenced the short journey through the cave network back into the Manor, but she didn't really need them. She felt better already. Soon, she'd see Marcus again. No one could deny they needed to go via Kelnariat now. She told Lord Maellwyn about their need to discuss what had happened, and he agreed to a kind of war council in his private antechamber.

When Lord Maellwyn pushed through the wooden door that led back inside the building proper, Kress hurried away to fetch Rael, Kiera, Meghan, Tarn and a number of Maellwyns. "I can't make any decision without a vote," Lord Maellwyn explained.

Claire tried to suppress nerves. She'd have to be like her father and tell her story convincingly to assure them she told the truth and that there was hope after all.

The party traversed up passageways until they entered an open space with a rectangular pool in its centre, silent men and women waiting in each corner. Claire guessed they were at the top of the estate because she saw the blue domed roof directly overhead. She looked around with interest. Lord Maellwyn's quarters were very different to her grandfather's. For one thing, painted murals ran all along the upper part of the walls, depicting berries and wine and dolphins diving. For another, the floor was made of polished white marble streaked with purple.

Before she could take much more in, Gareth indicated an archway to the left. "Through here."

She followed him into a new room, the two servitors still either side, little fold-out chairs dotted around a rectangular table. The footsteps of Maen and Gwenivere clattered close behind her. Lord Maellwyn indicated they should all take a cup from a basket perched on a wicker stool and dip it in a giant clay amphora of wine at the entryway before sitting. He sat at the head of the table, but not before asking the two servitors who'd assisted Claire to fetch some fresh fruit, bread and honey.

Claire sat gingerly on the brightly dyed cloth strip that formed the main section of her chair. It felt like she only sipped at her drink for a few minutes before six advisors arrived, including Kress and Jemroth, as well as Rael, Kiera, Meghan and Tarn. They sat in the spare seats around Lord Maellwyn, looking puzzled.

"Now," he said, fingers steepling, "to business. As everyone knows, we went to Merriam Beach to work Claire's spell a second time. She succeeded admirably."

"Except?" Jemroth frowned, leaning forward.

"Yes." Lord Maellwyn looked at Claire significantly. "What happened?"

"The Beast appeared," Gwenivere said. She looked at Claire with a small conspiratorial smile. "Amongst other things."

Claire took the Dream Mage's cue. "I was in the process of working the spell for the final time when I had a vision. Don't ask me how, because I don't know, but in it, I saw how to close the Rift."

Chaos. Rael shouted at Kress and another advisor while Kiera and Meghan whispered to each other. Maen pounded a fist on the table at Jemroth and still other advisors protested that such a thing was impossible. Claire tried raising her voice, but no one heard her over the cacophony.

"Silence," Lord Maellwyn's voice echoed throughout the room. "Silence," he repeated more politely as everyone turned his way. "Let the lady speak."

Claire smiled gratefully. "I saw the Rift and the shadows around it. Then the vision came. I saw that we need all four elements of *Iearth* to close it. That was when the Beast appeared, and when I saw it was frightened and angry, I knew I wasn't meant to have seen what I had. It tried to cover the sky so I couldn't keep watching but I could make out enough beyond it to know the truth." Her voice trembled as everyone leaned in close. "I saw who we need in our party to succeed. There was me, and then two others in Maellwyn attire; a young man using water magic and then," she frowned, "a man splitting the earth. I must admit that part didn't make much sense. I thought everyone with magical ability in House Domain has long since died."

"Indeed," Lord Maellwyn said. He wove his hand, "But go on. We'll get to that later."

"And then I saw Marcus. He was using air magic." She hurried on before anyone could interrupt. "I know he's a Dorran like me, but well, I thought and thought about it when we came back through the caves and I think I have the answer." She turned to Maen. "My grandmother was House Ushanan, right?"

"Yes, but—"

"So, she probably passed some of her magical blood on to Marcus. We need me and Marcus and someone powerful in Maellwyn magic, you, Lord Maellwyn, or you, Lord Gareth," she said, catching both their eyes. "And then someone from this House who has a bit of House Domain earth blood somewhere in their ancestry." She looked at Lord Maellwyn for confirmation.

To her surprise he turned to Jemroth, who had risen to his feet. "How can we trust that what you saw is true?" he demanded through bloodless lips.

Gwenivere pushed her chair back and stood, staring Jemroth down. "You forget that I too was watching, and I saw, heard and felt what Claire did. The Beast revealed itself to be an extension of the Rift and begged Claire to spare it, for if she closes that blight in the sky it ceases to exist. It is this that makes me believe the solution Claire saw is correct. The pair share a terrible bond; one will destroy, and the other be destroyed. I think the Beast appeared to cause trouble with Claire's spell, but instead, revealed too much of its mind and its fears." She looked around the table. "I think we can trust Claire's vision. We need all four elements to close the Rift."

"That means we need to go to Kelnariat after all," Maen said. He glanced at Claire with narrowed eyes. "How convenient."

"Nonetheless, you heard Gwenivere," Claire said. "I'm not making this up."

Lord Maellwyn drummed his fingers against the table. "Rescuing Marcus won't be easy. I'll send a message to my contact in Kelnariat. He'll be able to put you up, Claire, and help you find your brother."

Maen cleared his throat, and Lord Maellwyn look at him in inquiry. "Yes?"

"What of this person of your House with Domain blood? Does he or she exist? I don't see the point of haring off to the Riftlands without finding them, and that could take weeks of poring through records."

"It won't," Jemroth said with a sigh. "No," he said, as Lord Maellwyn moved to stop him. "The time for secrecy is past. I was a boy when my home was destroyed by Kelt. Lord Maellwyn found me on the edge of the battlefield, scared witless, and took me in." He spread his fingers wide, staring at them like they'd reveal something important if he concentrated hard enough. "I was too young to learn much of my true family's magic, but I can use basic spells. I have practised with Lord Maellwyn in private, knowing that someday the time to rebuild my House would come. I will go with you, Lady Claire." He closed his fingers into a fist. "And together we'll close the Rift."

"You have proof?" Maen asked.

Jemroth reached for the string around his neck. Claire, like everyone else, had assumed it contained a vial of seawater. Instead, he produced a metal pendant, a bronze coloured disc with a hole in its centre that the string passed through. Claire didn't need to hear the exclamations of shock to know what she was looking at; Jemroth wore the special metal of House Domain that Gareth had mentioned.

Kress looked from the metal to Jemroth and then to his lord in hurt confusion. "You never even hinted."

"I'm sorry I lied to everyone," Lord Maellwyn said, "but it wasn't my secret to give away and I didn't want Jemroth singled out. He was an orphan who deserved a chance to fit in with his new family." He sighed as he studied Jemroth. "Sometimes I still wonder if I did the right thing. I can't pretend to understand earth *learth*. I could have sent you to the Enchantment Weavers and they'd have known more about your past and how to harness your abilities, but they walk strange paths. It didn't seem right to send you to the mountains in isolation without children your own age to grow up with."

"I'm glad I was raised here," Jemroth replied gruffly. "You've never treated me unkindly or differently."

"But in my darkest hours I fear I have made you too much a Maellwyn. Your elementals have never appeared to you. It worries me."

"The gnomes will find me when they're ready, Lord Maellwyn. Perhaps I've yet to prove myself a true Domain." Jemroth grinned. "And what better way to demonstrate my right then by helping Claire on her quest?"

Claire couldn't stop staring at Lord Maellwyn's chief advisor. She'd thought Jemroth had an air about him that was different to everyone else, but she'd never have guessed he was the sole member left of a dead House. Still, everything was coming together. "When can we leave for Kelnariat?" she asked.

"We?" Lord Maellwyn asked.

Claire looked around the table. Maen, Meghan, Rael and Kiera were all shaking their heads. She felt like she was a child learning to swim, the board keeping her afloat pulled away before she was ready. "What is it?"

"It will have to be a small group that goes with you to the capital," Gwenivere explained gently. "Tarn and I are too easily recognised and Maen has been on many a diplomatic mission to Kelnariat over the years."

"What about Kiera or Rael or Meghan?" Claire asked, her concerns about being left alone rising.

"Meghan is old like me," Lord Maellwyn said. He smiled at Claire. "Though I am touched you consider me strong, I think younger blood is called for. My son shall go with you to Kelnariat."

"And Kiera and I are too easily recognised as Dorrans," Rael added. "Don't forget there is a price on our heads. No. You, Jemroth and Lord Gareth should go to Kelnariat alone. We'll meet you in the Riftlands."

Claire knew they only spoke the truth, but she didn't have to like it. She was losing her mentors and friends in one blow.

Gareth cleared his throat. "We should have a two-pronged mission in Kelnariat. We must rescue Claire's brother Marcus, but we should also try to find out who has turned Eidan against the Dorrans. It's no use closing the Rift if a House is immediately killed for their trouble."

"Yes," Lord Maellwyn agreed. "I think your best bet is to enter the city in disguise. Then, head straight for our safe house and our contact, Bron. He'll be able to tell you whether it's safe for you to reveal your identity inside the Council Building, Gareth. If it is, claim you're in Kelnariat to understand what has happened with Dorran House and to reaffirm our allegiance to Eidan. Learn what you can about why the man's gone rogue. If we can discover who's behind his sudden antagonism, we might be able to neutralise the threat they pose." He stroked his white beard. "The whole thing's bizarre, that an old friend and confident could turn like he has ..."

"It beggars' belief," Maen finished. "I know, but that's why your Bron could be of great help."

"If Gareth can go about as Lord Maellwyn's son, perhaps I could pretend to be a Maellwyn cousin serving Gareth and visiting the city for the first time? Servitors can learn all kinds of things without people noticing them," Claire mused.

Maen nodded. "It's a good idea. Keep your ears to the ground, but don't tarry too long in Kelnariat. As soon as you get Marcus, head to the Riftlands." He studied his wine cup for a moment, then looked up again. "I disagree with my good friend, Rael. I think one other should go, one who is not a Dorran and who can bring us a message if the need arises. Gareth, Jemroth and Claire are all needed to save Kelnarium so cannot waste time on messages, but this person could."

A thrill ran through Claire. There was still one other she counted as friend, and who wouldn't mind risk-taking if it meant getting answers about the murder of her family. "How about Lotte? She's not a Dorran, but a villager. She helped me when Eidan attacked and has stuck by us all this way." Claire kept her fingers crossed under the wooden table.

Maen frowned as he tried to remember Lotte's face but then his expression transfigured into a wide smile. "By the salamanders, she's perfect. No one will spare her a second glance."

Claire looked around the group eagerly. "So, it's agreed? Me and Lotte, Lord Gareth and Jemroth will head to Kelnariat straight away?"

"You'll need a few days to arrange things," Lord Maellwyn said, "and that gives Bron time to receive my letter and prepare, but otherwise, I'm for it."

Gwenivere cleared her throat. Claire's palms felt sweaty. She knew what was coming. "Before we progress further with plans, there's something Claire and I haven't told you."

"Oh?" Maen said to the ceiling. "The Saura help me, I'm beginning to wonder if I know anything at all."

"Claire's been sent nightmares by the Beast," Gwenivere continued. "In them, he tells her she will betray us. Before Rinn Taccala died, she spoke with it too. It told her the same thing; Claire will betray this world." She flung up a hand before anyone could interrupt. "I didn't want its words spreading discord, so I kept them to myself. Not to mention that I don't trust it not to have been playing mind games with Rinn and Claire."

"Why didn't you tell me about this, Claire?" The hurt in Maen's voice hit her like a blow. "I'm your teacher."

"Because I told her not to," Gwenivere said. "But we don't have time for recriminations. This is about next moves. I believe Claire is who we need to save Kelnarium, but I understand if others are worried."

Kress and Sleath scowled openly and Jemroth studied Claire looking so hawk-like, she felt like she was a mouse about to be eaten.

"What do you propose?" Lord Maellwyn asked Gwenivere with a faint smile. "I can see you have something in mind."

"Well, I'd be happier if the party visited the Enchantment Weavers before going to Kelnariat. You can ask them about Claire's role in the Rift as well as to weave Eidan a different future, one where he doesn't fear Dorran House. That way, we know where Claire stands, and you can avoid wasting time in Kelnariat if you don't need to. You'd simply pick up Marcus and keep going."

"No, there should be no delays," Claire interjected. She couldn't believe this. She needed to get to Kelnariat and Marcus as fast as possible before Eidan did something awful.

"It's only a slight detour and could save a world of trouble," Gwenivere said gently.

"Not to mention, it would mean all of us could get on with things secure in the knowledge you aren't about to destroy everything we've tried to protect," Tarn added. "Otherwise, doubt will plague us."

"What will you do if the Weavers say I'm the betrayer?" said Claire, desperate that another roadblock shouldn't come between her and Marcus.

"Then instead of going to Kelnariat, you will meet us at the Riftlands nearest the capital," Maen said. "We can discuss it then."

"And what will you be doing?" Claire demanded.

"We'll tell the common folk who'll listen about Eidan and his actions at Dorran Manor. That way, if the Enchantment Weavers cannot help, we have a way to deal with his sudden hatred of magical brethren once the Rift is closed. Many people respect and even love us. They will not want to believe the lies that are being spread. If we have to, we can get the people to rise up against Eidan."

"It is wisdom, Claire," Rael said as she scowled.

"We need to put it to a vote," Lord Maellwyn said, stroking his white beard. "Everyone in favour of caution and a visit to the Arras Ranges, raise your hand."

Claire could have groaned. Everyone but her had their hands in the air. *Well*, she thought, *uncomfortable journey up a snowy mountain range, here I come.*

Kiera held up the plain clay pot filled with dark sludge. It was the afternoon of their departure. Claire sat on the ground at Kiera's feet with her hair trailing down her back against an old blanket wrapped around her shoulders. Kiera's long fingers brushed through Claire's hair to distribute the dye evenly, and Claire relaxed, pushing the problem of the Beast aside. The brown dye applied in Autun had started to fade and needed touching up before her long journey.

"I'll miss you," Kiera said quietly. "Keep your wits about you and when this is over, we'll have a huge party before I have to say goodbye."

As Kiera massaged more of the dye into Claire's scalp, Claire cleared her throat against the lump forming in her throat. Something had bothered her ever since she'd met Kiera. "What did you really think of my dad, of James?"

"He was charming and funny, and he told the most brilliant tales. I remember when he first arrived, he'd tell Suranne and I stories every day. He'd tell us about little folk who stole milk and fruit in the night, or about the gods of the well and of the lake who never asked for anything but a memory. He told us of wars between gods and goddesses and of men lost in the hills, following fae lights into the otherworld, never to be seen again."

Claire laughed imagining her dad keeping two young teenagers transfixed with tales of Irish folklore.

"Did he remain a storyteller in your world? I've often wondered," Kiera asked.

"He became a journalist."

"A journalist? What's that?"

"A journalist writes news articles for the paper."

Kiera still looked lost.

"Never mind," Claire said. "Yes, he remained a storyteller."

"I wished for the longest time they'd stayed," Kiera went on, as though Claire hadn't answered. She gathered the last of the dye and spread it through Claire's hair in foamy scoops, then piled her curls over the top of each other to let the dye take. "There was a part of Suranne that never did quite fit in. I didn't ever want to admit it, but a part of me always knew she would go someplace far away on a grand adventure. When you get home, tell Suranne I forgive her and that I love her."

Before Claire could find the right words to answer Kiera, a loud thump on the door interrupted.

"Who is it?" Claire called.

"It's Jemroth, Lady Claire. The cart is prepared. When you are ready, get your things together. We leave before the light fades."

Chapter Twenty-Two

WITHIN AN HOUR OF TRAVERSING the dirt road, it began to drizzle, then pour down, the noise pitter-pattering against the oilskin cover protecting those inside the cart. Though Gareth insisted it was usual for travellers through the coastal pass to happen upon storms, he clutched at the vial around his neck like it was a good luck charm. Claire and Lotte huddled as near to each other as they could, wrapping themselves in the coloured blankets that softened the floor, and piling cushions to protect against sudden jolts caused by rut after rut in the road. Claire didn't envy Jemroth, who was driving. She doubted his poncho and hat would stay waterproof long and as to visibility, it was a wonder he could see more than a few feet in front of him.

She tried not to think about how nervous she was. Waving goodbye to Maen, Rael, Kiera, Meghan, Gwenivere, Tarn and Lord Maellwyn had been awful. She was glad they'd gotten their farewells out of the way quickly, but now she wished one of them were here to guide her. Though Jemroth was the eldest, she was the leader of the party, and responsible for everyone. She was worried about flooding and didn't know if she should command they stop and seek shelter. She wanted to sound like she knew what she was doing, but she also didn't have the knowledge and experience Jemroth and Gareth had of this environment.

"Have ya visited the Enchantment Weavers before?" Lotte asked Gareth, fingering at a tiny bulge in her cloak that Claire knew concealed the exile's bag of treasures.

"No, but Jemroth did many years ago when he first came of age. I thought it was simply a courtesy visit on behalf of my father but now I know my friend's real identity I wonder. Maybe he visited to ask them about his future as sole survivor of House Domain." He frowned at a sack of supplies by his feet. "Hopefully, the Enchantment Weavers aren't too hard to find. Jemroth said they've moved location since he met them. A snowstorm ruined the roof on their building a few years back and they built a better shelter elsewhere."

Before they could lapse back into silence, Claire fished for a new conversation starter. "Why don't you tell us a story, Gareth? If we've got to sit cramped and cold, we might as well take our mind off things, don't you think?"

"Sure, what kind of story?"

"Stuff about the magical Houses," she said eagerly. "Grandfather said there used to be tournaments and great loves and friendships. It sounded wonderful."

"Well, obviously that was all long before my time, but I'm told it was." He thought for a moment. "How about I tell you about House Domain and House Ushanan?"

Lotte pressed her hands together in anticipation. Claire frowned as she saw the tip of a feather peep out from her neckline. She'd have to talk to Lotte later about keeping her mother's necklace better hidden, preferably inside her pouch.

"Do. It'll come in awful handy later," Lotte said, unaware of Claire's disapproving glance. She'd become almost as invested in saving Kelnarium as everyone else, keen to be part of grand events as an exile who redeemed herself in the eyes of the world and changed history. She'd told Claire as much when she'd snuck into her bedroom so Claire could tell her everything that had transpired during Lord Maellwyn's meeting four nights ago.

Gareth smiled, putting his hands behind his head, and lounging back against a silver threaded cushion. "House Domain were great builders," he began. "With their ability to move and manipulate earth and land, they were some of the best in Kelnarium. When we reach Kelnariat, you'll see that the Council buildings were made by magic. That's the only way they could be built all crooked and stay upright. House Domain baked magic into the bricks to ensure the building would never topple and whispered spells into the ground to ensure no matter what wild climate troubled the city, it would stay strong and stable forevermore. One of their best builders, Shasta, led the team in Kelnariat. There's a statue of him in the main city square. Selk had it pulled down, but Praine restored it."

He paused to adjust a blanket around his shoulders. "As to House Ushanan, it's a pity they don't exist anymore, or they could have diverted this weather away from us."

"What else could they do?" Lotte asked, wide-eyed.

"They could float on wind and cloud if they wanted. Once in a great battle between our House and theirs, they used their *learth* to send their entire army into the sky." He smiled ruefully. "My people had no chance. Our spells couldn't reach them that high up. They shot arrows onto us and we were soundly defeated."

"The Houses used to fight?" Claire asked. She'd assumed they'd stuck together, and it was Selk and the creation of the Rift that had changed things. She tapped the edge of Gareth's leather boot with hers. "I bet if it came down to a fight between you and I, it'd be a tie."

"Speak for yourself," he said with a laugh.

Lotte rolled her eyes. "I don't need no magic. I'd beat ya both with me hands tied behind me back."

"Sure you would," Claire said. "Anyway, answer the question Gareth."

"Yes, they fought. In the early days of Kelnarium, it was for the usual silly things people fight over, land, resources, prestige. That's why the tournament was created nigh on three hundred years ago by two lovers from Maellwyn and Dorran Houses. Ava and Cerse bucked convention in becoming bond mates, and they became outcasts for it, forced to live in a small cottage in the Silent Vale. They saw how many were killed in pointless feuds and went to their respective heads of House to offer their idea for a new way. They were mocked and jeered out of the community a second time. It took years of campaigning for the idea to get off the ground, but in the end, when the priests gained more power and too many hot-blooded men and women died fighting their own kind, it was agreed a tournament could help."

Before Claire could ask how long ago the priests had come to power and why, they shuddered to a halt. Seconds later, Jemroth poked his head through the fastening, saying apologetically, "You'll need to get out. I think we're bogged."

Claire hastily whipped a cloak around her shoulders and jumped outside, Lotte and Gareth close behind. She saw at once Jemroth was correct. She fell to her knees to start burrowing the sticky mud out of the way. Lotte did the same from the other side.

As rain sheeted down, Jemroth held out both horses' bridles to Gareth to hold, then joined them. "What're you two doing? Let me use my magic." He rose his voice. "Gareth, when I give the word, get Agea and Livia to move forward."

Claire clambered out of the way. She'd forgotten Lord Maellwyn had said Jemroth knew some basic *learth* spells.

Lotte tugged at her arm, pulling her off the road and under cover of trees a little ahead. "It's a wee bit drier here," she said, as Jemroth closed his eyes and said clearly, "Gnomes, if you can hear me, aid me now."

As they watched, the mud peeled away from the wheel like skin from an apple. At Jemroth's command, Gareth guided the horses forwards. Slowly, but surely, the cart groaned forward, out of the hole.

Jemroth straightened, wiping sweat from his brow, then called out to Claire. "The downpours slowed. Can you make a fire where you are? We might as well have dinner, hey?"

"I can do that," she shouted back, then turned to warn Lotte to step aside to make room for the fire, but the girl was already slipping away among the bushes. "I'll see if I can find rabbit," she called by way of explanation.

Claire had the fire lit in no time. She went to fetch dried fruit, nuts, hard biscuit and cheese from a sack in the cart, but before she did, she nabbed some lumps of sugar out of a sack and headed for the front of the cart. With affectionate smiles for Agea and Livia, she fed them each a sweet cube, loving the way their tongues nudged her palm. When they were done, she glanced at the road ahead. Patches of sunshine had broken out and the clouds were grey instead of black. Two jagged mountain tops broke the cloud-line, a thin strip between them climbing up and up and up as far as she could see. She swayed with vertigo just looking at it as someone touched her arm.

"We'll eat quickly and be on our way while the daylight holds," Jemroth said, assessing the sky. "The pass is one-way, steep and narrow. If we skid, we'll go off the side of the cliff." He looked down to comb his fingers through Agea's mane. "I've noticed you love horses as much as I do," he said. "When we're through the mountains and on straighter road, I'll teach you to drive the cart. It's a useful skill and I think you'll take to it."

Claire couldn't help but feel a little proud. Jemroth hadn't offered to teach Lotte or Gareth, almost like he respected her, like their love of horses bonded them. She studied his face. She'd had little opportunity to talk to Jemroth after the meeting with Lord Maellwyn; the man had stridden about with such purpose, giving off an air of not wanting to chat, so she hadn't waylaid him. This was the first quiet moment they'd had together.

"How old were you when you lost everything?" she asked tentatively. "I can't imagine it." Part of her wished she could tell Jemroth about Lotte's experiences. The pair had a lot in common, but it wasn't her story to tell and she couldn't risk the exile being found out and abandoned.

"I was eight," Jemroth said grimly. "Old enough to remember the faces of my mother and father and my little sister, Jes. Too young to hold onto much more. Domain Manor was hewn from black granite, I remember that, and if I concentrate, I can recall the bronze lanterns and the green glowing lights that lit up the passageways, but I never saw our gnomes or journeyed into the quarry that contained these." He tugged at his tunic to reveal his bronze disc necklace. "I only have this because Lord Maellwyn liberated one from a fallen member of my House on the battlefield. Traditionally, it was only when one was presented before our elemental leader, the Gofannon, and recognised as true Domain that we were gifted one." He shrugged. "But when everything was lost, even the quarry, our gnomes and the Gofannon himself, rules had to be broken." He ran a hand over his forehead. "If only my elementals would appear. Then I'd know I was worthy."

Claire put a gentle hand on his shoulder. She thought of the times she'd seen the Saura in the sky and how her own elemental leader refused to speak with her though she was the current leader of Dorran House. "I'm sure you are. The time just has to be right." She remembered Lord Maellwyn's fears that he'd somehow changed Jemroth's fundamental nature and wondered how much of that fear had rubbed off onto her friend. "I don't think anyone could blame you for having to live such a fragmented life. It must be difficult, feeling half Maellwyn and half Domain but if Lord Maellwyn hadn't taken you in and protected you as he had, your House would be extinct and who knows how lonely your life might have been."

"Oh, I know," Jemroth said. "I owe him a great debt. He became a father figure to me. He was sympathetic and understanding. If his son grows to be half the man Lord Maellwyn is, he will be a great ruler." He smiled, then strode towards Livia and began to unharness her. Soon, he'd led her undercover and given her a nosebag.

Claire followed him with Agea, then collected the food. She, Gareth and Jemroth ate standing up around the small fire as they waited for Lotte to return.

"Lord Maellwyn mentioned a contact in Kelnariat," Claire said, scrounging for a topic of conversation. "Tell me more about the capital and what to expect." She grinned. "I wouldn't want to give us away with an obvious faux-pas."

"That won't happen," Gareth replied with a laugh. "But to answer your question, my father established a safe house in Kelnariat in the lead-up to Selk going on the offensive against magical brethren. One of my cousins without *learth* ability took over manning it a few years back. That's Bron, who we discussed at our meeting. He's apparently met a woman recently with a lot of coin and friends in town so his monthly reports to the Maellwyns have been even more detailed and useful than usual."

Lotte reappeared, a bloody, partly skinned rabbit swinging from her hands. She and Jemroth busied themselves cooking it, wrapping its flesh around sticks, while Claire asked Gareth if Bron had heard anything about Marcus.

"We left before this month's report arrived," Gareth explained, "but the rumours are that Marcus was popular in Kelnariat. There's gossip he's added two original paintings to the Council Gallery. A great honour."

"That sounds about right." Claire couldn't help a grin, but then she remembered how much danger her brother was in. "Tell me more about Eidan. After he became a merchant, I mean."

"He created a large empire trading in silk and glass, Kelnariat's key exports. His workers loved him. You've seen the scars on his face?" Gareth looked at Claire inquiringly and she nodded. "He got them defending his workers and a common coach from brigands on the road. Whatever else I want to say about him right now, I can't deny he's brave. What else can I tell you? He had a lot of long-term relationships, but no bond mates and no children. They say that's why he was able to throw himself so passionately into politics – he didn't have family to hold him back. He met a rich merchant woman named Alaya more recently and the pair were close for several years."

"They broke things off not long ago," Jemroth said, looking up from his work on the rabbit meat. "Only in the last year."

"Yes, it was a big scandal," Gareth agreed. Alaya alternated between insulting him from here to Southern Kelnarium and begging him to take her back, which did her no favours. Eidan didn't rise to her bait. He's always been reasonable. In Alaya's case, some would say too reasonable."

"But not in ours," Claire said, as she accepted a stick loaded with rabbit meat from Lotte.

No one had anything to say to that. They got on with the business of cooking their rabbit, then eating it.

Claire held her breath as the cart travelled along the road as it picked its way through tricky terrain. Though they'd set out with the sun shining, within an hour the rain had returned worse than before and now the cart moved at a slow crawl. She clutched at Lotte's hand as lightning cracked somewhere close by. "Should we stop? Isn't this too dangerous for Jemroth and the horses?"

"There's nowhere to stop," Gareth said through white lips. "We have to push on and hope it dies down."

As though nature had heard him, the rain beat like a drum overhead, making their cart sway with the wind, its cloth covering flapping wildly. They were jostled from side to side worse than ever. Claire gripped for purchase where wood met oilskin as a loud bang reverberated through the floor.

Claire hauled herself upright as wind hit her with full force. The wooden back of the cart had un-latched, at the same time tearing the oilskin rear wall attached to it, giving her a view of wide, open sky and exposing them to the elements. Lotte held onto the side where timber met oilskin too, using it to make her way towards the open door, now banging back and forth in the wind.

"Stop!" Gareth shouted.

Claire lunged forward and gripped Lotte by the back of her dress to try and restrain her. "Gareth's right," she shouted to make herself heard over the wind. "If we get jerked around and you're not careful, you'll fall and hurt yourself if you're lucky, or go over a steep ledge if you're not."

"We can't leave it open," Lotte shouted. She gestured at sacks of coin and their precious supplies. She didn't need to explain herself. Without them they'd be in real trouble.

"At least let me hold onto you," Claire insisted as she grabbed onto the waistband of Lotte's skirt. Then Claire craned her neck towards Gareth. "Here. Take my other hand and grip the side," she shouted to him.

As the cart continued to bounce along, they made a human chain, Lotte clambering right to the edge of the open cart. She flung sacks backwards first, then lent forward to close the wooden back. There was another bump and twist and with a hideous creak, they began to tilt. Jagged rocks far below stared at Claire.

"Move," Gareth screamed, face whiter than Claire had ever seen it, as a snap cracked through the air. All the muscles on his arms rippling, he hauled Claire and Lotte backwards, as sacks of food and skins of water toppled into emptiness. "By the Nereus, we're going to capsize."

They threw their whole weight against the far side of the cart as Jemroth shouted, his words snatched away by the howling wind.

"I think the harness connecting the horses to us has broken," Gareth gasped, "and Jemroth won't be able to pull us back from the ledge with his bare hands."

Claire closed her eyes rather than look at the steep drop below. What an ignoble way to die. She pressed harder against the wood, praying that their combined body weight would set them right. They teetered, but stayed balanced, though Claire knew they were on a knife edge.

A minute or two passed, though it felt like an eternity. Then, she heard shouts and hammering hooves coming closer and closer. Perhaps they weren't finished quite yet. Voices called to Jemroth; boots thudded as the newcomers dismounted.

"We've got you," a gruff voice said from outside the cart. Her new allies tugged and swore. Time seemed to slow, and she thought that any second their rescuers would make a mistake and they'd freefall, then smash onto the rocks below. She'd counted to two hundred in her head when at last they were pulled back from the edge so that the wheels rested on the track. Pressing a hand against her pounding heart, she climbed out of the cart, half-stumbling in the mud.

"That was a close one. Good thing we came this way," shouted one of the rescuers.

"Thanks," Claire stammered, as whoever had spoken flung a dry oilskin cloak over her own woollen one. She could barely make her rescuers out for the heavy rain getting in her eyes.

An arm moved around her. "You've had a nasty shock. Come sit over here." The mysterious stranger steered her away from the precipitous edge of the road to the shelter provided by a boulder. She sat at its foot, letting her head rest against her knees for a few seconds, then looked up as Lotte and Gareth came to sit beside her, Lotte quivering and Gareth bent forward as if to regain his breath, his face partially hidden.

They were surrounded by a party of four men, all clothed in coarse brown robes covered with oilskin coats and hoods. One man held onto Agea's bridle and Claire was relieved to see her four-legged friend was uninjured, if scared. A fifth man helped Jemroth bind Livia's leg, his hood falling back to reveal a partly shaven head. Once he was done, Jemroth took back both horse's bridles, looking relieved that they were relatively unscathed.

"Why're you travelling this route?" asked a man who wore a wreath of twisted leaves and berries around his head beneath his hood. He appeared to be the leader of the group; aside from the fact that he was the only one wearing a wreath, the other men stayed behind him and looked at him with reverential respect.

Luckily, they'd come up with a cover story in case something should go wrong. "My sister in Corinth Village is due with child," Claire explained, keeping her voice as colourless and unmemorable as she could. She gestured at Jemroth. "This is my husband. We were told this way is fastest."

The man shook his head, not unkindly. "Faster, but more dangerous. I hope you didn't pay hard coin for such terrible advice."

"Lucky for us ya was here, Yer Holiness," Lotte said.

Claire started. Of course. These men were priests. No wonder Jemroth and Gareth were keeping their heads down. She tried to hide her trepidation as she forced a weak smile.

"Most never come this way, and those that do have magical blood in their veins." The head priest spat at the ground as Claire stiffened. "As to us," he shrugged, "there are twin shrines to Brighid and Lugh on the outskirts of Maellwyn Village. You can journey there with us if you like. We'll keep you safe and even say a prayer for your sister. There's more than storm clouds to fear in these parts."

"What do you mean?" Claire demanded through trembling lips. Somehow, she could guess what they'd say next.

"There could be Maellwyns about," he said, "and in the direction you're journeying, other magical types too. A nice woman like you wants no truck in their ways. You're best off with us."

She pretended to consider his offer. "Thanks, but all the same, I'm worried for my sister. I promised her I'd come as fast as I could. If I go back with you now ..." She looked away delicately, faking tears.

The man peered at her, then glanced back at Jemroth, Lotte and Gareth as though he sought confirmation. His eyes widened as he took in Gareth, who had looked up to follow Claire's conversation, still holding his cloak across part of his face.

"Who's that?" he pointed imperiously.

"My cousin," Claire lied.

The man strode over to Gareth and knelt, placing a hand under the boy's chin, and forcing him to meet his stare as Gareth's cloak fell backwards. "I know you," he said. "You can't hide your eyes and hair."

"Wha' do 'ya mean? I'm jus' as she says." Gareth put on a mild accent to make his voice rougher.

"No," the man laughed. "You're really not." He released Gareth and stepped backwards, his hand at his side, brushing against a small scabbard. He addressed his men. "This boy is Lord Maellwyn's son." The men cursed and spat.

Claire didn't know where to look or what to do. She hadn't thought someone would recognise them before they'd even got started.

"What if I am?" Gareth said, giving up all pretence of being someone else. "It's not a crime."

"Not yet," the man sneered. "How much difference is there between you and a blasted Dorran when all's said and done?"

"A lot."

"I beg to differ." The man drew his dagger. "There's no one here but your accursed party, none to hear you scream, and I'd be doing Eidan a favour." Around him, his men drew their own makeshift weapons. "You others will be free to leave if you swear off your immoral ways and cleave to us."

"No!" Lotte yelled, as he drew his dagger back. Jemroth called out to his gnomes and Claire could have sworn she heard Gareth shout for the Merpeople's protection.

The time for hiding was past. There was no point journeying on without Gareth. Claire silently called on the Saura and her salamanders to aid her, then concentrated on the leader's dagger, remembering how Maen had told her she could heat up metal until it burnt the skin. She muttered under her breath, repeating Maen's instructions to calm herself and make sure she got the spell right. As the captain of the priests dropped his dagger with a howl, the ground heaved up around him and his fellow priests, sludge splattering into their eyes and mouth. Claire met Jemroth's amused glance as a roar sounded overhead.

Next to Jemroth, Gareth had both his hands raised in the air as water hurtled over the mountainside. Before Claire could scream, a swirling current surrounded the priests, sending them tumbling downhill along the path, the raging river somehow skirting around Claire, Lotte, Jemroth and the two horses.

Claire got to her feet, crafting scalding flame to lick at the backs of the fleeing priests, as rockfalls also pursued them. "They won't forget us in a hurry," she said with a laugh, tasting brine, loam and smoke on her tongue.

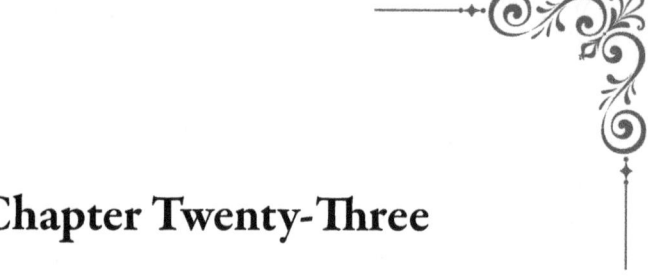

Chapter Twenty-Three

THEY MADE IT THROUGH the pass without meeting anyone else and on the fifth day of quiet travel began the steep climb up the Arras Ranges. With four days' worth of supplies having fallen off the cliff they were down to rations. It was hardest for Claire, Jemroth and Gareth, who had all used magic in fending off the priests. Their stomachs throbbed and they got snappier and snappier with each passing hour so that two days later, wrapped in every spare stitch of clothing they owned, they tumbled out of the cart, hungry, bruised and tousled.

Claire couldn't believe how flat it was at the top of the snowy mountain peak. Once he'd secured the horses, Jemroth pulled his hood around his ears and waved her forward as his breath misted. "The Enchantment Weavers lived in a lodge on that side when I knew them." He strode to his right, as the wind howled, and snowflakes whipped into his face.

Claire exchanged a doubtful glance with Lotte. She couldn't see evidence of life. Still, she made herself battle on, bowing her head against the wind. Within fifteen minutes, she knew their search was fruitless. There was no sign of buildings anywhere along the plateau at the top of the mountain.

"Let's think about this logically," she said, trying to ignore the damp seeping into her boots and the hollowness in her chest. "Where would you build a settlement on a mountain? Somewhere with proper shelter. Everyone, take a side each to look over and shout out if you see anything."

She strode over to the nearest mountain edge and made herself look over its precipice. A series of ledges rose to meet her and drifting from under them she thought she saw smoke. She narrowed her eyes, trying to pick out a route that would lead them down. White snow blinded her, but as she stared, an enormous salamander appeared, sudden warmth spreading through Claire from head to toe. "Help me find my way," Claire mouthed as the Saura's bulging eyes pinned onto hers, crimson and orange fire spouting behind the elemental leader's great head like a cloud. At last, the creature flicked a long molten gold tongue at two grey boulders, standing tall on the mountainside. Claire saluted the Saura, then straightened and turned back to the others. "I think there's a path," she called out. She fell to her knees and began to shovel snow aside, glad of her thick gloves. Her salamander protector had already vanished by the time first Lotte, then Gareth and Jemroth were helping too, everyone digging side by side.

Claire's fingers brushed against something hard. She was definitely onto something. *If I can dig deeper then ... yes!* Stone pavers peaked at her. Claire punched the air and silently thanked the Saura.

Soon, they'd uncovered the start of a trail. She waved at the others and they stopped, hands pressed into the smalls of their backs. "We'll need to leave the cart. It's too steep."

"What about Agea and Livia?" Jemroth asked.

Claire thought for a moment. "We can't leave them alone in a blizzard," she said. "They'll die. I know we could be about to walk a dangerous path, but there may be buildings further down the mountain that could shelter all of us. Besides, they're part of our party. We can't just abandon them."

The others nodded their agreement and ignoring thirst and her terrible hunger, she directed Jemroth and Gareth as they shoved the cart into a lee made by the peak, then they adjusted their coats and cloaks and set off on the near vertical path, each step painstakingly slow as they shoved snow aside.

Claire skidded numerous times and even fell over once, having to be half-dug out of the snow by Jemroth, but she was too excited at the prospect of warmth and shelter to do more than shrug and push on. She'd lost count of how long they'd trudged as her muscles strained and blinding white dazzled her vision, but at last they crossed under the ledges and Jemroth shouted, pointing ahead.

A sturdy rectangular building, a little like a small fortress, snow coating its domed cupola, greeted her. As they drew closer, she saw the structure was made of dark stone, almost the colour of rust. Claire led the way, the others falling into a neat line behind her. As she reached what she assumed was the entrance to the abode, she slid her glove off and rapped her hand against the heavy wood. No one answered, so she pushed against the door. It opened easily.

She stepped over the threshold, unsure what to expect. Would the Enchantment Weavers be friendly or standoffish, would they even be inside at all? She hoped so; she, her friends and the horses would die without new supplies soon. Someone had better be here after everything she and the others had been through to find them.

As her eyes adjusted to the muted gloom inside, the only light coming from lanterns hung from hooks on the stone walls and the flicker of flames up ahead, she couldn't help but draw in her breath. She'd stepped inside what looked to be a huge single-roomed shed reminding her of the old shearing sheds on some of the farms back home. The only real difference was that the roof of this place was a huge dome instead of the triangular shapes she was used to in Shale. To her left and right were wooden pens full of sheep, the ground strewn with hay, sweet-smelling and fresh. The sheep baas echoed in the cavernous space and Claire felt suddenly at home.

The brutal cold left her bones as the rest of the party entered the shed, Lotte hurriedly closing the door against the chill. The air was stuffy and smelt of lanolin and smoke, but it was also warm, and pleasant to hear the wind howling outside now it couldn't touch Claire.

Lotte clutched at her hand. "These people must be rollin' in coin to have so many livestock," she whispered.

Claire was too busy imagining she was back in Shale with her parents to register Lotte's comment at first. It took a moment to process. It didn't seem like so many sheep to her, but then she hadn't grown up in a fantasy world where wealth could be measured by the number of animals you owned.

A sudden cough echoed through the shed-like structure. Claire glanced ahead. She could just make out people at the other end of the building, the sheep pens and narrow walkway opening out into an open space. She nodded at Lotte, then Gareth and Jemroth, who was leading the horses, and strode further into the room until she stood before four women and four men all sitting on sheep-skin rugs with a wooden frame loom in their laps and wooden spindles and combs in their hands. Each was at a different stage of weaving a tapestry.

They wore grey tunics and dresses with a strange brown hat ending in frayed tassels over their heads. To their right, four tapestries hung from nails on the stone wall. Gareth looked at the nearest one longingly and Claire knew it had to be made by Marianne. It depicted a woman standing on a mountaintop, sheep surrounding her, as she stared down at the sea. Under the pictures, wood crackled inside an iron grate, the source of the smoke. Claire longed to rush over and stand as close as she could to it, but she remembered her manners in time as she sank into a curtsy.

"Welcome travellers," a young woman to the far left said without looking up from her work. Her voice was low but clear and she spoke with authority.

Jemroth cleared his throat as he stepped ahead of Claire, passing Agea and Livia's halters to her as he passed by. "We have come to ask for your help. I visited you many years ago to ask about my future."

"Ah yes, I remember. The hour is almost upon you when you must rebuild your House, Jemroth."

He bowed his head. "Even though my elementals haven't found me? Even though my *learth* talents are weak?"

"The Gofannon awaits you, young man, but you shall only meet the blacksmith when the time is right. The gnomes will find and lead you to him and he shall teach you all you would know."

"When?" Jemroth asked eagerly.

The woman smiled enigmatically. "Soon enough. Away from Maellwyn Manor, the gnomes will come to trust you, and when they do, we'll be ready. As you know, Lord Maellwyn entrusted us with Lord Domain's jasper ring and his green and bronze uniform. He had his friend washed and burnt, but he salvaged these things knowing their importance. They are to be yours. We have seen it in the weave." She paused, stopping to stare at Claire and the rest of her party. "But you have not introduced these strangers. Not all of them have the mark of a Maellwyn."

"No, good dame. Pardon my lack of courtesy. Beside me is Lady Claire, Suranne's daughter. She has come in Kelnarium's hour of need. Gwenivere, leader of the Dream Mages, had a second vision. The Rift explodes this year, taking all of Kelnarium with it, unless Claire closes it."

The woman continued to weave her wool. "I should not have thought you needed our help with her by your side. As I have told both Lord Dorran and Lord Maellwyn more than once, we cannot weave the Beast out of existence. It is not a person, and as such, we cannot touch it."

Claire took a step closer to the Weavers. "We didn't come for that, good dame," she said, adopting Jemroth's form of address. "We came because of Eidan."

"Why? He knows as well as the others what we can and cannot change."

"He's turned against us and attacked Dorran House," Jemroth explained. "Claire's grandfather is dead."

The Enchantment Weavers froze, their eyes boring into Claire's party.

"It's true," Claire said, shuffling from foot to foot under their intense scrutiny. "Eidan's put out proclamations saying that surviving Dorrans should be hanged, and I don't think it will be long until he turns on other magical brethren."

"How do you know this?" The young woman asked. "It is a serious accusation to make about the leader of Kelnarium."

"Because I was at Dorran Manor during the attack. I saw him murder Great-Uncle Aed." She clasped her hands. "Please, couldn't you weave Eidan a different future? One where he doesn't listen to whoever has fed him the lies that have led to this? I'm afraid for my brother, Marcus. We need him to close the Rift."

The woman began work again, as did the other Weavers. "What do you mean?"

"I had a vision. A member of all four Houses is needed for success. Somehow, Marcus has House Ushanan *learth* running through his veins, probably through my grandmother. If Eidan's madness means he kills Marcus, we're all doomed. Even if Marcus is alive, we'll have to go to Kelnariat to rescue him and could end up in terrible danger ourselves."

Lotte stepped forward before Jemroth could stop her. "Please," she begged. "Please help us."

The woman shook her head. "You don't know what you ask. Magic is dangerous these days."

"I know it is," Claire said, hoping she sounded braver than she felt, "and I wouldn't ask unless all of Kelnarium depended on this."

The Enchantment Weavers muttered amongst themselves, heads pressed together. At last, an old man spoke, his voice phlegmy. "We work our magic less and less these days." He waved towards the left corner of the shed towards piles of neatly folded cloth stacked from floor to ceiling. "This stuff isn't the stuff of people's lives. It is ordinary cloth we ask merchants to sell, but ..." He turned to the young woman who had first greeted Claire's party. "What do you think, Lyssa?"

Lyssa wove silently, as though she had not heard the older Enchantment Weaver. Claire thought she was thinking hard. At last, she looked up. "We don't have much choice. Even if you are mistaken in your vision, Claire, I can hear in your voice that what you say about your people being attacked is true. If Eidan turns on magical brethren, the merchants won't buy and sell to us and our little community will die. So yes, I will see if I can weave him a different future."

Lyssa got up and stepped into the corner of the shed, stooping to pick up something small. She returned with a spindle covered in strange carvings Claire didn't recognise. From Jemroth, Gareth and Lotte's expressions, it didn't seem like they did either. Lyssa sat and carefully picked up her loom again. Now Claire was watching closely, she noticed intricate flowers and vines carved into the frame of the Weaver's loom too.

Lyssa smiled at Claire. "This spindle and loom have magical properties. When I use them together, I can weave new lives and change destinies."

Before Claire could tell her how grateful she was for Lyssa's help, the woman's eyes became dreamy, like she was someplace far away and her hands speedily worked with almost invisible threads on the loom.

"Please. Take a seat," the old man said, gesturing to the skins laid on the floor by the fire as the other Weavers moved closer together to make room for the travellers. He smiled when Claire hesitated beside the horses. "Adair here will take care of your mounts. There's a spare pen and plenty of hay near the entrance to our abode."

Claire surrendered the halters gratefully to a younger Weaver who led them away, then sank to the floor.

"You must be weary after your journey and this will take some time," the older man said once Claire's whole party was seated. "There's fresh baked bread in a basket to the side of you. Help yourselves." He made a signal to one of the men next to him, who quickly rose to his feet.

Gareth snatched the bread, then tossed a piece to everyone, already cramming his into his mouth. Claire sat cross-legged on the floor, the silence and the stillness making her notice just how cold and tired and hungry she was. She ate three pieces before she felt sated enough to ask: "Why do you choose to live up here, so isolated from the world?"

"It's easier for us to live away from people. They do not like knowing that we can see and even change their futures, intimate secrets, affairs, unborn children, mortal sickness and even death. All of this we note and track. Before we sought refuge in the mountains, people offered payment if we'd interfere with those they hated by writing them awful futures. Some of us were tempted and did terrible things. Still other citizens accused us of changing their lives when even the smallest thing went wrong. It was easier, in the end, to stay away from civilisation."

Claire nodded her understanding even as she eyed Lyssa continuing to weave, the tapestry on the loom clear enough now for images to be seen. Claire could make out Eidan in its folds, him giving a speech to a cheering crowd, drinking wine in a chamber, sitting with her brother playing chess ...

Her breath caught at the sight of Marcus. Even just seeing him in woollen threads made him feel closer.

Now, Eidan slept, black all around him and then a riot of colours tangled together. Claire narrowed her eyes, trying to make out what it depicted. She saw its mouth first. With a small scream, heart thudding, she got to her feet. *It's only thread. Calm down.* Cheeks flushing, Claire made herself sit still.

Lyssa's eyes locked onto Claire's. Even as Claire watched, the Weaver's hand spasmed and the spindle fell from her fingers, landing with a thud against the paving stones. Leaving it where it lay, the Enchantment Weaver shuddered and came to stand before the travellers. "I'm sorry," she whispered. "I cannot change Eidan's future."

"What do you mean?" asked Claire.

"The Beast watches, blocking me from touching Eidan." She reached down to pick up her spindle, then tapped it thoughtfully. "I can try again with all of us, but I suspect the same thing will happen."

Claire let out a long breath. Perhaps they weren't beaten yet. "It would be wonderful if you could, but is it possible for you check if my brother is safe first, and can you weave him a future where he remains safe? After all, there's no future for all Kelnarium unless he's by my side."

"We can try. You'll have to sit quietly, and it may take a little longer." Lyssa glanced to the other seven Enchantment Weavers. "Maybe this time we should all work our magic." As one, her fellow Weavers got up to collect their specially carved looms and spindles from the same corner Lyssa had, then moved to sit again. "Let's begin," Lyssa said.

Fifteen or twenty minutes passed. Claire couldn't stop exchanging anxious glances with Jemroth, Gareth and Lotte. If Lyssa and the others couldn't change Eidan or Marcus's future, they'd have no choice but to head to a hostile Kelnariat as fast as they could, dangerous as it could prove to be.

Finally, Lyssa and the others looked up, shaking their heads. "Your brother is safe for now, but we cannot touch his future. The same shadow over Eidan is also over your brother."

"There's one last thing," Claire said softly, voice wobbling. "Can you see if I'm the betrayer the Beast claims? Will I save Kelnarium or destroy it?"

If Lyssa was surprised, she and her brethren hid it well. This time, it felt like it took an age for her and her fellow Enchantment Weavers to return from their vigorous weaving with an answer.

Lyssa's deep, grey eyes caught Claire's green ones. "I'm sorry, child. The Beast obscures all. Perhaps you will betray us. Perhaps you won't. We cannot tell one way or the other, but I can tell you this; there is no future for Kelnarium without you. The sign of the prophecy is upon you, even in the weave. If you do not close the Rift, no one else can."

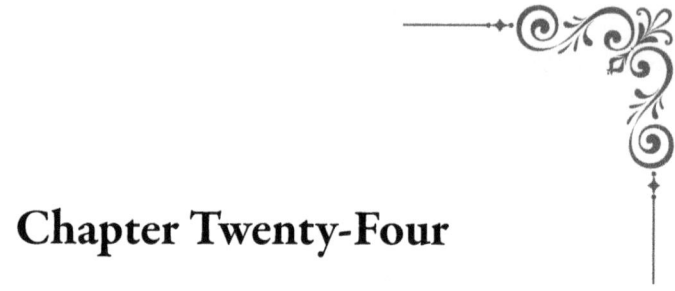

Chapter Twenty-Four

MUCH LATER, THE WEAVERS and travellers sat together in a circle around the grate, eating stew and drinking a boiling herb leaf brew. Claire wished they could get on their way, but the Enchantment Weavers had replenished their dwindled supplies with full drinking skins and bags of apples, dried meat and hard biscuit and it was dark by the time everything had been loaded into sacks to be hauled up the steep mountain path to where they'd left the cart. As Jemroth had pointed out to an impatient Claire, there was no point setting off in a snowstorm in the dead of night. They'd kill the horses for one thing. So she'd sat back in the thick woollen rugs and skins and tried to ignore the restless jitters that urged her forward.

At least the stew was tasty and warm. As she put the wooden spoon to her lips to catch the last dregs, Lyssa caught her eye. "You said you know which spell you need to close the Rift." There was a brightness to her expression that undermined her too casual tone.

Claire swallowed her mouthful of vegetables hastily. "I'd guessed before I had my vision that we needed to do the same thing Kelt did but in reverse. He shot hot and cold flames simultaneously into the sky." She paused. "I wasn't sure about where the other magical Houses fitted in, but I've had time to think on the road, and my feeling is that any spell of theirs will do as long as its next to mine and aimed into the heart of the Rift, because that's what happened the first time. Renegades from various Houses all stood beside Kelt."

"No," Lyssa said. "That's not what happened." Her eyes darted to the floor as the other Enchantment Weavers expressions darkened.

"What do you mean?" Claire cast her memory back to lessons with Lord Dorran. "How would you know? Granddad said you weren't involved."

"He never knew the truth," Lyssa said. "Kelt was an unusual man—and my friend." Lyssa got up and strode over to her pile of neatly folded tapestries, crouching to carefully sort through the heap until she pulled one out with a nod. She returned to the group, sitting next to Claire. "The Houses stayed away from us, but Kelt did not." She glanced at Gareth with a sad smile. "He was as hungry for knowledge as Marianne was. He knew he'd never rule House Dorran and wanted to find something else worthwhile to do, and so was a wonderful student."

"By the salamanders, are you saying you taught Kelt how to be an Enchantment Weaver?" Claire asked, shock making her voice quaver. She could tell from Jemroth and Gareth's wide eyes that this was news to them too.

"I made a dreadful mistake," Lyssa admitted. "I've told none but my own people. The shame was too great. Now it's time to break my silence." She took a deep breath. "I taught Kelt how to unite his *learth* with that of the other Houses and it is that action which made the Rift. Yes, he used his own spell, but he did it whilst drawing upon the strength of those around him, a skill I taught."

"But how can you know if you weren't there?"

"One of the men Kelt drew power from, one of his close companions, was untangled by Lord Dorran and taken back to his Manor to recover. He pretended he had no memory of how the Rift had formed, unable to admit his complicity in its creation and afraid that the curious would try to repeat the spell. Two months later, he rode to tell me of what had happened, knowing Kelt had learnt how to steer others magic from the Enchantment Weavers." She bowed her head, as though the weight of her story crushed her. "Kelt had assured him they'd win the battle without dangerous consequences. This man, Banna, wanted me to promise I wouldn't teach the skill to anyone else. I did so gladly."

"What do you mean by uniting *learth*?" Claire asked, her brain struggling with having so much new information to slot into place. It seemed everyone had played a part in Kelt's creation of the Rift – and that everyone felt responsible in their own way.

Lyssa unfurled the tapestry, then smoothed it out in front of her. Jemroth, Gareth and Lotte lent forward at the same time as Claire reached out to touch the bright colours.

"But it doesn't look like much of anything," Gareth said.

Claire had been about to say the same thing. The messy riot at her feet reminded her of modern art exhibitions. She traced her fingers against four separate lines of colour. One was bright red, another the blue green of the sea, yet another silver, and the last a rich brown, the colour of loam. As the lines continued, they wove into a complicated braid. "What does it depict?" she asked.

"The four Houses converging," Lyssa said. "They are woven of the same cloth and will return to the same when true peace spreads throughout the land. Kelt made me believe he had faith in this union, that he'd work hard for it. That is why I taught him how to combine with others in what we call a mind-mesh."

"I think I learnt the technique once. At least, I learnt how to connect with a Dream Mage's mind to get back to Shale?"

"Yes, it's the same skill. You see, we Enchantment Weavers and Dream Mages are tarred with the same brush. We're part of the same magical family, just as you and the other Houses are part of one community. Thanks to them, you are already halfway there."

Claire nodded, remembering Gwenivere telling her what felt like an eternity ago about *anam*, the magic of the soul. From what Lyssa was saying, *anam* was common to both Dream Mage and Enchantment Weaver.

She remembered Gwenivere's sharp rebuke, Maen's too, as she'd tried to draw on Rinn's magic to augment her own. "But I was told never to combine *learth* with someone not of my own House."

"Because of Kelt. The whole point of the *learth* dance as I taught it was to work together in joy and harmony, not with the rage he displayed that fateful day. Though some were willing companions in his mind-mesh, many more were dragged against their will." She bowed her head. "People like Lord Maellwyn's first wife."

Claire sat back on her heels. "You're saying that if I'm to have any hope of closing the Rift, you must teach me how to perform a mind-mesh, aren't you?" Her throat closed over and the air in the shed suddenly tasted stale.

"Not just you," Lyssa said. "If your vision is accurate and a representative from all four Houses is needed, then Lord Gareth, Jemroth and your brother will need to do so too."

Claire tried not to think about how carried away she'd been when Gwenivere, Rinn and Maen had tried to teach her similar. She'd enjoyed the feeling of power too much.

Gareth got to his feet, face blanched, no doubt thinking of Kelt. "Are you sure this is safe?"

"That's the wrong question," Claire said, pulling him back down beside her, even as her stomach sank. "The right one is can we afford not to learn. I suggest we have an early night and spend the next day or so practising. It won't take more than that, will it?"

Lyssa bowed her head. "I understand that you can't tarry long."

"You kind of need to picture your *learth* flowing through you without actually producing anything, so for example, I'm not looking to start a fire. You aren't trying to make water or rip up earth," Claire struggled to explain to a frustrated Gareth and Jemroth a day later as they stood near the grate in the Enchantment Weaver's home, the looms and spindles cleared away so the small party could practise their magic. Lotte stood with the other Enchantment Weavers, who silently watched proceedings with their backs to the wall. "Do the breathing exercises and picture *learth* escaping and when you open your eyes you should see the world differently." They'd been practising all morning, but so far, she was the only one able to get to the state you needed to connect with anyone else and there'd been a lot of cursing in the gnomes and the Mer-peoples name.

"Why don't we try with you first, Lady Claire? You'll be leading the mind-mesh spell anyway," Lyssa said, stepping forward to join the little circle.

Claire's stomach clenched. She'd known this moment would come, but she'd been delaying, telling herself it was more important to get Gareth and Jemroth up to speed.

Lotte smiled at her weakly. "It'll be fine." She moved to stand next to her, giving her hand a gentle squeeze.

"Thanks," Claire muttered. The exile had been unflaggingly cheerful, assisting Enchantment Weavers to carry supplies up the hill to the cart, petting the horses knowing Claire and Jemroth didn't have the chance to do so, and now was offering moral support from the sidelines. Claire was grateful as she closed her eyes.

Lyssa's voice came from her right. "Hold the image of those you seek to connect with in your thoughts and let the *learth* flow through you, but don't use it."

Claire gritted her teeth and did as Lyssa asked. She counted her breaths in and out until she reached ten. With each whoosh of air, Claire pictured *learth* escaping from her body in a steady stream. Thick mist stroking her skin and the familiar click in her ears told her she'd succeeded. Though her eyes were shut, she could see the shed in shades of bland grey, people marked out by colours rather than shapes.

"That's it," Lyssa whispered. "Connect with Gareth first."

Within seconds of picturing Gareth, Claire's mind hit against something hard with a painful clunk. Some kind of wall, maybe? It was silver-blue and rippled like sunlight dappling against reflective surfaces. Was this what Maellwyn *learth* looked like?

Out of nowhere, images of droplets, mist and waves crashing against a rocky beach spun past, faster and faster, until she felt sure she'd drown, her own flickering red *learth* mingling with the sparkling blue ocean.

-Stop. You're hurting me- Gareth's voice sounded in her mind.

Frantically, Claire tried to disentangle herself, but she didn't know how. The more she panicked and struggled, the more the ocean rose up and threatened to drown her.

-STOP- he roared.

With a hideous ripping noise, Claire fell away.

"You aren't concentrating," Lyssa's voce came from a long way off. "I told you to hover next to him, not dive through his defences."

"Sorry," Claire said aloud. "I didn't hear you."

She steadied her breathing. This time it took mere seconds to see her rope of red light extending into the air. Gareth's warm eyes filled her mind and before she could stop herself, she was disorientated, falling through a stream of blue and silver.

She saw a young boy crying for his mother as he imagined a beautiful woman with long dark hair standing beside him. She saw the same boy again, slightly older, standing barefoot in ocean waves as dolphins circled his feet.

She saw him a few years older again, periwinkle eyes and rough brown hair, his lips on a mermaid's.

-Get out!- Something tugged at the *learth* stream she'd created. Her spirit-self fell through an endless stream of colour. She couldn't stop the spiral. What was up and what was down? All blurred in the sickening tumble.

Marcus sat by Claire at the dam. He tossed a stone into the clay-coloured water.

"Why is our family so weird?" he asked, frowning at Claire.

"Don't know."

"Don't you ever wish we could be normal and... well... popular?"

She placed a hand on Marcus's shoulder as he shook his head in irritation.

"Hey. We've still got each other," she said.

Marcus smiled. "That's true. And we'll never stop believing in each other too."

Her stomach hooked as the memory shattered into splinters of painful light.

She was fourteen, behind the school toilets as boys and girls called out, mouths twisting in mockery.

"What's with your family, Claire?"

"Yeah, my mum says yours is a mad bitch."

"I hear your dad's a leftie toe-rag. No wonder you don't have money."

She cried and cried and cried.

-I'm sorry- Gareth's voice broke across the memory. -I'm so, so sorry-

She opened her eyes to clutch her head, rocking against the hard floor on her knees. Heat spread across her cheeks. She couldn't look up lest she catch Gareth's eye. He'd seen so much, and things that she'd have much rather stayed buried. It had been a long time since she'd thought about her first year of school, before she'd understood her family was different and friends were for other people.

"In the Gofannon's name, what happened?" Jemroth barked, no doubt dreading his own turn at the mind-mesh.

"We both lost control," Claire admitted, as a headache lanced across her temples.

Lyssa stood behind her, gently putting her hands on Claire's shoulders. "I had to separate you. Claire, next time, take a second to admire Lord Gareth's colours, hesitate before you dive into the mesh. You can't rush these things."

Claire nodded, begged for strength from the Saura, closed her eyes and tried again. This time, there was no sudden slam of contact. Bright shades of red soon twisted together in a tight braid and she concentrated on staying separate from Gareth's own cord twisting in the air. Sweat dripped down her face as she struggled not to get too close. Once she was confident she wasn't going to crash into Gareth's *learth*, she hovered closer and closer until at last their two cords connected with a gentle click. They were separate yet together at the same time.

-Praise the Nereus, I think this is working- Gareth crowed. -And it's beautiful. Look up-

As soon as he suggested it, their cord floated above the people hovering against the wall and the brazier and they sailed together through the roof. Their combined gaze took in a wide sky. Still higher they floated into a swathe of colour and light, the stars rising to meet them.

-What are you two doing? - Lyssa asked, but she was amused rather than upset. -Back to earth to join the chain with Jemroth, please -

For a few seconds, Claire flailed this way and that, but as soon as she thought of Lord Maellwyn's advisor, she flew back to solid ground, seeing Jemroth's golden brown and green cord waiting below. She imagined herself as a straight cord braided through with Gareth and Jemroth's colours. With a sudden click, she felt herself align with both.

Their combined power sung through her blood. In that moment, she knew no one could stop her; not Eidan, not the Beast, nobody. Finally, she was convinced that together they could win this thing.

Chapter Twenty-Five

THE NEXT MORNING, AT dawn, they departed from the Arras Ranges, a party of Enchantment Weavers heading the opposite direction to join with Gwenivere and the others at the Rift. Lyssa had explained she wanted to see the thing she had helped to create destroyed, and that perhaps it was time for the Enchantment Weavers long seclusion to end too. Claire and her party's own going had been slow down the rutted mountain track, but Jemroth had managed with skill and now, with the afternoon sun climbing higher, they were finally moving onto flatter, arable land. Soon, Jemroth would teach Claire how to drive the cart. There was just enough space on the wooden bench for Claire to sit beside him.

Lotte pulled back the curtain to look out on the countryside and farming hamlets. Peering over her shoulder, Claire could see towns in the distance, and even further off, a series of tall spires. Kelnariat. They'd be there by evening tomorrow, Gareth had said.

They trundled past a group of people camping along the side of the road. As they rolled past the tents, children ran behind them, their rags hanging in shreds as they called out. "Please! Something to eat."

Exiles. Claire dug into her pocket and flung some bread she'd been saving for a snack to the nearest child. Gareth didn't notice as Lotte's eyes flashed, but Claire did.

She reached out and squeezed Lotte's hand. "Before I leave this place, I'll try and change your people's situation, I promise. If I'm Kelnarium's saviour, I can't be brushed aside when I demand change. There'd be a kind of symbolism in it too. The exiles were punished for their involvement in the creation of the Rift, but if it's finished, doesn't that mean the punishment should end as well?"

Lotte looked at Claire, sad and angry and despairing all at once. "My people made a mistake and they've never stopped paying for it," she whispered. "It ain't easy for people to forget. When'll they forgive?"

"Very soon," Claire said firmly. "Trust me."

"What are you two whispering about?"

Claire had forgotten for a moment that Gareth was still inside the cart. She tried to smile but it came out more like a grimace. "I'm excited to be reunited with Marcus. I was telling Lotte about him."

Lotte continued to clutch at Claire's hand as she bit her lip. Small children ran alongside the cart in the mud and stared after the party pitifully.

"I meant to apologise again, Claire," he said, looking uncomfortable, "for seeing those memories when we combined *learth*. I can't stop thinking about how unhappy you looked. How could anyone treat you, a powerful magical user, in such a base way?"

"There's no hint of magic about me in Shale. I'm as ordinary as anything there. As for why they're mean – Dad told me that's what being a teenager is about. The worst years of your life, he said. But then, I think maybe he just claimed that to make me feel better. Our family isn't well liked back home." Much like the exiles. If she could change their lot, she would, and that might take changing one person's mind at a time. She might as well start with Gareth.

"Teenagers?" he asked, sliding nearer to her.

"Our word for a young person who isn't a child," Claire explained. "Anyway, as a teenager, you have to deal with constant whispers, gossip, judgment of people, because of things you have no control over." She thought of Liz and wished the pang of disappointment and shame would go away. Surely it had been long enough. "People are two-faced or do things that make no sense. It makes you feel hurt and humiliated, like you're dirty and unclean."

"But why would people want to make you feel like that?"

Claire shrugged, staring at the wooden floor. "My family was never what you could call conventional. Maybe kids my age were jealous of us or they were afraid because we seemed different." She nodded towards the children outside. "Back home, I might as well be an exile. Just as unfairly treated as they are."

"Unfairly treated?" he asked. "They're descendants of assassins. I'm sure your grandfather told you they deserve everything they get."

"He did, and I disagreed with him," Claire said. "Kids were nasty to me because my parents are seen as weirdos in Shale, not because of anything I'd done." Claire kept her voice low so that Jemroth, driving out the front, wouldn't overhear them. "You must ask yourself, Gareth, is it fair that you visit the sins of the parents onto the children? Doesn't that make you every bit as twisted as the exiles who murdered your people for coin?"

"That's not true," Gareth said, his voice rising. "You don't understand us at all."

Claire sighed as Lotte stared at nothing. "Maybe I don't, but I do know you'll only bolster their hatred for Maellwyn House and later, when they face better times, they'll turn on you. Better to show kindness now and create a better Kelnarium tomorrow."

Gareth looked unconvinced, but at least he was no longer angry, and she could tell that he was considering what she said.

Lotte caught Claire's eye. "Thanks," she mouthed.

They rode on in awkward silence for a bit, until Lotte broke the strained atmosphere. "About Marcus," she said, "What's the plan when we get to Kelnariat?"

"Yes, Gareth," Claire said, relieved that some of the tension in the cart had dissipated. "Let's go over the plan one more time." They all knew it off by heart, but it gave them something to focus on that wasn't their differences.

Gareth glanced at Lotte, then Claire. "As soon as we get inside Kelnariat, we'll find Bron and have a proper discussion. He'll give us all the information about Marcus; if he's locked up or not, where he is, and what the situation is in the city for Maellwyn House. If it's safe, he'll get me a token to get inside the Council Buildings without too much comment. Envoys get given a plain brass token to have free range of the Buildings. I've used them once or twice before, and I've never had any trouble."

But that was before farms and villages were supposedly razed by a magical House. Somehow, Claire didn't think things would be as simple as Gareth made out.

They fell back into tense silence, the cart moving slower and slower as the road widened and they had to share it with other traffic as it wound its way through fields sporting healthy crops and dotted with larger buildings, until Jemroth came to a sudden halt. Claire let the curtain fall back into place at the back as he swivelled around to address them.

"We're going to have to stop," he said, voice strained. "There's a shrine to Brighid up ahead and a bunch of priests are watching who says a prayer and who doesn't. It'll be better if we don't draw attention to ourselves. Claire, all we have to do is get out, keep our heads down, join the line and mutter something quietly when we get to the front."

Claire did as she was told, following Jemroth and the others even as her nerves jangled, her fingers closing over the coin she'd grabbed to give up in offering. As they joined the queue to get to the small wooden shrine, colourful flowers placed in heaps in front of it, she couldn't help but listen to the people in front of her, many muttering about Dorran House and criminals. She was thankful her hair was dyed and that she was dressed as a simple farmer's wife. She couldn't help but notice that for every person who seemed neutral or indifferent to the magical brethren of Kelnarium, there was another two or three spouting furious rhetoric worthy of a newspaper tabloid back home.

"Did you hear about Candmere Farm? Not a single person or animal spared. It's Kelt all over again," one woman said, her dark hair piled in braids.

Her partner shook his head. "It'll be a relief when Eidan declares the lot of them criminals. If a Dorran dared show their face near me ..."

Claire couldn't listen any longer. Things had better not be this ugly in Kelnariat or Gareth would have no hope of doing anything under his own name and then how would they get inside the Council Buildings to find Marcus? As she knelt in front of the shrine and took in the carved Brighid's full lips and wavy hair, the same way Jemroth had done before her, she said a brief prayer to the Saura, asking that Bron would have a solution to everything. If he didn't, her future wasn't worth thinking about.

They reached Kelnariat the next afternoon, Claire getting a chance to drive the cart with help from Jemroth before they'd stopped overnight in Heath Town. The talk had been just as ugly there, and all four of them had been glad to leave at first light, the strain of trying to pretend they were as anti-magic as everyone else at the inn awful. At least the weather was good. Jemroth had pulled half the cart's covering back so they could watch the passing landscape. As they meandered along the Teranth River, Claire took in the tall sailing ships and merchant barges caressing each shore, wishing she could be sunbaking on a deck without a care in the world.

Lotte grabbed at her arm. "That man's being fanned by a massive peacock feather," She laughed. "Can ya imagine?"

"When this is over, I bet we could ask for anything we wanted and Kelnarium would oblige," Gareth said, leaning over to join their conversation. "I'll ask for hot chocolate every day for a month and the softest cushions and I'll hole up in my bedroom and sleep. What about you?"

Lotte bit her lower lip. "Someplace to live. A real home."

"I thought you were visiting Dorran parts and had a home in Corinth Village?"

"I did, but I left it 'coz there's nothing left for such as me there," Lotte lied glibly. "I don't wanna live in a city, but a village is dull as stagnant water."

"Hey," Gareth considered, "maybe you could live with me at Maellwyn Manor." His shoulder brushed against Lotte's. "I'm sure you'd find something you liked doing there and there are always things happening." His face lit up. "I could show you the dolphins and the mermaids." He leant forward from the cart to tap Jemroth on the shoulder. "What about you?" he asked softly when Jemroth turned around. "What'll you do when this adventure's finished?"

"Hmm, I'd go on a pilgrimage to where my House lived and died. Build memorial cairns, try and find clues as to where the Gofannon has gone. As I've been driving the cart, I keep thinking I've half-glimpsed my gnomes, but then I blink, and the image vanishes. Without them, it may take a long time to find the remains of House Domain."

"What do your gnomes look like?" Claire asked curiously. "Maybe we could all keep an eye out for you. I know they don't like to appear before people who don't share their *learth*, but it's worth a shot?"

"Yeah," Lotte added, "and then we could help ya find ya home together when all this is over."

Jemroth sucked at his cheek thoughtfully. "All I have is second-hand knowledge from Lord Maellwyn and Lyssa and *they* heard descriptions from their Domain friends, but I'll tell you what I know: the gnomes were naked, their skin mottled brown and dark green all the better to camouflage into passing scenery. Their noses were the red of cherries and their cheeks were dusky. They had black bristly hair and beards and moustaches, and their eyes were black and dangerous. They weren't cute and cuddly, you see, or even human, but rather quick-tempered and violent. Not even fully trained Domain's found them easy to love, but they were ours." His eyes twinkled. "Do you three still want to help me find my place when we've closed the Rift and risk coming across one with a metal axe?"

"We're not scared. Sure thing," Lotte and Gareth chorused as Claire tried not to feel left out. It would be fun to stay in Kelnarium but she couldn't leave her parents wondering what had happened to her and Marcus forever.

"Quiet back there," Jemroth warned. "We've nearly reached the gates."

Claire pitched in with the others to cover the cart again, just in case, then scurried to the front to peer outside over Jemroth's head.

Up ahead the city's ragstone walls rose, dull and grey, the colourful silver and green flag of Kelnariat with silkworm and coloured glass stitched in the centre flying at every sixth crenellation. The walls rose up to five times her height, and beyond that she saw the tips of white and brown roofs, here and there tall grey stone buildings and in the centre of the tumble of structures, a gleaming building rising crookedly into the sky, with such height it made her stomach turn to think about being at the top of it looking down. Gareth noticed her stare and told her it was the main Council Building before lapsing back into silence. Sentries in leather caps and holding metal spears bound with blue ties strode along the walls.

Soon the wide road ended at a large stone gateway with two large doors pulled back and two circular and towering turrets at either side. Four sentries, all dressed in black hose and tunics with silver linked chainmail vests and steel metal boots waved them lazily through the checkpoint as soon as Jemroth explained they were visiting a cousin about to give birth. One even offered his congratulations.

Beyond the gates, the road narrowed and was paved with cobblestone and Claire couldn't help but jerk from side to side with the rough movement of the cart. The smell of horse dung, sewage and smoke was pungent as she peered outside at the narrow wooden town houses and the coloured silk coverings of market stalls. Chickens and children ran about in the mud. Washing hung on ramshackle balconies, ragged and worn.

Within twenty minutes, they were nearer the city centre, the skyscraper Council Buildings drawing ever closer. Claire could see they were arranged in a semi-circle with the main tower in the centre. Claire could make out its unnatural angles. House Domain had built the tower to look like a standing 'K' with the sheer sides revealing glass windows with people scurrying overhead like ants. The whole complex looked like its own mini city.

"The main building is where meetings and the important business of government takes place," Gareth explained under his breath. "Those other buildings are accommodation for the Council and for staff and Kelnarium's army and for guests too, each with storehouses and kitchens and laundries. If they needed to, they could stay self-sufficient for many months without ever setting foot in the rest of the city."

The townhouses surrounding these buildings were richer looking than those in the outer city, less ramshackle and with delicate carvings around windowsills and doors, and the markets were sparkling clean and the inns and shopfronts freshly painted. Yellow silks were draped across every house and market. Even over the pebbled street, swathes of the stuff swung overhead, tied from one end of the street to the other.

"We might have a problem," Gareth said.

Claire turned to him in surprise. "What is it?"

"The yellow flags indicate an important funeral is taking place," he said grimly. "It's going to take longer than I thought to get through to Bron. Look ahead."

Crowds of people blocked the road up ahead, all dressed in yellow silks and linens and cottons. A man dressed like the sentries at the city's entrance diverted traffic. Many travellers stood in huddles or gave up on pushing through, abandoning their vehicles and joining the throng.

Jemroth twisted around. "We'll never get through this. You might as well get out and see what it's all about."

Gareth flung long yellow scarves at the two girls. "Drape them around your shoulders. We always keep some spare for our visits to Kelnariat. Someone old and important usually dies when you least expect it." He grinned. "Thank goodness the silks didn't tip over the cliff with our supplies."

Once they were all blinking in the sunlight, Jemroth directed the horses and cart into a line to his right at the guard's orders, then changed into a yellow tunic himself.

"This is the main city square," Gareth whispered in Claire and Lotte's ears as they surged ahead with the roiling crowd. Soon, no one could move.

Surrounded by a sea of daffodil, saffron and lemon yellows, Claire stood on tiptoe, craning her neck to see to the front. The crowd ended at the foot of a dais, the main Council Building with its blue glass and dark-brown brick rising high into the clouds behind it. A strip of yellow silk hung from a window halfway up the building and shimmered all the way down to the platform. A group of men and women stood on the platform, and Claire's breath caught in recognition of the person standing in the centre.

Eidan waited behind a dark brown podium, the symbol of the city's silkworm carved into the front. He was surrounded by the eleven other Council members, who her grandfather had explained at a dinner that seemed long ago were elected from the major cities and towns across Kelnarium. All wore yellow from head to toe with their gold armbands of office visible. Out to the front and left of the platform, stacked high so the crowd could get a good view, a body lay wrapped in yellow cotton cloth tied to a wooden pyre by yellow ties. Wooden torches were alight all around the pyre and another guard with head bowed waited solemnly in front of the body.

Eidan raised his hands, palm upwards, in what she supposed was a greeting. He alone wore hose and tunic of plain black, a battered bronze badge pinned on the right side of his chest. As she watched, a young man was ushered up onto the podium beside Eidan, his clothing bright, his hair perfectly slicked. His blue eyes scanned the crowd.

Claire cried out before she could stop herself, recognising Marcus even at this distance. As Lotte turned to her and frowned, Claire bit her tongue. She'd known that Marcus was alive, but part of her hadn't really believed it, yet here he was. He wasn't in a prison cell or mistreated. He looked unharmed, and why was he standing next to Eidan like they were allies? Unless he was being forced to stand there? Maybe Eidan was going to do something horrible to him while Claire was forced to look on. The square was too packed to get closer to the front and she couldn't have a complicated discussion with Lotte, Jemroth and Gareth in this noisy crush. She'd have to watch and wait and hope.

"My friends," Eidan began, "We gather today to acknowledge the death of Rinn Taccala. She was one of us, an ally to me, a friend of this city." The crowd cheered, even as Claire went cold. She hadn't expected the important dignitary to be Rinn. Tears threatened to spill as she remembered the kindness of the Dream Mage. "Yes, friends, she will be sorely missed," Eidan went on.

"This can't be good," Lotte muttered into Claire's ear.

"Lotte's right," Gareth murmured. "If Eidan is giving Rinn a state funeral then it's certainly not out of a sudden sense of decency or kindness. She wasn't important enough to get this kind of attention. He's up to something."

He fell silent as Eidan gesticulated at the air to emphasise his next point and people in the crowd gaped up at him, hanging on to his every word. "But you do not yet know the extent of her sacrifice. Many of you may well be asking yourselves where the Dream Mages are, her colleagues, her friends and her family?" His voice took on an incredulous tone. "Surely her own kind would be here, at her funeral, surely yes, citizens?"

Whispers broke out in the crowd.

"They have made themselves scarce with good reason. Rinn Taccala was foully murdered by her own brethren and Dorran House in a conspiracy designed to silence her because she disagreed with innocent people's livelihoods being destroyed. Rest assured that all shall be revealed in time – I shall not let this matter rest."

The crowd gasped as one, followed by fury that rose like the buzzing drone of bees. Claire was glad that Gwenivere and Tarn had not tried to enter the city. If these people had spotted them now, she felt sure they'd have torn them apart with their bare hands.

"And so, my friends," Eidan proclaimed, his voice rising, "over the departed soul of Rinn Taccala, we proclaim the Dream Mages criminals. Some fifty in Kelnariat are imprisoned and awaiting execution. As to their leader and her small party that carried out the deed at Dorran House, they are outlaws and must pay the price. Indeed, the same price that poor, honest Rinn was forced to pay. That of death to be meted out on sight. And what of Dorran

House, you might well ask? I and my faithful guards took care of them in Rinn's name and they are finished. I am honoured to have been able to make our lives safer."

As Eidan stretched his arms out to the crowd, they began to cheer. The sounds of their chanting filled Claire's ears and made her gut twist, their anger as potent as any intoxicating drug.

"Eidan! Eidan! Eidan!"

Marcus grasped Eidan's hand and together they stepped forward, raising their arms to the sky. Then, Eidan indicated that the guard should approach Rinn Taccala's pyre and the people sighed as the funeral process returned to normalcy. Eidan intoned something as the guard flung perfumed oil over Rinn's body and set her alight, thick, sweet smelling smoke coiling overhead.

Many of the dignitaries in the front row shuffled impatiently, like they were bored now the grandiose speech was over. Claire's fingers itched to slap someone, *anyone*. This wasn't a political game, even if Eidan made it one. Rinn Taccala *mattered*. Claire's tears blinded her. She tried to shrug Gareth off as he clutched at her arm.

"Listen. We have to come away," he whispered.

"Why?" Lotte asked. "Things was gettin' mighty interesting."

"We have to get to Bron," Gareth explained. "Don't you see? Eidan condemning the Dream Mages on top of the anger towards Dorran House already spreading through Kelnarium will make things more dangerous for all of the magical community, including Maellwyn House. By the Nereus, things are far worse than I thought."

Chapter Twenty-Six

CLAIRE FELT CLAUSTROPHOBIC as their party and even the cart, Agea and Livia were dwarfed by narrow, tall houses and shopfronts, uneven cobblestones leading them on to the Maellwyn safe house. She'd hurriedly told the others about Marcus, but they were every bit as confused as she was as to why he was on the podium with Eidan. There was nothing for it but to find Bron and hope he could explain everything. Wooden footbridges criss-crossed overhead as they headed closer to the Teranth River again, along the way small stalls popping up run by old women, heads covered in dark shawls. Many of the women stared after Claire's party, dull-eyed.

"We could afford nicer accommodation than Bron's," Gareth explained, "but we didn't want to draw attention to ourselves by purchasing a grand house, which would have been talked about."

The stench of refuse, open sewers and old meat assaulted Claire's nostrils as they turned onto a dark street where cracked signs swayed in the gentle breeze, advertising this apothecary or that grocer. Further down, the wooden houses had been built by the Teranth River's edge, in front of which tiny rowboats were tied to wooden posts. A girl a few years younger than Claire leapt into her boat, full to the brim with stained brown packages, so that the prow bowed into the river at a dangerous angle, and began to row under a stone archway to the busy open water. No doubt the primary trade of such small boats was taking supplies and wares to the bigger boats.

Jemroth halted in front of the oldest, most ramshackle dwelling on the street. The windows were scratched and dirty and the wooden walls had been slapped together with little care so they bent at odd angles with gaps here and there.

On the right-hand side, a tiny shed had been added. Jemroth unhitched the horses and headed straight to the shed, muttering to them affectionately as he slipped a hand into his pocket to draw out a few slices of dried apple. Claire couldn't help a grin as he fed the pair his treat. The man loved horses as much as she did.

Gareth signalled that Claire and Lotte should follow him to the front door, where he tapped a scratched bronze knocker. Claire couldn't help but glance back at the shed where Jemroth had left Agea and Livia and now tugged the cart through the door, thrusting a large oilskin over it to shield it from view and from the elements. Though travelling inside hadn't always been comfortable, she'd gotten used to its known quantity.

She forced herself to concentrate as the door opened.

"Come through, come through," a man's voice greeted them from inside, a dull navy cloak flung about his shoulders so that his features were hidden. "Quickly."

Claire had barely put both feet over the black, dirt-stained threshold before the door slammed shut behind her. The man pulled back his cloak to reveal someone of about middle age with salt and pepper curls. His cheeks were ruddy and salt stained, but his brown eyes sparkled with sudden joy and in his smile, Claire could see a small likeness between him and Gareth. This had to be Bron.

"Thank goodness you came here straight away. The city's a powder keg."

"We know, and I think I speak for all of us when I say we're mighty pleased to see you," Gareth said, as Claire glanced about the bare room, noting it was bare but for a table and some rickety chairs at its centre and a set of steep stairs leading to the next level. "We got caught up in Rinn's state funeral."

"Take a seat," Bron said, shaking his head. "The whole thing's a bad business."

Claire and Lotte followed Gareth to the table, already set with pewter tankards and a chipped jug. She peered inside to find a straw-coloured liquid, the same colour as the fine sand that lined the floor. She poured some in her tankard and took a cautious sip. She didn't much like the taste, but it did send warmth shooting through her. The door scraped quietly as Jemroth slipped inside and joined them. He sat at the table with a smile, expelling an audible sigh of relief.

When everyone had poured themselves a drink, Bron folded his arms in front of him. "You'd best head straight home."

"We can't do that," Claire said. Hadn't Lord Maellwyn explained things to Bron in his letter? "Don't you understand our urgency?"

"You must be Lady Claire," he said smoothly. "Lord Maellwyn was not foolish enough to commit everything to paper. He merely told me you needed to come as part of Gwenivere's prophecy, but Kelnarium isn't in terrible need yet and surely whatever you need to do isn't so important you'd risk everything to stay?"

"We don't have a choice," Claire said, realising Bron didn't know about Gwenivere's second prophecy. "I was summoned to Kelnarium because Gwenivere foresaw that the Rift will explode this year unless I can close it. If that's not Kelnarium's greatest hour of need, I don't know what is." Bron's face turned a sickly grey but he didn't interrupt her as she pushed on. "And I can't do it alone. I need Gareth and Jemroth to use their magic, but I also need my brother, Marcus, too. We need all four elemental Houses and—"

"Wait," said Bron, looking disbelieving. "Did you say all four Houses? How, when there are no survivors of House Domain or House Ushanan?"

Jemroth cleared his throat, leaning forward to show the metal disc dangling from his neck. "Lord Maellwyn rescued me from the battlefield thirty years ago and rebadged me a Maellwyn, but I am of House Domain. I apologise for the lie."

Bron stared at him in surprise.

"And we think Marcus is part House Ushanan through my grandmother, Lady Dorran," Claire continued impatiently. "So, you see, we can't leave Kelnariat without him."

Bron wiped sweat from his brow, and Claire knew he was about to deliver bad news. Her imagination jumped to Marcus in danger and she took a drink to steady herself.

"The Nereus have mercy on me for being the bearer of such ill tidings, but Marcus is one of them now," he said.

Claire blinked, then rubbed at both ears, sure she'd misheard. "I'm sorry. What did you say?"

Bron turned pitying eyes her way. "Him and Eidan are thick as thieves. He's by Eidan's side at every public event, usually ones criticising magical brethren. And what's more, he's proud to be there."

Claire felt her mouth drop. She couldn't deny the truth of Bron's words. Hadn't she and the others seen Marcus at Rinn's funeral a mere hour or so ago? He hadn't looked bothered standing beside Kelnarium's leader. Her stomach lurched.

"How long has this been going on?" Gareth demanded. "The anti-magic stuff, I mean."

Bron thought for a moment. "About a week after Marcus showed in Kelnariat, things heated up, for he and Eidan have been profuse in their harsh criticism of Lord Dorran and his entire House."

"You can't be suggesting Marcus was the one behind Eidan's change in attitude towards us?" stated Claire, incredulous. *It's impossible*, she thought. But then she remembered how everyone in Dorran House had said Marcus hadn't fitted in. *There must have been a misunderstanding and Marcus must have been angry and upset when he met Eidan, and whoever had been in Eidan's ear had gotten inside Marcus's too.* Nothing else made sense.

Before she could say so, she heard the door open for a third time. She swivelled around to see a feminine figure in a brown skirt and a stiff white yoked shirt, a long navy coloured veil framing her heart-shaped face and covering her hair.

"Ah, my wife," Bron said, filling another cup. "When she's not attending to business, she's got her ear to the ground for Lord Maellwyn."

Gareth had mentioned his cousin meeting a rich woman, though she didn't look wealthy with her plain spun cotton clothing. Claire watched her cross to Bron's side. She pulled the wimple back to reveal lustrous brown curls. Bron stretched out a hand to cover hers where she rested it on the wood. "My clever Alaya, what news today?"

Gareth and Jemroth's eyes widened. It took a Claire a second to understand why, but then she remembered. Alaya was the name of Eidan's ex-girlfriend. Yet neither Gareth or Jemroth had mentioned her being the same person Bron had married. She exchanged knowing looks with Lotte. She'd bet hard coin and a few precious Dorran salamanders into the bargain that the Maellwyns hadn't known about Bron's liaison with someone so closely affiliated with Eidan. She suppressed a shiver. Hopefully Bron knew what he was doing.

"The public funeral of Rinn Taccala has set everyone upside down," Alaya replied. "First, the villages and farms destroyed and now knowledge that the magical brethren turn on their own? It's no surprise to me that fewer and fewer speak kindly of your kind and those that would fear reprisal. Soon, we shall have no allies left in the city." Her beautiful blue eyes darted about the table. "Is this Lord Gareth and his party?"

"Yes." Bron quickly introduced everyone and filled his wife in on what they'd discussed so far. Claire could see Gareth was just as uneasy as she was, his eyes narrowing as they locked with Alaya's.

"Do you know who's behind Eidan's sudden change of heart towards magical users? His actions don't make any sense. Someone has to be using him for their own ends, but what are they?" Claire asked, eager to dispel the negative undercurrents in the room. "It sounded like you thought it was my brother earlier, Bron."

"Not necessarily. For one thing, the little jibes against magic began before Marcus arrived in Kelnarium; Eidan's soldiers diced in the popular taverns and made small comments, or gossiped at market stores, which was worse, for shopkeepers spread it around faster than soldiers could. Council servitors talked of a changed mood in the building, and there were public comments against the Dream Mages from Wallis and Heath, though I took little notice of them, for they have long bleated to Eidan about a desire to return to the days of Selk. No, this began before Marcus."

"But with who?" mused Gareth as Claire slumped back into her chair. "Eidan was a dear friend, not just Kelnarium's leader."

Bron exchanged a tired look with Alaya. "We don't know. It doesn't matter how often I pump my contacts for information or Alaya flings coin and ale everywhere, no one can say what caused Eidan's change in policy. We have almost started to believe that he has turned on magic of his own volition."

"That's absurd," Gareth said. "Unthinkable. For that to happen, he'd have to be mad, and we've seen no signs of it."

"You should not trust Eidan overmuch," Alaya said bitterly. "I, of all people, know this. You don't like me," she said, fixing her gaze on Gareth. "No doubt you've heard the rumours of how I pined after Eidan and think me a troublemaker who'd be better off keeping her mouth shut. Those were lies to make me look the fool instead of him."

"But he did ditch you," Claire blurted without thinking.

Alaya glared at Claire. "*Excuse* me. *I* 'ditched', to use your peculiar phrasing, him. He was a very charismatic man. When he fixed his attention on me, it felt like I was the only person in the universe that mattered, but as time went on, he cared for me less and less. It was as though I was someone half real to him, and when his mind wasn't elsewhere, and he saw me, I no longer pleased him. I had to leave."

"You think we shouldn't trust Eidan because of how he lied about your relationship?" Jemroth asked.

"He's a deep man. He tells people what they want to hear, all the while pushing them closer to his aims."

"Which are what exactly?" Lotte asked.

"I don't know." Alaya bit her top lip. "To be honest, something changed within him while we were together. In the end, the things that had appealed to him, that brought him pleasure, held nothing for him anymore. I was afraid to find out why and I hadn't yet met Bron so I didn't realise how important knowing such information would prove to be. At the time, I just wanted to get out with my life intact."

"The way you talk about him ... it's like he scared you," Claire said. "What happened?"

"He never touched me, never hurt me, but," Alaya's brow furrowed, "there were times when I woke at night unbeknownst to him to find him looking at me in a way that frightened me more than I can say." She put a hand to her throat. "And in those times, I thought him capable of strangling me. Those flashes I saw, they became more and more frequent, and I knew that if I asked or said something he didn't like ..."

Bron reached out to wrap an arm around her shoulders. "Don't think of it, love. That part of your life is done." He turned back to Gareth and Claire. "We must figure out what you'll do next."

"I need to get into the Council Buildings to see Marcus," Claire said. "I'm not sure he even knows I'm in Kelnarium. I can't see him being happy that Eidan intended to kill his sister, no matter how justified Eidan felt he was. Given they're still friends, Eidan must have kept my presence in Dorran House from him."

"His mind is made up," Bron said firmly. "You will never change it."

"I'm family," Claire said. "I'll explain everything that's happened, and he'll see he has no choice but to continue on with us. If nothing else, he can't get home without me and Gwenivere."

"Claire's right," Gareth said. "She has to try at any rate, 'else we're all doomed. Yes, it's risky, but what choice do we have?"

Bron sighed. "If your minds are set, then I bow to your will. I'll write to the Council today notifying them of your arrival in the city. When they send through the token, you'll have access to the Council Buildings. At least Eidan hasn't named Maellwyn House as public enemies. Not yet anyway."

"What about accommodation?" Gareth mused. "We don't want to compromise the safe house."

"I don't think you should stay at the emissary accommodation. There are too many prying eyes," Bron said. "I'll book the Spotted Duck, an expensive inn near the Council Buildings. The token and any message the Council may wish to send can go there. If you need Alaya or I, we have our own house in the same district. Ask the innkeep and he'll tell you the address. Are we agreed?"

Everyone nodded and Bron rose to fetch paper and ink, leaning forward to shake everyone's hand. "For goodness sake, be careful, and may the Merpeople grant you good luck." His expression told Claire he was convinced they'd need it.

Chapter Twenty-Seven

THEY HURRIED TO THE Council Buildings, Gareth nervously fingering the gilt-edged invitation in his pocket, alongside the silver key for their luxurious accommodation at the Spotted Duck. There was to be a grand reception hosted by Eidan tonight, and Kelnarium's leader had invited the Maellwyn party, the letter arriving alongside a generic Council token. Though none of them were too confident about walking into what felt like the lion's den, there wasn't really any other option to get to Marcus, and offending the Council wasn't a sure path to success in anyone's book.

Gareth and Jemroth wore white linen tunics to the knees with cobalt cloaks over the top secured at their shoulders with the Maellwyn silver brooch and silver circlets in their close-cropped hair. Claire smoothed down her own plain cotton dress, a silver wave embroidered on the chest to indicate she belonged to Gareth's House, then checked her braided bun stayed in place. She glanced at Lotte, who wore matching Maellwyn attire and gave her an encouraging smile. Lotte wasn't used to wearing such expensive fabrics, but it was necessary for their plan to succeed. The idea was that while Gareth and Jemroth cautiously socialised, Claire and Lotte would attend to them, fetching them drinks and food, while keeping their eyes and ears open for Marcus. At the first sign of trouble, they'd all head for the Council Building exit and the safe house.

Gareth led the way as they neared the semi-circular Council Complex. Now that the square in front of the complex wasn't crowded, Claire saw that a high barricade ran around the buildings, made of smooth, thick glass. Her scared reflection stared back at her as they approached it.

"Is this more magic?" she asked Gareth.

"They say that Shasta of House Domain cast a spell on these walls, yes. They'll never shatter. Glass is one of the main trades of Kelnariat, so it's a symbol of the city too."

He indicated she should follow him to a point in the barricade just ahead, where pricks of light showed through a thin rectangular line guarded by another two sentries. They barely glanced at the party as Gareth held out his envoy token and the invitation. The man checking over the paperwork frowned but handed them back and waved them through.

"A Maellwyn envoy?" Claire heard one sentry say, as they touched the glass door and it swung open to let them pass. "Good luck to them. I suspect it won't be a warm welcome they'll receive from Eidan."

Claire suppressed a shudder and walked a little quicker. She knew their plan was risky, but they had no choice but to push on with it.

A red brick path led them straight to the main Council building where a plain brown carpet had been placed at the entrance, a black spider spinning a silver web embroidered across it. Men and women wearing colourful silk garments and bright jewellery entered the structure alongside poorer folk in their best homespun cotton tunics and hose or dresses. There seemed no method as to who had received an invitation, as disparate group after disparate group was waved through the large purple painted door.

"I didn't realise so many were coming to tonight's event," Gareth said as he handed over his token and invitation for a second time to a man in uniform who was checking guests of a list.

The man with the guest list smiled. "Eidan's invited a huge cross section of the city to his reception. You mustn't have been here long if you don't know Eidan likes to give a warm welcome to all classes and all types." He looked up, taking in Gareth's attire, his eyes resting a few seconds too long on his silver badge. His mouth twisted as he turned away. "Go through. Jalarch here will take you to the Ballroom."

A young boy in black silk scurried forward, bowing first to Gareth and then to the rest of the party. Claire tried not to feel like the lurid door was an omen as the boy led them through, terror emanating from him like he thought Gareth would turn him into a frog at any moment.

No one spoke as they hurried through corridor after corridor lined with thick and plush carpets, paintings and tapestries. Claire almost forgot her purpose as Kelnarium's history and culture passed her by. It all looked so interesting; she could have spent hours wandering through the building. She lost count of how many elaborate and steep staircases they took and sharp corners they turned and only realised they were in the upper part of the building when she glanced out of one of the glass windows. Her head spun at the height they'd climbed.

With a final right turn, the boy, Jalarch, led them to a gold embossed leather table, with a harassed, bald man, and a wide entryway just behind it. Gareth proffered the invite to the man who waved them on at the sight of Eidan's seal with a pained sigh.

As Claire stepped inside the Ballroom, she could barely hide her awe. She'd never seen such a large room – she estimated that there were as least two hundred people inside, but she could imagine another hundred fitting easily. Noise threatened to overwhelm for a moment as loud conversations and raucous laughter echoed in the open space.

And as to the aesthetics? She was stunned by the room's beauty. The marble floor was chequered black and white like a chess board. Tall and wide colonnades supported the ceiling, which had been painted with images of gold-rimmed clouds, flocks of colourful birds, trees with vines in a forest of wild creatures and at the very centre of the ceiling, an old woman with bark for skin reaching out a mottled hand to grasp at a man with clear brow and a gold armband, the man seeming to stare out at Claire, self-assured and calm.

Around the edges of the hall, long tables had been joined together and groaned with all kinds of delightful food; fresh fruit in bowls, platters and platters of every kind of meat imaginable, each with their own fancy hand-painted ceramic jugs filled with gravy. Then there were salads and roasted vegetables in silver trays. And at one end of the room were tables loaded with cakes and jellies and ice creams and sugar spun sweets. Servants scurried in every direction, replenishing the tables when they threatened to get low and proffering wine and ale to anyone whose cup looked empty.

Claire made herself take a breath. She couldn't stand here gaping. Where was Gareth? He'd explained to her and Lotte that their role was to fetch food and hold drinks for him and Jemroth. She glanced about, spotting Lotte shooting her warning looks a few metres ahead and rushed over, keeping her expression blank and respectful like the other servants bustling around her. She'd just reached Gareth's side when a man with the symbol of the city stitched on his tunic thumped a wooden staff against the sparkling clean marble. "Councillor Eidan, I present to you Lord Gareth Maellwyn and his father's trusted advisor, Jemroth."

Eidan stood in a semi-circle with his councillors. They cast hard, steel-like glances at Gareth. Two of the men, dressed in garish red and green silk tunic and hose and with well-trimmed beards and oiled moustaches, looked at Gareth with outright hatred. Claire wondered if the pair were the councilmen Gwenivere and then Bron had mentioned, Wallis and Heath. One of the female councillor's noticed her frank stares and raised a brow.

Claire's chest pounded as she remembered to keep her eyes downcast. A real servant wouldn't be so impudent. Out of the corner of her eye, she saw Eidan's gaze slide past Jemroth, Lotte and Claire to rest on Gareth. With a fruity laugh, he raised his golden goblet to the group. "Welcome to Kelnariat," he said. "It's been too long since a Maellwyn has graced our halls."

"I have come to Kelnariat remembering your friendship with my family," Gareth said with a careful bow. "And trust everyone tonight knows we are not of the same ilk as Dorran House."

"It's evident you share nothing in common with the recalcitrants I have been forced to deal with," Eidan said, but a note of faint menace underlay his words. His smile turned cold. "But you must be hungry. Let one of your servitors fetch you a plate so we might talk."

Gareth inclined his head and stepped forward. Taking that as her cue, Claire shuffled over to the nearest table, selecting a range of meats and vegetables and a handful of salted nuts for Gareth to nibble on. She returned to stand unobtrusively next to Gareth, holding his plate and his goblet until he wanted either.

"And how is your dear father?" Eidan was asking.

"He is well, Councillor."

"Interesting." He turned to his other Council members, blocking the Maellwyn party from the rest of his conversation as it flowed on without them.

Claire could tell from the way Gareth's lips had thinned he wasn't happy about the insult, but he turned and strode casually to the far end of the room, Claire trailing along behind.

He eased into a colonnade, then held out a hand for his drink as she inched closer. "Did you see the expressions on Wallis and Heath's faces? They could have melted lead."

"They were the ones in the garish colours?" Claire guessed.

"Yes. Wallis is from Heli City, an hour or so ride from here and Heath is the next town along, Potsmat. Both are too close to the Riftlands for comfort and they've taken their anxiety out on us, needing someone to blame to keep their people from rebelling."

A tall man and woman whom Claire recognised as Councillors brushed past in a swirl of blue and purple silks, heads bowed in animated conversation.

"That was Pilla from Cora Town and Saskia from Reeve Town," murmured Gareth. "Both are moderates. Their prosperous districts are in a hamlet near Maellwyn Manor and they enjoy roaring trade with us and with Maellwyn Village. It isn't in *their* interests to make us enemies." Gareth grinned, "They've got Maellwyn blood a few generations back through a great-great grandmother and a great-uncle respectively. I wouldn't be surprised if they were discussing ways to make sure Eidan stays neutral towards my people."

Claire blinked at the sudden onslaught of information. "This is all very interesting, Gareth, but we're getting distracted. I need to find Marcus. He's got to be here somewhere. Can you start circulating the floor and I'll keep an eye out." The quicker she could get in her brother's ear and explain the whole situation, the quicker they could get away from the city and its tangle of politics.

It took her and Gareth three or four turns about the crowded hall, and Claire's head stuffed full of myriad new facts about councillors and their complicated allegiances, before they found Marcus ensconced in a knot of men and women dressed as brightly as parrots. She and Gareth edged closer to their conversation, both pretending to admire the patterned rose and gold coloured wallpaper behind Marcus.

Claire had to remind herself to stop staring. She wanted to drink every element of her brother in now they were so close. He looked so different in his expensive forest-green tunic and hose, his hair neat and brushed, and yet so familiar she wanted to run and throw her arms around him. Just in time, she stopped herself, looking to the ground before he could notice her.

"Thanks for that little tour of the Council Gallery. Your paintings are the best I've seen," Claire heard an older man say. "Is your world full of people with your skill?"

Her brother was enjoying the attention, his chest swelling with pride. "No, but my whole family paints except for Dad." He considered for a moment. "Though I'm probably the best at it. Mum's work is too abstract, and Claire never puts in the time."

Claire wanted to rush forward and protest. She put just as much effort into painting as Marcus did these days. He was always off with Laura or playing footie. What a rotten liar.

She checked herself as a woman wearing a necklace of large shards of coloured glass elbowed the man aside. "I loved the painting we saw of the city. It's nothing like one of ours. Everything looks so foreign." She affected a delighted shiver.

"Oh, that's a city called Sydney," Marcus said. "And yes, my world is definitely different." He brushed his fringe out of his face, the way he did when he wanted to kiss Laura.

Claire gasped. She couldn't help it. He was flirting with this woman like he would in Shale with his girlfriend. It was almost like he wasn't missing his old life at all. She pulled herself together with a small shake of her shoulders. What an uncharitable thought. Of course Marcus was as worried about everyone back home as Claire was. She needed to inch closer and catch his attention somehow. Once she could whisper her real identity and explain everything that had happened, he'd have to come away with her.

She was still trying to figure out a plan – should she accidentally sidle up to him and spill wine on his tunic or pretend she had a message for him? – when the crowd surrounding Marcus parted. Her heart sank as Eidan swept past her in his signature black silk. He paused at Marcus's side; an arm wrapped around her brother's shoulders, saying to the gathered crowd, "You can't monopolise all of my young friend's time."

Through her lowered lashes, Claire noticed that Marcus didn't shrink away from the sudden embrace. In fact, as Marcus raised his goblet to chink against Eidan's, a delighted grin dimpled his cheeks and making him look more roguishly handsome than usual. Claire had to admit Bron that had been right; Marcus was hand in glove with Kelnarium's leader. She bit her lip. She'd have to think extra hard about how she worded her story when she caught up with Marcus later.

"It's time for a speech," Eidan said loudly, interrupting her thoughts, as he steered Marcus away from the group. She stepped out of their way; eyes trained on the floor. She counted to ten and then followed Marcus's sandalled feet.

Before she'd gotten more than two half-steps, fingers pinched into her arm. "Oww," she hissed, as Gareth took her elbow and firmly guided her aside, then led her to the edge of the room.

"We don't want him to notice us right now," he murmured in her ear as she leaned against cold marble, "Can't you hear how quiet it's gotten? We don't want to draw attention to ourselves."

Claire saw right away that he was correct. Servants ushered people into neat lines facing where Eidan stood on a raised dais, a similar podium to the one he'd used at Rinn's funeral standing in front of him. Marcus stood beside him, a hard look marring his usually pleasant features.

"I thank everyone for coming to my little event," Eidan began, his voice reverberating through the enormous room. "As I've always said, I want Kelnarium to be a place that welcomes everyone, no matter who they are, how rich or how poor." He turned to Marcus with a grin. "Or even what world they're from."

He looked back to the tittering crowd, suddenly serious again, his gaze sweeping the audience until it came to rest upon Gareth. "The only people who are not welcome are those who would try to undermine our community, who would harm others and spread fear."

The crowd shuffled as everyone craned to see where Eidan stared, angry mutters rising as they saw the object of his attention was a Maellwyn.

"I have no tolerance for such people, and you shouldn't either," he continued. "Their time in this world is ending." He indicated Marcus. "My friend tells of a world where magic does not exist and yet people still get by. We can emulate this place. Is that not so, Marcus?"

"It would be easy," Marcus said eagerly his voice raised so everyone could hear. "Why, I learnt in school that we once lived like you do now but minus the magic, and now we've got loads more technology than you do to make our lives better. If we can modernise, so can you!"

"Thank you, Marcus," Eidan said gravely. "This young man tells the truth. His paintings of his home gifted to the Council prove it. Here, now, with all strata of Kelnariat society bearing witness, I make a new promise to Kelnarium; I shall modernise us and make sure we are a population that is self-sufficient. There is no need for magic in our great city any longer." *Or anywhere,* he seemed to add silently.

Gareth shook beside her, his skin jolting against her arm. "This is a complete insult. He's suggesting we're no longer relevant."

"We have to get to Marcus away," Claire said, as Eidan climbed down from the podium and the crowd parted into small cliques once more, talking eagerly of their future. Space opened around her and Gareth as people did their level best to steer clear of those so obviously out of favour with Kelnariat's leader.

Gareth shook his head. "This is hopeless. You've seen how they are. The pair are apparently inseparable. Let's find Jemroth and Lotte and head back to Bron. We need to discuss a new plan for getting to Marcus."

Claire wanted to protest, but she saw as well as Gareth did that Eidan and Marcus whispered to each other near the exit, eyes sparkling and with no obvious intention to break away and join another group.

She searched instead for Lotte and Jemroth. A few seconds later, Jemroth strode over, his forehead creased. "I can't find Lotte anywhere."

"You can't have lost her," Claire chided. "I saw her trailing you close as a shadow earlier."

"Search the crowd all you like," Jemroth insisted. "I can't see her."

She glanced around but as the chatter grew louder and she searched the sea of heads, Lotte was nowhere to be seen. Something made her swivel back to the wide arched doorway, ice sliding down her spine.

Eidan swept through on his way out with Marcus, dragging someone else in tow by her elbow. Claire recognised her terrified face immediately.

Lotte.

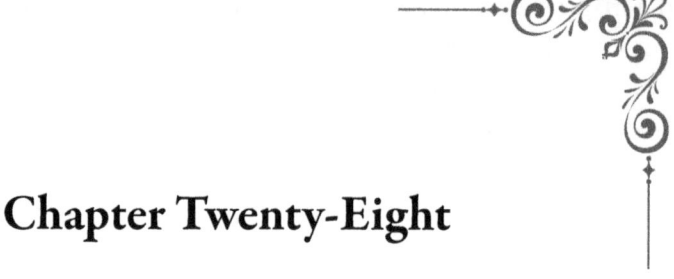

Chapter Twenty-Eight

THE URGENT GROUP TOOK to a shadowed backstreet, trying to find someplace they could speak in private, Gareth and Jemroth half-supporting Lotte between them. She hadn't stopped shaking since she'd finally made it back to the Ballroom, a nail-biting hour after she'd left with Eidan. As soon as she'd found Claire, she'd hissed in her ear they needed to leave and find somewhere to talk, fast. Thinking quickly, Claire had asked for Gareth's cloak pin. When he'd asked why she needed it, she'd clutched it tight in her fist explaining, "I need an excuse to come back tomorrow so I can find Marcus." She'd waited until they'd descended halfway down the building before dropping it surreptitiously in a corner. After that, she'd breathed easier as they swept out the front door amongst the throng of other departing guests and hurried through the Council Complex to the city itself, Jemroth leading them through side street after side street until they'd left the wealthier part of Kelnariat far behind.

At last, Jemroth paused in a wide cobblestone street beside a wooden pillar for tying horses to, dragging the others in close. "What happened?"

Gareth flung an arm about Lotte's shoulder. "Yes, are you all right? Are you hurt? We saw you following Eidan and—"

"Let Lotte speak," Claire said gently.

Her friend's eyes were wide with fright. "Eidan knows about ya, Claire. Somehow he knows yer alive."

A sudden roaring in Claire's ears and pounding at her temple made it hard to concentrate. How could Eidan know? *The Saura, if you can hear me, protect us.*

"Take a deep breath and start from the beginning," Gareth said.

Though his advice was meant for Lotte, Claire used Maen's breathing exercises to slow her own racing heart.

"No, not here," Jemroth said. "Let's get back to the inn. We don't want to be overheard."

"We can't do that," Lotte said. "Eidan knows we're staying at the Spotted Duck thanks to the invite and the token. He's sent men to intercept ya. He promised me I'd be unharmed, but only if I lead ya onto their swords."

"Then we should go straight to the safe house instead," Claire said.

As Gareth and Jemroth murmured assent, Lotte caught her eye, shaking hard as she mouthed something between stiff lips.

"You'll have to speak up. Take another breath," Claire said, taking Lotte's cold hand in hers.

"He knows about the safe house too. I dunno how but I'll swear on anything ya like he does."

Claire felt like a bucket of icy water had been thrown over her head. "But that's not possible. Not unless—"

"Someone's betrayed us," Jemroth finished her sentence for her. "But that means we've lost everything." His voice broke. "Even the poor horses. They'll become another trophy in Eidan's stable. They won't settle after how well they were treated with us."

Claire put a steadying hand on Jemroth's shoulder, swallowing past the lump in her own throat. She hated to imagine Livia and Agea in Eidan's grasp, but they had to accept the pair were lost to them. "I'm sorry," she murmured, "but we need to find shelter. We can mourn what we've lost later. I can't believe this of Bron. I thought he was our friend."

Gareth's stare flicked from Claire to Jemroth and back. "If you're suggesting for one second that Bron was the one to sell us out ..." he said hotly.

Claire's stomach roiled as the truth of Gareth's words hit her. Bron wouldn't, but what about Alaya? She'd been connected to Eidan after all, and not all that long ago. Her scalp and neck prickled as Jemroth's eyes met hers and he gave a small nod. It was good to know that he shared her suspicions.

"We need to find somewhere we can talk properly," Jemroth said. He paused, peering into Lotte's face. "Though there's something I want to know first. Why did Eidan take you into his confidence? For all he knows, you're of Maellwyn House and no amount of coin would break your loyalty to us."

"He knew I wasn't one of ya. Mebbe I didn't hold meself correctly or had a different look. I dunno." Lotte wrung her hands together. "I had no choice but to tell him a version of the truth; I told him I weren't really a Maellwyn servitor, that I'd joined ya on the outskirts of the city when yer'd seen me wearily walking on the main road, sobbing that my sister would give birth before ever I made it to Kelnariat. I said ya took pity on me and lemme ride in your cart and offered me a position for coin while ya was staying in the city 'coz yer old servitor got sick."

Claire wanted to hug Lotte. She knew that the best lies were the simple ones. She'd only had to adjust her cover story a little.

"By the Mer-people, that was some quick thinking," Gareth said quietly. "Good work."

"If the safe house is compromised, what should we do about Bron?" Claire asked.

"He knew the risks," Gareth said. "If he wasn't the one who sold us out to Eidan, and I don't believe for a second he did, he's probably dead, but even if he isn't, we can't afford to lose sight of why we're here. If we can find a change of clothes so it's not so obvious that we're Maellwyn, I'll purchase quill and ink and parchment and write to father to warn him about what's happened. Lotte can take the message. That's why she was chosen to come along after all, but the rest of us need to push on."

Claire felt sick. She didn't want to be separated from Lotte. What's more, she couldn't stop thinking about everything they'd lost with the safe house and their room at the Spotted Duck in Eidan's hand; their horses, Livia and Agea, the cart, their coin and supplies, even Lotte's bag of memories. The exile had left it on her bedside table, unable to conceal it beneath her thin servant's attire. Claire would have to go on foot to the Rift and if Eidan's men followed after, they'd soon catch up. What were they going to do? She glanced up the street frantically. Not too far along, someone's washing hung on a rickety balcony, swaying in the gentle breeze.

"Gareth's right. In half decent light, anyone will recognise our clothes and report us to Eidan." She pointed at the washing overhead. "Who's the best climber?"

Lotte raised her hand.

Claire outlined her plan. Lotte would shimmy up the side of the townhouse and filch some clothes. They'd have to put whatever Lotte could scrounge over their Maellwyn outfits and leave anything too bulky like their cloaks and the servitor dresses she and Lotte wore at the porch. They couldn't afford to pay a few coins in apology for stealing, but perhaps the family could cut up what they'd left behind and create something new to make up for it.

Claire, Gareth and Jemroth watched in agonising silence as Lotte swung up the edge of the townhouse, grasping at uneven wooden slats for purchase. She made it back down without mishap and soon they were pulling large tunics and baggy hose over whatever they could salvage of their own costumes.

Soon they were on the move again, the poorer residential streets giving way to the commercial district, busy even at this hour of the night. Jemroth led them into a narrow strip decorated with warm yellow lights strung across balconies. Stools and small tables scattered along the street were occupied by men and women drinking ale and laughing.

He stopped at a cramped tavern, hordes of revellers hanging out of windows and spilling onto the street. A woman stood next to an oaken barrel by the wooden door. Jemroth flung her the few coins he had kept in his pocket, holding up four fingers. The woman barely reacted, merely dipping brass tankards into the ale barrel and passing them over.

When everyone had their drink, Jemroth jerked his head outside to where buskers played flutes as dancers swung about on the cobblestones and those on the sidelines clapped and cheered. He shoved his way through the crowd to an empty patch of wall and lent against it with arms crossed. They huddled in close.

"Now, Lotte. Tell us exactly what happened," Claire said, as quietly as she could manage. "Word for word. How did he know about me?"

"I dunno who told him about ya, but as to what happened, well," Lotte said, white-faced, "after I'd sold him on my cover, he said as he'd pay me handsomely and that I'd be doing my civic duty if I told him where ya were, Claire. He described ya and asked me if I'd seen Gareth and Jemroth talking to someone who matched yer appearance. I lied. Said I hadn't seen ya, but perhaps as yer'd come to meet them whilst I'd been out with my sister."

"You did good work tonight," Claire said, her fingers trembling against her tankard. "Your quick thinking probably saved our lives. Now, first things first, how much coin do we have between us." They reached into pockets and pooled their meagre amounts. She looked at Gareth and Jemroth expectantly. "Is it enough?"

The pair shook their heads. "We couldn't buy a quarter of a horse with that."

Claire swallowed. She had to stay strong and find a way out of this mess. "Is it enough for accommodation?"

Jemroth grinned. "Sure. The piss-poor kind."

"It'll do," she said. "Do you know which area of the city we should start looking? Let's get some rest and then we'll figure out what we should do in the morning."

As Jemroth led them once more down back streets and into the poorer end of the city, Claire and Lotte fell a little behind the others. Lotte gripped tight to Claire's hand, her breath too heavy and eyes too huge in her small face. She reminded Claire of Suranne, sitting on the couch waiting for news of Marcus.

"There's more isn't there?" Claire said grimly. "Fess up."

Lotte turned. "Oh, Claire. I didn't wanna lie to the others, but I didn't know what else to do. I couldn't tell 'em I'm an exile now, could I?"

Claire felt like the air had been slammed out of her. "What? Eidan knows you're an exile? That's impossible!"

With a guilty glance ahead, Lotte pulled back her cotton tunic to reveal her mother's feather, quartz and bead necklace nestled at her chest. "Someone bumped me, and I poured wine all over the floor. Another servant flung me a cleaning rag and when I knelt, it musta slipped out, and Eidan saw."

"You shouldn't be wearing it," Claire hissed. "If Gareth or Jemroth had been the ones to—"

"I know, Claire. I just wanted to feel close to me mam and she told me to never take it off, remember? I thought I could be extra careful. That no one would ever have to know." She swallowed, "Thank goodness I did 'coz now my pouch is gone an' all."

Claire squeezed Lotte's hand. "I'm sorry." She sighed. "There's no use either of us crying over spilt milk. Go on."

"Eidan pulled me aside and said that if I was a Maellwyn he was a Dorran. He said he recognised the necklace's make. He said he'd make it worth my while to follow him to another part of the building. I didn't know what else to do. When we was alone, he said he could guess why I'd joined with Gareth and the others, that I wanted revenge for the death of me people at the hands of a magical House. I agreed with him, o'course, and begged him not to gimme away. I said I joined with ya on the road and had been biding my time ever since until I could stab ya in the dark." She paused reflectively. "He enjoyed my bloodthirsty nature an' all. As a kid, I spent loads of time thinking up what I'd do to Dorrans so it weren't hard to be convincing."

Claire glanced ahead but Gareth and Jemroth didn't look back. She wondered what they'd think about her and Lotte with their heads bent so close together in private conversation. They needed to wrap things up before one of them noticed and asked awkward questions. "Then what happened?"

"He said as he'd sent guards to the places we'd frequented in the city. I pretended I didn't know what he meant when he mentioned the safe house. Then he said I'd get to watch the Maellwyns squeal because he'd sent men to torture 'em for yer whereabouts. All I had to do was make sure ya went straight there after the reception. I asked him why he hated ya as much as we exiles did, and he spouted all that bilge about wanting to protect Kelnarium." Her sweaty palm clutched harder at Claire's own. "What if Jemroth and Gareth figure out I haven't told 'em the full story?"

"They won't," Claire said.

"But someone told Eidan yer alive and in the city. I'll swear on anything ya like it weren't me, but what if they figure out who I really am and think I was the one as betrayed ya? They're Maellwyns! They ain't gonna believe it were Bron or Alaya!"

Chapter Twenty-Nine

CLAIRE ENTERED THE Council building, Gareth's envoy token in the palm of her hand. They'd found a dirty but cheap inn to sleep in last night, and today, while Gareth searched for parchment and quill to send a message to Lord Maellwyn, Jemroth scouted for suitable horses to get them to the Rift and Lotte went to steal supplies, Claire had gone to find Marcus on the pretence of retrieving Gareth's lost brooch. She was dressed in the plain dress and shawl she'd stolen yesterday, passing herself off as some lord's servant. In the daylight, the crisp white painted walls and ceiling in the Council building dazzled, and the plush rugs felt deliciously warm as her boots sank in deep. Sunshine falling through enormous, elegant glass-paned windows filled the foyer with light. Stairways and corridors led from the foyer, but no doubt the tall guard pacing the space was meant to prevent just anybody heading further into the building, for all that he looked relaxed. There was a wooden counter to her left, behind which sat an elderly man wearing pea-sized spectacles. He looked up. "Yes?" he wheezed.

She passed him the token. He held it up to the light like he thought she'd forged it. "My master dropped a brooch last night at the reception, Sir. He was taken on a tour of the Council Gallery to look at some paintings and he remembers his cloak catching against a colonnade on the way out. He believes it's there."

"And who is your master?" he said, his customer service smile vanishing now that he knew she was a servitor.

"Councillor Pilla Brent, Sir," Claire lied, picking the first name she remembered from the reception.

The man said nothing, merely picking up a ledger and consulting it for what felt like agonising minutes. Claire was sure he'd hear her beating heart. Any second, he'd tell her she wasn't a real servant or deny her entry. Sweat prickled her back and she was about to turn tail and flee when at last, the man looked up.

"All is in order," he said. "You may go."

Claire turned away and took a step, but then stopped and turned to face the counter again.

"Well? What are you waiting for? Get on with you," the man said sharply.

"I ... I don't remember the way," Claire stammered.

"Walk down that corridor," he said, pointing, "and take your third left and then a second right and take the stairs to the top floor, third room on the right." He glared at her, adding sarcastically, "Can you remember that, or should I write the instructions on your hand in ink?"

"No, I can remember," Claire said.

As she hurried through the corridor the man had indicated, Claire shivered. Men and women dressed in sentry uniform marched past in twos and threes, but all looked bored rather than confrontational. Claire doubted they'd spare more than a glance for a servant girl, yet still she was afraid. Lotte's fear in the street last night had been contagious.

And then there was the doubt growing in the back of her mind. *Someone* had betrayed them to Eidan. Was it Bron and Alaya as she so badly wanted to believe, no matter how horrible their underhandedness, or was it Lotte after all? As Claire had lain awake with the rats scurrying about, she'd remembered Liz and how kind she'd been until she'd turned on her. Was Lotte the same?

To make matters worse, overnight Claire had dreamt of the Beast as her dream-self floated paralysed. The corruption of its flesh had spread since she'd last seen it. Spools of spit dripped onto her cheek, yet her limbs wouldn't obey to wipe the smears away. Its stench overpowered, making her stomach roil, even in the dream.

The Beast's rotting, tattered flesh reached out, picking her up with incorporeal hands and tossing her into the wide, empty cavern of its mouth. It had laughed, then cried 'Betrayer,' the sound rattling through her entire body until she felt she couldn't bear it a second longer and she'd woken up.

As Claire took the third right and the second left, a wide stairwell greeting her at the end of the corridor, she prayed to the Saura Gwenivere was right about the Beast. *Surely, he's simply sending the dreams to mess with me,* she told herself. She puffed up the stairs, glancing from side to side in case

Marcus passed her by. She hoped she found him soon. She didn't want to get lost inside this enormous building trying to find him. She made herself push her problems aside. She needed her wits about her.

She paused for a moment at the top landing, leaning against the railing, waiting for her heart rate to slow, then made herself walk sedately to her right, counting rooms as she crept along the corridor. Within minutes she'd found the Council Gallery, its doorway ajar, painted white and overlaid with silver gilt. She pressed against the door, hoping it wouldn't screech. To her relief, it appeared well-oiled and she was able to slip inside silently, suppressing an awed gasp.

The floor was squeaky clean and polished within an inch of its life. The ceiling was so high, she didn't know how anyone had managed to get to the roof to paint the plaster gold. The walls were covered in a deep red brocade, floral patterns embossed onto the fabric. Paintings hung in rows everywhere she looked. She recognised a few of Marcus's right away.

The centre of the gallery featured long rectangular divans, on which a group of men and women sat as they drew on sheets of paper with intense concentration. If any of them had heard her enter, they didn't acknowledge it. A young man walked slowly from person to person, looking over their shoulders at the art produced and stopping to make quiet comments. Though his face was partially in shadow, Claire recognised him immediately. Marcus, teaching his regular painting class just as Bron had said.

As though he felt her stare, he looked up, eyes meeting Claire's with shocked recognition. She had to get in quickly before he blurted out that she was his sister.

There was nothing for it. She stepped forward. She could only hope Marcus would recognise the urgency and the need for secrecy in her eyes. "Greetings, Mr Marcus, Sir. Excuse me, but my master has sent me to fetch his brooch. He believes you found it?"

The people around Marcus looked up curiously, some staring at Claire in open enquiry.

His eyes glistened as he placed his artwork beside him, got to his feet and began to stretch his arms out. "She's –"

"A servitor of Councillor Pilla," Claire finished for him.

He frowned at Claire, but she frowned back, willing him to understand. *Not here, Marcus. Please. Get the message.*

He considered for a moment, then turned to the prospective artists surrounding him. "I must fetch the good councillor's brooch. I'll be back shortly to check over your work, never fear."

"No rush, Master Marcus," one man said cheerfully. "You're not our slave. It's near enough to lunch, anyway."

"Keep going," Marcus said shortly, "I'll be back as fast as I can. It's a small thing I can do to make up for ... for ..."

The man placed a hand on Marcus's shoulder. "You don't have to keep working yourself into the ground to prove you're not your grandfather," he said. "We know you're not like him. You're one of us."

Claire turned away, lest someone see the pain in her eyes at the mention of Lord Dorran.

Soon, Marcus was in front of her, gesturing for her to follow him outside.

In the hallway, Claire resisted the urge to hug her brother. "Is there someplace we can talk where we won't be overhead?"

He nodded tersely, grabbing her arm, and tugging her inside a tiny study four doors down from the Gallery. "What the hell's going on? Why're you here?" He pushed her into a wicker chair complete with plush purple cushion, then took the second chair behind the polished desk.

"I love you too," Claire said sarcastically, even as her voice wobbled. She'd longed for this moment ever since Marcus had vanished. She'd missed him so much. Her eyes misted.

"Don't cry, Sis," he said uncomfortably. "I'm just surprised. I bet darling Grandpa dragged you to Kelnarium too?"

"Don't speak of him like that. He's dead. And yes. He summoned me because of the prophecy."

"Stuff him and his prophecy. It's a load of rubbish." He waved his hand, dismissing it. "Never mind all that. How's Mum and Dad? Did they miss me? Do they know where we are?"

"It was awful when you left. We were so miserable, but they knew you'd been summoned. I feel so bad for them waiting for us to return. That's why I'm here. Unless you and I and some of the magical brethren close the Rift, all

Kelnarium will be destroyed. We need to do that and then we can go home, so you see, you need to help us and—"

"Woah, slow down, Sis. Don't tell me you believe those crazies threatening to create a second Rift? Still, if it'll make you feel better, let's go find Eidan and you can tell him your story."

"What? No, Marcus, we mustn't. I don't know what lies Eidan's fed you, but he's known about me being in Kelnarium for weeks. He would have killed me inside Dorran Manor if he'd found me."

"What on Earth are you on about?" Marcus said crossly. "There's no way Eidan knew you were with Grandfather. He'd never hurt me or someone I'm close to. We're friends and I've told him all about you."

"I'm telling you; he knew about me and that I'm needed to close the Rift, and he didn't want me to succeed. I ran for my life. I was so scared, Marcus. I thought he must have killed you or had you locked up."

"This is all a stupid misunderstanding." Marcus reached forward to clasp her hand where it rested against the desk. "Come with me and he'll explain everything, you'll see."

She narrowed her eyes. "What exactly has Eidan told you? About the carnage at Dorran Manor? About the Dream Mages?"

"Why, the same as what he's told everyone at the war council today," Marcus said. "That there was a conspiracy to overthrow the government spearheaded by Grandfather. That the Dream Mages were working hand in glove with him."

"That's all wrong," Claire insisted, frustration making her harsh. "Kelnarium dies unless we close the Rift, which means unless you come away with me, you and I die too."

"Don't tell me you believe that rubbish," he scoffed. "I wouldn't trust a word those Dorrans say. They aren't nice people, Sis."

"They told me you guys got off on the wrong foot and I get that your lack of magic didn't help matters, but Grandfather summoned first you, and then me to Kelnarium, because this year the Rift will explode taking all Kelnarium with it. He believed it, but more importantly, so do I."

"Look, I'm sure Grandfather filled your head with nonsense about Eidan and made out you were important with his *learth* magic and chosen-one prophecy guff, but it's all absurd lies. I don't blame you for falling for them. I can see why this would all be appealing to a little girl like you."

Claire itched to slap her brother. *Little girl? Who was he kidding?* "Listen to me, will you? Eidan is the Big Bad, the Super Villain, the Mr Downright Evil, whatever you want to call it. He murdered Grandfather."

"*Killed* him because he was a traitor," Marcus explained patiently.

"No. *Murdered* him because Eidan's up to no good."

"Bullshit."

"How can you be so cold? You're related to Lord Dorran too!"

"I wish I wasn't," he said, raising his voice, half-getting up from his chair. He took a deep breath, starting again more calmly. "I woke up in Kelnarium without so much as a by your leave and then Grandfather's stupid captain turned up to take me to the Manor and when I said I wasn't coming and I didn't believe a word of his crap about magic and Mum, he waved his sword around so I was forced to go with him. We rode past a camp and the bile I had to listen to … It would have made you sick! No wonder Mum got away from them and never looked back."

"I don't think it was like that."

"And then," Marcus went on hotly, like Claire hadn't spoken, "I was berated day in and day out. I got told what a disappointment I was and to apply myself to magic. What was the point? When I reminded them they'd told me I had the only slightest of talents for it, they'd go on and on about how every *learth* soul was precious and I had a duty as a Dorran to learn what I could. I danced a jig when they finally sent me to Eidan. When he told me about Grandfather's real plans for me, I felt sick to my stomach. I'd seen how they treated those poor exiles, but to use family in such a heinous way?"

"I hated how they treated the exiles too, but you've got things all wrong, Marcus. Our grandmother was from House Ushanan which uses air magic, and her blood runs in your veins. That's probably why you weren't great at fire magic. You're meant to close the Rift with me using air *learth*. Now let's go."

He stared at her like she'd gone mad. "I don't think so. That traitor, our grandfather, has brainwashed you. Come and see Eidan and he'll set you straight."

He got up to stand beside Claire, tugging at her arm, but she pulled out of his grasp, her chair screeching across the floor as she twisted out of reach.

"You silly idiot," he hissed in her face.

"No, you're the idiot," Claire said. "By the salamanders, why won't you listen?"

"Because you sound insane!"

"You're blinded by your faith in Eidan. Why can't you see it?"

"You're blinded by your need to feel accepted. Can't *you* see it?"

"I thought you'd be glad to meet me again," Claire said, tears streaming down her cheeks.

"I am. Very. I just wish you hadn't arrived spouting garbage," Marcus said.

"I'm telling the truth," she said defiantly. "Back home, my word would have been enough."

"We're not home, are we?" he said.

"Which is why we need to stick together. Eidan can't get you back to Shale. But me and the surviving Dream Mages can."

"That's where you're wrong," he said, eyes shining. "Eidan has promised to get me back as soon as he's dealt with the rag-tag magical army in the Riftlands."

Claire's stomach dropped. Surely Marcus could only be referring to one thing: Maen and Gwenivere and the rest of the magical brethren waiting for Claire. "What're you talking about?" Her voice shook.

"They're turning the countryside against the Council and now the farmers and villagers and even some townspeople are demanding answers from Eidan. If he doesn't comply, it will be open war. He's responding in kind with his own army. And then he'll do a magical working with his spirit friend at the Rift to get me back to Shale. We leave tomorrow morning."

"What spirit friend?" Claire could barely get the words out. She had a bad feeling she knew the answer.

"I don't know," Marcus said airily. "It comes to Eidan in dreams and helps him. That's how he knew some people survived Dorran Manor. His spirit friend saw them and showed them to Eidan in a dream."

Claire felt like Marcus had punched her in the gut. Eidan was allied with the Beast? Why? And as to Maen and Gwenivere, and the rest of their party, there was no time to lose. She had to get back to the inn and find a way to warn them of what was coming.

"As soon as Eidan deals with the renegades, I can go home. You've got the explosion stuff wrong. Eidan's explained it. To get to Shale, there'll be a big bang, but no one will get hurt. It's all part of the magical working," Marcus went on. "Seriously, we can go home together and if you know magic, maybe you could help Eidan defeat those idiots defying him. Think of how many soldiers lives you could save. Now, will you come?"

Claire was stunned. How could she experience so many emotions within a few minutes? Shock, joy, relief, and now, crushing disappointment and hurt. Marcus had everything so very wrong, but he was too sure of himself to listen to her. It was no use. She couldn't waste any more time.

"I can't, Marcus. I wish you'd understand. I've spent weeks trying to find you. All I've thought about is your rescue, and I get here and don't know you anymore."

"And I don't know you. Believe me, Eidan cares about Kelnarium. He won't let it be destroyed. If you won't come meet him, what will you do? Go back to his enemies? To *my* enemies?"

"I don't have a choice. Please, Marcus. Won't you at least speak with them?"

"No," he said coldly as he stood up. "You've picked the losing side and you'll look like a fool when you come crawling back admitting it."

His insults stung, but she couldn't rise to his bait. She got to her feet, acutely aware of the danger she was now in. "Please, Marcus. Don't tell Eidan that I visited you today. If you don't do this for me, I'll never ever forgive you."

He stopped, undecided. After a short pause that seemed an eternity, he nodded. "If it means so much to you my lips are sealed." After a moment of strained silence, he flung himself at Claire, hugging her warmly. "And it *is* good to see you, Sis. I'm so glad you're safe."

She hugged him tightly. "I feel just the same."

He sighed. "You know where to find me if you change your mind about Eidan and decide to trust me." He stepped back and held her hands. "Now go. Before someone comes."

Chapter Thirty

CLAIRE TOOK THE STAIRS to the loft of the inn two at a time, banging open the door to see Lotte, Jemroth and Gareth sitting cross-legged on the wooden floorboards, flinging about a set of dice and laughing. Their grins peeled away as they took in Claire. No doubt she looked miserable. She couldn't understand Marcus's stubbornness, but she knew her family. There was no point arguing once his mind was made up. She hated to be the bearer of bad news, but she couldn't deny the facts; there was no way her brother would help them. She made herself sit on her dirty hay mattress bed and took a deep breath.

Gareth peered at the open door. "So, no Marcus?"

Lotte stared wide-eyed, like she'd already read Claire's mood and knew something ominous was coming, and Jemroth sat up straight like a schoolkid paying attention to his teacher.

"He wouldn't come," she said. "Eidan's claimed he can get him back to Shale without the help of magical users and has told him a pack of lies about Dorran Manor and Grandfather. Marcus thinks I'm his misguided little sister," she couldn't help but sniff at the memory, "and I've been sucked in by you magical brethren to fight against Kelnarium's government. He thinks you'll threaten creating a second Rift to take power."

"What's Eidan playing at?" Jemroth growled.

Claire shrugged hopelessly. She wished she knew the answer. There had to be a logical reason for Eidan's behaviour. If only she knew what it was.

"Marcus won't come?" Gareth repeated, as though he hadn't registered Claire and Jemroth's exchange. "But then," his face blanched, "what're we going to do? Will he tell Eidan about us?"

Claire pressed a hand to her throbbing temple. "I don't think so. He's family and he promised he wouldn't, and we never break our promises to each other. But that's not everything I learnt from Marcus."

"What else could go wrong?" Gareth groaned.

"Eidan's in league with the Beast that keeps haunting my dreams, the one that's a kind of extension of the Rift—"

"It can't be true," Gareth said, looking shocked.

"I'm afraid it is," Claire confirmed. "Marcus wasn't lying. I can always tell." She couldn't help but give a small smile remembering the time he'd told Suranne he hadn't eaten the last chocolate bar in the cupboard. Claire had noticed the way his voice had quavered and gone high-pitched with false indignance. Her smile vanished. There'd been none of that during their reunion today.

"Then the Beast must have bewitched him or something," Gareth protested. "Why else would Eidan risk Kelnarium's future and his own life? Why else would he throw away years of friendship and peace? I simply can't understand it."

"I can't either," Claire admitted. "Perhaps the Beast has told him that magical users do want a coup and that the Rift has to explode to get Marcus home and he believes it. That's what he's told Marcus – that there'll be an explosion, sure, but it's part of the natural working and nothing to fear. Either he's leading my brother a merry dance or the Beast is feeding Eidan lies. Whichever's the truth, Marcus reckons the Beast will get him to Shale once Eidan's dealt with … with," she had to pause to stop rushing her words.

She pressed her palms hard into sticks of straw that poked through the cover of the mattress, welcoming the scratches. "Somehow, he knows about Gwenivere, Maen and the others. They've been telling farmers, villagers and towns about what happened at Dorran Manor, just like they said they would. People from all walks of life have gone with their party to the Riftlands, promising to follow them into Kelnariat to demand answers of Eidan." Claire closed her eyes.

"And? I'd bet the gnomes there's more to this story," Jemroth prompted.

Claire nodded, opening her eyes again. "Marcus was at a war council today. Eidan is assembling his army to leave tomorrow. He'll catch our friends and their makeshift resistance group by surprise unless we can warn them."

"We have to find horses and get away from the city," Lotte said, fingers picking at a rent in her plain dress. "When I were a-stealing, Eidan's soldiers was crawling everywhere. I were mighty glad me face were covered."

Claire's stomach sank. She'd seen a lot of soldiers too coming back from the Council buildings. She supposed it made sense that when Eidan hadn't found them at the Spotted Duck or the safe house, he'd sent his people to comb the city.

"There was wanted posters and all, Claire, worse than in Autun." Lotte went on. "Citizens and soldiers alike are to arrest us on sight." She rubbed thumb and forefinger together. "And the reward is high."

Claire pressed her lips together tightly. They needed to get out of the city fast. She turned to Jemroth. "Did you find any horses?"

He shook his head, pain flickering across his face for a second. Claire guessed he thought of the four-legged friends they'd lost not so long ago. "The best horses are those in the rich end of Kelnariat, but sentries patrol those streets even on days when Maellwyns haven't escaped Eidan's grasp, and punishment is more severe if you're caught for theft in that part of the city." He shot Claire a wry smile. "It won't be possible for us to steal horses, at least without a good plan and careful disguises. One horse will be far easier to steal than many."

"And what do we do about Marcus?" Gareth said. "We can't close the Rift without him."

"He's made up his mind for now," Claire said. "He needs a few days to think over our version of events."

"We don't have a few days!" cried Lotte.

"I know," Claire admitted. "On the way back to the inn, I thought and thought about what we should do next, and every choice seems bad. At first, I thought we should make a run for the others at the Riftlands, but if we don't have Marcus, we can't close the Rift and the Beast will ensure it explodes destroying Kelnarium. If we stay here, we run the risk of getting caught and our friends being murdered before we can persuade Marcus to come away with us."

"And the Rift will still explode," Gareth said gloomily, "because once his enemies are killed, Eidan and Marcus will ride for its centre, poor Marcus thinking he's about to get sent home and who knows what Eidan thinks will happen."

"We'll have to separate," Lotte said, though she didn't look enthused. "I was gonna return to Lord Maellwyn to report what happened with the safe house. Mebbe that's not a good idea now and we should stick together." She perked up. "I stole cured meat and hard biscuits from a market earlier. Not much, but if I go now to get more supplies, mebbe it'd be enough?" She turned inquiringly to Jemroth.

"You'll need skins of water and food supplies for three days tied to the saddle and risk half-killing the horse. Still," Jemroth sighed, "it may be our only option."

"What about your father, Gareth?" Claire asked. "I think we should still get a message to him. If he can send Maellwyns to our aid, it would help. Maybe Lotte should go to him as originally planned and one of you should warn the others. I'll join you as soon as I persuade Marcus I'm right about Eidan."

Gareth reached behind him to pull forward an elegant quill and a sealed pitch-black pot of ink. His lips curved into a sudden frown. "What's that?" He pointed a finger at something poking out beneath Lotte's mattress.

A bit of white feather and a wooden bead were visible. Claire met Lotte's eyes with horror. How could Lotte have been so stupid? Claire had told her to be careful after Eidan. Then again, they'd been so tired last night, perhaps Lotte had taken the necklace off after all the excitement of the evening and hadn't remembered to put it back around her neck.

"Nuthin'," Lotte said hastily, trying to kick the necklace back with her foot. "I found it at market when I went a-stealing and thought it pretty. I know I shouldna have done it, but it's so sweet."

"You're lying," Jemroth said, getting to his feet. "I've seen jewellery like that once before." He turned grimly to Gareth. "In the exile camp near Dorran Manor." Hard eyes met Claire's. "Where did you say you met this girl again?"

"I ... at the edge of Dorran territory, escaping from the village," Claire stammered.

Jemroth strode over to Lotte and shoved her aside. In a trice, he was on his knees feeling about under her mattress. When he resurfaced triumphantly, necklace in hand, Claire gasped at the hatred in his face.

"Gareth and I aren't fools, even if you think we are, exile," he spat. "Someone gave away our safe house to Eidan, and I'm willing to bet a Maellwyn dolphin it wasn't Bron or Alaya."

"What're you saying?" Claire managed through stiff lips.

"She's the one who went off with Eidan alone," Gareth said. "We only have her word for what happened at their meeting."

But Jemroth was staring at Claire. "Lady Claire or no Lady Claire," he said slowly, "I won't have you keeping secrets from me or from Gareth. Lotte's an exile and you don't look a bit surprised. How long have you known the truth?"

Claire knew guilt clouded her face. For a second, doubt ate at her. Had she done the wrong thing in keeping Lotte's secret? Jemroth did have a point. The exile could have set them all up, laughing at Claire's naivety all along. No – Lotte was no Liz. She wouldn't sell Claire out the second a better friend came along. And Claire was no Liz either. She'd decided to trust Lotte, and that meant sticking by her.

"From the start," she said defiantly. "I haven't told the truth until now, but I didn't learn about Grandfather's meeting with Eidan from Aed either. I eavesdropped from a passageway above them, and frightened by what I heard, ran away from Dorran Manor."

"But Maen said you were hidden on the Manor grounds in a stable when it was attacked."

"Like I said, I lied," Claire said. "I got as far as Lotte's exile camp and rescued her." Out of the corner of her eye, she saw Lotte huddle against the wall, eyes wide with fright. "I couldn't tell Maen where I'd been without giving her away. She's my friend and she's on our side. She could have given us up more than once, but she didn't."

"If this is true, I have nothing more to say to you," Jemroth said.

"But I do," Gareth said. He stood and began to pace the tiny loft, bending his head to avoid low beams. "Why didn't you tell me?"

"Because I knew anyone of a magical House would act as you are now," Claire said. "Because I knew you wouldn't listen to me."

"I might have listened if you'd tried to talk."

"From the way you spoke about exiles in the cart on the way to Kelnariat, I doubt it."

"*She's* the enemy," Gareth hissed, pointing at Lotte, who shrank back closing her eyes.

"No," Claire said. "Eidan and the Rift are the real enemies."

"*Her* people were assassins for hire! They murdered your ancestors and *she's* one of them."

"*She* never harmed anyone. They harmed her." Claire glanced at Lotte. "Tell them that you mean no harm. Tell them you didn't sell us out."

Lotte opened her eyes and colour rushed into her face as she leapt to her feet. "Why should I, Claire? My family were murdered by Eidan, jus' as yers were. How he'd laugh if he saw us turnin' on each other."

Gareth gaped. "What's she talking about?"

"I don't speak for her."

He turned to Lotte and grudgingly repeated his question as Jemroth scowled.

"I was mindin' me own business in our camp when men in Dorran colours came down the slope on horses a-whooping and a-yelling. Some of us came out to try and placate 'em and even as we did, we saw they carried lit branches in one hand. They set the whole camp alight, and any one they could catch too. They formed a barricade so as we couldn't escape. We screamed and screamed as these men laughed and laughed. They left us for dead in burning piles. I were at the bottom of one when Claire found me." Lotte's lips twisted at the awful memory.

"I used magic to save her," Claire said, remembering the horror of that day. "We both lay under a smoking sky, too exhausted to move. Next morning, I managed to convince Lotte that I wasn't a threat to her." She paused, unsure whether to mention the Crian or not. After a moment's thought, she erred on the side of caution, even though Jemroth and Gareth might consider the omission lying. Who knew how they'd react to Claire talking to a mysterious spirit on top of finding out Lotte's real identity?

"I stuck with Claire," Lotte went on with a shrug of her shoulders. "I had nothin' and no one left and she saved me. What were I to do? At Autun, I admit I thought about sellin' the Dorrans out for coin when I saw as there was a bounty on their heads, but before I could make up my mind to do it, I overhead Claire, Gwenivere, Rael and Maen talking about the prophecy and how Kelnarium would die without Claire closing the Rift. I ain't stupid. What's the point of coin if yer dead and can't spend it? 'Sides, I thought mebbe I'd be able to help the exiles if I aided ya 'cos I'd be part of the winning side and Claire promised."

"You promised what exactly?" Gareth demanded, folding his arms.

"That I'd change things for the exiles," Claire said calmly. "My Mum regretted how she'd treated them, and I know she'd be proud of me doing this. The past is finished. Lotte isn't responsible for whatever her people did years and years ago. It's time for everyone to move on. Trust your heart, not what you've been told. Before you knew Lotte was an exile, you looked at her with respect."

"When I thought she was one of us," Gareth said.

"She *is* one of us, Gareth."

"Leave it, Claire," Lotte said. "I don't need 'em to believe me. If no one wants me, I'll make me own way in Kelnariat and good luck to y'all."

"By the Gofannon, I don't think so," Jemroth said, as he gripped Lotte's arm tight, a knife suddenly at her throat.

Chapter Thirty-One

CLAIRE GOT TO HER FEET. "Put that down, Jemroth," she said, a tone of authority she'd never heard before in her voice. "If you touch her, I'll be forced to use *learth*, and I promise you it'll hurt." Before anyone could stop her, she stretched out her fingers, flames gleaming at their tips. She shot one at his feet, forcing him to leap backwards in surprise.

"You'd turn on us for her?" Jemroth demanded incredulously.

Claire sighed as she doused the flame. "I've had quite enough of murder. Do what I say and stop being an idiot, Jemroth. I'm ashamed of you. You and Lotte have more in common than you think. You've both lost your families and homes for starters."

Mouth hanging open, Jemroth did as he was told. Lotte glared at him, then glanced at Claire gratefully. Claire was sure if Jemroth wasn't still in the way with a knife on the floor, she'd have peeled off the wall and hugged her.

Gareth hauled Jemroth to his feet, grabbing the knife and pocketing it with his spare hand, then tugging the advisor to his end of the loft. Claire noticed Jemroth stared at his feet as if ashamed as both he and Gareth sank onto a mattress.

As the awkward silence grew, she cleared her throat. "We'll put that little episode behind us. Jemroth, I'll never mention it again." She paused. "Assuming it never happens again."

"Fine," Gareth answered for him, sounding strained. "But what are we going to do about her?" At Claire's glare, he backtracked. "I mean, about Lotte. I don't trust her, and you can't make me. I, for one, don't want her going to my father on her own lest we get a repeat of Dorran Manor—"

"For the last time, I ain't the enemy!" Lotte said, red in the face and looking ready to launch herself at someone.

"She would say that, wouldn't she," Gareth said, nudging Jemroth in the side so the sulky man looked up. He nodded his agreement.

Claire put her hands on her hips, fixing him with a hard stare. "Then what do you propose? I won't let you hurt Lotte. If you insist on stupid prejudices colouring everything, we're doomed."

"Then she'll have to stay with us," Gareth said. "No messages to my father and no going anywhere else alone either. We stick together."

"Right, and Eidan wins. What a brilliant plan," Claire scoffed.

Gareth flushed, falling into silence. Jemroth stared at the floorboards like he was praying, and Lotte had her arms crossed, wearing a mutinous expression. Claire wanted to scream as she sank back into her own mattress. Everything was coming unstuck. Even if Lotte had betrayed them to Eidan, she didn't deserve death. That would make Claire and the others as bad as Kelnarium's leader. But how could they succeed now? Someone had to take a message to Gwenivere and the others.

She racked her brains, carefully going over everything Marcus had told her. Maybe there was something she could use from that conversation ...

Yes! She restrained a squeal. What a wonderful idea. Risky, absolutely, but if it worked ...

"I've got something," she said, trying to sound casual, even as adrenaline coursed through her like a sugar hit. "Marcus said Eidan's preparing his army." The others blinked at her, dull-eyed and sulky. "If you insist on keeping an eye on Lotte, why don't we go with them to the Rift?"

"How?" Gareth asked, looking blank. "None of us are soldiers and we don't have the right uniform or weapons. The army would know we were fakes straight away." He thought for a moment. "Unless you meant we could knock a couple out in town and steal their identities. I suppose that could work."

"*She* could run off and warn Eidan of our presence at any moment," Jemroth said, jerking his head at Lotte, who glowered back at him. "We'd have to guard her round the clock and that might look a little obvious. Armies are disciplined. They don't do things out of the ordinary unless they've been ordered to, or they're spies. We'll be caught."

"No," Claire said, sure her eyes were shining with glee. "We're all good with looking after horses and –"

"I ain't," Lotte interrupted.

"Well, I'm sure you could manage organising supplies and that sort of thing. Unless history class has led me astray, armies have baggage trains." The others stared at her in confusion and she could have burst with impatience. "Isn't it obvious? We join Eidan's army that way. In the textbooks I read, no one ever notices them. They're the servitors, so why should they? We'll be behind the main army too, so there's less chance of Eidan or Marcus noticing us." She glanced at her friend. "And if Lotte is who you say – sorry, I don't think you are, but I've got to make the argument – the three of us will have time to grab a horse and ride away. And," she finished triumphantly, "I can try talking to Marcus and persuade him to come away with us and as soon as I succeed, we can ride hard for Gwenivere and the others." She looked from person to person. "Well? What do you think?"

"It's pretty audacious," Gareth said slowly, "but it could work and at least we'd be close to Eidan and all the action."

Jemroth grinned nastily, darting a glance at Lotte. "And it will be easier to keep an eye on this one in such an environment. The baggage train is a disordered mess compared to the main army."

"What do you think, Lotte?" Claire asked, ignoring Jemroth's hostility.

The exile shrugged. "Nothin' I can say will change those two's mind so it's as good an idea as any, only how'll we join? Won't Eidan have people already, especially if he intends to set off tomorrow? Isn't that what Marcus said?"

Claire nodded, pulling herself together. "There isn't a second to waste. Pack up your things. Take only what you need and can carry without drawing too much attention to yourself." She squared her shoulders, trying to look and sound confident. "We head for the Council Buildings. I still have the token to get into the complex and we can find the stables from there."

As soon as they got inside the complex, Claire knew where to go. Men and women in black and grey cotton with the symbol of the city stitched on their chest hurried with baskets of food and drinking skins towards a point to the left of the main building. Not all of them were in uniforms so she and the others could hopefully blend in. Claire made sure the others were right behind her, and set off in the same direction, a small bag of coins tied through her belt sitting hot against her skin. She'd elected to leave most of their stolen supplies behind, taking only what they could fit into pockets. They had to be able to run if they needed to. Lotte had nothing but spare coin, dry biscuits, and hard cheese. Gareth and Jemroth had added tiny daggers to their boots. They kept their heads down.

Claire picked her way past the side of the building, letting servants brush past her. In front of them rose squat mud-brick buildings. It was here that supplies were dumped, men with long, unravelled parchment scrolls marking items off on lists, then directing people to take them in hessian sacks to the nearby sheds. Claire glanced about, trying to spot the stables. A woman pushed past her, leading three horses by the reins. Hoping no one would look at her too carefully in the bustle, she followed close behind the animals, with Lotte, Gareth and Jemroth close behind.

Every step felt closer to discovery. When someone shoved at Claire, she was sure they would call out and ask her what she thought she was doing, especially as she wasn't carrying anything useful to the war effort. Yet somehow, she made it into the darkness of an empty stable, straw and dirt packed to make a hard surface and wooden stalls stretching out as far as she could see. To her right, troughs full to the brim with feed waited.

Now, for the hardest part. Convincing someone to let them come along. Luckily, she'd thought of a plan as she'd wended her way through the city. She'd claim Wallis had sent her party to join the army as a sign of support for Eidan's new anti-magic policy. With the councillor well known for his fanaticism, hopefully no one would question her story. Then, she thought, as she untied her bag of coins and settled it in her hand, people could always be bribed.

Lotte, Jemroth and Gareth jingled their own coin behind her, the agreed signal to indicate someone was coming.

Claire spun around to come face to face with an irritated looking overseer, the metal on his belt gleaming from polish and his attire crisp. "What're you doing?" He demanded belligerently as Lotte, Gareth and Jemroth tried to give nothing away in their expressions. "I've no time for slackers." He squinted and stepped closer, "And why aren't you in uniform?"

Claire clasped her hands together, wishing her heart wasn't beating quite so loudly. "Please, Sir, Wallis sent us to help with the horses. I'm one of the best in his stable."

"I've received no word," he snarled.

Claire held out the bag of coin. "He sent this too, for the overseer who will take his people on."

The man's eyes lit up with greed. He snatched the bag out of Claire's hand. "If you can manage the war horse on the end, I'll take you. Brighid knows, half the servitors I've been sent are lazy brats and the other half piss themselves at the barest mention of magic." He peered at Claire. "Are you scared, girl?"

Claire decided for a half-truth. "A little," she admitted, "but Wallis says the people of Kelnariat are made of stronger stuff than those as use magic and we'll catch them unawares and beat them bloody before the week's out."

"Hm," the overseer said. "Get to the far stall and let me see what you're made of. His name's Luln and he needs a brush and a feed." He turned to Gareth and the others and pointed to the following stalls, then clicked his fingers. "And you three can do the same with the next few along."

Claire did as she was told, trudging to the wooden door, and reaching for the bulky bolt. She wasn't too nervous. She and Marcus had ridden horses since they were four and she'd met her fair share of temperamental creatures. She made sure she side-stepped as the door swung open. Sure enough, the horse kicked out the second he saw her. Making crooning noises, Claire cautiously entered his stall, grabbing the brush from a wooden plank at eye height as she did so.

She brushed Luln as gently as she could, feeling the horse calm at her gentle touch. Soon, she was able to lead him outside to the troughs of oats and barley she'd seen on her way in. Jemroth followed less than a minute later with Gareth close behind, their own horses tall and proud.

Come on, Lotte! Claire thought as the overseer shifted his feet like he grew bored. This was the riskiest part of her plan. The exile hadn't ever ridden horses or even really been around them until she'd met Claire and joined the Dorrans. The man was tapping his boot heel hard now. Claire had to do something fast. She reached for *learth*, aiming cold flame at the far end of the stable. Within seconds, the overseer screamed, and she knew her spell had worked. As he ran outside shouting for buckets of water, she quickly doused her working, a bit of sweat dripping down her neck as the smell of burnt meat faded.

She gripped Gareth by the elbow as he gaped. "Take off your shirt and pretend you put it out. I'll help Lotte."

Without waiting for acknowledgement, she raced for Lotte's stall. Her friend stood white-faced, backed into a corner as her horse snorted belligerently her direction.

"It's all right," Claire whispered. She grabbed the horse's halter and led it outside, thrusting the rope into Jemroth's hands, then headed back for Lotte.

Lotte shook like a leaf. "I can't do this. I'll have to wait in Kelnariat for ya to close the Rift."

"I don't think so," Gareth's voice came from behind her.

Claire made a quick decision. She could tell from Gareth's face he didn't believe Lotte and thought this was a ruse to get away from them. "Get the rest of your coin together," she said shortly. "We'll bribe the overseer to let Lotte take care of rations, and you too, so you can keep an eye on her, not that she needs it."

"But—"

Claire could see Gareth was upset about having to do anything with the exile, but Claire didn't care. She'd had enough. She didn't have time for more arguments. "Maen and then your father made me the leader of this group. You'll do as you're told."

Chapter Thirty-Two

CLAIRE COULDN'T HELP but feel content as she sat at the front of a cart directing her two horses onwards. Thank goodness Jemroth had taught her the basics of driving. She was no expert, but she could manage. Three quarters of the day had passed since Eidan had ordered his army out of the city at first light. The sun was high in the sky and the gentle clip-clop of hooves against the wide dirt road was soothing after the drama of yesterday. Lotte and Gareth were inside her cart, cramped alongside animal skin tents, warm blankets and coats, while Jemroth was driving a cart a spot or two behind her in the snaking army line. The rest of the baggage train stretched out for miles ahead and behind, carrying tents, weapons, bandages, food and other medical supplies.

They'd passed through two towns and crossed the river at a wide stone bridge around mid-morning. The land had been green and fertile, dotted with farmhouses and villages, farmers glancing up and smiling or waving in cheerful acknowledgement as they slowly passed. However, as the afternoon wore on, farmhouses became few and far between, the road grew rocky and ill-kept and the ground harder and more unforgiving. As dusk fell, Eidan called a halt, and overseers commanded coats and blankets be distributed as an unnatural chill descended.

Claire glanced behind her and Jemroth waved before getting on with settling his horses. She copied his movements, the action of soothing her own mounts reminding her of home and relaxing her nerves too, then she went to help with setting up tents. Lotte followed her at a careful distance while Gareth took Jemroth's lead to tend to the many horses in the baggage train. The falling darkness was somehow comforting as Claire struck at peg after peg. As she worked, she kept an eye out for Marcus. The sooner she could speak with him the better.

Sidling closer to the vanguard – the other servants didn't protest as she was clearly doing more than her fair share of work – she was inconspicuous in a sea of other plainly uniformed men and women, her dyed brown hair pulled back in a ponytail. As she toiled, red dots bloomed into life as campfires were lit, smoke and the crackle of burning kindling filling the air. The sight was a little magical and Claire could almost forget the danger she was in. With a sigh, she tore her gaze away, reminding herself to look for Marcus. Men and women in leather uniforms with the symbol of Kelnariat stitched at their chest huddled in groups, some leaning against spears or with arms crossed, others sitting in circles and munching on dried meat.

Squinting, she saw Eidan and some of his advisors, including Heath, standing by an enormous animal hide tent covered with a purple silk overlay. Her breath caught as she saw Marcus standing at his right. As she stared, Marcus looked up, his eyes meeting hers. He took an uncertain half-step back from the others, then made a muttered excuse, heading right for her.

Her heart hammered. She hoped he'd had the sense to say nothing to Eidan about her presence or she'd have to make a wild run for it. She made sure Marcus still had his gaze trained on her as she ducked behind a cluster of tents so Eidan was no longer in view.

She barely had time to compose herself and think through what she'd say before Marcus poked his head around the tent, his hands outstretched. "I knew you'd see sense, Claire! Come and meet Eidan!"

Claire groaned. She should have predicted this. Her brother had said she should come see him again if she changed her mind and she *was* in Eidan's war camp. "What did you tell him, Marcus?" she hissed, sliding her fingers out of his grasp.

He blinked, caught off guard. "Nothing," he said. "I promised I wouldn't, but why does that matter now?"

"I'm not here to switch sides," she said, figuring it was better to be blunt. There was no sugar coating this. "I came to ask you to listen. You need to come away with me. It's the only way we can get home."

His face flushed in the half-light and his fist clenched and unclenched at his side. "Not this again, Sis. Just admit you're wrong."

Claire pulled Marcus close to her side as a knot of soldiers ambled past, heading for a pile of blankets laid out in a circle. "I'm not. You and Eidan are being misled. The Beast is a creature of the Rift and will be destroyed with it. It can't take you back to Shale. It wants to survive so it's telling you what you want to hear."

"I ... how can you be so sure?"

"It's visited me in nightmares and when I perform bigger spells. It came to the Dream Mages too. It killed Rinn Taccala, no matter what Eidan claims."

"You keep going on about having magical talent, but I haven't seen the proof."

Claire lit a cold flame in the palm of her hand. "There. Will that do?"

Marcus's eyes widened in shock, but then to her surprise he turned away, lips twisted like the sight pained him. When he finally swung back to face her, he sounded strained, like he suppressed tears. "If this is true, you must come and tell Eidan what you know. It will be safer for you. The Council will know you mean well. Not only that, but your friends will also regain their lost status too." He looked about the cluster of tents near them like he'd find a troupe of Claire's allies behind an open flap.

Claire considered his words. If Eidan was a total innocent in what was happening in Kelnarium, then Marcus's plan was a good one, but the truth was she didn't know what motivated the leader. Worse, she feared the hatred and distrust of magical brethren that he'd engendered in his people had taken on a life of its own. Even if Eidan believed her, there'd be others keen to snuff out her life. Wallis and Heath for a start.

She shook her head regretfully. "It's too risky. We're better off going now and when everything is fixed, if Eidan's friendship means so much to you, we can go back and explain the situation to him before Gwenivere sends us to Shale."

"I can't run off without so much as a message," Marcus said uncomfortably.

"Why?" Claire asked. Who cared about upsetting someone when a whole world was at stake?

"Like you'd understand, Claire," he said, face screwing up in anger. "He treated me like his equal from the first; he recognised my talents, he listened to me, he's taken me under his wing. He knows I deserve more than a backwater country town like Shale, that I'm smart and talented and charismatic."

Claire had never thought of Marcus as being conceited before but as he stood next to her with arms folded over his chest, his lips in a sulky pout, she couldn't help but think that Kelnarium had brought out the worst in him.

"For all I know, Eidan is in league with the Beast knowing full well what the outcome will be," she said. "Have you stopped to consider that you wrote off Grandfather too quickly and put too much stock in Eidan? He isn't the Mr Perfect you make him out to be. He murdered the Dorrans and I'm fairly certain he paid men to murder the villagers and exiles around Kelnariat and Dorran Manor."

"Why on Earth would he destroy his own people, his own world?"

"I don't know. Right now, it doesn't matter because he's a murderer, however he justifies that to himself and to you."

"So? I believe Eidan will get me home. I believe Mum went to our world with Dad to get away from our shitty Kelnarium relatives. I believe she's been obsessed with her charity work ever since as a kind of atonement. I believe if she were here, she'd tell you to do what I say because I'm the oldest."

"Mum only left because Dad wasn't coping away from Shale," Claire said. "Yeah, I agree she felt bad about how her family treated the exiles, but that doesn't mean she stopped loving her Dorran relatives."

Marcus looked mutinous. "That's not what Eidan told me."

Claire rolled her eyes. "Because he's totally unbiased when it comes to the Dorrans." She paused for breath as uncharitable thoughts loomed. She had a horrible feeling she understood why Marcus had turned away at the sight of her *learth* ability. "You know what I think?"

"What?"

"You're jealous that Kelnarium needs me instead of you. You can't stand being bad at something for once. I bet at Dorran Manor, you couldn't handle sucking at magic and because it wouldn't come easy, you didn't try. I bet you hated people not falling at your feet in adulation. Get over your hurt pride, Marcus, and do the right thing."

He reeled back like she'd slapped him, then studied her face carefully. "So, what you're saying is you won't see Eidan." His voice held a nasty edge. "Not now, not ever, come hell or high water. It's your way or the highway. Fine, but let me remind you, I'm the eldest and our parents would want me to look after you. If I need to tell Eidan you're in his camp to save you from yourself, I will."

"What do you mean?" Her skin prickled. "Don't give me away, Marcus. You can't."

"I'll do what I think's best," Marcus replied.

"No," Claire said bitterly. "You don't want to admit I'm correct about Eidan and the Beast because if you do, you'll have to admit you've been a bit of an idiot. Not only that, you don't want to tarnish your precious Kelnariat reputation, which is what will happen if Eidan finds out I'm alive and working against him."

The guilt in her brother's eyes told her that she was right.

"Get away from me," she said.

"But—" he began.

"Go."

Marcus stared, lips parted in shock.

So much had changed since she and Marcus had spent that day in Shale's National Park. Back then, they'd been close. Now, she and Marcus were stuck on two opposing sides, each convinced that the other was in the wrong. Could Claire find a way to bridge that gap? As Marcus stumbled away from her, hurt and confusion in his eyes and tears glistening on his cheeks, she knew it was no use. Her brother's pride would never let him admit he'd made a terrible mistake in trusting Eidan.

Chapter Thirty-Three

CLAIRE WORKED SIDE by side with the boy she was paired with, removing saddles from horses and brushing them down before putting on warm blankets for the night. Earlier, she'd quickly told the others about Marcus as they ate dry biscuit and Jemroth took care of his own horse; they'd looked so glum she'd told them to find something to do beyond mope. She patted the glossy chestnut coat of the horse in front of her, trying not to think about Peony in Shale. She wondered if her beloved pet would even remember her by the time she returned to her farmhouse.

It was no use thinking like that. Claire had to pull herself together. She'd wait until they were nearer the Rift and then steal a horse and ride hard for Gwenivere. They'd have to come up with a way to close the blasted thing without Marcus.

The boy next to her cleared his throat shyly. She glanced up. "You dropped your brush," he said, "and you didn't notice." He pulled a sympathetic face. "I've seen how hard you work. I can take care of this." He waved at the rows of horses tied to wooden stakes hammered into the ground. "Get some rest."

"I know I won't get to sleep," Claire explained shortly. "I'd rather help." She bent to pick up the brush.

The boy pushed floppy blonde curls back from his forehead. "You're scared?"

It took Claire a moment to understand what he meant. For many of the servants, the fear of bumping into magical brethren was ever present. She shook her head.

"I am," he admitted. He held out a rough palm. "My name's Gav. You?"

"Clera," she said, using the fake name she'd used in Autun. She shot him a grudging smile. "I guess I'm a little scared."

"I reckon you're one of those people who works themselves to the bone to keep fear at bay."

"Yeah, something like that."

"They're people of flesh and blood like you and me," he said, reaching out to put a comforting hand on her arm. "I like to remind myself of that when I feel my heart racing."

Claire stopped brushing her horse. "What do you mean?"

"I'm one of Eidan's personal servitor's," he said, straightening to his full height with chest out, "and this horse is his. Did you know?"

Claire made her eyes go wide. "No. What a beautiful creature." It wasn't a lie. Eidan's horse was tall and muscly with a shining coat of coal black.

"Yeah," Gav said. "He's a real beauty. Everything of Eidan's is. You should see his apartments in the Council Building."

"If it's anything like Wallis's ..." Claire lied.

"Oh, *him*," Gav said. "I had to take a message there once and his are nothing compared to Eidan's; he's got damask and brocade bedding, curtains and walls, more gold and silver than you can poke a stick at, trays and trays of mead and honey and cheese and grapes. I'm hungry just thinking about it. Not that he likes it overmuch," he sighed. "Eidan prefers the simple life, but the rules of office are such that he must look the part and that's my point. You don't have to worry about magic with Eidan to protect us. He doesn't stand for that sort of thing at all. He's big on protecting common people because at his core he's one of us."

Claire remembered the way Eidan had spoken at Rinn's funeral and the rumours flying around Kelnariat's streets about him raising his sword for the poor and the innocent, a real Robin Hood figure, and wasn't all that surprised that Gav spouted the same rhetoric.

"Those magical types are pretty powerful though," she said absently, unbuckling a strap.

"Yeah, but so's Eidan. I've seen how he's dealt with them before."

Claire stiffened, the horse's saddle slipping to one side. With a muttered curse, she caught it and adjusted her stance. She was overreacting. Gav was probably just referring to a public event. It wasn't likely that a servant like him would have been at Dorran Manor. If he had been involved in her

Grandfather's murder, why she'd ... she'd ... there was nothing she could do. "With magical brethren?" she asked cautiously, willing herself to calm down.

"Yeah," Gav said. He dropped his voice conspiratorially. "I've found remains of Dorran uniforms stashed at the back of his office cupboard before. I bet he killed a bunch of those marauders, don't you?"

Claire bit her tongue to prevent herself giving something away. She was willing to bet hard coin on those uniforms being used by some of Eidan's men to masquerade as Dorrans.

"And then, there was a man arrested by Eidan. One of those Maellwyns."

Gav had to mean Bron. Claire nearly stopped breathing. "Was this recent?" she asked, trying to sound casual.

"Oh no," Gav explained. "Two weeks back."

Two weeks back? But that was before Claire and the others had even arrived in Kelnariat. Did this mean Bron had been the traitor all along?

"Eidan had a lot of 'chats' with him and," he said proudly, "I was kneeling beside him with the torture implements. The Maellwyn soon talked. Apparently, there was some girl and her friends coming to the city from their Manor to wreak havoc. Eidan wanted this Bron to sell her out when she arrived. He tried to deny Eidan, but see, he had a bond mate in town and Eidan isn't afraid to twist the knife when he has to."

"You mean he threatened him with hurting his wife? But that's ... that's barbaric," Claire stammered.

"It's what we must do to protect our own," Gav said, obviously unaware of her inner turmoil. "But that doesn't make it pretty." He reached out to pat her shoulder. "I hated every second I watched it happen, truth be told," and indeed his dark eyes were haunted. "His screams still haunt my dreams, yet we had no choice."

Wrong! Claire wanted to scream. *You and everyone else have been duped by Eidan and you'll all pay for it.* But there was no point. She'd merely give herself away.

"What happened to him?" she asked. "Is he dead?" She hoped she sounded eager enough that Gav would assume she wanted to know more out of fear of magic.

"I don't think so, but Eidan isn't likely to tell me much either. I suppose he'll be hanged in a public execution once we get back from the Riftlands, unless he expires in his cell first."

"Good," Claire said. If Bron was still alive, she and the others could eventually get to Kelnariat and rescue him.

Inside, thoughts rolled like ocean waves. She wondered how the others would feel about Bron being the real traitor, albeit under duress. All alone in a big city with no magical talent to defend himself, what else could he have done? *Die for the cause*, a nasty voice whispered. Claire suppressed it, even as she suspected that might be how Gareth and Jemroth would feel. As for her? If Alaya had truly been threatened by Eidan, Claire couldn't blame Bron for giving the game away. She had to talk to the others.

She got the saddle off the horse and smiled weakly at Gav. "Do you mind if I take that break after all? I'm suddenly exhausted." At his sympathetic nod, she hurried to the centre of the hodgepodge army camp, only running once she was well out of Gav's sight.

She found Gareth, Jemroth and Lotte with their backs to a cart, thick blankets wrapped around their shoulders. Lotte was pressed tight between Gareth and Jemroth, looking uncomfortable and trapped. *Well*, Claire thought, *soon they'll have to give her a break.*

Gareth glanced up at Claire's heavy footsteps. He flung her a spare blanket and pointed beside him.

Taking the blanket, Claire wrapped it around herself but instead of sitting beside him, she sat directly in front of the trio, ignoring the chilly wind at her back. "I learnt something about Eidan and Bron," she whispered. "One of Eidan's boys thought I was afraid of magic and I let him believe it. He tried to reassure me that magical brethren were no match for the Council, telling me Eidan had tortured a Maellwyn two weeks ago and threatened his wife. Eidan learnt I was alive at Maellwyn Manor and planning to come to the capital thanks to a tip-off from the Beast. Marcus mentioned that in Kelnariat – the Beast coming to Eidan in dreams. When Eidan knew I was alive, he picked up Bron."

Even in the half-light, Claire could see Gareth's eyes widen. Jemroth's expression was unreadable.

Lotte lent forward. "Yer sayin' Bron were the one as gave the safe house away?"

"Impossible," Gareth snapped. "I never did believe it, even when you two tried your best to convince us. Maellwyn House is a close-knit family, same as Dorran House."

"I'm sorry, Gareth," Claire said gently. "Bron sold us out to Eidan. As far as the boy, Gav, knows, Bron's in a cell in Kelnariat awaiting execution. Don't be too hard on him when you meet him again. They tortured him and threatened Alaya." She fixed Gareth and Jemroth with stern glares. "But that's to worry about another day. The upshot of all this is Lotte is innocent. You owe her an apology."

Jemroth frowned. "But she's still an exile and a sworn enemy of our people." He prodded Lotte's side. "Everyone knows she'd stab as soon as look at us."

"Why?" Claire demanded. "She wants to survive this as much as the rest of us, which means we have to live, at least until the Rift is closed."

"There's nothing stopping her turning on us afterwards," Gareth said darkly.

Claire wanted to throw something. These two would keep finding excuse after excuse to distrust Lotte and she could see nothing she could say would make them change their minds. She shook her head apologetically at her friend, but the exile didn't notice, being too busy staring into the distance, lips pressed in a mutinous line.

Chapter Thirty-Four

THE SUN WAS CHILLY and the land black, dry and hard, not a single farmer, house or crop in sight. No birds, no insects, no wild animals either. Claire recognised the barren oddness of the landscape from her original summons to Kelnarium. After three days of steady travel, they'd reached the borders of the Riftlands. The army draped themselves in thick coats and furs, stamping their boots against the cold. If Claire was any judge, overnight there'd be frost. Red spots formed in cheeks and people rubbed their hands and blew on them. Claire shivered against four layers, a head covering and her scarf as well as a blanket over her knees.

The novelty of the road had worn off. Claire's muscles ached from stiffness and she was tired of the emptiness stretching out forever and of the endless chores to be completed as soon as Eidan called a halt. As she steered her horses, Claire cursed Eidan, her grandfather, Marcus, even her parents for getting her into this mess. Why her? But then, deep down she knew she wasn't serious. Who'd want to live a normal life mired in school lessons? She might die trying to save Kelnarium, but she'd have learnt *learth*, tried some cool spells, even met wondrous salamanders and other magical creatures. And she'd met Lotte, who despite the suspicion of the others, genuinely seemed to still want Claire as a friend. All of that counted for something.

She glanced at the sky; primary colours blending with cloud letting her know they were almost at the Rift. She traced the shadows it generated and squinted at one in the distance. An enormous shadowy human figure stood at the horizon, and though Claire couldn't be sure from that distance, the outline looked remarkably like someone she knew. As though sensing her attention, the shadow darted away, shrouded in mist. Perhaps Claire was overtired and had imagined the Crian's silhouette. Even as she stared, the Saura appeared overhead, its great tail curling and uncurling as it raised its webbed foot in greeting. Claire wondered if the Dorran fire elemental had scared the Crian off. It blinked in silence and vanished.

Turning her thoughts back to her main task, she thought of Marcus again. She'd avoided him, figuring he could find her if he wanted to chat. She wished he wasn't so stubborn. Although each night, she and Lotte had sat cramped next to each other and whispered about what to do, they hadn't been able to think of a better plan beyond stealing a horse and riding away. If Claire couldn't think of something by tomorrow morning, she'd have to set off.

Tears prickled. Damn Marcus. Why couldn't she do this without him? She remembered the way the Beast had looked at the Maellwyns secret place when she'd seen who she needed to help her defeat it once and for all; there'd been fear and despair in its eyes and something else too, an odd furtiveness she'd never questioned.

Claire sat up, jerking the reins so hard the horses almost clattered to a halt. "Sorry pals," she whispered, a slow smile creeping at her growing excitement. Why hadn't she thought of this before? The Beast didn't want her to close the Rift because it died with it. Gwenivere and she had discussed the nightmares it sent might be a double-edged sword. Even if they contained elements of truth, they were designed to unsettle Claire. Why couldn't the vision she'd been sent when she was performing magic have been the same? She barely noticed the baggage train slowing to set up camp, members of the army wheeling back to give directives.

The secret place was the first time Claire had tried Kelt's spell with others. What if the Beast had come in a panic because she was closer to cracking the puzzle of how to close the Rift and in its panic, it'd shown her the solution unwittingly? The pair had a connection to each other that couldn't be easily severed. When it had realised what it had done, it had misdirected her with Marcus, knowing how much she idolised him. If she was right, she didn't need Marcus at all. Anyone from House Ushanan would do.

She slumped in defeat. It was a wonderful theory, but there wasn't anyone else left with air *learth*. She was grasping at straws.

Lotte rapped at the barrier between Claire and the rest of the cart. "Are ya going to stop, or d'ya want us to slam into the next person?"

Claire's eyes widened. With a sharp cluck and tight tug, she brought their cart to a halt, heart beating hard at how close she'd come to causing an accident and injuring the precious horses. She dismounted and undid the harnesses, joining in with the hustle and bustle of setting up for the evening, her mind circling back to her theory as she pushed through mundane chores. If only Lord Maellwyn had picked up a stray Ushanan like he'd done with Jemroth and House Domain, but Claire hadn't met a single person who had a drop of their blood beyond herself and her brother.

As she handed out stale biscuit and strips of dried salted meat to waiting soldiers, Lotte joined her. "I wish they'd stop treatin' me as though I'm rotting fish," she sighed.

"Ignore them," Claire said through clenched teeth, knowing Lotte referred to Gareth and Jemroth.

A captain waved them over and told them to help distribute skins of water and hand out cups of beer to the men. "They deserve it," he said. "We'll face the enemy tomorrow."

As Claire and Lotte set off in the direction of the supplies, Lotte muttered under her breath, so Claire had to lean in to hear. "I hate this. I can't even leave. I've no money, no home, no family. Yer all I got. Mebbe me family was cursed."

"Don't be silly."

"Me mam lost everything too," Lotte said. "All her brothers and sisters, cousins and friends killed."

Claire stopped, suddenly realising she'd heard something significant, something that had been in front of her all along. "What'd you say?" She reached forward to clutch Lotte's arm, ignoring her surprised "Ouch."

"They was all killed somewhere west of here."

"Listen, Lotte. This is important. You said your Mum stumbled into your camp and that's how she met your father. She never revealed her real identity, right?"

"Nope," Lotte shrugged. "She wouldn't talk about it, but Da thought she'd escaped from a bad bonding or somethin' 'coz one morning, a week after he took her in, he caught her flinging a ring in the river. Real silver with a turquoise stone he said. He told me when I was young not to poke and pry. He said Ma were scarred by what happened and she wanted to leave it behind, that rich men ain't always the best bond mates. Hey, where're ya going?"

But Claire was already running through the camp to find the others, thoughts whizzing like popcorn. Was it possible Lotte's mother had flung away a ring just like the one Claire wore hidden around her own neck, making her not just a member of House Ushanan, but the heir to its Lord? Perhaps she'd been caught up in Kelt's spell and, traumatised by what she'd seen and done, run away once she'd been freed of his control, wanting nothing more than to leave that life behind. Claire could understand a desire to never touch magic again after an event like that and it would explain her desire to throw the ring away too, a symbol of her past vanished forever.

And then she remembered something else, triggered perhaps by her unexpected sighting of the Crian earlier; Lotte explaining that the Melinor and their queen had helped her from childhood, as she had also helped her mother. Perhaps the Melinor were the magical brethren affiliated with Ushanan House, just as Dorran House had salamanders, Maellwyn House had its Mer people and Domain House its gnomes. She was sure she had enough evidence to demonstrate Lotte's mother had been the last surviving magical member of House Ushanan and that made Lotte …

Claire began to sprint.

Only when Jemroth and Gareth were inside their halted cart away from listening ears would Claire ask the questions that clamoured to spill out. "I haven't been entirely honest with you," she admitted, flinging blankets at the pair and wrapping one around herself. Gareth stared at her expectantly while Jemroth played with a loose woollen thread on his coat. "What can you tell me of the Crian and her Melinor?" she asked.

"The Crian?" Jemroth barked. He put a hand over his mouth and forced himself to take a breath, then repeated his question again, softer.

"So, you know of her?" Claire said.

"Know of her?" Gareth repeated, a strained note in his voice. "Everyone at Maellwyn Manor has learnt of that foul spirit and her kind. I'm surprised you didn't hear about her from your grandfather. She's no friend of Dorran House either."

Claire suppressed a shiver. The Crian had never come up in history classes, but she'd also never asked Maen anything further, albeit at Lotte's request. Her friend had explained she'd overheard Rael bad-mouthing the Crian and was afraid of how the Dorran's would treat her if they knew she spoke with the creature. "Tell me about her, and the Melinor," she said firmly.

"Why?" Gareth demanded.

She closed her eyes for a moment, offering up a silent apology to Lotte. The time for secrecy was over. "When I ran away from Grandfather, and found Lotte in the exile camp, the Crian appeared. She warned me there was danger at the Manor and whisked me and Lotte there, leaving us outside. I didn't ask Maen about her because we were escaping from certain death at Eidan's hands." She fixed Gareth with a stern glare. "So why do Maellwyn House and Dorran House hate the Melinor?"

Gareth's mouth opened and closed like a floundering fish. Finally, he pressed his lips together and squeezed his eyes shut. To Claire's surprise tears appeared at the corner of his eyes.

Claire laid a hand gently on his back. "I'm sorry for asking a painful question, but I wouldn't press you like this unless it was important."

Gareth wiped away his tears. He swallowed and opened his eyes. "I told you my father's first wife died at the battle that created the Rift, alongside many other Maellwyns, including my aunt and uncle."

"Yes, I remember," Claire said encouragingly. Her uncle and a host of Dorrans had died too.

"Perhaps Lord Dorran and my father could have stopped Kelt and his monstrous working if they'd made it to the battlefield in time."

"Sure, but how was the Crian involved?"

"I'm getting to that," he said, unable to meet her eyes. "You know how each House has its own magical creatures?"

"Yes," Claire said. She hugged herself under her blanket, certain her theory was about to be proved correct.

"Well, House Ushanan's creatures were the Melinor spirits, ruled over by their queen, known as the Crian. Historically, the magical creatures stay out of politics and decision-making. Whatever their House says and does, they support, only we thought with Selk and the certain bloodshed coming the Crian would change her mind." He looked up. "My father and your grandfather begged her for help to make it to House Ushanan and the battlefield to stop Kelt doing what they knew he was planning. She could have whisked them where they needed to go, as she did for you. She refused."

"Why?" Claire was amazed. If the Crian could have prevented Kelt from making his spell, Claire might never have needed to come to Kelnarium.

"Because House Ushanan, like House Domain, didn't sign Selk's treaty, preferring war to capitulation. We were ranged to stop it and she knew it. She would not betray her House for us, no matter how hard we begged her, even though it meant their downfall. The rest, as you know, is history. Our Houses were too late to stop the spell." He frowned. "We knew she and her kind hid themselves in the Silent Vale after the Rift was formed. No one has seen hide nor hair of her since. Until you."

Claire sensed the truth in Gareth's story. Why else had the Crian, an elemental leader who, like the rest of the elementals, was only meant to speak with her own kind's Lord or Lady, spoken to her? Had it been because of the Crian's guilt over her role in the Rift's creation? She remembered Gareth saying at Maellwyn Manor that the special object of House Ushanan was quartz and shivered as Lotte's mum's necklace swam before her, complete with feathers, beads and crystal. Why had Lotte's mother insisted her daughter always keep the necklace on her person? What if the House Ushanan necklace was the rusting silver chain and quartz and the exiled style beads and feathers had been used to disguise that fact? It all added up. "How do you test someone for *learth*?"

He stared at her uncomprehending as Jemroth's eyes widened.

"Why did the Crian help you?" Gareth asked at last.

"Because she saw I had the mark of another world about me and I told her about Gwenivere's second prophecy. I believe that like Lyssa, she wanted to make amends for her part in the Rift's formation," she said. "Now, please, answer me; how do I test someone for *learth*?"

Gareth stared at her, then shook his head wearily, like the force of her personality was too much for him. "Hold your hand out, palm parallel to the person your testings face, get into the meditative state as though you're going to join magic with someone else and when you open your eyes, you'll see an aura about them."

"Like with Maen or with you and Jemroth?" she asked eagerly. "The different colours, I mean?"

"Yes, like that—"

But Claire was already on her feet, snatching a heel of bread and dried meat ready to re-join Lotte.

Fifteen minutes later, she found her friend wending her way back through the camp.

"Yer making me dizzy with how often ya appear and disappear," Lotte said, though she didn't sound too annoyed.

Claire angled her head towards a patch of tents near the horses tethered for the night. Arm in arm, the pair reached the quieter spot Claire had indicated, barely anyone about but for a knot of servants huddled together for warmth. Now that they were almost on top of the Rift, the army stayed tight knit.

"What's all this about?" Lotte demanded.

"I never told anyone about the Crian, just like I promised you," Claire whispered, dragging Lotte to sit beside her, in the shadow of a bulky tent. "Until tonight."

"What? Why'd ya blab?" Lotte said, startled.

"Shh, keep your voice down," Claire said, looking around furtively, but no one even glanced their way.

Lotte relaxed, seeming to reconsider what Claire had done. "I 'spose now they know I'm an exile it don't matter."

"I told them because of what you said earlier, about your mother."

"What about her?" Lotte shrugged.

"I think she was of a magical House called Ushanan. The House of Air." Claire gripped Lotte's arm excitedly. "If I'm right, we can use you instead of Marcus to close the Rift."

Lotte laughed scornfully. "Now yer reaching. I can't be magical. I'm an exile, remember?"

"If your mum was caught up in Kelt's spell, and she was the only House Ushanan survivor, it would explain why she never mentioned her past. Besides, I've been thinking about the Crian. You see, each House has its own magical creature that's kind of like their emblem. House Ushanan's are the Melinor spirits. Gareth just confirmed it." She rushed on at Lotte's sceptical expression. "And that's not all. *Learth* users possessed objects to signify their House." She pulled her tunic aside to show Lotte her salamander egg pendant. "This is mine. Jemroth's is his bronze disc and Gareth's is his vial of seawater. You're not meant to take them off because they connect us with our elementals and our magic. House Ushanan's was quartz crystal, and there are some of them on your mum's necklace. It can't all be a coincidence and she was insistent you keep it. Then there's the turquoise ring your dad mentioned. Each House ruler had a special ring. My grandfather's was an opal ring, for example. All this points to one thing: I think your mum was the daughter of House Ushanan's Lord."

"It's too much to hope for," Lotte said, clasping her hands together. "If I do have magical ability like ya, Gareth and Jemroth'll have to trust me." She looked towards the horizon. "I always did wonder why the Crian and her kind helped me but vanished at the merest presence of another exile." Her face fell. "But why didn't she help me mam much?"

Claire thought hard. "Perhaps because your mum wanted to sever all ties with her past. But we don't need to keep fruitlessly conjecturing. There's a way I can check who you really are. Maen tested my magical strength when I first arrived in Kelnarium. Gareth told me how to do it. Will you let me test you?"

Lotte laughed. "Are ya crazy? 'Course ya can. What do I do?"

"You don't have to do anything except wait. I'm going to close my eyes and draw on *learth*. If anyone notices us, give me a good shake and I'll come back.

Claire sat on her heels, silently asking the Saura to grant her courage. She was hoping the spell was such a small one the Beast wouldn't appear, but she couldn't guarantee it. She started the process, emptying her mind of anything but the gentle rise and fall of her chest. Soon, she felt ready to open her eyes. The world was tinged with a whitish fog. She could barely make out the tents and the soldiers were rimmed with shadow. Between them, pale phantoms walked about. Her own *learth* was a vibrant crimson in the darkness.

She fixed her attention ahead of her. Amongst the surrounding dullness, Lotte glowed, tinged with bright silver and pure white. As Claire stretched her hand out, it felt like an electrical charge whipped through her body and her blood sang, like calling to like.

She'd only half believed her own theory, scared to hope too hard after so many disappointments and setbacks, but her vision wasn't lying. Lotte had magical ability, and a lot of it too if Claire was any judge.

As she rushed back to share the wonderful news, she made the mistake of looking up. The sky's strange colours hadn't dulled. Instead, the terrifying vibrancy of the Rift's shifting reds, blues, greens and yellows physically hurt, its beauty a thousand times stronger because she saw the world through *learth*.

Even as she watched, familiar tendrils reached towards her, the Beast's loud laugh so crippling it felt like a thousand blows to the head; only this time she heard hysteria and fear beneath the cackles. Lotte *was* key to everything and the creature knew it.

Chapter Thirty-Five

THE DAWN BLOOMED CLEAR and bright. Claire could see for miles when she looked outside their moving cart, an early morning breeze having blown away the campfire smoke. The landscape was tough as nails with black patches stretching out on either side of the baggage train, but it was the sight above her that was spellbinding. The sky gleamed with strong primary colours. Scarring the horizon, a long black crack ran along its entire width. Smoke wisped at its torn edges.

"The Rift," Lotte breathed, as she peered outside the cart's curtain over Claire's shoulder.

Gareth ignored them. Though last night Claire and Lotte had shared the good news about Lotte's latent magical ability, neither he nor Jemroth had been too pleased. Claire longed to pull a face at him, but she knew it wouldn't help.

"We've no time to lose," she said to Lotte instead, letting the curtain fall back into place and pretending she hadn't heard Jemroth's pained sighs up ahead where he directed the horses. Eidan's servant boy had taken pity on Claire this morning, thinking her overworked given he'd watched her pretend to stagger away from him back to camp the previous evening. He'd taken over driving her cart when the baggage train had begun to move again which had suited Claire perfectly because now she, Lotte, Gareth and Jemroth were all together as they neared their final destination. "Like I explained yesterday, I don't know the first thing about House Ushanan spells, but Lyssa taught us how to connect and draw on each other's *learth* as Kelt did and that's all you'll need to learn to help me close the Rift."

Gareth sniffed and turned away.

Claire raised her voice. "And you, Gareth, shall help. When Lotte and I can connect, you must add yourself to the braid."

He muttered something under his breath but didn't deny her.

She turned her attention back to Lotte. "Plump up some blankets and lie down. Breathe in and out slowly like you saw me do in the mountains with Lyssa." She waited for Lotte to do as she asked, the exile's eyes wide with interest.

They had a few hours before they reached Gwenivere's party, so Claire had decided now was the time to practise. This was their one shot to get it right. As soon as the army made ready for battle, Claire and the others would have no choice but to try and close the Rift, regardless of how prepared they felt. Or how on-board Gareth and Jemroth were with Claire's plan to use Lotte.

"I'll be right next to you," she made herself go on, crossing her legs, arm brushing against the basket of bread and cheese she'd taken out of the supplies bag to ensure all of them could restore their strength after the working. "Now, when I do this, I imagine fire flowing through and beyond me and let the power rush through my body. I know it's there, but I don't use it. Then, when I open my eyes, the world is changed, tinged with *learth*. How is it for you, Gareth?"

She counted ten seconds passing before he turned around and answered. "I do the same as you, only I imagine water coursing through my bloodstream."

"And Jemroth?"

"I think his is less concrete than ours. More about the acknowledgement of his flesh and the connection it has to our world." He forced a smile. "I'd say his method relates most to House Ushanan because air is just as all-present." He shuffled closer to Lotte and Claire, his sudden helpfulness a form of apology. "I think we'll need to experiment. Lotte, once you're in that meditative state, notice how the air touches your skin and your reaction to it. Are you warmer at its presence? You'll feel *learth* as an extension of yourself."

Claire shot him a grateful grin. "Good one. Lotte, are you OK to start?"

"As 'OK' as I'll ever be," she said. "But I ain't completely in the dark." She laughed as Claire shot her a puzzled glance. "The Crian taught me how to summon her and honestly, it sounds like she were gettin' me to draw on magic. I'd sense this kind of disturbance in the air and a pull in my chest and do this breathing stuff like yer describing."

Claire studied her face for a moment, then nodded. "Lie back and tell me when you're ready for instructions."

She closed her own eyes, feeling feverish. At first, flashes of thought swirled, making it impossible to concentrate. The Beast, Marcus, Grandfather, Eidan, Lotte and Gareth. Fear, anger, frustration, sadness and hope. She was so close to winning this thing.

She willed all thought away as Lotte whispered, "Ready."

Claire counted out loud until she heard Lotte's breathing fall into a steady rhythm. "Imagine the wind on your face and caressing your skin. Imagine the air as a physical thing," Claire began.

The cart rocked and Jemroth shouted out in alarm, sudden force ripping around Claire and making her hair stand on end. She opened her eyes to find Lotte looking apologetic and Gareth's cheeks pale as goose bumps formed up his arms.

"Sorry. That weren't meant to happen," Lotte explained.

"I don't know. A mini tornado is pretty cool," Claire laughed the incident off as she flung a hunk of bread to Lotte. "Eat that, then try again. You don't want to recreate what you imagine. You want to feel it become part of you."

"Yep. Got it."

Though they repeated the exercise many times with varying results (the worst result being when Lotte accidentally cut off their air supply) eventually Lotte figured out how to access *learth* without using it.

At Lotte's peaceful expression, Claire's shoulders slumped to normal height. Contemplating what she'd do if Lotte couldn't get the hang of this technique hadn't been fun. Now their real challenge could begin.

Claire imagined burning fire deep within her, spreading through her veins, taking her consciousness with it so it was freed into her surroundings. She heard a sharp click. In the blackness of her mind, she saw a streaming rope of red and orange rush out of her mouth, her hands, her legs to float around the cart.

She pictured Lotte, her unique blend of silver and pearly white, and wanted to crow when she saw Lotte's colours rise to meet her. *Perfect*, she thought, and before her friend could get any closer, she twined her own essence into Lotte's ethereal stream, remembering to keep her mind disengaged unlike when she'd first practised this with Gareth.

-Hello- she sounded.

-Is that ya, Claire?- Lotte's awed voice echoed back.

-Yes. Stay with me. I'm going to get Gareth to join us. No- she hastened as Lotte began to fade in and out. -Keep concentrating on me- She waited for her friend's colours to re-establish themselves before glancing about the silvery cart for Gareth.

His essence hovered nearby, familiar blues calling to her. Gingerly, he wended his way closer, pausing over hers and Lotte's combined braid. Before Claire could wonder what it was he waited for, something slammed against her mind.

Lotte panicked, slipping this way and that like an eel while Gareth came dangerously close to dive bombing her memories again. Head aching and colours threatening to splinter, it took all Claire's energy and skill to keep the three of them wound tight. Any second, she'd lose them, any second ...

-Stop it-she screamed, pressure building in a band around her forehead and temples. -You're hurting me-

-Can't help it-Lotte sounded. -Nothin's workin' right-

-I can't either- Gareth called. -Without a Dream Mage to watch over us and this close to the Rift, I fear our magic is too unstable-

Claire gritted her teeth -At least there's no sign of the Beast yet-

-Don't tempt fate-

The colours of the Rift opened impossibly before her, as though the roof of the cart no longer existed; the hard ground beneath it cast in planes of shadow and light. How could she see outdoors when she was seated on a wooden floor with animal hide coverings stretched above her? Even as she pondered, the landscape stretched out wider.

-Don't think of it- sounded Gareth sharply. –Think of Lotte and I-

Claire tried to, but every time she conjured up Lotte's elven face, fear of the incoming Beast drowned the images out and cast her like a floating buoy back to the yawning cavern of the Rift. Traitorous thoughts infected her like spores. The last time she'd lost control of a major working, she'd almost killed a man. And if she lost either of the two people enmeshed with her today ...

-Come on- Gareth growled.

-Trying- Pain ripped through Claire's fingers as she dug them into the wood in a bid to distract herself. Every time she focused on Gareth by the ocean or Lotte threading her mother's necklace through reverent palms, the Beast's cackle and Sleath's burnt face ripped through it like a match curling up paper and blackening the words and images held on its creamy page.

-Quick- Gareth's voice sounded. –End the spell-

Something ripped at her mind and she scrunched her eyes shut, biting down so hard on her tongue she tasted blood. As stinging tears squeezed from the corners of her eyes, the Beast hovered above her with the rent of the Rift behind it like a hungry crack, about to eat them all.

-End it! By the Nereus, you'll kill us all-

In rising alarm, Claire forced herself to think of Gareth. The braid they'd carefully woven remained intact. She un-wove Gareth first, peeling his essence out of the braid. With his experience in *learth*, he could dive straight back into a working to help her. Then, she turned her attention to Lotte. The exile's terror manifested as a slipperiness.

-Stay still- Claire screamed in exasperation, not daring to check where the Beast was in relation to her, even as its cackle reverberated through her whole body. At last, Lotte was separate to Claire, but how much time did Claire herself have to escape?

She tried to reel her cord back inside herself, but she found it hard to concentrate on the *learth* singing through her blood. The Beast followed, sending colour after colour chasing her; spears of multi-coloured light that dazzled and would have delighted in any other circumstance.

A spear made of garish lime, psychedelic blue and eyepopping red pierced her and sent her sprawling upwards.

Gareth screamed. Something sharp dug into Claire's corporeal flesh. Agony bloomed as hard pressure made her tingle. The feelings grounded her. What was she doing? Up was down and down was up as she sailed through unnatural sky. She was getting further and further away from Eidan's baggage train. If she didn't do something, she'd die.

With a vicious wrench, Claire ripped away from the Beast. Colours fell around her like rain.

She opened her eyes to find a shadowed Gareth standing over her.

"Sorry for the pinches and punches. I've never been so terrified in my life," Gareth said. "You were nearly lost altogether."

"Thank you for saving me," Claire said, voice shaking. She thanked the salamanders she had such good friends.

"We shouldn't have tried to do this," he said, hand to his forehead. "Lotte's too inexperienced and the Rift's too unstable." He indicated Lotte as he slumped backwards. She lay passed out on a pile of coats. "This whole thing's hopeless."

But Claire only half took in Lotte's too chalky skin and dilated pupils. Instead, she stared beyond her. The cart had come to a halt, the cow skin covering at its back burnt away, cinders and smoke curling around its edges. "Did I do that?" She stretched out a trembling finger.

Gareth didn't look up. "Do what?"

Claire inched closer to the scorched hole. Within a few footsteps she saw right outside. Rings of fire surrounded the horses and carts behind them, men and women frozen in terror.

Sleath rose before her like a warning. *I won't let this happen a second time.* She held out a palm, gritted her teeth against the screaming and reached for each flame one by one, pinching them out. It took her a good five minutes, but soon, there was no evidence of her out of control *learth* working beyond soot and ash, curling rank smoke and the kicking of spooked horses. She was so relieved she didn't even care everyone stared at her open-mouthed or that Jemroth was cursing up front.

"What're you doing?" Gareth shouted.

"Saving them," she said, shocked at his anger. "I'll not be responsible for more innocents losing their life."

Gareth's hand connected with her shoulder and pulled her back to face him. He hauled her to the ground, so hard she was sure she'd bruise at the knees. "Take it easy," she said indignantly. "Are you trying to break a bone?"

"Are you stupid?" Gareth hissed. "The fires mean magic, and now you're putting them out, they'll know we're responsible. What do you think happens to those with *learth* in this camp? I'd say we have about five minutes before an alarm's sounded. How useful do you think our magic will be against an entire army? The ground is so unforgiving here it will take Jemroth ages to work a spell. I'd have to melt ice before I could do something remotely useful with *learth* and Lotte is out cold."

Claire felt the colour drain from her face. "I ... I didn't think. I was so afraid for them I—"

"What in Lugh's name is going on here?" a growling voice sounded from behind her. She'd been so busy arguing, she hadn't heard Jemroth's shouts snuff out.

Heart pounding, Claire swung around to find the overseer who'd hired her holding a knife to a well-trussed Jemroth's throat, three other soldiers ranged behind him.

Chapter Thirty-Six

CLAIRE FLEXED HER WRISTS to test the rope bonds, but the overseer knew his knots too well. He'd tied them so tight that the rope cut into her wrists and she gritted her teeth against the pain. As the burly overseer had stood over them mockingly, she'd considered setting the man's clothing alight, but she'd hesitated the barest moment too long, afraid that if she was too slow or the man reacted quickly, he and his soldiers would kill Jemroth before she could overwhelm them. It hadn't taken the soldiers long to truss the four magic users like chickens for the oven. Everyone that is, except Lotte, who was still unconscious on the floor of the wagon.

"What did you do to her?" the overseer had snapped. Turning to a soldier, he'd muttered, "She's nothing but a slip of a servitor." With a click of his fingers, he ordered the soldier to check Lotte's pulse.

"Still breathing," the man confirmed.

"Good. Pass me that water skin."

Claire could have crowed with delight. They thought Lotte wasn't with them. Now if only the exile would wake up. She hardly dared breathe or even make it too obvious she was watching as the overseer tipped half a skin of water over Lotte's face.

Lotte's eyes shot open. "Wha—" she spluttered.

The overseer crouched beside her. "It's all right. You're safe now."

"Safe? But—" Lotte's expression clouded over.

"Don't try to talk. We know what happened. She," the overseer glanced over his shoulder at Claire, "used magic. I assume you rumbled to her being more than she seemed and that's the reason for the fireworks display."

Through lowered lashes, Claire scouted out how much attention was on her. Not much. *Say yes*, she mouthed at her friend.

"I ... yeah."

"Can you get up to come with us?"

Lotte shook her head weakly, eyes wide.

"Mph," he uttered as he stood again. "I'll need to leave you then so I can tell Eidan the good news, but I'll make sure you're well rewarded for this morning's work." He swivelled around to Gareth, Jemroth and Claire. "And this lot won't touch you, I promise. These three men," the soldiers started forward at his words, "will sit crouched beside them with a knife. Any hint of funny business from one of them and they'll find themselves with slit throats faster than they can croak the words of a fancy spell."

Claire struggled against her bonds for the show of it and he laughed. She settled for a sneer as one of the soldiers took up position beside her, heavy hand at her neck and a gleam of steel too close to the skin for comfort. She swallowed nervously.

"Sit tight," the overseer said, admiring his handiwork. "Won't Eidan be pleased when I tell him I've found spies in our camp." He spat at Claire's feet and walked towards the front of the cart. "We'll be back quick smart. You won't get a chance to miss us."

He turned, as out of the corner of her eye, Claire saw Lotte wink. Hope burgeoned. Lotte was many things, but she wasn't stupid. Her friend must have faked exhaustion to fool the overseer into complacency and now, Claire could tell from Lotte's fierce expression, he'd pay for his assumptions.

The overseer got as far as leaning down to jump out of the cart before he fell to his knees, clawing at his throat, the veins in his forehead bulging. To Claire's delight, the man holding a knife to her neck immediately followed suit and two more resounding thuds let her know a similar thing had happened to the other guards. She breathed deeply. The air seemed a little thinner than usual, with a minty freshness which cut through the taste left by Claire's own fire magic, but otherwise she felt fine. Somehow, Lotte had found a way to cut off their enemy's air supply, and theirs alone. If Claire's hands had been unbound, she'd have punched upwards in victory.

She glanced over at Lotte. The girl had stumbled to her feet, legs wobbly but face resolute. As Claire watched, she reached down to her boots, a thin bronze knife sliding out to sit firm in her rigid hand. Without a word, she shuffled over to Jemroth and the soldier who had fallen to his knees, cheeks red and sweat pouring off him as he struggled to breathe. Before anyone could say a word, the thin knife plunged and twisted at the man's heart, killing him.

Claire was sure the horror in Jemroth and Gareth's face was reflected in her own. She couldn't just watch as Lotte's sudden feral brutality consumed her. "Stop," she cried. "These men have been lied to by Eidan. They don't know any better and they're defenceless. Knock them out and tie them up. We don't need to kill them."

"Witch," the overseer gasped, a clenched fist shaking against the wood as Lotte stared blankly at Claire, eyes filled with a terrible darkness.

"Listen to me, not to him," Claire tried again, desperation threading through her words. Lotte's emptiness scared her. "This isn't who you are. Don't you want to finish what we've started in the right way?"

"The only thing I want no one can ever return to me," Lotte said, her voice filled with bitterness. "Eidan, and those as thoughtlessly obey him, took 'em away forever."

Claire knew she meant her family and felt a pang of sadness. Once this was over, poor Lotte deserved all the happiness life could bring, but for now Claire had to snap her out of her strange mood. "I know it's hard, Lotte, but revenge won't bring your family back. There's rope in that corner. Bind Eidan's men and free us, then let's get out of here."

Lotte blinked, her knife dripping blood onto the cart's floorboards. Shadows crossed her face, but at last, she nodded, normal colour returning to her cheeks and her eyes clearer. Within minutes, she'd tied up all four guards, then hurried over to slice through Claire's bonds. "I'm sorry," she whispered. "I dunno what came over me. I were so mad."

Claire massaged her wrists and then her ankles as she was freed. "I understand. Your family meant a lot to you just like mine does to me, but I'm glad you stopped the bloodshed." She smiled up at Lotte, hoping to smooth things over. "We all owe you our thanks. We'd have been dead meat without your quick thinking."

"I should have trusted you when Claire first asked me to," Gareth's small voice came from further in the cart. "I've never been more grateful to be proved wrong about someone."

Lotte got to her feet with a start and quickly freed Gareth while Claire grabbed some bread from a supply bag and began to eat. She watched as the pair eyed each other like they'd never met before. Gareth offered a hand to the surprised girl and Lotte quickly grasped it in a firm grip.

"I'm sorry for being a nasty piece of work where you were concerned," Gareth said. "I let prejudice blind me, and then when Claire found out Bron was the one to sell us out and that you were House Ushanan, I was too proud to admit I'd made a mistake." He caught Lotte's eyes with a solemn stare. "Now I see that you're as good as anyone from Maellwyn House, exile or no exile."

Lotte gave an abashed, "Thanks," in response.

"Hey," Jemroth grumbled from opposite them. "This is all very touching, but my limbs are so cramped I might end up with serious damage if you don't free me soon." He paused, clearing his throat, his tone becoming contrite. "I'm sorry too, Lotte. I persuaded Gareth he shouldn't trust you, even when he wanted to waver. Forgive me?"

Lotte grinned, "Sure." Soon, she'd freed Jemroth too and the pair and Gareth stared at Claire expectantly. "What now?"

Impatience burned within Claire, making it hard to concentrate. "Someone will raise the alarm about fire appearing out of nowhere and Eidan and his advisors will eventually figure out an overseer is missing and when they put two and two together ..."

"We should run," Jemroth said. "Grab some horses and get to Gwenivere."

"No!" Claire said. "This plain is empty for miles and miles. Eidan would notice our horses and follow us. There's no point doing anything until we close the Rift, because once we've succeeded in that, it doesn't matter if we live or die. At least Kelnarium itself will be saved." She flung bread and cheese at each of them. "Swallow that. Fast."

When they'd done so, she reached out to rest one hand on Lotte's own and the other on Gareth's. "We must end it, here and now. By the Saura, by the Nereus, by the Gofannon and by the Crian." She drank in each of their faces in turn as they all linked hands; Lotte grim but ready for anything, Gareth shaken but prepared, even Jemroth, his healthy scepticism overridden by loyalty.

"I'll count us in," she said, hoping she sounded braver than she felt. "No matter what happens, try to stay with the spell." She paused, sorting through words to find the right ones to say. "And before we do this, I want you to know, you're all amazing. I couldn't have made it this far without every single one of you. Yes, we've all got on each other's nerves and made mistakes, but we've picked ourselves up again and tried our best. Gareth, you were a huge help to me when I accidentally injured Sleath and Jemroth, your knowledge of Kelnariat was invaluable. As for Lotte ..." Her throat closed over. She wanted to say so much. How Lotte had mended her brokenness over Liz, how she'd believed in Claire and followed her even when she hadn't had to, how she'd thought quickly and got them out of rough situations every time. "Just thanks," she said at last. "For everything."

Lotte grinned. "No problem."

Claire closed her eyes. "One, two, three, four ..." She'd just managed to connect to *learth* and weave with Lotte when Gareth's own cord sped towards them far too fast. Before she could yell at him to slow down, he collided with her.

-They're here- He howled. –Go-

Claire managed to untangle Lotte and herself, head throbbing. Somehow, she made herself open her eyes and take in the cart. Nothing. What was Gareth playing at?

She whirled around, stumbling to her feet and dragging Lotte up alongside her. Gareth and Jemroth already raced ahead. Their urgency told her there was no time for questions. Something was wrong.

Claire followed them as they leapt outside the cart. Her mind raced as she clutched Lotte's hand tightly. Which way to run? The land was barren in every direction. North, South, East and –

She came face to face with a soldier. Without a moment's hesitation, Claire prepared to hurl fire at him, only for him to step aside as many hands clutched at her arms. With a smirk, one of Eidan's councillors closed the gap between them. She recognised him right away, his cruel eyes and beaked nose distinctive. Wallis.

A whole troop of muscular soldiers surrounded him, brandishing brass headed spears and long blades.

He eyed her hungrily. "Eidan wishes to speak to you."

Lotte punched and kicked wildly as soldiers lifted her off the ground.

"Use a spell," Claire screamed.

She conjured up her own flames, letting them lick at men's cloaks and tunics, but there were too many of them. She had to think smarter. Remembering Maen's lessons, she ran through her options and couldn't help but grin. She had just the thing. *Salamanders, aid me,* she thought as she put her plan in motion.

She knew she'd heated up the ground when Wallis howled, dancing about like his shoes were made of blades. As Lotte squeezed air from lungs and Claire heated land and blood, painstakingly slowly they pushed through the wall of human flesh separating them from freedom. *Almost there*, Claire thought. *A couple of metres more and—*

"Stop!" Someone cried from behind.

Claire spun around. A second man dressed in councillor garb had Gareth on his knees, melted ice pooling at their feet where Gareth had started to work a spell, his neck tipped back as the man held him by his hair. It was Wallis's right-hand man, Heath.

"Surrender or I smash his necklace," Heath called. Gareth's shirt had come unlaced and his vial hung loose, bared for all to see.

Behind Gareth, Jemroth had managed to create fissures in the earth, preparing to crack the land asunder, but at Heath's words he paused, letting his hands fall to his sides, then be bound in front of him.

Claire glanced back at Lotte in desperation. Her friend struggled as many hands clutched at her dress and at her own long hair. "Give it up, Lotte," she said quietly. "It's no use."

She let her spell die out and made herself stand still while she was bound yet again.

"Gullible fool," Heath crowed behind her. "Take that one to Eidan and kill the others."

Her heart slammed. What had she done? Behind her, Gareth cried out. Seconds later, something smashed, Heath's laughter ringing in her ears as she was swivelled around to face him.

Gareth sprawled, grimy and pale, the rope at his neck no longer attached to its vial. He patted his palms along the hard ground, ignoring glass shards sticking into his skin in his frantic race to recapture lost seawater. Without it, and this far away from the sea, he would die in hours, even if Heath didn't kill him first.

Chapter Thirty-Seven

EIDAN'S PURPLE AND gold silk tent sat behind a long patch of black ground. Claire kept her gaze straight ahead, her expression set, as she tried not to slip on the difficult terrain.

"After you, Lady Claire," Wallis sneered as he opened the tent flap to let her enter.

She stiffened, a cold fist squeezing about her heart. She'd assumed the alarm had been sounded by a servant and that Eidan was only interested in her as the leader of a band of magical brethren spies who had infiltrated the camp. She hadn't imagined he'd know her real identity. How could he? If Bron had said something, why hadn't Eidan acted earlier?

She ducked to enter the tent and let her boots sink into the animal skin that covered the floor, as Wallis's soldiers blocked the entrance behind her. That didn't matter. She could blast a fire ball through the tent and make a run for it. With a grin, she straightened. She'd go down fighting, even if without the others she couldn't create the spell to destroy the Rift.

Eidan sat on a fold-out leather chair, garbed in his usual plain black. Behind him, Marcus stood with his arms folded, a mixture of pity and smugness underlying his stern expression.

Claire stared at her brother, hardly able to believe it. She would have told anyone Marcus wasn't capable of such betrayal and yet there was the evidence of her own eyes to contend with. It was lucky Claire's hands were tied, or she'd have punched her brother *hard*. As it was, she seriously considered setting his hair on fire, and what's more she reckoned any salamanders watching would cheer her on. "You," she managed through choking rage. "You gave me your word." To her dismay, tears brimmed.

"I told you, Sis," Marcus said sadly, stepping out from behind Eidan to stand by his side. "You picked the losing team. I have to look out for you."

It's what our parents would want. I'd agonised over telling Eidan ever since we met in Kelnariat but when word came from the baggage train of magical brethren using spells, I knew it was you, and I knew I needed to act."

"You idiot!" Claire yelled. "You've ruined everything. Don't you realise my friends will die?"

"They deserve it," Marcus said.

"Like you, they're criminals," Eidan added.

Claire tried to keep her expression calm. "What do you mean? I've done nothing wrong."

"Drop the innocent act, Lady Claire," Eidan said scornfully. "You destroyed a cart, injured some servitors and tried to kill my soldiers carrying out their lawful duty."

"I didn't want to hurt anyone," she said. "We were trying to close the Rift before Kelnarium is destroyed. I lost control because of your friend, the Beast. As to your men, we only attacked them because they were attacking us. Let me and my friends go, and your world has a future." Telling the truth might be futile, but she had to try. "I don't know what you believe, Eidan, but this is your last chance to save yourself and everyone else."

Marcus shrugged helplessly. "She was like this in the capital. No matter what I said, she was convinced all she's been told is true."

Eidan glanced between Marcus and Claire, then clicked his fingers, and the soldiers, led by Wallis, left, only two soldiers staying behind to guard the entrance to the tent.

With the odds a little more even, Claire felt better. Now that things had come to a head, she was weightless, fearless. "What will you do to me?" she asked Eidan.

"You leave me no choice but to kill you. My apologies, Marcus, but your sister will ruin everything unless she's dispatched."

"What?" Marcus's eyes widened and his face went white. "That's not the bargain you and I made."

Claire wanted to shake him. Why had she never noticed in Shale how stupid her brother could be?

Eidan brushed a weary hand over his beard. "In other circumstances … but no matter. It must be done. I thought you were like me and that you'd understand that to be a great leader sacrifices must be made. If Kelnarium is to modernise like you and I planned, your sister must go."

"But you said you'd try to get her on side," Marcus protested, hurrying around Eidan and crossing the tent to stand beside Claire. "Can't you keep her tied up and captive until the Beast is ready and then he can send us both back? She's already admitted she can't touch the Rift without her friends, and you're going to kill them."

Eidan frowned. "Our friend won't be happy if we do as you suggest, and I can't have it turning on my people. Not only that, but it also won't take you to your world unless Lady Claire is dead." He shrugged at Claire. "For some reason, it really hates you."

Marcus's cheeks paled. "You never told me."

"Because I suspected you would react this way."

"Can you blame me?" He began to untie Claire's bonds. "I won't stand by and watch my sister die."

"The Beast hasn't told you everything anyway," Claire said. "It's told you it can get you home in a big explosion, right?"

"Yeah," Marcus muttered as with one final tug the rope dropped from Claire's wrist.

"The Beast cares about its own survival," Claire went on as she rubbed at her wrists. "It's an extension of the Rift and knows that if my friends and I close it, it dies. It's manipulating both of you. The explosion it describes is the one that will destroy your world, Eidan, just as Gwenivere foretold. Do you really want to be responsible for that?"

"You're lying," Eidan said coldly. "I have spoken to the Beast myself and know what it intends, unlike someone who relies on the garbled nonsense of magical folk."

Marcus stepped back from Claire, looking doubtfully from her to his mentor, clearly unable to decide who to believe.

Taking advantage of Marcus's indecision, Eidan strolled over to Claire, placing his fingers under her chin so she was forced to stare into his eyes. His breath was warm on her face, making her shudder. "The Beast is my friend. It showed me in dreams you'd survived the attack on your grandfather and that you were on your way to Kelnariat with the Maellwyns. Without its knowledge, I would never have known that you lived. You're trying to put a gulf between us. When Gwenivere first approached me with her latest prophecy, the Beast told me not to trust her, that she was looking for a way to show me up as weak, so I'd lose the capital. She and her kind have always been jealous of my power. I pretended to support her to the hilt, but already I'd made plans ..."

Marcus looked troubled. "A creature that demands my sister's blood doesn't sound super trustworthy to me. If there's even the smallest possibility Claire's correct, we've made a terrible mistake."

"Especially," Claire snapped as she stepped back out of the range of Eidan's touch, "when I know you fabricated the story of Dorran bandits ravaging the countryside and small towns. One of your servitor's saw our uniforms in your chambers in Kelnariat. It was your men attacking your own people, wasn't it, to set magical users up? Why? They were your friends."

Eidan's expression was suddenly as petulant as any naughty schoolkid's. "They never liked me. It was all an act."

Marcus looked at Claire, teeth bruising his lip. "Wait. What's this about *Eidan's men* attacking ordinary citizens?" He switched his gaze to Kelnarium's leader. "I thought the reason we weren't asking the magical brethren for help was because they don't have Kelnarium's best interests at heart and they'd make me do terrible magical works in their name." Without taking his eyes off his mentor, he spoke to his sister. "Are you saying that was a lie too, Claire?"

"You've got to be kidding me!" Claire burst out, feeling like a lit fuse about to run out. By the Saura, how could Eidan and Marcus both have everything so wrong?

She made herself take a deep breath, running over everything Eidan had just said, the ghost of understanding beckoning. She remembered Gwenivere saying something about Eidan testing to be a Dream Mage and how lucky it had been he'd gotten over his teen grudge when he'd failed to make the grade to learn magic. What if he never had? "You never forgave her, did you?" Claire whispered, staring straight into his eyes.

Eidan's eyes narrowed, and he stepped back like she'd hit him. "I should have been their leader. I'd have overtaken Gwenivere in a few years, but she saw my power and was afraid. Too threatened to train me, she sent me away."

"No," Claire said. "You had the barest glimmer; dangerous to you and others if trained."

"Wrong," he screamed, saliva hitting her cheeks. "My grandparents knew. They told me I was my great-uncle, the former leader of the Dream Mages, reborn, and I knew it was the truth. They never lived down the shame I brought them. They spent their remaining days faded and bitter, their family dreams destroyed, and it was all Gwenivere's fault."

Claire calmly wiped the back of her hand across her face and shook her head in disbelief. "For ages I thought someone had put you up to persecuting us; Wallis or Heath or someone else, but you did it all yourself, and for such petty reasons. I bet the Beast didn't have to spend long persuading you Gwenivere's vision was false. You believed it easily because you wanted it to be so."

"I detest magic with every fibre of my being," Eidan spat, pounding a fist against the palm of his other hand. "I've dreamt of revenge on Gwenivere, your grandfather, the rest of them who all laughed at me, for years and then the Beast came to me and said it could help me create a world where magic was stamped out, a world like the one you and Marcus are from. I agreed right away and look at how our alliance has paid off." He laughed. "Take Bron. Once I knew you were on your way to Kelnariat, I enlisted his services immediately, knowing he couldn't bear to see Alaya threatened. He thought I'd be a pushover when he sent me his letter saying he hadn't understood the true danger Kelnarium was in. He was deeply shocked when I tortured him to get the information I needed, but he didn't know he'd been tricked by Gwenivere and all the others. I stand by the Beast. Kelnarium dies if I let magical renegades dictate government."

"And you're fine that the Beast told you to murder me."

"Yes," Eidan said, but he couldn't meet her eyes.

Marcus rushed forward before Claire could stop him. "But you told me these magical brethren were out to destabilise the Council. That's why we attacked them. Are you saying it was all a front so you could get back at them?"

Eidan grinned. "I figured I could have a bit of fun before I stamped them out for good." He rubbed his hands together. "My grandparents died before I could show them how wrong they were to give up on me." He paused at Marcus's growing look of horror. "Look, boy, I like you, but I'm no fool. I knew you'd baulk if I told you everything."

Marcus stepped backwards, tugging at Claire by her cloak. "I've made a big mistake."

"You haven't, Marcus. Trust me. I'm your friend," Eidan protested. "Together, you and I can make Kelnarium great like your world. It's a shame about your sister, but, well," he shrugged. "These things happen."

Marcus stared at Eidan like he'd never seen him before. "But she's my sister. I can't let you kill her in front of me. And you're a terrible friend, keeping secrets from me like you have. You should have told me the truth. If I'd known I would never have encouraged you to go along with the Beast's plan." He turned to Claire. "Time to leave, Sis."

"I like you, Marcus, but you're getting in my way." Eidan's fingers reached under his cloak as he stepped closer to Claire. He withdrew them to show a gleaming, bronze blade in his hand. "Time to say goodbye. I won't have you ruining my plans when I'm so close to success."

Chapter Thirty-Eight

BEFORE CLAIRE COULD reach for *learth*, Marcus bulldozed into Eidan's side, the crazed Council leader's knife entering Marcus's fleshy thigh. The pair fell to the ground, wrestling each other in a mix of blood, sweat and desperate animal grunts. Claire glanced at the tent flap. The pair were so noisy, someone would come inside to check on their leader. Sure enough, one of the soldiers was striding inside, sword at the ready. She had to access *learth* quickly. Within seconds, Claire had conjured fire at the man's feet, blocking his way further into the tent. The soldier stared at her with bulging eyes, clearly terrified. Claire let herself smile coldly at him as she let the flames grow higher. With a shout, he turned tail and fled.

Adrenaline pumping as she let her spell flicker out, Claire grabbed Marcus's cloak and hauled him back, kicking hard at Eidan's wildly swinging blade. Its edge sliced through her left boot and hit the sole of her foot. She ignored the smarting cut. If she could get Marcus out of the way she could get the fireworks started. Literally. Before those two soldiers came back with reinforcements.

But Marcus pulled away from her and got back in the fray, swinging muscly arms in every direction, forcing Claire to duck. "Watch it," she said as she narrowly missed another punch. She'd never seen her brother so fuelled by anger, but then they were both members of the O'Connor family, and they stuck together. Besides, his stinging embarrassment at how he had been taken in by Eidan would spur him on. She bit back exasperation. This was no time for heroics. Physical prowess had nothing on magic and if Marcus would just move …

"Get out of the way," she yelled.

Before Marcus could react, Eidan's arm snaked towards his ankle. He winked at Claire.

She tried to fling fire to wipe the smirk off his face if nothing else, but it was too late. Marcus and Eidan were so entangled she couldn't aim for one without injuring the other. "Watch out," she cried, as Eidan tugged and Marcus fell to his knees at his side.

"Don't underestimate me, boy," Eidan spat throwing an arm around Marcus's shoulder and holding the bronze knife at his throat. The knife scored Marcus's neck with the sharp edge. Beads of blood trickled across his neckline.

"Stop," Claire howled, her breathing ragged. "Please don't kill him."

"You'd offer yourself in his place?"

"Of course." She limped over to the pair, ignoring Marcus's shocked protests.

"Good," Eidan sneered. He shoved Marcus aside and Claire knelt in her brother's place. Eidan wrenched her long hair back so that her neck was exposed to his blade. She tried not to flinch. She couldn't bear to give him a moment of satisfaction. Even so, blackness filled her. If Eidan killed her now, she'd never see Mum or Dad again. She'd never swim in the ocean or paint or go for walks in the National Park. She'd never again exist in her own world.

"I want my face to be the last thing that you see on this earth," he said as Marcus sobbed from the tent entrance.

Something hot brushed past her neck and she winced, knowing it was the knife. She bit her tongue to stop herself from crying out. Her thoughts were so scattered she couldn't reach for *learth* properly. Instead, she pictured her family smiling and laughing at a Christmas lunch as she waited for the end.

But the fatal blow never fell.

"Get your hands off her," a calm voice came from outside the tent, "or I'll set you on fire."

Eidan flung Claire away even as her own heart swelled. She'd recognise that voice anywhere. She got to her feet clumsily, wincing at the pain shooting up from her left foot as she glanced at the open tent flap.

Lord Dorran stood in the entryway, his tattered cloak swaying a little from the wind at his back. His white hair was whiter than she remembered, his wrinkles deeper, but his chest rose and fell with real breath. Somehow, against all the odds, he lived.

"Grandfather!" she cried. No wonder the Saura hadn't spoken with her on her journey to the Riftlands. The real leader of Dorran House had never truly died.

His face stopped her from sprinting to fling her arms around him. He stepped into the tent. Marcus hurried over to stand beside him uncertainly.

"But you're dead," Eidan gasped. "I killed you."

"You shouldn't believe everything you see," Lord Dorran replied, striding to loom over Eidan. "It was my beloved brother Aed you murdered that terrible day. He's been my double for years."

"You never said."

"Luckily. I've long suspected there wasn't something quite right about you."

"But Maen said you gave him your ring and Lords of Houses don't do that unless they know their time is spent," Claire said, pulling aside her tunic to reveal the ring about her neck. "He was convinced ... we were all certain you'd died."

"I led some of the children to safety," Lord Dorran explained. "I needed Maen and the others to follow you and I knew the Dorran survivors would scatter unless someone stayed behind to help them regroup. I would have reached you sooner if it wasn't for Eidan's soldiers rounding up the last of the Dorrans. I had to protect everyone and then get them to safety. By the time I made it to Maellwyn Manor, you were long gone." He shot Claire a look. "But this is no time for explanations. Move."

Claire hurled herself aside, just as Dorran sent a stream of flame at Eidan. The Councilman howled as his hand met red-hot heat and the smell of barbecued flesh filled the air.

Marcus broke away from Lord Dorran to join Claire, face white. He grabbed her arms and helped her to her feet.

"Give up, Eidan," Dorran said. "Call your army off and let my granddaughter finish the task she was born for."

Eidan's lips twisted. "No. You want me to give in so you can take over Kelnariat."

The pair circled each other like uncoiled snakes. Eidan turned to look at Claire as his hand slid into the pocket of his robe.

"Watch out," Claire screamed.

Dorran took no notice, laughing as he sketched flaming rings around himself and the other man, barring Claire and Marcus from interfering. "You took everything from me. Or nearly everything. You won't take my grandchildren too."

"So sure?" Eidan sneered. He pulled his hand free to reveal another sharp knife.

Unheeding, Dorran smirked and brought both the palms of his hands together as though to finish the Councillor off in columns of purifying *learth*. Before his palms could touch, the knife left Eidan's hand and hit Lord Dorran deep in the chest.

Claire shook Marcus off, walking into the silk fabric sides of the tent with her hands pressed to her lips in a silent scream as Lord Dorran spiralled backwards, mouth open in a puzzled "O." His spell began to gutter out.

Eidan had already darted aside. There wasn't a moment to lose. Claire held her palm out and reached for her grandfather's flames, shaping them into high walls that blocked off any possible escape route. Once the council leader was surrounded, she sent fireball after fireball at Eidan's feet, so powerful that he was blasted backwards into the side of the tent.

She turned her back on him to rush to Lord Dorran's side. She'd deal with Eidan properly in a moment. For now, he was going nowhere.

"What are you waiting for? Finish him off," her grandfather screamed, blood leaking from his stomach in a horrible reconstruction of Aed's death. "He can't be allowed to live if we're to save Kelnarium."

Claire's feet glued to the tent floor. Tears slid down her cheeks in ashy tracks. She moved a hand forward as though to touch her grandfather, her thoughts racing. Eidan had done terrible things. She couldn't deny that. But she'd stopped Lotte from murdering his men mere hours ago. Was she a hypocrite to kill Eidan now? Then again, she'd attacked soldiers earlier with magic, albeit in self-defence. She didn't like it, but perhaps she had no choice. After all, everyone in Kelnarium's lives was at stake.

"Do it," Lord Dorran gasped one more time. "He'll show you no mercy if he survives and our world will die."

"Hold on," she whispered, digging her nails into her palms. She was strong enough to do this. She straightened and headed right through the wall of flame, making it part at her presence.

Eidan laughed. "You don't have the guts to get rid of me."

Claire stood tall. "I absolutely do. I'm a Dorran."

She concentrated on the nearest wall of *learth*, letting herself become one with it, embracing it within and outside of her; hot and red and strong, her limbs tingling. With each breath she felt the heat leap with her mind in a complex dance. Then she sent it raining down on Eidan's head. His screams set her teeth on edge. The sound of flesh crackling and the scent of it cooking made her want to vomit, but she made herself watch as Eidan's lips stretched in a rictus as skin peeled and blistered. This man would have murdered her grandfather, Marcus, her friends, and an entire world for an imagined slight. In his madness, he'd left Claire no other choice.

A knife whizzed past Claire's ear to crash into Eidan's heart. His eyes turned glassy and his lips moved as though he wanted to say something, then he fell to the burning rug, finally lifeless. Claire let her spell fade away as a heavy hand landed on her shoulder.

"I couldn't let his death weigh on you alone," Marcus said in her ear. "He was my problem as much as yours."

"Thank you," she whispered as her hand found his. It was horrible, but she was glad they shared responsibility for Eidan's death. It meant that in Shale, there'd be someone to understand, and she also knew it was Marcus's way of saying sorry. She closed her eyes for a moment. She wanted to say so much more. She wanted Marcus to know she forgave him. She'd never see him the same way again, but it didn't matter. He was still her brother. But there'd be time for heavy conversations later. She released his hand, saying, "There's one more thing I need to do, Marcus."

As she hurried over to Lord Dorran, blood bubbling at his lips, she thought of the Saura. The elemental leader had been following Claire's journey, waiting for the moment when Claire would finally take up the mantle of leader of House Dorran. "Help me," Claire whispered, summoning up every scrap of energy she had left. "Ruler of the salamanders, I call on you now."

At first nothing happened, then the air grew furnace hot and she felt greasy smoke thicken and settle against her sweaty skin. A soft buzzing filled her ears as the Saura manifested, dazzling Claire with its brightness and its heat. "Please," Claire whispered to the giant salamander stretching from floor to tent ceiling, bulging eyes simultaneously distant and kind. "Lend him some of your strength."

We will do so, a voice sounded in her mind, scratchy and dry as old leaves. *The other elementals are here too, all helping to distract Eidan's men. Leave your grandfather to us. It is time for you to do what you came for.*

Suddenly, salamanders appeared on the ground, slithering over to Lord Dorran, covering him from head to toe. Their webbed feet stroked Lord Dorran's forehead and mouth. Their tongues whipped against his shoulders as they crowded over him, touching his stomach. Marcus's eyes widened as the knife wound closed over in seconds and the colour in their grandfather's face returned to normal.

"Help him up and follow me to the Rift," Claire commanded her brother as she pushed back the tent flap to see Melinor wraiths, salamanders, Merpeople and angry little men she took to be gnomes streaming outside Eidan's tent.

Without waiting to see if he acknowledged her, she sprinted outside. The camp was already in uproar. Elementals pulled up tent pegs, spooked horses, and surrounded gibbering soldiers. Without a clear chain of command, they left Claire alone. Most were too terrified to recognise her, let alone care where she headed. She crammed abandoned strips of meat in her mouth and as soon as she was clear of the camp, ran straight for the magnificent colours and rock-hard plains at the centre of the Rift.

Chapter Thirty-Nine

CLAIRE SWORE AS SHE slid across a patch of hard black diamond. Light reflected every direction and her eyes ached from the glare and the impossible colours of the Rift above her. She hunched her shoulders against the wind and kept going. Calls echoed behind her and she wondered what the soldiers were doing. Had someone recovered their wits and raised the alarm? Were Eidan's men after her even now?

She risked a glance over her shoulder and nearly cried out, the sickening wave in her stomach vanishing. Jemroth and Lotte supported Gareth as they crossed the barren landscape coming towards her. They'd escaped after all.

Lotte raised a hand to shade her eyes, her face white as she stared at Claire. "Wait for us," she called out.

But Claire was already grinning and running back to them lopsidedly thanks to the cut in her foot. "How did you escape Eidan's men?" she asked as she reached them. In the distance, an eldritch mist blanketed the camp. Two shadowy figures stumbled beyond its foggy tendrils. Marcus supporting Lord Dorran.

Jemroth paused for breath, muscles straining. "If it hadn't been for Lotte's quick thinking, we'd all be dead." He shot his erstwhile enemy a genuine smile. With tired grunts, he and Lotte began to walk forward again, half-carrying Gareth between them. Jemroth glanced at Claire. "She closed off their air supply again."

"Then the Crian and her Melinor came to help me," said Lotte. "It was them as scared most of the guards away."

"It wasn't just them that came," Jemroth said, his eyes full of wonder and joy. "I saw them properly, my gnomes, I mean. They helped us because finally they must recognise me as a true member of House Domain. The Mer-people were there too, and even some salamanders, but, Claire, I saw the gnomes. I'm going to find the Gofannon when this is over with. I know it."

Claire couldn't help but find his hope infectious. "And now Eidan's dead. We've almost achieved everything we set out to do."

Gareth barely reacted but the others smiled in tired relief as they trudged on, Claire barely keeping pace as she limped beside them.

"We saw ya runnin' out of his tent at record speed," Lotte said, her voice straining from physical exertion, "so we followed ya. Only, we didn't know what to do about Gareth. He's been floppy, pale and weak since his vial smashed."

"You know he'll die unless he goes home soon," Jemroth said quietly, his former excitement evaporating like it had never existed. He glanced at Lotte and the pair halted, chests heaving.

"He can't die," Claire whispered on the verge of tears at the thought of her friend leaving Kelnarium forever. "We need him." Her distress knotted her stomach. It wasn't fair. Gareth was her age. He deserved to live a full life.

Gareth looked up, eyes shadowed. "I might as well use the last of my energy on one final spell. Don't feel bad for me. I've accepted my fate. I had long ago when the Mer-people first told me this might be my end."

Claire pulled herself together. He was right. They had a job to do. "Then let's get going. It would have been easier with Gwenivere and the others, but we can't wait any longer."

They picked their way slowly and carefully across the cold, hard ground, pausing for breath and for Jemroth and Lotte to adjust their grip on Gareth every now and then. Soon, they stood directly under the Rift, the sky glowering and a massive crack filled with smoke sitting above them like a yawning mouth. They placed Gareth down carefully, then Jemroth and Lotte stood back, looking at Claire.

"We've come so far," Claire said slowly, "and overcome hate and fear and prejudice. Let's stand together at the end as good friends. No matter what happens next, that mattered." She paused, looking at each member of the group in turn. A weary Jemroth first, then sickly Gareth, his head slumping forward over his lap, and finally Lotte, who stood straight and tall and whose gaze never faltered. And then she looked away and set her gaze up at the blazing black smoking crack in the sky, surrounded by a patchwork quilt of colour. "Well," she said. "It's time to look death in the eye."

She sank to the ground next to Gareth, placing a hand on his knee. Her stomach was hollow with hunger, but they were nowhere near supplies. She had energy for this last working and then she was done. The others sat facing Claire and each other, reaching out to hold hands. Directly above, ribbons of colour dazzled her vision.

Claire squinted at the crack with trepidation. If she stood on tiptoe and stretched, she felt as though she could almost grasp the inside of the Rift. Her stomach somersaulted at the thought of the Beast attacking, but it couldn't be helped. This time, she'd be ready. She tried to push thoughts of Sleath and magic spiralling out of control back of mind too. What happened would happen. She couldn't keep second guessing the future. "Let's begin," she said.

"If we don't make it ..." Lotte said.

"Our elementals watch over us. We'll be fine." Claire was proud that her firm voice made her sound braver than she felt.

The group closed their eyes. Claire pushed thoughts of Marcus, of her parents and of her grandfather away. Her mind had to be blank. Her chest rose and fell. In and out. In and out. In and out.

She opened her eyes to the spirit plane as she heard the rushed click of her *learth* thread leaving her body. She concentrated on joining with Jemroth first, then Gareth, his thread fainter than she'd ever seen it. Finally, she turned her attention to Lotte. Gingerly, she wove the exile's thread into their rope. As soon as all four minds were joined, Claire forced herself to stare deep into the pit of the Rift. Yellows and reds and blues mingled at its edges.

Power tingled through her, sending charges of electricity through her body. Her head felt clearer than it had in days. Hunger and thirst and exhaustion faded. She drew on everyone's combined *learth* and aimed up into the heart of the Rift.

With a rush of wind, the Beast came, an enormous mud coloured creature in the sky. It considered the thread glittering in front of it. For tense seconds, it hovered, surrounded by glistening light, then dove directly into them. Heavy and fetid, it cackled with delight as Claire screamed at what felt like hundreds of glass pieces splintering in her head. Nails drove through her mind and her hold on the others slipped, cords unravelling around her and whipping left and right with wild abandon.

-I have you at last- the Beast chortled as Claire soared upward into the shattering colours of the Rift.

-Remember Kelt, Claire- Gareth sounded, faint and far away as the last of his blue skeins undid from Claire. -Hold on-

How could Claire have forgotten her task? She tried to regain her hold on the others but even as she made the attempt, their threads slid like oil through her mind.

-Concentrate- Jemroth sounded desperately, clutching tight.

She reached deep within herself, knowing there'd be no second chances to get this right. Gareth, Jemroth and Lotte's lives were in her hands. She couldn't fail them. Just as she managed to forge their threads back into a braided line, The Beast began to laugh.

–Betrayer. Your time is up-

Claire screwed her eyes up tighter and shook her head defiantly. Somehow, she managed to find her voice through her exhaustion as she angled the *learth* directly at the mad creature.

-No. Yours is-

With all of her might she shot a steady stream of flames its way, the others' air and mist and rock woven into it, the taste of fresh mint and cooking meat, wet loam and sea salt itching at her nostrils.

The Beast screamed on impact. Colour fractured as it swelled tall and for a second Claire thought they'd failed. Then, in a great burst of sparks and brown muck wisping away, the thing began to disintegrate.

Elation sang through her veins. Claire was so close. She pictured some of her happiest moments; the accomplishment she'd felt learning *learth* with Maen, the way it had felt to have Lotte stick by her, Gareth's kind face when she'd made a terrible mistake at Maellwyn Manor, Jemroth sharing his love of horses with her and showing her how to drive the cart, the way all four of them had banded together despite so much violence. As the joy swelled within her, so did *learth* power. She pictured bushfires and campfires and grates and matches and candles and turned them all hot, then cold. A fierce grin spreading, she aimed them all directly into the chasm of the Rift, as remnants of the Beast floated first this way, then that, ineffectual at last.

With a loud crack and the smell of sulphur and charred flesh, the rent across the skyline slowly, painfully, started to slide shut. Claire waited until only a lightly limned sliver remained before ending the spell and releasing the others, collapsing alongside her friends.

Chapter Forty

EVERY PART OF CLAIRE ached. Someone brushed against her shoulder and supported her head. The smallest movement made Claire feel as though she were filled with lead, but at last she managed to sit upright. She glanced upwards. Every scrap of the Beast had vanished. The sky was a more normal shade of blue, the sickly colours that made the Riftlands so distinctive already fading.

She scanned the circle. Jemroth knelt beside her, tired but calm. Lotte rubbed at her temples, blinking away confusion, like she'd only just regained consciousness herself. That was to be expected for a relatively untrained *learth* user. Gareth remained on the ground, his face now an unnatural green-grey.

Claire crawled to Gareth's side. She flinched at his drained and pale face and the deep, dark shadows under his eyes. He'd been too long without seawater and performing a great magical working had hastened his deterioration. With a jolt of certainty, she knew this was the end of his journey. She wished he didn't have to die in this forsaken place, devoid of warmth or humanity or life.

She smoothed his hair back and wiped sweat off his forehead with the edge of her tunic. "This isn't fair. We should be rejoicing together that your world is safe."

He smiled weakly. "I'm content. We did what we came to do. Won't you all come and sit by me until the end comes? I'd die happy knowing my friends are with me."

Lotte and Jemroth joined Claire and Gareth; Jemroth getting to his feet and moving with a slight dragging limp, Lotte crawling on hands and knees. There was nothing to say. Gareth's breath grew shallower and shallower, his eyes closed, and his heart beat sluggish.

"It will be soon," Jemroth said softly. "I—" but his sentence was interrupted by shouts.

Claire turned around. To their left, and in the distance, Marcus half-stumbled, half-walked as he supported Lord Dorran, the Saura watching over them as they headed towards her, but he wasn't the one making all the racket. Cresting the edge of the land beneath the nearly closed Rift, a group of people entered her line of vision, coming up behind her brother and grandfather and sweeping them up into their party. Soon, their features were easier to make out. Shaggy horses of every colour ridden by men and women in a motley collection of robes, tunics, cloaks and hose came to a halt alongside five wooden carts. Everyone clapped and cheered. Their joy was infectious, making Claire want to join in with the raucous din. This must be the army Eidan had mentioned to Marcus, which meant Gwenivere and Maen and the others must be inside the carts.

Indeed, as she studied the tableaux, four men and women tumbled out of the first cart in a mess of wool skeins.

"Enchantment Weavers," Lotte cried in delight.

Her friend was right. Before Claire had a chance to take in their arrival, the incorporeal and ghost-like Melinor, led by their Crian, surrounded the group of four. Within seconds, the Nereus appeared over Gareth, his expression grave as he tried to flick incorporeal seawater from his seaweed green and rusty red tail onto the boy's cheeks. Salamanders clung to Claire's arms, poured into her lap, clutched to strands of hair as three little gnomes clutched at Jemroth's tunic, faces screwed up and red from frustration. They hit at Jemroth's knees with tiny metal axes, making rents in his pants.

Jemroth's eyes widened. "They're talking to me," he explained in wonder. "Can you hear them?" When Claire shook his head, he rushed on. "They want me to follow them right now. The Gofannon waits for me, just as Lyssa said." His face fell. "But I can't. Not yet. I won't leave Gareth."

Clearly unhappy, the gnomes hit Jemroth harder and he fell silent, no doubt trying to reason with them.

"We did as you bid, Lotte. Oh, what fun we had in that camp," the Crian trilled, ignoring the other elementals as she glanced between both Lotte and Claire. "There'll be no trouble from that quarter. They turned tail and fled."

She frowned, glancing down at Gareth, saliva spooling out of the corner of his mouth. "But this boy is dying, though I see no mortal wound."

"One of Eidan's councillors smashed his vial of seawater," Claire explained, "and he can't survive without it." Wait, that wasn't strictly true. She was speaking to the Crian after all. Maybe Gareth had a chance. "Can you whisk him to Maellwyn Manor like you whisked me where I needed to go all those weeks past?"

"What you ask is unusual, but because you saved the last surviving member of House Ushanan, and because you helped me wash out my guilt, I will let you command me." The Crian looked sideways at the Nereus. "That is, if my actions are acceptable to the leader of the water elementals. I know my place."

The ancient mermaid's lips pursed as he thought, but at last, he nodded. "Do this," he said aloud, his words deep and rumbling, "and I shall forgive you for your part in Kelt and the Rift."

The Crian smiled, her face transformed into something fierce and beautiful. "It shall be done."

"Good. I go now to alert Maellwyn Manor to its heir's arrival." Before anyone could react, the Nereus vanished.

Claire lent forward, gripping tight to Gareth's fingers. "Thanks for everything. I'll never forget you." His faint answering smile assured her he heard and understood. "When you're better, help Lotte and Jemroth and the others rebuild. All three of you will be the leaders of a magical House and you've had the most training and experience for the role, Gareth. Be gentle and kind the way you were to me when we first met, share your thoughtful nature and your intelligence with them." She bent closer and kissed his cheek, then stood. "Get back," she waved to Lotte and Jemroth. She looked up at the Crian. "Take him home."

A cold mist crashed over her, its damp stealing through flesh and into bone. Claire couldn't see a thing. When the fog cleared, the Crian, her Melinor and Gareth were gone. Jemroth and Lotte's cheeks glistened with tears as Lotte started forward.

Even as she did, something flashed across Claire's vision. The silver thread that remained of the Rift glowed and dazzled, narrower now than it had been ten minutes ago. She shivered, struggling to her feet as a knot of people hurried over, baskets of food on their shoulders, Marcus and Lord Dorran amongst them. She recognised everyone immediately. "Maen! Meghan! Gwenivere! Tarn! Rael! Kiera!" she called. "Thank goodness you're safe too." The Enchantment Weavers, headed by Lyssa, trailed behind at a short distance. Lyssa carried a bundle in her arms, though from this distance Claire couldn't make out what it was. More wet tears trickled down her cheeks, though this time they were ones of relief.

Kiera ran forward smiling, putting her arms firmly around Claire. "I was so afraid," she murmured into Claire's hair.

Rael laughed, passing Claire a honey cake when she let Kiera go. "With good reason. We wouldn't have stood a chance against Eidan's army. I could have led these good farmers and villagers, but there would have been bloodshed. My scouts saw the camp and we were trying to decide when to reveal ourselves. The distraction in Eidan's camp meant we could come out of hiding and make our way towards you."

"Whatever you pulled off, it worked a treat," Maen added, kneeling to offer water skins and cake to Jemroth and Lotte.

"It seems not everyone liked Eidan's sudden change of policy towards magical brethren." Gwenivere waved behind her. "These people joined us and will help tell the truth about what happened at Dorran Manor. It won't be easy preventing a civil war but I think we're up to the challenge."

She ground to a halt as Lord Dorran reached Claire's side, still leaning on Marcus for support, the Saura standing over him in a halo of red and orange flame. He was closely followed by Lyssa and the Enchantment Weavers, who formed a semi-circle behind him. Lord Dorran smiled proudly at Claire, but his eyes were tired.

Gwenivere turned to him with her own small smile. "Lord Dorran, I didn't notice you amongst the crowd. We thought you killed at Dorran Manor and as to you, Marcus, I didn't think Claire would find you alive, let alone rescue you."

"I wasn't rescued," Marcus explained, as he stared at the ground and Lord Dorran frowned in disappointment, his breathing ragged. "I was on Eidan's side right up until he almost murdered Claire and I realised what he really was." He groaned. "I've been a total idiot, but who was I meant to believe? The man and his fellow magical brethren who had kidnapped me without so much as a by your leave, or the man who promised me safety and security and eventually a way back home?" At Claire's look, he flushed. "No, that's not fair. I had a chance to help Claire in Kelnariat but I wouldn't listen to her. I was jealous, so I didn't want to believe her. I couldn't handle being wrong as well as less talented at something for once."

Claire took pity on him as she licked crumbs off her fingers. Out of the corner of her eye, she saw Lotte and Jemroth get to their feet, rejuvenated by the food, Jemroth clutching at his gnomes as they refused to let go of his clothing. "But Marcus did some good in the end. He helped kill Eidan. We had to when he wouldn't listen to reason. And then I called on the Saura and the other elementals came too, and the Crian—"

"The Crian was here?" Maen spluttered.

"She and her Melinor helped the other elementals cause destruction in Eidan's camp."

"What the Crian did there is no coming back from. She is no friend of ours, now or ever."

"Says who?" Claire asked, hands on hips. "She accepts her role in creating the Rift and she has played her part in closing it. She helped me more than once, and just now she saved Gareth's life."

"Or says she did," Maen shot back.

"Have ya learnt nothing from the creation of the Rift?" Lotte huffed. "If we're to make a better Kelnarium, everyone must stand united; the four Houses and Dream Mages, Melinor and Enchantment Weavers, farming folk and ..." she took a deep breath, "exiles."

Shocked faces stared at Lotte.

"Yep," she went on, "I'm an exile. Go on. Look at me with disgust." She paused, folding her arms, "and then get over it. I'm one of 'em thanks to me da, but I'm the last survivor of House Ushanan too thanks to me mam. I helped Claire close the Rift, I'm the leader of a magical House and I'll find my people and rebuild, but I'll protect the exiles too, for part of 'em be in me."

She stared at everyone defiantly as Jemroth strode to her side, a hand resting on Lotte's shoulder. He'd managed to dislodge the gnomes and they stood behind him in a huddle, discussing something in inaudible mutters. "I don't doubt she'll succeed," Jemroth said. "She's too determined and too talented in *learth* to fail. Besides, I'll support her every step of the way in whatever she chooses to do. I, too, am leader of a magical house." He glanced at Lyssa. "Ask this good dame or Lord Maellwyn if you don't believe me." He paused as Lyssa stepped forward.

Now the Enchantment Weaver was closer, Claire saw she held a neatly folded green and bronze uniform in her hands, a gold ring with a jasper stone as its centrepiece sitting neatly atop the clothing.

"Lord Maellwyn gave me these for safekeeping after the battle with Kelt," she said, her voice ringing with authority. "Lord Jemroth is exactly who he claims. After today, he shall go seek the Gofannon and rebuild House Domain. We have woven it."

Jemroth took the items Lyssa proffered with a small bow, the gnomes hugging his ankles again, this time in obvious excitement. "Lotte and I have big jobs ahead of us, but we're not alone," he said gravely. "We have each other. All four of us do; Claire, Gareth, Lotte and me."

Claire's voice was the most confident she'd ever heard it. "They're both right. What's more, today can be about more than closing the Rift. We can heal past wounds. With Eidan gone there will be new rulers in Kelnariat. Don't let a tyrant take Eidan's place."

Silence sat heavy on the group, though Claire noticed her grandfather looked thoughtful as the Saura whispered something in his ear. Claire supposed she shouldn't be too hard on them. Their whole world had flipped upside down with Claire's arrival in Kelnarium.

Lyssa came forward to peer into Lotte's face, then turned back to Lord Dorran and Maen, seemingly pleased with what she'd read in their expressions. "I agree with Lady Claire. This could be the start of a new age. All of us, if we work together, can make sure it's a time of happiness and prosperity, of good governance and of peace between our peoples, including those we have once mistrusted." She nodded at Claire. "You'll stay to rebuild with the other current and future leaders of the magical Houses, of course. I'm sure Lords Dorran and Maellwyn will help all of you."

"Yes," Lord Dorran said, having finally recovered his breath. "I, at least, am prepared to put past prejudices behind me to guide you young people as you learn what it means to rule a House. Stay, Claire. Think of it as a balancing of the scales. Your mother in Shale in exchange for you in Kelnarium."

He glanced kindly at Marcus. "You're welcome to try and find a place with us too. You're our family and we forgive you."

"Claire and Lotte will both help shape our future," Jemroth added enthusiastically. "There's nothing those two and me and Gareth can't do when we put our minds to it. First things first, we have to get Lotte her grey and purple House Ushanan uniform. There're paintings at Maellwyn Manor of how they used to look. We'll journey back there together to make sure Gareth is safe and study those images and then we'll head to Kelnariat to sort out Kelnarium's government and get new clothes made by the finest tailors into the bargain. Then, I'm off to find my old home and my elemental leader. I know I'll succeed with you three at my side."

Lyssa smiled. "You and Lotte will both make fine leaders, as will Claire when she takes over the position from her grandfather."

The picture everyone painted was so tempting. For a second, Claire almost considered staying in Kelnarium – it would be easier, she'd have status and magic and friends – but then she thought of her parents longing for her to come home. She couldn't do that to them. Before she could fish for the right words to explain, Meghan stepped forward to fling a blanket about her shoulders. "Perhaps this land will change now that the Rift is closing," she said.

Claire looked up at the sky. The crack had closed to a whisp. She couldn't wait any longer.

"Are you listening?" Lyssa asked. Claire met her eyes with a start as the Enchantment Weaver went on. "Don't you agree it is you who can build a new Kelnarium?"

She gaped. "Me? I ... I can't stay here." She thought again of her parents.

"Please," Lotte cried. "We have to make sure no one lets us slip back into old habits."

Her grandfather stepped forward. "And we can be a family without impending doom getting in the way."

"I have a life in Shale, one I can't keep running from," Claire said sadly. "Once the Rift closes, I can't get home." She stared upwards. "And it's almost shut."

"Is there really much for you there?" Meghan asked gently. "I know there's your parents, but other than them, you've never said a good word about the place, and think about how much you could do."

Claire chewed the inside of her lips. "Marcus and I don't belong here, just as Gareth doesn't belong away from Maellwyn Manor. We have to go home," she insisted, looking at her brother, who was staring at the ground, abashed.

Silence descended like a heavy blanket. No one looked at each other.

Finally, Kiera spoke. "If Claire wants to go home, we should respect her wishes." Her bright eyes sparked with something Claire couldn't quite place.

Claire smiled at Kiera, then reached for Marcus's hand. Her brother groaned as he looked up to meet Lord Dorran's eyes. "I'm useless at *learth* - Maen said so often enough - but leave me behind. Perhaps I can atone for my dreadful mistakes."

"Think of Mum and Dad and me trying to justify letting you stay," Claire said. "Not to mention, Laura will be devastated. Get over your fear of failure. Gwenivere will make sure we make it back in one piece." She shot the Dream Mage leader a stern glance. "Won't you?"

Gwenivere nodded, wide-eyed. "It's the same as when we practised at Dorran Manor, only this time it's the real thing. Are you sure about this? On the way, you'll lose all your considerable *learth* ability, as your mother did. You'll never see your salamanders again."

"If that's the price we must pay to see her again, I'll pay it gladly." Besides, part of her knew she'd gained something other than magic in Kelnarium. She'd learnt to interact with all kinds of people and more importantly, she'd learnt how to lead them. She'd take those skills home and use them and she'd be less afraid. She interlaced her fingers with her brother's, then glanced over her shoulder at Rael and Kiera. There were tears in both their eyes.

"We'll be fine," she insisted with a false, bright smile. "Shale isn't as bad as all that."

Before anyone could argue, the others rushed forward, flinging their arms about the pair. Finally, Lord Dorran hugged them both tight. "I'll miss you," he said gruffly. "I was wrong to be so hard on you, Marcus and Claire, you were everything I wanted and needed you to be. Tell your mother ..." He paused. "Tell her that I love her."

"I'll tell her," Claire said, carefully removing the Dorran ring from around her neck to return it to its rightful owner. She held onto the second necklace she wore, her Dorran pendant. She'd look at it in Shale and remember her grandfather. "But something tells me she already knows."

He slid her hands away from his as the Saura's leathery voice sounded in Claire's mind. *You did well, child. Do not fear for your grandfather. I shall look after him as I've always done, and there'll be a new heir to House Dorran in time.*

Thank you, Claire sounded back. *But there's one more thing worrying me. When Jemroth finds the Gofannon, help the Nereus to persuade him to forgive the Crian. She made a mistake but that's in the past now. All four of you elemental leaders are strongest when you work together. Am I right?*

There was a long silence and then a humbled, *Yes. I will do as you ask.*

Finally satisfied, Claire let herself be drawn back to the main party. Biting back more tears, she nodded at everyone, then gazed up at the sky as Gwenivere and Tarn picked their way closer to her and Marcus, slow and mournful as any funeral procession.

Before they reached her, Lotte and Jemroth both broke ranks, flinging their arms around Claire.

"Every time I see a beautiful horse, I'll think of you," Jemroth said gruffly as he and Lotte let go of Claire's shoulders, his gnomes standing to the side and waiting patiently now they knew Jemroth was ready to take up his mission.

Claire held back tears but managed a small grin. "I'll do the same in Shale. I could always rely on you, Jemroth. If I find someone half as trustworthy as you back home I'll consider myself lucky." He nodded, then sniffed as Claire turned to Lotte.

"Things'll be different now, thanks to ya," Lotte said. "I'll make sure they happen the way we promised each other they would. Jemroth and Gareth will too."

Claire gripped her friend's shoulders tight. She never wanted to let go, but she knew that if she didn't leave now, she never would. "You're my best friend, Lotte," she said. "Even if I never see you again, no one in my world can ever replace you."

She scoffed two more honey cakes to try and prevent burn-out after so much magic use, then drank in everyone's faces one more time, trying to commit each to memory, focussing last on Jemroth, solid and dependable, then Lotte, impulsive and fierce. She'd never forget either of them.

"I'm ready." Closing her eyes, she reached for Marcus. His pinky-red *learth* threads were faint, but she was able to connect with him easily. Gwenivere and Tarn soon wrapped around them in skeins of silver.

-Call fire- Gwenivere sounded.

Drawing on Marcus's limited strength too, Claire created a corridor of the stuff in the remaining silver thread above her. As she did, Gwenivere and Tarn conjured a golden light that overlaid everything. The crack widened a fraction. Beyond it, wind tore at grey streams billowing across the sky. Blinding white light hurt Claire's eyes and lightning crackled, its electric tang combining with the scent of cooked meat.

-That's your path. Stay straight and true. Goodbye- Gwenivere sounded in Claire's mind.

Claire felt like she'd been pushed off a vast cliff as she tumbled wildly through the woven mesh of light and colour, hair whipping into her face as she clutched her brother. If she'd thought her journey harsh when she'd first come to Kelnarium, now was a mad rush of energy making it harder and harder to hold onto *learth*.

She tried to centre herself. As their descent gained velocity, Claire's eyes opened of their own volition and she saw the hard ground below them.

The ground of another world. Hers.

Magic itched through her blood and skin, demanding to be used. Somehow, Claire knew they'd die if they didn't reach for *learth* now.

She grasped at Marcus's mind. At first, she thought it was barricaded to her, but his *learth* was still active, if faint. She prodded. There was no time for delicacy.

-Make the smallest spark. Anything-

His attempt was pathetic, but Claire augmented his efforts with her own considerable power. Magic tore through her like a spear as she shot flames high above them. Even as she fell, she stretched out onto tiptoes, her hands stretching back for Kelnarium. She ignored the voice that begged her to hold on. Being ordinary was a small price to pay if she could be reunited with her family again.

She waited until the more natural red-brown dirt of the National Park rushed up to meet her and then she flung hers and Marcus's combined skeins of *learth* high into the sky. Her ears popped and lightning flashed overhead as the Rift closed forever.

Then she hit the ground.

The wind stopped tearing at her unprotected skin and the dust and the ash settled so that she could open her eyes. Marcus lay face down in mud beside her; dirty and sooty, hair sticking up every which way. Claire knew she must look a similar fright.

The sky was unblemished, a near perfect cornflower blue, thick branches of gum trees weaving all around them. Gasping for deep lungfuls of air, Claire choked on hysterical laughter. "We did it, Marcus."

Half-sobbing, half-coughing, Marcus tried to stand up. "Thanks to you, Sis!" he croaked.

Her green eyes met his blue ones as she smiled. "Don't expect me to follow after you every time you vanish into another universe."

He punched her arm playfully. "You won't be able to help yourself."

She linked her arm in his. Supporting each other, they took an unsteady step forward.

"I'll never forget what I did," Marcus said. "It happened in another world, but I'll never stop feeling guilty that I doubted you."

Claire shook her head. "Everyone makes mistakes. It's part of growing up, I suppose." Even so, she knew something had changed between them forever; no longer would he be her knowledgeable older brother, forever the leader. In another world she had found she was made of stronger stuff.

"Shall we?" Marcus asked.

She nodded. "I wonder how much time has passed in Shale?"

He began to walk, slowly at first, but then surer as his strength returned and the shock wore off. "We'll find out soon enough."

As they neared the end of the dam trail and the path widened into the familiar grass across from their house, Marcus broke into a run, calling to her to hurry, laughter lines appearing across his face.

Claire raced to catch up, so that arm in arm they unlatched the screen door to the farmhouse. At first the silence seemed claustrophobic, but then Mum and Dad rushed forward; both wearier and more careworn then when Claire had seen them last. In their crushing embrace, Claire could push thoughts of all she had left behind away, her love for home filling her like water rushing into a deep well.

Epilogue – Three months later

CLAIRE WRAPPED HER arms around her knees, facing the ruined tree where Marcus had gone missing what felt a lifetime ago. She could barely make out the soot or the scuff marks against the bough and the dirt anymore and the air was crisp and fresh instead of metallic and burnt. Beside her, Marcus worked his mouth funny directions, like he wanted to tell her something. Since their return from Kelnarium, the times they felt closest were sitting alone by the dam, as they did now. She waited patiently for Marcus to speak.

"It hasn't been the same since we came back," he said, fiddling with a pebble he'd found on the track. "You don't want to do everything with me the way you used to."

Claire didn't answer. Something had snapped inside her with Marcus's betrayal. His shine was tarnished.

He flung the pebble into the dam. "I miss it." He looked up, finally meeting her eyes, voice breaking. "Do you?"

"No," she said truthfully.

"I'm sorry," he said. "Not just for refusing to listen in Kelnarium or for dobbing you in to Eidan, but for treating you pretty shittily in Shale long before we ever knew other worlds existed. I took you for granted. I wanted your adulation even as I told myself you were my pesky little sis. That wasn't fair."

"It's fine," Claire said, reaching out to touch his bare arm. "I don't need you the way I used to. Kelnarium taught me things about myself I hadn't thought possible. Really, you don't need to keep apologising. I've never been happier."

He turned away like she'd slapped him. "I know," he mumbled, "but I miss mucking about together. I miss our adventures. Will things ever go back to the way they were?"

Claire smiled, as a girl in a faded cotton sundress wended her way down the trail towards them, her brown hair wisping every which way. Ella. Claire remembered the way she'd avoided her at the supermarket aeons ago, afraid of more stinging remarks or another failed friendship. How wrong she'd been. Ella, it turned out, loved painting and baking as much as Claire and Suranne did, and she'd long been in awe of the way Claire's family did stuff for charity without shouting it from the rooftops the way some families did. This school term, the pair had struck up a friendship.

"Claire?" Marcus prompted.

"Things can't go back to how they were," she said a little impatiently, as Ella broke into a grin at Claire's enthusiastic wave. She turned back to Marcus. "I'll always love you, silly. No matter what, you're my brother, but I have to have my own life too." She tilted her head towards Ella. "This afternoon I promised my friend we'd help Mum with cooking some lasagne. I'd better go." She got to her feet. "Don't mope about too long. I also promised Ella you'd take us on a trail ride tonight and I've told her you're the coolest brother ever when you're away from the schoolyard. Don't let me down. I'm counting on you."

He took a deep breath and nodded. "I wouldn't miss it for the world."

And this time, Claire knew he meant it.

Acknowledgements

This novel has existed in many iterations and was the first full length story I ever wrote. I owe big thanks to Angela Slatter for providing extremely helpful structural and line edits early on, alongside some great tips for planning novels in the future so the next one doesn't take more than a decade to write and publish! I also want to thank my betas Mathilde, Holly and Eleanor and my second editor, Kate McAllan. Kate did a lot of extra work to really make this novel shine and I can't express how helpful her thoughtful feedback was. Big thanks as well to Gillian and Tim who proofed the manuscript and to Holly and Tim for their work on my awesome cover. I love it!!! Finally, to my friends, family and faithful social media followers who have always supported me; thanks, I love you and this story, as with every other, is for you.

About the Author

Maureen Flynn lives on the East Coast of NSW on Dharawal nation land. She is an avid speculative fiction and crime fiction lover, writer and fan. She has finally taken up part time work at her local library so she can dedicate more hours of her day to working on novels and short stories. Her short stories have featured in publications by CSFG, Specul8 and Deadset Press and she is working on a new YA fantasy series to be released in 2022. You can find her at https://maureenflynnauthor.com or connect with her on her social media.

    Facebook: https://www.facebook.com/maureenflynnauthor
    Instagram: https://www.instagram.com/maureenflynnauthor
    Twitter: https://twitter.com/InkAshling

Lightning Source UK Ltd.
Milton Keynes UK
UKHW010736180522
403171UK00001B/35